Slay

A FREYA NOVEL

MATTHEW LAURENCE

⟨Imprint⟩
MAKE YOUR MARK

NEW YORK

[Imprint]
MAKE YOUR MARK

A part of Macmillan Publishing Group, LLC
175 Fifth Avenue, New York, NY 10010

SLAY: A FREYA NOVEL. Copyright © 2018 by Rovio Entertainment, Ltd. All rights reserved. Printed in the United States of America.

Library of Congress Control Number: 2017945054
ISBN 978-1-250-08819-2 (hardcover) / ISBN 978-1-250-08820-8 (ebook)

Our books may be purchased in bulk for promotional, educational, or business use. Please contact your local bookseller or the Macmillan Corporate and Premium Sales Department at (800) 221-7945 ext. 5442 or by e-mail at MacmillanSpecialMarkets @macmillan.com.

Book design by Ellen Duda

Imprint logo designed by Amanda Spielman

First edition, 2018

10 9 8 7 6 5 4 3 2 1

fiercereads.com

Bookish burglars, stay your hands,
resign yourselves to safer plans.
Take not from gods the spotlight,
lest you become the next they smite.

For those who believed in me, and you,
who believed in Freya

1

BURNING BRIGHT
FREYA

The lava hasn't even cooled yet.

Fat drops of rain hiss on the glowing pit of molten slag that used to be the home of my enemies. I inhale deeply, savoring the smell of steam mixed with a hint of sulfur, then let out a contented sigh. Long ropes of bright yellow caution tape flutter in the wind, while rows of police barricades present a more permanent deterrence to the hordes of onlookers at Florida's first volcanic crater. I'm just another face in the crowd, one more tourist huddled under an umbrella, gawking at the scene. The only difference is that this is all my doing, the remnants of my first battle with a conspiracy arrogant enough to exploit the gods themselves.

Did I mention I was a goddess? I'm not sure if you knew that already.

My name is Sara Vanadi, but that wasn't always the case. I used to be Freya, goddess of love, beauty, battle, and a host of other glorious things. I abandoned that title when my worshippers abandoned me. I tried to retire, to hide and live in peace. Then a man visited me and changed everything. His name was Garen, and he tore my life apart. I fled him and the people he worked for, a company named Finemdi. They wished to contain the gods, to shackle us all, and I'm certain you know how I felt about *that*. So I sought to destroy them in turn, and, well, I'm still at it. I've been joined in this quest by a new high priest—a mortal named Nathan—and new divine allies.

"Look! There's where I flew the convertible in!" an exuberant voice yells from beside me. I turn to its source, a young Hawaiian girl in a flowery dress, and give a look that pleads for silence. "Sorry," Hi'iaka squeaks, her voice a whisper on the air. A windswept spirit of nature, she doesn't exactly define *restraint*. I glance around, anxious, but luckily the other tourists either didn't hear or have decided to ignore us. So far so good. Finemdi might have written off this place as a total loss, but that doesn't mean they aren't watching its remains.

Nathan shifts nervously beside me, and I can tell he's thinking the same thing. The two of us nearly died in that pit a month ago; it was only thanks to Hi'iaka and her sisters we didn't. About as literal a deus ex machina as you can get, come to think. I can tell Nathan's not very keen on getting captured and starting the whole thing over again, but I had to come.

I got a letter, you see.

It was addressed to me—to *Freya*, actually—and its contents were short and to the point: *Meet me where my father died. Saturday, 2:00 p.m. I'll find you there.* I knew exactly who'd written it, and despite the danger, I couldn't help myself; I had to know what she wanted. So here I am, standing in the rain under a cheerful polka-dot umbrella, waiting for her to make an appearance.

"Now there's a thing of beauty," Pele, goddess of fire and most famous of the three sisters, says with a nod at the sizzling lake of rock. "Fine work for such a tectonically dull land, eh?"

Nāmaka, the third sister, pulls an exaggerated smile. "Did you create a *volcano*, Pele?" she says, voice dripping with sarcasm. "Why, I'm surprised you've never mentioned it. Especially not *every day for the last four weeks*."

Pele pauses to look at her sister, then smirks. "Well, where do I begin? First, I sunk my mind beneath the Caribbean plate, searching for the sweet music of magma. . . ."

"Ugh," Nāmaka says, giving her hair an irritated flick that shakes droplets at her sibling. A water spirit, she's the only one of us without an umbrella. Pele glares in response and sticks out her tongue before turning back to the crater to admire her handiwork.

I hope my contact shows up soon. Even with a few choice illusions (courtesy of yours truly) concealing their elemental natures, the sisters aren't exactly the most inconspicuous creatures. At least Sekhmet, my fourth divine companion, understands the occasional need for self-control—and *she's* the Egyptian goddess of righteous wrath. Her leonine features are also hidden under a disguise, an enchantment she was granted long ago, and she's been quiet since we arrived.

That said, I can tell she shares my discomfort; her illusory cheeks are contracting oddly, trembling as she twitches hidden whiskers. This place just doesn't feel safe, even behind the anonymity of the crowd. I feel like I've returned to the scene of the crime, an amateur thief displaying a rather classic lapse in judgment. Maybe this was a bad idea. I'm considering a retreat when Nathan stumbles against me with a grunt of surprise.

"What the—" he starts to say. Then his words are stifled by a gasp as he realizes there's a teenage girl standing next to him who definitely wasn't there a split second before. She's no enemy of ours,

3

though, and I relax the moment I identify her. Unassuming and awkward, she's precisely who I'd hoped to see.

"Hello, Samantha," I say with genuine warmth.

This scientific prodigy is the only employee of Finemdi's I can trust. Her father was Gideon Drass, an all-around vile individual and, up until I murdered him in a waterfall of lava last month, Finemdi's CEO. Samantha has had a rather tragic past, what with her dad sacrificing her mom to a god of darkness and being a colossal ass. There was an upside to all that misfortune, though: It made her only too happy to help us destroy her employer and father. Of course, as tends to happen in these stories, things got complicated. During my recent adventure, I discovered her mother had actually become a vessel to *contain* that god of darkness . . . and I may have inadvertently released it to wreak havoc upon the world.

I'd prefer to keep that little tidbit a secret as far as Samantha's concerned. You understand.

"Hi, everyone!" she says cheerfully, turning to take in my new pantheon and adjusting her glasses.

They all mumble their greetings in hushed tones, looking around to see if anyone noticed a lady appearing out of thin air. Samantha picks up on it and shakes her head. "Got it covered. There's an illusion of random tourists here right now."

"Nice!" Hi'iaka exclaims. "Just how many tricks *do* you have up your sleeve?"

"In charge of divine admissions, remember?" Samantha says, pointing at herself. "You wouldn't believe how many artifacts I managed to sneak out before Impulse Station went up in flames."

"We made off with a pretty good haul ourselves," I say, thinking of the truckload of mystic widgets the Hawaiian sisters managed to steal.

4

She chuckles at that. "Wasn't like anyone else was going to use it." She holds out a hand to Nathan. "Oh, and we haven't been properly introduced."

My friend shakes it and smiles. "Nathan Kence," he says. "High priest and Web designer."

"Samantha Drass," she replies with a laugh. "Scientist of the divine."

A tiny frown creases my forehead at her cheer. The Samantha I knew was a wallflower, sweet but interpersonally inept. She might have had a calculating streak, but you could never mistake it for social confidence. This girl is bubbly and forthright, so unless that reserve was just another emotional wall she'd built, I'd say there's been a seismic shift in her personality in just a handful of weeks. Then again, she's always been a little hard to read. Maybe her tyrant of a father was keeping her down? I toss the idea back and forth, then mentally shrug away my doubts—I've always been a trusting goddess, and right now I'm just happy to see that Samantha is alive and well.

Sekhmet, on the other hand, is about as far as you can get from "trusting," but since she was locked up at Finemdi until I showed, she never really got to know Samantha. All she says is, "It is good to see you again. I am pleased you chose the path of virtuous strength. The craven submission you displayed when I first awoke in Impulse Station was most disagreeable."

Samantha's good cheer fades a little as she recalls the memory. "Er, yes, thank you. I believe you promised to, um—"

"Flay you alive in the burning winds of the Sahara," Sekhmet says with a too-wide smile.

"Ah. Yes, that was it," Samantha says.

"Fortunate indeed you chose another path, *yes?*"

Samantha pauses for a moment, seeming unable to find the right words. Finally, she just nods at the Egyptian goddess before turning to me. "Well, I'm sure you're wondering why I wanted to see you."

I give her arm a friendly tap. "I'm just glad you're alive, really."

"And kicking," she says. Again, so confident. "So listen, before I get to the real reason I asked to meet you, I wanted to talk about Finemdi."

"Oh?" This should be good.

"They're transferring me. Meridian One, in New York—it's their headquarters. Makes Impulse Station look like a strip mall. More security, more researchers, more everything. It's where the board meets and where they keep their most-trusted gods. When you think you're ready—or want to catch up—look for me there. I'm not about to start planting bombs, but I'm willing to do what I can for you as long as I can keep working on my, um, project." She gives my friends an apprehensive glance as she finishes.

I know what she means, and why she's reluctant to say more. Samantha's been trying to resurrect her mother as a god for the past few years, using Finemdi's stable of shackled believers to worship the woman into existence. It hasn't been going well.

"I hope you find success up there," I say, and mean it. What she's doing may be an abomination, but then, what's been done to her is worse. Besides, after dealing with Finemdi's industrial approach to magic, my bar for divine outrage has been set pretty high. "Do you know what they're going to have you do?"

She shrugs. "After they debrief me about this place"—she jerks her head at the lava pool—"they'll probably just put me back on artifact identification and divine intake. Anyway, the main reason I brought you here is . . . hang on . . ." She reaches into the satchel at her side and begins rummaging around. "This!" she exclaims as she retrieves a thick manila envelope. She holds it out to me. "Here you go."

"What's in it?" I ask, moving to open it.

"Wait until you're home," she says, holding up a hand. "You're going to want a quiet place to think about what's in there. Besides my contact info, I've included something you'll find very interesting—a bit of research I've been doing on the side. Finemdi doesn't have a clue, but I knew you'd want to see it."

"Um, okay. Thanks, Samantha," I say, stuffing the envelope into my bag. It's not a great fit—I went with "cute" today, not spacious.

"Oh!" Samantha says, snapping her fingers. "Something else I need to do: Make sure you understand just how dangerous Finemdi can be."

Nathan chuckles at that. "Yeah, they seemed all sunshine and snuggles before."

Samantha pushes her glasses up on her nose and gives him a pitying look. "How much do you *really* know about them? You have no frame of reference for the level of power they can bring to bear. They get enraged when somebody so much as pokes their hive with a stick, and you've taken a baseball bat to it."

I have to laugh. "I'm liking that image."

"So Finemdi's all crazied-up," Nathan says. "What does that actually *mean*?"

"It means they're more suspicious of their gods than ever before, they're investigating every lead they can find, and they're dead set on hunting down whoever's responsible. Actually, it's just about . . ." She checks her watch. "Yes, in another minute, they're going to be here."

That gets my attention. "*What?!*" I hiss, eyes darting around.

"Shh, keep your voice down!" Samantha snaps. "Look, you need to see what a real Finemdi operation is like—not some lone specialist going after a girl in a mental hospital. They barely considered you a god, Sara. You need to understand who you're dealing with, because

I need you out there and fighting, not captured or killed because you underestimated these people."

"Why do you—"

"Just listen—when they get here, everyone is going to drop, including me. *All* of you need to pretend to fall asleep with the rest of them, but land so you can still see what's going on."

She looks up, frowning, then nods. "Okay, they're a little early. Get ready, and whatever you do, don't—"

Her eyes roll up in her head and she crumples to the pavement along with Nathan and every other tourist around us. I spin around, bewildered, before practically throwing myself onto the asphalt. My still-conscious friends follow suit, each pantomiming their own personal fainting spell.

There's a massive bass rumble in the air, a shuddering that jars reality and thrums in my bones. The gray skies ripple and flex, waves and eddies distorting the air like the surface of a storm-tossed sea. An enormous . . . *flipper* descends from the sky, a mottled green arc of wizened leather that has to be at least a hundred feet long. I'm so focused on it I almost miss that there are four of them in all, spaced in an ellipse above the pit. Then the clouds part farther, revealing the plated underside of a colossal beast. An enormous pitted head lowers from above, jutting in front of the shell, and as it opens its beak to yawn, I realize it's a turtle—a gigantic, floating *turtle*.

I stifle the urge to laugh, but just barely. Keep it together, Sara. This is serious. Sure, your mortal enemies fly around on a *freaking turtle*, but—*no*, I need to stop thinking about this. The more I consider it, the closer I get to hysterics.

The creature continues its descent from the roiling heavens. I can just make out a woman perched atop its head, still as a statue. She's jet-black, as if carved from flawless obsidian. A bunker-like structure rises from above the turtle's back and I can see guards patrolling its perimeter, on the lookout for any threats. Then there's movement on the side closest to the lava pool, and as I watch, a thickset, well-built man with a great bushy beard walks to the edge of the shell. He's clad in nothing but a heavy blacksmith's apron and limps as he moves; one of his legs is twisted and lame.

With that last clue, I'm able to put a name to him: Hephaestus, Greek god of the forge.

He halts for a moment, leaning over to peer into the pool, then throws himself in with a graceless swan dive. His body smashes through the thin crust on the surface of the molten lake, vanishing in a spray of liquid rock.

"What's he doing?" Hi'iaka's voice whispers to me. A spirit of the wind, she's controlling the air to carry her voice to our ears alone.

Ordinarily, it would be a brilliant idea. Ordinarily, the little spark of divinity she's using to do it would be about as noticeable as a mouse's sneeze for anyone with the sense to look for such things. But there's a flying turtle above us with a Finemdi-run outpost lashed to its back. Ordinary has gone out the window, booked a ticket to the moon, and left our world behind.

With a deep, mournful whine, the turtle shifts to stare down at us, its body spinning in the air. It begins drifting closer, zeroing in on the errant whiff of magic it somehow senses. The Finemdi guards on its back are yelling, calling to their companions and rushing to get a better look at what their ride has found. The flippers lift up, moving out to the side so the turtle can drift lower without touching the pool of lava below. It's getting even closer now, enough for me to make out hundreds of years of wear and tear, a reptilian face of impossible character and age. Its eyes are great black ovals, their darkness made all the more striking by irises that shine like the stars of a distant galaxy.

Those captivating eyes can't be more than fifty feet away now, and getting closer by the second. The ebon woman perched atop the turtle's head is peering around as well, trying to find the source of her pet's interest. She's hauntingly beautiful, her midnight features refined yet brushed with a touch of warmth. Any moment now, I fear they'll spot us—that the turtle will somehow realize what we truly are, and all my beautiful dreams of vengeance will come crashing down.

Then the smoldering lake beneath the creature churns, the darker rock on the surface heaving and cracking. An enormous geyser of lava erupts from deep within the pool, spouting up to splash against the turtle's belly. Its roar of pain is titanic—a bellow that drowns out every other sound and makes me shudder in sympathy. With stunning speed, the beast rears back and launches itself away from the pool, soaring up hundreds of feet in an eyeblink. The guards on its back cry out in surprise and panic as they lose their footing. Several of them topple from their perches and fall, screaming, before they crash into the lava below with thick, satisfying *plop*s.

"Now!" Pele shrieks, picking herself off the ground and running. "C'mon, move!"

I lie there dumbly for a moment as my friends scramble from the pavement, trying to understand what could have possibly made the lava do that. Then I snap out of it, berating myself with the realization that Pele's the reason there's even a lake to begin with. *Idiot!* I spring to my feet, grab Nathan's arm, and haul him over my shoulder. I look for Samantha, but she's nowhere to be found. Assuming she's been saved by one of her many contingencies, I hightail it after my friends. As I run, Nathan's body jiggling on my shoulder with every footfall, the part of my brain that's not concerned with side-stepping a field of torpid tourists amuses itself with the fact that I've been getting a lot of experience carrying my poor priest's unconscious body lately.

I spare a glance behind us as we reach the parking lot; the turtle is still spiraling high into the skies, flecks of lava dripping from its stomach, enraged howls escaping from its maw.

"An excellent distraction!" Sekhmet yells at Pele as she jogs alongside us.

"Yeah, brilliant!" Hiʻiaka adds.

Pele grins at that and puts on an extra burst of speed, aiming for our Honda at the back of the lot. Nāmaka just shakes her head, though whether she's frustrated at our nearly getting caught or Pele getting something new to brag about, I'm not sure. We all reach the car at roughly the same time (I suspect Sekhmet was holding herself back for us). I fumble in my bag for the keys, spending a few heart-stopping seconds fishing around in the mess of makeup, receipts, trinkets, and mini Toblerone bars for the little tangle of metal before I wrench it out with a cry and click the button to unlock the doors. I practically toss Nathan into the backseat, and we all pile into the car. I slam the door closed, turn the key in the ignition, and peel out of the lot as quickly as I dare. Driving is still new to me, but I refuse to err on the side of safety.

A few minutes later, as we merge onto more populated roads, I feel some of the tension in the car begin to fade. There's no sign of the turtle, or any other form of pursuit. "Hey, girls?" Hiʻiaka says, chuckling nervously. "I think I can guess what Ms. Drass was about to say before she fell asleep."

I laugh a little too much at that—we all do, really—but I can't help myself. I didn't get up today expecting to narrowly escape the attentions of a Finemdi assault squad . . . to say nothing of the *turtle*. That thought just makes me laugh even harder, and it's to the sound of our relieved mirth that Nathan finally awakes with a groan.

"What the hell just happened?" he moans from the car's floor. "And why are you all laughing?"

"Sky turtle," I manage to squeak out before a new wave of amusement consumes us. When it finally dies down enough for us to concentrate, we fill Nathan in on what he missed.

"Wish I could've seen *that*," he murmurs, sounding a little jealous.

"Yeah, wasn't something I've encountered before," I say. "Sekhmet? Any ideas?" My friend has been rather quiet the entire ride.

She nods, seeming unsettled. "I believe that was the personal conveyance of the ebon goddess we saw. She is Yamī—a Hindu deity. The Tibetans revere her as ruler of all the female spirits in Naraka, their purgatory."

She pauses, displaying a rare moment of apprehension. It occurs to me that she doesn't want to voice her next thought. When she does at last, I can see why. "It bodes ill for us that Finemdi controls such gods. How many can they truly call their own? How many are left beyond their walls?"

The remaining humor flees the car in the face of those sobering questions. We ride in silence for an awkward minute. Finally, Hi'iaka breaks it, trying to focus us on something a little less depressing. "So what's in the package?" she asks.

"Oh yeah," I mutter, patting my overstuffed bag. "Must've been important. Let's check it out when we get inside the apartment."

I pull into our usual space, and we hurry out of the car, dashing across the parking lot as if any time spent in the open will call Finemdi down onto our heads. Then, safe in our cramped little condo,

I haul out the envelope and tear it open. Two things spill out: a note card with Samantha's e-mail address, and the political section of the *Washington Post* newspaper, dated from over two weeks ago.

I begin leafing through it. "Why would she . . . ?"

My confusion ends the moment I spot a particular article. The image above it has been circled in red. It's captioned with the innocuous phrase *Gen. Theo Ariston seeks a new life in the private sector* and shows a stern man standing in front of a government building, looking official. Beside it, Samantha's neat handwriting reads, *Who do you think he just joined?*

I gasp, and the paper falls from my hands. He may be wearing a military dress uniform, but I would recognize that chiseled face anywhere.

Sekhmet touches my shoulder and leans in to examine the image, eyes narrowing. "Can it be?" she whispers.

I nod, an odd mix of excitement and anger coursing through me.

"Who is he, Sara?" Nathan asks, picking up the paper and frowning at the picture.

I glance at my friend, a wicked smile tugging my features. At last. *At last.* "A dead man," I say, laughing at the absurdity of it all.

I take a moment to gather my thoughts, and then I begin the story of how I lost everything.

13

ONCE UPON A TIME

FREYA

The world was mine, once. Maybe twice. It's hard to remember. Here I am, a god, a shining, egotistical force of nature, yet fallen so far from what I once was that I don't even want to use the *name* my followers gave me. Haven't you wondered how that happened? How I came to accept my fate, to pull away from the world and hunker down in the shadows like a wounded animal?

Well, I was wounded, of course.

Long ago, I tried to play kingmaker, to use my immortality to meddle in the affairs of man. My pantheon had begun its decline, but our power was far from gone. I thought I could do what no human could, that with my magic, agelessness, and experience, I could create an empire to stand the test of time. My hand would always be there, guiding an endless procession of rulers.

In my arrogance, I actually believed I was the only god to try this.

Let me paint you a picture: I sit behind a dozen thrones, hidden ruler of Scandinavia and England, beloved queen, courtesan, and seer. Then a horde of ignorant barbarians arrives from lands beyond, from across the southern sea, and challenges my kingdom. Our armies meet at a spot of my choosing, on high ground that gives us the advantage. I ride out beside my king, shield our forces with an impenetrable spell, and wait for our foes to come and die.

They oblige me. They fall in droves, unable to assault the hill, their arrows and spears turned aside by my wondrous magic. Then, as the rabble retreats, a single man walks forth, clad in odd segmented plates of armor, glittering bands of steel covering his bright red tunic. A skirt of studded leather straps bounces around his legs, and he clutches a short, thick sword in one white-knuckled hand. He brushes our arrows from his skin as if they were irritating flies, his stride unbroken by the hail of weaponry that rains upon him. As he nears my wards, I catch the jagged pulse of divinity writhing beneath the crested helm that shadows his eyes. Then he plunges his sword into my barrier, gives it a twist, and shatters it like glass.

I walk forward to meet him, long sword in hand and spells of battle on my lips. We lay waste to each other and the land around us, our fight tearing open the earth and turning men to mist. I besiege him with living lightning, bathe his forces in hurricanes of fire, and resurrect my fallen almost as fast as he can kill them. Golems of blood and steel rise at my command, glacial winds of razor ice howl across the battlefield, and our weapons clash with the speed and strength of thunderclaps. Impossible devastation flows from me, a torrent of magic and violence that scars the skies and nips at the foundations of reality.

And it's not enough.

I am a god of war, but far too late I realize he is one as well, and this conflict has only fueled him. *He* is battle personified, a creature undiluted by concepts such as love and fertility, and in this arena, he is my better. In the end, a brutal slash of his blade removes one of my arms, a spinning thrust pierces my heart, and a final sweep takes off my head.

My view of the landscape tumbles and bounces crazily before I come to rest on a thick patch of grass halfway down the hill. At first it's peaceful, a welcome rest from the haze of battle and the pressures of command. Then rough fingers plunge into my hair and I'm wrenched from the grasses, raised into the air until I am brought face-to-face with my attacker. I sway before him, a crisp fall wind rustling my golden locks.

His eyes are burning pits, his features noble yet enraged; a berserker carved from marble. "Your little island is mine," he grates in the Norman tongue. "And you will make a fine trophy."

"I am no man's prize," I say with all the disdain a decapitated head can manage. It's not much.

He laughs at that, a booming, humorless bellow that carries over the sound of my people being crushed by his army's counterattack. "Pathetic girl, I am the Destroyer of Men, the Stormer of Walls, the Lord of War." He sneers and brings me closer. "The *world* is my prize."

The terrible thing is, he's right.

My neck is capped in molten gold and enchanted with ruinous magic, preventing me from re-forming through the beliefs of my followers. For a hundred years, I rest on his mantel as he conquers the known world in the name of countless mortal rulers, always seeking new wars, new bloodshed. In the end, I'm traded away with a host of other trinkets. I don't know if he simply forgot about me, or this is just another form of disrespect. Whatever the reason, I've escaped in the hands of unscrupulous traders, and through no guile of my own.

I should be outraged at the idea, but decades of imprisonment and humiliation have blunted my sense of self-importance. I can feel my worshippers dwindling, my strength fading. Christianity is spreading, its missionaries slithering through my homelands, and I have no one to blame but myself. I dared to meddle in the affairs of other realms, reached too far for power, and this is where it has led me—if I had remained with my pantheon, if I had been there to answer the prayers of my people, I might still have their belief. At the very least, I certainly wouldn't be a disembodied head on a pile of treasure, being sold for a handful of coins.

Besides self-loathing, I actually feel a stirring of excitement. The end seems in sight. My hope is that my new owners consider my head worthless, that the gold on my neck is all they really want. If they pry it off and melt it down, they'll free me in the process. Yet all too soon, it becomes clear the enchantments are too strong for these mortals to sever. Though my surroundings have changed, I remain a prisoner. The years crawl by as I'm passed from owner to owner, nothing more than a bizarre curio traveling Europe in the collections of nobles and scoundrels alike. The days blur into a crushing mix of boredom and disgrace while my power evaporates like blood into the seas. The only constant, the only thing I can hold on to, is my hatred for the god who did this. I swear a thousand times, to all the fates that touch this world, that his suffering will be cruel beyond reason and last days beyond counting.

Finally, another *decade* after I was first sold, I wind up in Egypt, a gift to a powerful lord. Servants bring me to his home with other expensive gifts and leave me in a receiving room overseen by a bookkeeper with a checklist. Rolled carpets, jade statues, bolts of cloth, chests of spices, and lockboxes of jewelry are piled here, awaiting categorization. I sit on a velvet pillow within a curled brass

17

enclosure, waiting my turn with the bookkeeper. As I wonder if I'll be jammed in storage somewhere or placed high on a shelf to gather dust, a door leading farther into the manor swings open and a beautiful woman enters.

She has a dark, olive-skinned complexion, wide-set eyes, and icy, regal features. She is dressed in jewel-studded robes and a golden snake-headed circlet nestles in her thick black hair. She is haunting grandeur wrapped around brutality, breathtaking in her majesty and ferocity. This is a predator, a hunter, a warrior queen. The bookkeeper bows his head in greeting, which seems silly, like a rabbit waving at a wolf. "Greetings, Lady Rashida," he says with great respect in Coptic.

"Is this everything?" the woman asks, gaze darting over every trinket and bauble.

"Indeed," he replies. "All the gifts for our master."

"*Your* master," she snaps. "*My* compatriot."

"Of course, of course," he says, grimacing. "I did not intend offense, dear lady."

She gives him a baleful stare, locking him in place for an awful second. Then she shakes her head in disgust. "Get out. Finish your tallies later."

He nods and backs away, all but dashing from the room. The woman sighs as he leaves, then begins examining each of the items. She doesn't spend much time with anything, doesn't seem to care about the wealth in front of her, sparing but a moment for each piece before moving on to the next. She runs a hand over the bolts of cloth, taps the ornate statues, fiddles with the jewelry and spices, every movement cold and precise.

At least, until she turns to me.

The moment her eyes lock on to my brass cage, her composure

changes completely. She hunches over, features freezing, arms drifting down to her sides, looking like she's ready to pounce. She stays like that for a minute, studying me. Then she stalks forward, picks up my cage, and rips it open in one smooth motion. Brass pieces clatter against the floor as she holds my pillow up to eye level and snarls.

"You come to my lands wrapped in darkness. The scent of ruin hangs heavy about you," she says softly. "What are you, wretched thing? Tell me now, for you will never have the chance again."

She's a god. I can finally feel it, now that she's so close; I can sense her divinity through the haze of spells inside my head. My mouth drops open in surprise, but nothing emerges—I haven't spoken in over a century.

I'm not even sure I can.

"A spy? An assassin?" she asks, intense. "Who holds your reins, and why have they sent you?"

Her question strikes a nerve deep inside me. My *reins?* I may have spent more than a hundred years as a beheaded toy, but never for a second was I the servant of another. The warrior maiden in me, the Valkyrie, rises for the first time in ages, incensed at the notion, and with her return, I find my voice. "I am no one's *pet,*" I spit, the words hoarse and hollow. "I am shackled, yes, but not by choice—*never by choice.*"

Her eyes grow wide, and I feel her judgment like the glare of the sun. "A fighter, I see. But if it is not choice that brings you here, then what?"

"Defeat," I say, looking away as the grief floods me. "I defied my nature, and for a hundred years, I have suffered for it."

The woman gives me a voracious smile that seems to bare too many teeth. "Do you desire freedom, then?"

19

Of course I do. But something tells me this woman is looking for a different reply. She wants to hear what the Valkyrie's answer would be, and I am all too happy to give it. "I want *revenge*," I hiss.

The woman's smile changes, shifts from hostile to joyous. "A goddess sits before me," she whispers. "Broken by her past and hidden by vile spells, but a goddess all the same. I shall release you, little fighter. I shall hear your story, become a part of it, and one day, rejoice in its bloody end."

She holds me by the hair with her left hand, letting the pillow drop away, and brings up her right. Wicked claws sprout from her fingertips, and she digs them into the golden seal on my neck. With a roar, she tears it from me. The enchantments collapse in a calamitous burst of sparks, and I feel relief for the first time in a century. At last, the pain in my mind is silenced. She sets me down and I begin to change, to reassume the form chosen by my dwindling pool of believers. Veins writhe and flex, spilling out of my neck like crimson roots. Bones click, skin stretches, and blood thunders as my body rebuilds itself. Weak as I am, I know it will take hours, but in the end, I will be whole again.

My eyes close, and we stay quiet for a time as I enjoy the simple peace of freedom. Then my curiosity grows, forcing me to break the silence. "Who are you?" I ask the woman as I re-form.

"I am the protector, the One Before Whom Evil Trembles," she says, bending down beside me. "I am Sekhmet, and you are welcome in my lands."

"Thank you," I whisper, and I see in her eyes she understands the depths of my gratitude.

"And you, little fighter?"

I sigh. "Freya, though I feel unworthy of the name."

She shrugs. "Then choose another, and *fight* for the honor of returning to the old one."

That brings a smile to my lips. "Perhaps I shall."

"*Who?*" she asks, leaning in, and I can tell she isn't wondering what my new name will be. "Who did this? Who must die? The promise of death sings in my soul, and I would know the name of your foe, a title for this hymn of destruction."

A hundred years of hate fill me as I recall the man. My powers wither, my pantheon fades in lands far removed, and all I have left is my revenge. He must die. How else can I have any right to call myself a god? My eyes narrow, and I clench a half-formed fist as I spit his name.

"*Ares.*"

"I looked, believe me," I say to my friends. "For centuries, I sought him, and for centuries, I was denied. Sekhmet became a good friend of mine, and our adventures could fill libraries." I glance at her, smiling.

"But never again did I catch the barest whisper of Ares. My strength dwindled and, alongside it, the call for vengeance. I pulled away, withdrew from the divine, and, as I traveled the New World, became convinced my quest was pointless. In the end, I committed myself to a mental hospital in Florida, intent on spending the rest of my existence there."

"And that's where I came in," Nathan adds, a touch of wonder in his voice.

"Precisely, my priest," I say in a soft voice, feeling a little awed by my own sprawling history.

"And now he's working with Finemdi?" Nāmaka says. "That's what Samantha's little note means, yes?"

"Must be," I say. "She reviews most of the new gods they get—I'm guessing he joined up voluntarily, but she probably still had to give him a once-over."

"Fine, wonderful, but think about your shared history—that's *nine hundred years* gone," Nāmaka says. "How would Samantha even know *any* of it? And *why* would she send you after Ares? None of this makes any sense."

These are excellent, excellent questions. Questions I'd almost certainly be asking if our roles were reversed. But my head is filled with the glorious drumbeat of battle, drowning out pesky things like logic and self-control. So I brush away Nāmaka's completely reasonable—and incredibly important—queries with the first thing that pops into my head.

"She probably came across an account of what happened as part of, like, research she was doing for Ares's intake evaluation. I'm sure it showed up in a history book somewhere."

Yeah, that sounds plausible. *Surrrrre.*

"She's my friend—she would have known how much I want him dead, how much I would appreciate the chance to take revenge." Makes perfect sense.

"If you say so," Nāmaka says, doubtful.

"So where does that leave us? I mean, we kind of have a lot on our plate already, don't we?" Nathan asks.

"There's only one place it can possibly lead, my priest," I reply, a solemn tone creeping into my voice. I get up and walk to our computer. I jiggle the mouse so it comes out of sleep mode, head to the Web browser, and type *General Theo Ariston* into the search engine. The first hit is a *Wikipedia* entry for the man. I click it, bringing up his page, and feel a dark smile spread across my face as his picture appears on the right-hand side. Cold and dour, yet with a hint of bloodlust visible even now, it can be no one else. This is my nemesis. The reason my power has vanished, my faith has fled, and now . . . well, now I can feel him becoming something else entirely. My will is bending itself around the idea, all my effort focusing itself on this one glorious thought. The urges of love are a distant cry now. If I were human, I might mourn the plague of hatred that bubbles within me.

But I'm not.

"We are going to find him and destroy him."

3

EMBERS OF WAR

NATHAN

Here we go.

With mounting worry, Nathan watches as his goddess loses herself to the siren song of payback.

"It's going to be incredible," she's saying, eyes glazed with fearsome joy. "I'm going to eat his heart. Like, literally rip it out of his stupid uniform, show it to him, and then *eat the damn thing*."

Nathan looks to the others in the room, hoping to find a bit of support. The Valkyrie in his goddess is clearly taking charge, while love and beauty, laughter and life—the things he adores her for—are being kicked to the curb. Sekhmet, of course, sports a mile-wide grin, those dazzling features of hers bathed in delight at Freya's dreams of violence. At least the Hawaiian sisters seem to share Nathan's appalled outlook.

"Gross," Hi'iaka says, scrunching up her broad nose. "So, what, we're just gonna traipse off to kill this Theo guy because he's actually some jerk-ass Greek god I've never even heard of?"

Nathan breathes a sigh of relief, thankful for some common sense. The girl is clearly trying to steer the conversation toward less-brutal topics. A goddess of nature like her siblings, she's a step removed from the passions of humanity, and that seems to include centuries-old vendettas.

"Really?" Nāmaka says, incredulous. "He's all over your beloved gadgets. Didn't you fight him in a video game? And what about that silly show with the warrior princess?"

"Oh yeaaaah . . ." Hiʻiaka murmurs.

"Comics, too," Nathan says, figuring now was as good a time as any to jump in. "But Hiʻiaka's on the right track—are we really going to drop everything and go tearing *through* Finemdi just to get to this guy?"

Freya turns a cold smile on her auburn-haired high priest.

"Yes," she says in the voice of a goddess, all steel and arrogance.

A crash of thunder wouldn't be out of place, Nathan thinks.

"I've waited over *nine hundred years* for this," she continues. "How many of your lifetimes is that? If you think my vendetta against Finemdi matters in the face of his sins, then you cannot fathom the depths of my hatred."

Nathan's lips twist into a grimace. Since he met Freya at the Inward Care Center several months ago, he's learned a great deal about the true nature of the world, not to mention a handful of spells—*freaking spells*—but the sinking feeling in his gut tells him he still doesn't quite understand how gods work. After all, hadn't Ares obliterated her when she was near the height of her power? And now she wants to try her luck again, from the bottom of the celestial barrel?

He feels sick.

"Can we . . . not?" he says, trying to package his extreme dislike into something more palatable than gagging in front of five goddesses. "I mean, really—think about this. You've waited so long. What's the hurry?"

"It's not like I have him booked for next weekend," Freya says, frowning. "I know I need power—and probably a plan. I may be obsessive, but I'm not an idiot."

"I know that, but is this what you really want to sink yourself into? Revenge? Hatred? You're a god of love, not—"

"I'm more than that," she replies, soft and dangerous. "More than love, and more than capable of—"

"Then be more than *this*, Sara," Nathan says, wishing he could keep the pleading tone out of his voice. "It makes *no sense* for you to focus everything on settling this score right now, especially when you've got *the rest* of Finemdi to deal with, too. Remember them?"

"You don't—" Freya starts to snap, but then she stops herself, closes her eyes, and inhales sharply. "Nathan," she begins in a calmer voice. "This is part of who I am."

"That doesn't make it any less of a terrible idea," he counters. "I mean, Nāmaka's totally right: If Samantha knew enough to send you this article, she'd *have* to know you'd want to drop everything to go after Ares. Why would she do that? What does she get out of it?"

Freya blinks at that, and Nathan entertains a moment of hope that paranoia might win out over a thousand years of deep-rooted divinity. Then Freya shakes her head, saying, "Nothing. She's trying to do a favor for a friend—that's all."

Nathan stifles a groan. "Even if that's the case, you know these stories," he points out. "How often do they *ever* end well?"

"Nathan," Freya says, a blend of frustration and finality in her voice. "This tale is already being written. I'm on the path. Now,

I'd really like to walk it with you, but one way or another, I *will* walk it."

Nathan turns to share a worried look with the Hawaiian sisters, but they seem content to stay out of the argument. *Nature spirits*, he thinks, letting out a small sigh. The sisters were born to neutrality in much the same way Freya was wired for vengeance. It's a part of what they are, and behind those flashing forget-me-not eyes and pale, flawless Norse features, Nathan has the sneaking suspicion Freya knows this is just as bad an idea as he does.

And then it hits him. He stiffens, suddenly realizing why all his arguments, all the reason and logic in the world don't matter: This isn't about them. It's all wrapped up with centuries of dogma, a tower of belief rising from the past that leaves little room for Freya to defy the expectations of her followers.

Gods aren't born, after all, Nathan remembers—they're *made*. Every last one, from his goddess and her allies to the prisoners and collaborators behind Finemdi's walls has a *purpose*. Belief doesn't just empower gods; it *defines* them, and though Freya's long absence from the spotlight has granted her a bit of leeway in obeying the calls of her portfolio, it clearly isn't enough to overcome this.

She has to hunt Ares as surely as every human heart has to beat.

And so, even though every part of Nathan wants to object, to charm, beg, and plead his god away from her decision, he instead bows to it and says, "Okay, Sara. I'm with you. Wherever you go, or whatever you're after, I'm with you."

It doesn't feel great, but slamming his head against that unyielding bedrock of faith is worse.

His words bring a genuine smile to her lips, which almost—*almost*—makes the choice feel right. "Thank you," she says. Then an odd look flashes across her face, an out-of-character blend of regret and self-doubt, and though it's gone in an eyeblink, it's enough for Nathan to realize he's seen it on her once before: The night he agreed to help her take down Finemdi.

She thinks she might be influencing me again.

It makes sense. She'd been worried his agreement then was a result of her influence, of the pressure all gods exude on the people and places around them. Following Freya (or any god, for that matter) meant risking a little of one's personality, of surrendering a part of oneself to their power. That kind of thing apparently went double for him: As Freya's high priest, their connection meant he got more than magic. According to her, he has a much higher chance of experiencing those changes.

Not that he's noticed anything yet.

Then a soft, cold little part of him asks, "Would you?"

The thought gives him pause, because it's painfully, terrifyingly true. After all, Freya herself had told him it might happen, had seemed worried *sick* about the possibility. How subtle was it? Could his choice of religion have influenced him already?

How much of any *of this is my own free will? And if it's not me . . . how will I ever know?*

"And don't worry," Freya adds, pulling him out of his head with a touch on the shoulder. "We're going to be smart about this. I won't drag my friends into a battle I can't win."

He gives a tired laugh. "I know. It just seems . . . fast, that's all."

"She's waited long enough, I think," Sekhmet says, flashing him an enormous smile. "As have I."

Nathan blushes at the attention. He's still unsure if he finds Sekhmet appealing or petrifying, but when a beautiful lady beams at you, it's hard not to feel *something*. He settles for returning a grin.

Freya nods at her words, then seems to fidget for a moment before returning her attention to "General Theo's" *Wikipedia* article. She looks embarrassed, though by what, Nathan can't quite tell. She's just won the argument, after all—shouldn't that make her happy? Are there other reasons she's leapt on this opportunity beyond a bitter past? He knows she's been having trouble with her goal of destroying Finemdi . . . perhaps Ares is a way of ignoring those difficulties.

A few weeks ago, when he agreed to help her and the other goddesses wipe the company from the face of the earth, what they'd all failed to realize at the time was just how *large* global conspiracies could be. Even worse, they had no idea who Finemdi's true leader—some mysterious "chairman"—actually was, so it wasn't like there was a figurehead all lined up to assassinate.

Would've been nice, Nathan thinks, not liking the hint of irritation he can feel trickling out of his god.

He doesn't like it, but he *does* understand, at least a little. For a creature like Freya, defined in part by passion, confrontation, and war, being unable to act on *any* of those things must have been frustrating beyond imagination. With Finemdi, not only did she not know where to begin, but she didn't have the power to do something about it even if she *did*.

His god had been resigned to gathering belief, waiting until she was strong enough to divine the future and cheat her way into a plan, but now . . . now Ares represents the perfect outlet for her rage: a simple, tangible foe upon which to focus all her attention. He's even working *with* their enemies! How perfect is that?

But it means Freya can't see—or convince herself—that Finemdi *as a whole* is the greater threat, and focusing on a single employee of theirs isn't exactly the best use of time.

Just goes to show how well gods listen to voices of reason, Nathan thinks. *Especially their own.*

Pele leans in to read the webpage over Freya's shoulder. "Handsome fellow," she says after a moment. "Little cold for my liking, though."

"Figures," Hiʻiaka says with a snort.

Pele sighs. "Like *you* want to date him."

"He has a father?" Freya says, still reading the article. She clicks a link titled "David Ariston," and Nathan leans closer to see what comes up. The picture on the following page is much older, but clearly of the exact same person.

"Decorated World War Two officer and descendant of famed Civil War leader Alfred Ariston," he reads.

Freya clicks the new name. The picture is faded and grainy this time, but still unmistakably Ares in a period uniform. Nāmaka shakes her head. "He's masquerading as an entire family? How do mortals miss this? Doesn't anyone suspect?"

"Of course not," Freya says. "Why would they? Why would any of them go looking for magic when they know the world would laugh at them for it? Isn't 'family resemblance' all the excuse they need?"

Hiʻiaka nudges Nathan. "You people need to work on your imaginations."

"I'll make sure to bring it up in our next newsletter," Nathan says with a half smile.

"You have a—Ooh, sarcasm. Hilarious," Hiʻiaka says, hair snapping in a sudden, irritated gust. Nathan snorts a little at that. He enjoys messing with the nature spirits, and Hiʻiaka's naiveté makes her a fun target.

"He's been a part of every American conflict since they started keeping records," Freya says, still skimming the articles.

"Must love fighting," Pele remarks.

"Well, he is the Lord of War," Freya says in a mocking tone. Then her eyes widen. "Oh, son of a—" She pushes away from the computer and spins to face her friends. "I know *exactly* what the bastard's doing. You know how we've been working for Disney the past few weeks, right? Lapping up belief?"

The other goddesses nod, looks of gratitude popping onto their faces as they do. Not long before their recent showdown with Finemdi, Freya started a job at the local theme parks as a princess—a choice that amused Nathan to no end. There, she'd discovered some of her youngest visitors believed so earnestly in her as a fictional character that she was charged ever so slightly by the strength of that conviction. She'd said it was like gaining a fraction of a worshipper every time, all without them even knowing her true name. When Sekhmet and the Hawaiian sisters joined up, she'd let them in on her little secret and helped them get similar jobs.

At Finemdi, Freya and Nathan had learned that gods need concentrated worship to form, but after that, just about any form of belief directed at them was fair game—particularly if it was catalyzed by something related to their specialty. Dionysus was a good example of how powerful a god could get that way, and Nathan frowns at the memory. A jackass god of merriment and madness they'd met at the parks, he drew his strength from revelry and entertainment. They weren't sure where he'd gone in the aftermath of Impulse Station, but considering how much strength he'd drawn through his position at Disney, it was a safe bet he made it out just fine.

"We all have our areas of expertise," Freya continues. "Ares . . . well, he's figured out the perfect way to empower himself from his."

Sekhmet's mouth drops open. "You mean to imply—"

"War is his answer to humanity's cynicism," Freya says, nodding grimly. "They may not believe in him anymore, but he knows the call of battle will never fade." She looks at Nathan as she finishes, prompting him to put two and two together.

It doesn't take long. "Wh-wait, you mean *he's* the reason we're still blasting craters out of the Middle East?" Nathan says, shocked by the implications.

Freya gives him an approving smile, and Nathan feels a surge of pride for making the leap. "I think he's the reason for more than that. *Look* at this," she says, gesturing at the monitor. "I'm sure it goes back centuries. All these stalemates and endless wars, prolonged conflicts and global tensions. He's been wallowing in warfare like a pig in mud, using his military connections to keep the planet in peril."

"Then why join Finemdi? What more can they offer him?" Nathan asks, feeling dismayed by the idea of a god with that kind of obsession anywhere *near* the conspiracy. The lives Ares had destroyed over the centuries, all to fuel the fires of conflict . . . it staggers him to imagine the scope of the suffering that could be placed at that monster's feet, and for the first time since Freya laid out her hateful plans, he feels they might actually be a good idea.

Sekhmet lets out a humorless laugh. "A challenge," she says.

The room turns to her, curious.

"Look at what has become of war," she says. "Commanders no longer lead the charge—they sit in meetings and observe the results of orders from half a world away through spy satellites and drones. That is not what a creature like Ares craves. He will miss *battle*, the chance to test himself in combat. Finemdi can provide all this and more, can promise he will face *gods* firsthand, not men and their toys from behind a desk."

Nathan notices Freya nodding at that, but as much as he hates being the voice of dissent with this group, something doesn't feel right about that line of thinking. "So he'd give up on the military for *that*?" he says. "I mean, he's got access to *nukes*—why wouldn't he just stay with the government and try to kick-start World War Three?"

"I am aware of your ghastly atomic weapons," Sekhmet says, shaking her head. "Enough to know that Ares does not desire a nuclear exchange. He needs humanity alive and fighting, not slaughtered in a radioactive flash."

Pele makes a little gasp of understanding, drawing the connection at last. "So he can feed on them. But a *world* of conflict? For centuries?" She turns back to Freya. "How strong is he, Sara? We were born in all our glory through the worship of thousands. Now you're telling us Ares has managed to draw on the strength of *billions*?"

"Merciful Ra," Sekhmet breathes, brow crinkling as she does the divine math. "Of what feats could such an abomination be capable?"

"Sky's the limit," Hi'iaka says. "And *this* is our monster of the week? Come on, Sara. Be the better god and let it go. We've already got a global conspiracy to kill. Gotta go big picture on this one."

Nathan can't help shaking his head at the notion. Hi'iaka's right, of course, and deep down, he's sure Freya knows it . . . but that battle has already been lost. He understands the fury that seizes her soul at the thought of Ares. She won't be able to take the high road, no matter how much all those years of hiding have eased off the call of divinity. The principles of her faith don't just influence her; they *define* her.

She's trapped, he thinks.

A half second later, Freya simply shrugs and says, "No, my friend. I can't."

"You sure?" Hi'iaka pushes, and Nathan wants to snort at the impossibility of arguing. That ship sailed the moment Ares put a sword through Freya's neck. "We've got a good thing going here."

"Am I sure?" his goddess repeats with cold disdain. "I will set this world alight if I can catch him in the flames."

And that's that, Nathan thinks to himself, unable to keep a little stirring of glee out of his head. Maybe it *is* the influence of their link, but this new endeavor carries an undeniable thrill, the brutal simplicity of the plan calling to him in much the same way it must for Freya herself.

Find Ares. Kill Ares.

How very . . . neat.

Hi'iaka shares an unhappy look with her siblings, then turns to Nathan and Sekhmet. He just shrugs and moves to stand beside his goddess. Sekhmet, meanwhile, practically glows with anticipation, claws unsheathed and whiskers twitching as if there's a chance of finding Ares outside the front door.

An awkward moment of silence passes as everyone judges just how committed the rest of the room is to the endeavor. Then Pele speaks up, regret filling her voice. "I fear this is a path you must walk without us, my friends. We will support you if we can, but our place is here. We must restore ourselves in these parks and, in time, face the larger threat of Finemdi as a whole. Know that we do not consider this an ending—merely a different trail. The moment you wish to rejoin our cause, you will be welcomed with open arms."

Nāmaka and Hi'iaka nod, and Nathan knows Pele speaks for both of them. He's a little disappointed but bears the trio no ill will. They don't have as strong of a commitment to Freya as he does.

No turning back.

"I look forward to that day," Freya says. "But there's no reason to make this feel so final. I don't even have a plan, so I'm not going anywhere just yet."

Pele smiles, clearly relieved this hasn't caused a rift between them. "Good!" she chirps. She stands there and fidgets a moment longer, glowing eyes flickering with uncertainty before she moves away. "Well. I'll, um, let you three get to your plotting, then. Come on, girls."

Hi'iaka turns back before she exits the room to say, "Oh, and we're having breaded pork cutlets with cabbage and rice for dinner!"

Nāmaka sticks her head in to add, "And I'm making mai tais!"

Then the three are gone, leaving Nathan, Sekhmet, and Freya to their dreams of revenge. Nathan shakes his head. "I'll never get used to that."

Freya snorts. "What, their mood shifts?"

"It's like living with hyperactive kids."

"They are nature spirits," Sekhmet says with a shrug. "Children of the earth, yes, but children nonetheless."

"I'm a little surprised at your reaction, too," Nathan says, turning to her. "Thought you'd consider that a 'betrayal,' of sorts."

Sekhmet smirks, and a husky laugh pours from her throat. "My specialty, yes? Well, priest, there must be *trust* before there can be betrayal. They are friends, to be sure, but only a fool would rely on such . . . *whimsical* creatures in matters of life and death."

Nathan remains silent a moment before he says, "Sekhmet, you nearly killed the pizza delivery guy last week because he was late."

"*He promised it would be thirty minutes or less!*" she snarls, whipping her head around to glare daggers at him.

"Okay, okay, just, uh, commenting, is all. Only a comment," he says, putting up his hands. *Smooth, Nathan.*

"Hmph," she replies, staring him down for another second before turning back to Freya. "What next?" she asks.

Freya blinks. "Now isn't *that* the question of the century?" she says, shifting to look at Nathan.

"Yeah, you're going to need to give me some time on that one," Nathan says, wishing he had a better answer. *Any* answer, really.

"If Ares truly *has* become the beast we fear, my vengeance won't come easily," Freya says, idly tapping the keyboard beside her. "I need strength, and a lot more of it than even a decade at these parks will provide. I need people to believe *in* me, not *at* me. I need worshippers again."

"But how?" Sekhmet asks, sounding a little distraught. Nathan has a feeling she's spent a long time considering that very problem. "How do you reveal yourself to the disbelievers of this modern world and not die in an onslaught of cynicism? There's no room for new religions now, no appreciation for magic and wonder. The only fantasies humankind will accept in this day and age are of their own creation: books, movies, and games built to *entertain*, not answer prayers."

"Well, magic isn't gone, if you think of it that way," Nathan says, drawing their attention. "Sure, yeah, the rules have changed, but people *will* believe. I mean, I'm still waiting for my Hogwarts letter. It's just . . . we don't buy new gods anymore. We never lost our faith; these days, it just goes elsewhere."

"Why is that?" Freya asks, a blend of frustration and curiosity in her voice. "Why can you so easily accept a fictional character from behind the safety of the page or silver screen but can't bring yourselves to embrace the *real* wonders that walk among you?"

"Hey, *I* did."

"Yeah, but you needed me standing in front of you to do it," she says, frowning. "And okay, you'll allow fictional characters and settings and such into your hearts, so fine, maybe there's belief there, *maybe* even worship of a sort, but it's *celebrity* worship, not—"

She stops mid-sentence, mouth agape as a thought strikes her. "Oh," she murmurs, a smile curving the edges of her lips.

"What?" Sekhmet asks. "What is it?"

"I think I know how to gain the strength I need to destroy Ares." She laughs. "I know how to get worshippers. *True* worshippers, Sekhmet, not mental patients or distant cultists."

The goddess's eyes grow wide, and Nathan can practically *feel* the desire radiate from her. "*How?*" she whispers.

Freya turns to the computer and pulls up a map of the United States. Then, she traces a line from Florida to California, to a dot labeled LOS ANGELES.

"I'm going to be a star."

CHASING THE SUN
FREYA

Our farewell party has gotten a little out of control. Actually, it got out of control a few hours ago. Now it's approaching "really fun natural disaster."

Finding an isolated place in central Florida isn't much harder than driving thirty minutes away from civilization, so we weren't too concerned about random onlookers walking into our midst . . . but I'm starting to worry this will show up on satellite. What began as a mash-up of Hawaiian luau, Egyptian banquet, and Viking feast has devolved into a drinks-fueled, magic-boosted, music-blasted riot. I may be a minor player, but the other goddesses with me have more than enough mystic might to compensate. Have you ever seen three drunken nature spirits and a berserker cat goddess compete to see who can do a better job of firing up a party?

Besides the five of us, we've also brought a few dozen of our friends from Disney to this isolated patch of forest. I've made a lot of great connections in my time there, and there's no way I'm abandoning them without a little good-bye celebration. We *were* a tiny bit concerned about letting them see us wield our supernatural skills, however, so I agreed to use a touch of my gift to befuddle their memories. Most people seem to think this is a test for a new Disney attraction, anyway, but just to be on the safe side, we also had everyone leave their cell phones in their cars. After Sekhmet ferreted out the handful of social media addicts who tried to hold on to their gadgets, food and drinks began to flow, and my friends cut loose.

Waitresses of sculpted water mingle with the revelers, wielding platters of barbecued meats and fizzing drinks. Each moves with Nāmaka's liquid grace, and the concoctions they bear are tweaked and tuned to intoxicating perfection. Pele dances before a grand fire pit, surrounded by a throng of ecstatic revelers caught up in her addiction to music and movement. Balls of light twinkle and throb high above us, ten thousand flaming fireflies pulsing in time with the beat and lending the event a unique, arcane rave atmosphere. The songs themselves shake the trees with their power, amplified, channeled, and enhanced by Hiʻiaka's mastery of wind and air.

Sekhmet has already torn through a lake of cocktails and is in the process of entertaining a crowd of awestruck cast members by dueling an escalating series of elemental golems. Forged by the Hawaiian sisters from water, wind, and fire, the beasts steam and slosh in an enormous fighting arena prepared by the Egyptian goddess herself, pummeling wood and earth with thunderous blows in their single-minded attempts to flatten her.

Hiʻiaka protects the onlookers with an invisible screen of air currents, but they still jump whenever a particularly large chunk of rock or tree slams against the barrier. Nathan, at least, is far from the chaos, DJing the event and trying to ignore the rising madness around him. Every time I spot him looking up from the rented controllers and turntables, I can tell by his look of increasingly bewildered awe that things are rocketing out of hand.

With all four goddesses trying to one-up one another and our mortal friends getting increasingly hammered, I really hope nobody gets hurt. Or at least, I *would*, if I were present enough to string that many thoughts together. I may not be able to throw down with my empowered allies, but I've been saving up some lovely illusions for this event, and dancing through a field of living fireworks, towering giantesses, and kaleidoscopic cats while pounding mojitos isn't the sort of thing that inspires sobriety. Oh, well. Sekhmet has the gift of healing, so come what may, we'll probably make it through the night without any fatalities.

"Love the fire moths!" I shout to Pele as my pack of dancers crashes into hers.

"The go-go giants were a nice touch!" she replies, grinning as she bounces a nearby reveler with one lovely hip.

"I really am going to miss you, you know," I say, moving to dance with her. "All of you."

"Oh, sweet little Viking, you'll return to us!" she says with a laugh. "Tonight, we celebrate a choice, a quest, and our friendship—and when you return, we'll do it all again!"

"Any excuse for a party?" I ask, hair bouncing as the air thrums.

Inferno eyes blaze with glee. "*Life* is all the excuse you need!" she yells. "Make sure you remember that while you're out there on your big adventure!"

"How could I forget?" I say, throwing back my head and letting the music wash over me.

Ironically, that's fairly close to the last thing I can recall with any real certainty. The rest of the night is a very loud, very awesome blur. I'm pretty sure I remember tossing Sekhmet a can of beer and cheering as she shotgunned it while ripping the head off another battle golem. There might have been a drinking contest with Nāmaka at one point (always a bad idea), and I seem to recall a few rounds of ear-blasting karaoke with Hiʻiaka. I might've grabbed Nathan's butt, too. Actually, I think I grabbed a *lot* of butts.

By the time the sun rises on the remains of the most shamelessly wonderful evening I've had in centuries, we're all dead to the world. The day that follows is a long and quiet one, and while I bounce back almost as quickly as my fellow goddesses, Nathan sleeps through the entire thing. A shame, because our flight leaves the following morning.

I'm actually a little worried about it. Not because I have a problem with flying, mind you; it's just that I've never tried to sneak mystic artifacts through airport security before.

After stumbling home from the party, we finished our packing and started divvying up our haul from Finemdi. It's a frustrating pile of wonders: glowing talismans, enchanted tools, inscrutable tomes . . . all of it pilfered from their armory, all of it valuable beyond measure, and all of it completely unidentified. Despite the fact that none of us know what the things actually *do*, we aren't about to leave a stockpile of potential "Get Out of Jail Free" cards lying around, so we pour them onto the dining room table and go in a circle, each of us taking a piece until it's all divided.

Sekhmet crams her share into her luggage, and I do the same for mine, mixing in a pile of spell components I've been building with the help of Amazon.com and some of the local markets. Since I'm too weak to dish out major magic without keeling over, I've gotten in the habit of attaching a host of useful spells to keywords (I use breeds of pigs so they won't go boom in casual conversation) and casting them over the course of hours. It's a bit of a hassle, requires tons of weird and wonderful ingredients, and most of them are fairly utilitarian—summoning, tracking, illusions, and so on—but considering how much they helped me back at Impulse Station, I'm wary of letting even the least of them fade. I've even got a casting schedule set up in my phone; my very modern Mímir.

Once every mystical party favor and reagent is packed away, we do our best to get one last night of solid slumber, then prepare to say good-bye. Despite centuries of practice at it, leaving friends behind never seems to suck any less. Sure, Sekhmet gets to be all stoic about it, but I'm a mess. In spite of everything, part of me really wishes we could stay. Amid sniffles and hugs in our kitchen the following morning, Pele repeats her command to find celebration whenever I can, Nāmaka cries and asks if we can take a swim in the Pacific for her, and Hi'iaka gives me, Sekhmet, and Nathan big hugs, tweaks my nose, and tells us we'll be back before we know it.

I hope she's right.

A few last jokes and heartfelt sentiments, and then, far sooner than I would have liked, we're dragging our many suitcases to the curb, packing ourselves into a taxi, and taking a quiet, nervous drive to Orlando International. Even at this early hour, the airport's a buzzing hive of tourists, families, and business travelers.

I try to restrain my sniffles as we make our way toward security. I miss those girls already. Sure, they might have been flaky and naive, but they are also joyful, talkative creatures who just want to have fun with life. Now I'm standing in a line of bedraggled tourists, getting eyeballed by apathetic TSA agents, and hoping I don't set off any red flags. The last thing I need is to be detained and have somebody run a background check on me. Or worse, Sekhmet. Do you think there's a chance in hell of them strip-searching her? There'll be blood on the walls in a heartbeat.

Nathan sighs and shuffles forward a step. He looks exhausted. I think the combination of an early-morning flight and our earth-shaking festivities have taken a toll on my poor priest. Maybe it's because it's been ages since someone's thrown a party in my honor, but thinking back on the whole event is getting me choked up all over again. I grimace as a new pang of loss stabs me. Why am I hurting myself like this? Now I miss those delightful spirits even more.

"Please remove any laptops from your carry-ons and place them in a separate bin," one of the agents says. Nathan complies sleepily, retrieving his computer from its satchel bag.

Glad to have something else to think about, I hoist my rolling pink suitcase onto the baggage conveyer, square my shoulders, and move toward the metal detector. Nathan walks through without a problem, and the TSA agent beyond beckons me forward. Out of the corner of my eye, I watch as my possessions disappear into the uncertain darkness of the baggage scanner.

Nothing beeps as I walk through the detector, and I allow myself a sigh of relief. I move to the left and wait anxiously for my suitcase to emerge. The belt stops, jerks back for a heart-stopping moment, and then mercifully pushes its boxy prisoners into the light. I pull my things down the line and begin stowing everything away, when an agent speaks up.

"Ma'am, we're going to have to ask you to step aside."

My blood freezes. It's not *what* he says that terrifies me—it's the person he's addressing it *to*.

There's a horrible, horrible pause that goes on for far too long, and as my head pivots to take in the scene, I hear her reply at last: "Excuse me, but may I inquire as to *why?*" Sekhmet says it slowly, enunciating each word as if she's speaking to a child.

This is not going to end well.

"We'd like to ask you a few questions about your carry-on, ma'am," the man replies, unaware of the monumental danger. "Right this way."

He holds up a hand. Sekhmet's eyes dart to it as if she's considering how easy it would be to rip it off and feed it to him. Then she inclines her head in the slightest of nods and follows him to a secondary security area partially fenced in by glass screens. The man has her carry-on with him, a dark tan rolling bag I picked out for her after an exasperating trip to the mall. (It took us *four hours* to find something halfway decent—I love the girl, but it's staggering how indecisive she can be when it comes to fashion.) The agent places the bag on a small table between them and unzips it. Sekhmet bristles at what she must consider an appalling invasion of her privacy, but thankfully that's all she does.

I move to get a better look. Frowning, Nathan follows me. The agent, wearing a dark blue uniform that probably offers little to no protection against brutally sharp claws, reaches in, fishes around for a moment, and then closes his fingers around something. He nods to himself and moves to withdraw the object. A bit of metal shines in his hand as he pulls back—and keeps pulling. It takes a moment before I realize it's an enormous *knife*, with a blade that seems to go on forever.

My heart stops. Part of me wants to scream obscenities at the woman.

"Ma'am, you can't take this on the plane," he says in a weary tone, turning the weapon over in his hands. It's obviously ancient and priceless beyond measure, its hilt decorated with polished bands of lapis lazuli and the business end of it hidden by a sheath of beaten gold. Hundreds of tiny Egyptian characters have been carved into the precious metal, the life's work of an absurdly skilled craftsman.

"What? Don't be silly," she says in a haughty tone. "How else am I to know it's secure?"

"Passengers aren't allowed to bring weapons on the plane, ma'am," he replies.

"Well, that's fine, then," she says with a sharp nod. "I have no intention of using it as such at this time."

The TSA agent sighs, obviously used to dealing with obstinate passengers. *I'm* seething. I think I remember her getting a package from overseas a week ago—*this* has to be what was in it. Really, Sekhmet? *REALLY?*

"Ma'am, it's still a knife," the agent says. "Now you can either take the item back and check it in your luggage, give it to a friend to take home, leave it in your car, or mail it."

"I will do no such thing," she says, rearing back. "Do you have the barest notion of how long I have searched for this? It is one of the few relics to survive the fall of my faith and I will *never*—"

"*Hi,*" I say, butting in to stand beside her. I glance down at his name tag. "Gary, is it? This is a friend of mine. She's new to this whole 'air travel' thing, and I'm very sorry about all this."

"That's fine, ma'am, but we still can't let her board with the knife."

"Impertinent mongrel—!" Sekhmet begins, but I elbow her in the side to cut her off and lean in, focusing my will upon the man.

I didn't want to have to do this. I don't know who's paying attention or if this might alert some Finemdi sleeper agent, but I *do* know there are cameras watching . . . and that I don't have much of a choice.

I'm a goddess of love, first and foremost, and even at my weakest, the one thing I'll always be able to do is tweak how others feel about me. Now, after my successes at Disney, it's child's play to flood the man's brain with adoration. In just a second, his look of glazed irritation vanishes, his cheeks flush, and I can feel a heady soup of affection bubble in his brain.

"So you two are friends?" Gary asks in a completely different tone.

"Yes," I say, scooting around Sekhmet to stand directly in front of him. "Would it be too much trouble to bend the rules for us? Just this once? It's such a teensy little thing, isn't it?"

"Huh?" he murmurs. Then he notices the knife in his hand. "Oh, this? Ha, it's like, from a gift shop or something, right? Sure, this couldn't hurt anyone."

I hold up a hand for it and he lowers the weapon onto my waiting palm. As soon as he lets go, I jam it back into Sekhmet's bag and zip the thing closed.

"Was there anything else I could help you with?" Gary asks.

"Nope!" I chirp, giving Sekhmet a meaningful look as I hold out the suitcase for her. "You've been a huge help. Such a sweetheart."

"Aww." Gary scratches the back of his head, looking embarrassed. "It's nothing."

"So we're good to go? We do have a flight to catch. . . ."

"Oh, right, yeah, of course. Better get moving. Sorry about all this." He leans in, lowering his voice and jerking his head at the agents monitoring the baggage scanners. "They can get real uptight. Don't mind 'em."

"Already forgotten," I say, flashing him a smile.

"Say, you, ah, wanna get drinks sometime?" he asks as we gather our things and begin moving away.

"Sure thing, Gary!" I reply with a wave. "Next time!"

He grins and returns the gesture. I give Sekhmet—who still looks highly annoyed—a friendly shove, and then we're off, heading for the elevated shuttle that will take us to our terminal. She manages to restrain herself until we're standing by the sliding doors that will open when our tram arrives. She turns to me with a glare and says, "That was beneath us."

"Beneath—Sekhmet, you tried to bring a giant freaking *knife* on the plane!"

"And what of it? If I wished to cause harm, I would certainly not use such a precious bauble."

I roll my eyes. "Well, they don't know you can sprout *razor-sharp claws*, now do they?"

"Even so, how dare they suspect me of lawless behavior—I am beyond reproach, my fury saved only for the deserving."

"We are not in *ancient Egypt* anymore, Sekhmet!" I snap, feeling myself getting angrier by the second.

"Oh, look, here's the tram," Nathan says, trying to ignore us.

"We talked about this," I say as we begin moving onto the shuttle. "We need. To lie. Low." I plop onto the little shelf at the front of the car, keeping my bag between my knees. Sekhmet moves to stand beside me, frowning.

"Yes," she says after a moment, some of the rage behind her eyes subsiding. "Yes, we—we have greater threats whose punishment I will not jeopardize." She sighs and shakes her head. "I apologize. I do not wish to be a burden. Even after all these years, it is difficult to accept how much our world has changed."

I nod, looking out the window at the approaching terminal. There's not much else to say to that, so I decide to bring the conversation back to the little oddity in her suitcase. Somehow, I doubt she'll mind changing the topic. "So what's the deal with the knife, anyway?" I ask her.

"The—? Ah, yes," she says, actually looking a little sheepish. "An old artifact of mine. A gift, actually, from Ninurta." She gives me an appraising look. "Do you know of him?"

I frown. "Vaguely. Assyrian?"

"Close. Sumerian. God of war and agriculture. He bequeathed it to me after I, ah, bested him."

I glance at Sekhmet as our shuttle glides to a stop and the doors open. She seems a little too self-satisfied for that "bequeathing" to have come from anything other than Ninurta's bloody remains. Such a delightful woman. "How'd you get it back?" I ask. "I assume Finemdi didn't let you keep it."

She shakes her head as we head out into the terminal and begin looking for our gate. "No, I lost it long before my capture."

"Then where'd you find it?"

She sighs. "eBay."

Nathan snorts, barely managing to turn an obvious laugh into a coughing fit. Sekhmet glares at him. "It was very difficult!" she snaps. "Some wretched individual tried to steal it from me at the last moment; the price raised in a matter of seconds!"

My priest looks like he might be in danger of pulling a muscle trying to keep quiet. Finally, he manages to choke down his mirth and says in a strained voice, "I'm sorry. It's just that the idea of a god having to deal with auction sniping is, well, absurd." He pauses a moment, then adds, "Wonderfully absurd."

Sekhmet huffs and turns her attention back to navigating the crowds of travelers. As we're padding down a long carpeted hallway, our rolling suitcases making a satisfying hum, I lean in and whisper to her, "Plan on telling me what the knife *actually* does? I know you're not *that* sentimental. You wouldn't seek it out if you didn't think it would be useful."

She turns to peer at me with a curious expression. "You touched it, did you not?"

"Yeah, for all of five seconds," I say.

Sekhmet's features contort into a ghastly smile. Despite the illusion of a Nile queen, I get the sense I'm facing a mouthful of long, curving teeth. "There is an intelligence within it, a ghost of prophecy and power. The weapon is meant for the hands of a warrior who will wage this world's last battle. I couldn't care less about the magic it provides—I only wish to ensure I play a role in such a conflict."

"Oh," I say. I suppose I should have guessed. As a goddess of warfare, destruction, and judgment, she must have found the words *final war* utterly irresistible. I keep forgetting I'm dealing with an intractable relic here. I really need to do something about this.

"Listen, Sekhmet, I have a favor to ask of you," I say as we near our gate.

"Name it, little fighter," she replies in an instant.

"When we get to LA, I want you to relax."

"Relax? I'm not sure I—"

"Let your guard down. Get a pedicure. Go to the beach. See a movie. Be a civilian." Part of that shouldn't be too hard; I know she's utterly addicted to action movies. You should see the way her eyes light up when they're on. I swear she's watched some of her favorites a hundred times.

Even still, she responds with a frown that remaps her forehead in wrinkles. "You're joking, of course."

"I am *not*," I say with a shake of my head. "I know you—you're going to want to sink your fangs into a villain the second we land.

This isn't that kind of adventure. We need to deal with producers and socialites, not barbarian hordes. I'm going to need your help, and if you want to be able to provide it, you're going to need to dial back the bloodlust."

"If it helps, I can show you around the city," Nathan says, sounding oddly hopeful. "All the hot spots. It'll be fun."

"But—but Ares . . ." she sputters, ignoring him.

"*Will be dealt with.* We're going to LA to stock up on belief, remember?"

She wavers a moment, then persists. You don't know stubborn until you've talked to a god. "Yes, but I can still—"

"You *can't*, Sekhmet." I think my tone is getting really close to pleading at this point. "No fighting. No *threatening*. I need you to be a tourist."

She thinks it over a moment. "I can't even—?"

"*Need*, Sekhmet."

She blows out her breath in a sigh, then looks away. As she does, we reach our gate at last. Our flight's not ready to board yet, so we find a few seats together and settle in to wait for its arrival. Sekhmet sits down and immediately begins drumming her elegant fingers on her bag. I can see the gears turning.

"Centuries ago, I swore to help you achieve vengeance," she says at last. "That promise is now one of my oldest unfulfilled oaths, so if indulging in such . . . *frivolity* is how it must be resolved, then I will learn." She looks me in the eyes as she finishes speaking, and I see the stoic resolve there, like she's agreed to march through the gates of hell for me. Geez, Sekhmet, it's just a pedicure.

"Thank you, my friend," I say, holding her gaze. Despite how silly it all feels, I'm sincerely grateful—I know how hard it is for a god to change his or her ways, even if it's only for a little while.

She nods at that, then sits back in her chair to watch the airplanes outside taxi beneath the hot sun. A few minutes pass in silence until a flight attendant's voice echoes overhead, crackling out of a loudspeaker to let us know they're about to begin boarding. It's only a few moments more before we're walking down the ramp toward our plane; we're flying first-class, after all. I made sure to buy the tickets in person, and—surprise, surprise—the agent liked me enough to give us all an upgrade.

We stow our carry-ons in the overhead bins and settle into our large, luxurious seats. Nathan and I are sitting together, and Sekhmet's just across the aisle. I flip the window shade up and look over the tarmac, letting the Florida sun play on my face one last time. A sense of nostalgia fills me as I realize I'm leaving here for the first time in decades. My true home will always be in the far north, in the verdant bloom of spring and breathtaking cold of winter, but this place is not without its charms.

"Ooh, the screens flip out of the armrests!" Nathan says, showing his focus is on more immediate luxuries. "And can you believe this leg room?"

"Trivialities," Sekhmet mutters, yet I can't help but notice the little smile that curves her lips as she settles into her own chair. She may not *need* the amenities of first class, but she's still a god at heart, and we have a thing for special treatment.

"First time riding up front?" I ask Nathan.

He nods. "Never took many flights to begin with. We were all about the road trips."

"Oh? How were those?"

"When my dad was alive? Great." He pauses. "There . . . weren't many after."

"The soldier?" Sekhmet asks, perking up from across the aisle.

"My dad? Um, yeah . . . ?" Nathan says, seeming a little taken aback by her attention.

"You do not speak of him often."

"Kinda try not to," he says, shrugging. "I mean, I can't tell you how much I miss him, but I don't want to be that guy who's always moping after his dead dad, y'know?"

She watches him a moment, then nods. "I often forget you are of warrior blood," she says, giving him an approving smile. "The occasional reminder is not . . . undesirable."

Nathan's face goes through an interesting mix of confusion and appreciation at that, while Sekhmet simply leans back into her chair, still smiling. For my part, I focus on the food and drinks menu we get as first-class passengers, mentally ticking off the things I want to try.

The rest of the passengers finish loading, each seeming to fix us with a jealous stare as they pass on their way to coach. Then there are a few clicks and bumps and the plane taxis away from the terminal, heading for the runway. Nathan taps my arm after a few minutes. "So besides not drawing attention to ourselves, how else how can we help you when we get there?" he asks.

I lean around him to look at Sekhmet. She's still pressed back in her chair, eyes shut: the picture of tranquility. You might think an ancient creature of the desert would hate flying, but gods don't scare easily—it's hard to worry about a crash when you know you'll just regenerate. The whine of the engines increases to a dull roar as the plane readies itself for takeoff, and I turn back to Nathan. "Uh, well, I'll definitely need someone to help me coordinate everything, which I bet you can do. As for Sekhmet—"

"She'll still be with us, right?" he says as the plane shoots forward, on its way to the skies. He seems surprisingly concerned about her. "Maybe a bodyguard?" he adds.

"She'd be great at that," I say over the sound of the aircraft rumbling. "Actually, it might not be a bad idea to call that her cover. When she's not 'enduring' her vacation, though, what I'll really need her to do is sift truth from lies. I've read enough about the entertainment industry to expect plenty of the latter in the days to come." The rumbles fade, and there's a gentle lurch as the plane takes off.

Nathan nods, looking relieved. Then a slight frown makes an appearance. "Wait, just 'coordination'? Like, schedules? That's it?"

"Um, that's not . . . enough?" I say, feeling slow.

"You haven't thought about what I'll be doing at all, have you?" he says, toeing the line between amusement and frustration.

"It's cute, right?" I say, then slip into a Valley girl parody. "Forgetful girls are, like, so totally cute."

"Totes adorbs," he drawls, trying to mimic the accent. Then he sighs. "I really *do* want to help, Sara," he adds in a normal register. "Palling around with gods is basically the best thing ever, but even so, it's hard not feeling a little . . . unnecessary."

I wince at that, and rub his arm. "Nathan, you—*all* of you—are everything. We. Serve. You. Some of us might do that in some really jerky ways, but we're all made by mortals, *for* mortals. I am nothing without you. Never forget that."

That fun, easygoing smile of his makes a reappearance. "Okay, that *is* nice to hear, but c'mon—I want to do more than stand around and look pretty."

"And here I thought you'd found your calling," I say, giving him a shoulder bump. "Okay, you're right. High priests should always be more than window dressing. And I know exactly what's going to set you apart. Remember those spells I've been teaching you?"

He snorts. "You can only burn your eyebrows off so many times before that kind of thing sinks in."

"Well, it's time to crank it into overdrive. You're my chosen representative here in the world. When you cast those little flame spheres and cantrips, you're tapping into whatever empowers me, right?"

"Pixie dust, rainbows, and M•A•C lipstick, right."

I poke him. "Well, train enough at it, and you'll be able to do a *lot* more. I'm a goddess of magic, and that means my followers are supposed to be able to conjure some pretty impressive stuff. Every spell still goes through me, but until I get a line on some solid belief, your potential is actually higher than mine right now."

"What, seriously?"

I nod. "The power of my clerics was never precisely tied to my own—just validated by it. Belief made me, *and* it can supercharge you. Starting to get the picture?"

"Yeah," he breathes, then laughs. "And starting to wonder what the holdup on the phenomenal cosmic power was."

I give him a bashful smile. "Eh, things got busy. Then aimless. Then busy again." I shrug. "Gods are not the best friends, in case you were wondering. But I'm committed to this: We're going to use every shred of downtime we have to make you a high priest worthy of the name."

"Now *that* is a plan," he says, nodding eagerly. "Only problem I can see with it is how hard it's going to make falling asleep on this flight—I was keyed-up about this adventure before, but now . . . ?"

"Perils of priesthood," I say with a grin.

He laughs at that, and we fall into easy chatter as the ground sneaks away beneath us, an intricate model reaching for the horizon. Not even five minutes pass before I have to stifle a bit of laughter as our conversation trails off and his eyelids begin inching down. Thrilled he may be, but an all-night god party is not something one recovers from in a single day. He'll probably be out for most of the flight.

I unfold my complimentary blanket and tuck it over him, then turn away from my friend and stare out the window, gleefully watching the clouds beyond and the land beneath. It's glorious, a miracle of technology made possible in the last century alone. To someone who's lived over a thousand years, this kind of change is simply astonishing—and just a bit saddening. People seem all too ready to take such wonders for granted, after all. I glance around the first-class cabin, looking at the other travelers absorbed in their newspapers and notebooks, ignoring the fact that what they're doing right this moment would have been impossible at nearly any other point in human history.

I'll find a way to impress them, to leave a mark on the collective consciousness of mankind they won't be able to shrug off so easily. Just wait, people. Just wait.

I watch through the window a bit longer, then recline in my chair and pull a fashion magazine out of my bag. It's a long flight to LA— might as well read up on the latest styles. Part of me itches with glee at all the shopping I'll need to do. There's a brand-new scene out there, and I'll have to look my best if I want to fit in.

This is so exciting! Celebrity status and Hollywood stardom are waiting for me. The call of fame has been a part of my soul since before the concept even existed, and now I'll be chasing the dream that's already ensnared thousands of would-be starlets. I might just have the edge on all of them, though, because while I'm probably not the finest singer or actress, I *am* the most beautiful goddess in the world. And if that's not enough, I can always force people to love me, so hey, I've probably got this in the bag.

I allow a self-satisfied smirk to make an appearance on my lips, feeling like the answers to my many problems are just a few hours away. With all this smug certainty, it's a wonder alarm bells aren't going off in my head. I've certainly been around long enough to know better. Gods may have the market cornered on cockiness, after all, but that doesn't mean we're immune to good old hubris-induced disasters.

And there really *is* something I'm missing here, incidentally. It's the reason I got so upset with Sekhmet earlier, and the reason I was so uneasy about using my gift to get us through security: the fear that someone was watching.

As it turns out, someone was.

STAR POWER

FREYA

Maybe I'm still out of touch. Like all gods, my origins are in the fields and freeholds, in the unknown wildernesses of a time when the largest city in the entire world might—*might*—hold a million souls. Los Angeles has a population almost *four times* that size in its center alone, and the number skyrockets to nearly *thirteen million* when you include the surrounding metropolitan areas. Florida as a *state* isn't much bigger, relatively speaking.

I thought I was "with it" and hip to the modern era, but this is mind-boggling in the extreme. The seething mass of hopes and dreams around me isn't the real surprise, either. I mean, I've been to big cities before, but this place has a certain extra "spice" to it that feels about as far removed from the stoic superstition of the past as you can get. Where do I even begin? The reckless cab ride through a congested sea of automotive anger? Or perhaps the walk all tourists must take down Hollywood Boulevard? There, I was distracted from a pink cowboy and a collection of superheroes by Sekhmet decking an overly pushy man thrusting stacks of CDs at her while a homeless gentleman screamed expletives and informed us he was going to "see what Thomas Edison" had to say about the affair. This place mixes the best and worst of humanity in a blender of glitz and urban sprawl, and I have to admit it's fairly addictive.

There's an *honesty* here I never realized I was missing, a sense that whoever you are or whatever you do, it's okay: There's a place for you. Every culture, every fetish, every lifestyle . . . every last one is accepted somewhere in this sprawling land of sun and sin. Those vapid socialites you've all read about in the tabloids? They aren't fake here; they're *authentically shallow*, seemingly unburdened by the need to hide their greed and vanity behind a thin veneer of social convention. I can appreciate that, I really can. As a creature who can already sense the hidden hopes and desires of mankind, I see it as a refreshing change of pace.

I grin as we finish our first tour of the city, the sunset in my eyes as we descend from the heights of Mulholland Drive, down Laurel Canyon Boulevard, and into the heart of West Hollywood. The brands, the movie posters, the *people*—oh, oh, this is too much. I think I'm tearing up a bit as I open myself to it and realize just how closely the heart of this city beats in time with my own.

Vanity. Fertility. Love. Magic. Even *war* has its place here. Has there ever been a better fit?

"Sara, are you okay?" Nathan asks. The leather beneath him squeaks as he leans forward—we traded in our taxi for a limousine once we were in the city proper. It seemed appropriate.

I bring up a hand and wipe at my eyes, drawing away fingertips coated in shimmering yellow. Tears of gold. Laughter bubbles out of me, colored with shock and delight. How long has it been since they did *that*?

"It's this place," I say, giggling like an idiot. "It's just so . . . *me*."

Sekhmet, standing up in the center of the passenger compartment so she can look out the sunroof, raps the metal to get our attention. "They have a zoo!" she yells so we can hear. She folds her knees, pulling herself back down and pointing out the window at a billboard. She has a silly smile, too—I think this is her first ride in a limo. "I wish to go, when there is time. It has been ages since I spoke to my kin."

Nathan opens his mouth in confusion, muttering, "I took her to Animal Kingdom last week!" Then he points at my glittering fingers and says, "What does it mean, Sara?"

"I guess those months at Disney really helped. The little touches of my myths are returning," I say, admiring the golden gleam. "It's just the beginning, too. Look around us. Did you know they call this place the City of Dreams? How utterly perfect can you get?"

He smiles, seeming relieved they're not tears of sorrow. "It does seem like a good fit. Why haven't you tried to come out here before?"

I shrug. "I don't know. I mean, there are a lot of cities in the world. How was I supposed to know they made one for me?"

"Nobody told you? How inconsiderate."

"I know!" I say, laughing.

Our ride pulls up at the Sunset Tower Hotel. An art deco fixture of West Hollywood since the 1930s, it felt like a rather appropriate place to stay while we got our bearings. That, and the spa is supposed to be *amazing*. A valet helps us with our luggage while we check in at reception, and before long, we're unlocking our adjoining suites and settling in. Booking even one room here isn't cheap, let alone three, but my much-improved magic and talents of persuasion have made money little more than an annoyance. Nathan tells me this is a rather perfect outlook for my new profession-to-be.

I bounce on the edge of my bed after the valet leaves, giddy. The view of the city is gorgeous, and I can almost see my name plastered on its endless billboards and silver screens already, a world bent in worship to my glory. I'll be able to *help* again, to answer prayers, delight in the offerings of my devoted followers, and watch as their sparks of faith kindle an inferno.

Can you imagine it? Can you fathom how much I've lost? My entire reason for being, stripped from me for *generations*, and now it seems within reach again. My eyes burn, and I don't even need to look to know those golden tears have returned. It's so bittersweet— the pain of loss and the hope of triumph, all bound together by one city and the promise it holds.

By the time Nathan and Sekhmet join me after touring their own rooms, I've cleaned up and added some gold-smudged tissues to the trash. Both seem nearly as excited as I am.

"A fantastic battlefield you've chosen, little fighter," Sekhmet says, holding her hands out at the view beyond my suite's windows, then clenching her fists. "Can you not feel the conflict in the air? The raw hatred, the passion and ferocity? My blood *sings* in this strange place."

"That could just be the reality shows alone," Nathan says, moving to stand beside me. "Not that I'm complaining; this is pretty amazing. Once you get past the theme parks, Orlando's hot spots start spreading out. Here, well, feels like there's something cool around every corner. So what's next? After the jet lag's gone, I mean."

I look at him, notice the dark circles under his eyes. I don't think he slept well on the flight, and considering how drained *I* felt after our going-away party, he's probably running on fumes. My poor priest. Mortals always suffer when they try to keep up with gods.

Well, now that we're actually here and taking the first steps on the road to stardom, the pressure for vengeance feels . . . distant. What's the harm in giving us all a chance to relax? It could do everyone some good, even Sekhmet.

I glance at the woman, who's currently staring at the city as if it were a delicious wildebeest, just waiting to get pounced and eaten. *Especially* Sekhmet, come to think.

"A prebattle treat, I'd say." I riffle through my bag and pull out the hotel's pamphlet for the CURE Salon & Spa, waving it at my two companions.

Nathan's features soften. "That sounds—"

"Frivolous," Sekhmet snaps. "Our enemies can only gain strength while we delay."

"You promised," I say, raising an eyebrow.

"But—"

"I'm going to start adding spa services every time you protest."

Her eyes widen. "Wait, you actually expect *me* to—"

"Relaxation-flow massage, thirty minutes," I say, reading out of the pamphlet.

"For *me*? Is this—"

"Deep tissue, sixty minutes."

She snarls.

"Aromatherapy add-on."

"I refuse to be—"

"Soak. Lavender ocean bliss."

She opens her mouth as if she wants to say more, seeming impossibly pissed. I hold up the pamphlet like a talisman and give her a meaningful look. She wavers, fingers flexing as her eyes dart between me and the brochure. Then, incredibly, she backs down, eyes bulging as if she can't believe she's actually agreeing to enjoy herself.

She gives me a sharp, violent nod. "So it shall be," she rasps, conceding the victory.

It's a spa treatment, I want to scream. Instead, I give her what she wants, inclining my head in acceptance as the honorable victor. I hold out the pamphlet to Nathan, who looks like he's been trying to hold back laughter the entire time. "Pick what you'd like from there. We'll book it for tonight and have dinner afterward. I'll make sure we get to hop any reservation lists."

"And our plans?" Sekhmet asks.

"Once we're settled, with clear heads and full bellies," I say.

She grumbles something that sounds like "Asgardians," then nods and stalks back to the window. Nathan gives her a wary smile and buries himself in the spa brochure. After a few minutes' discussion, we pick some truly decadent-sounding treatments and head out to book our appointments in person.

I can't wait, to be honest—it's been too long since I was properly spoiled. I'm a *god*, after all. Bring on the massages, aromatic oils, and half-naked manservants! If you're going to be queen of the world, you ought to be treated like it.

My swagger ends two steps into the spa. The receptionist looks up as we enter and fixes me with a patient smile. "Welcome to CURE," she says. "How can I help you?"

I just stare, openmouthed. The girl looks utterly normal—pretty, with a stylish haircut, tight-fitting clothes from top designers, and a runner's build—except for one thing: The searing violet letters standing out on her forehead that read, SAYETH "HŌRAIOS" FOR PROPER SERVICE.

Nathan looks completely unfazed, but I feel Sekhmet stiffen

beside me. Somehow, this girl has been branded with a message intended only for immortals, or at least those with eyes for magic.

"Is . . . everything all right?" the girl asks, picking up on our confusion.

"I think so," I say, unable to tear my eyes away from the message. It moves with her, little motes of bubbling purple light drifting behind the letters. "Have you—Uh, that is—" I circle my forehead with one finger. "Can you tell me about your, um . . ."

"My skin treatment?" she asks, looking pleased. "Looks really clear, doesn't it? If you're having trouble with breakouts, I can recommend a few really nice—"

"Hōraios," Sekhmet interrupts, looking very curious.

"Hey!" I say, annoyed. "We don't know what—"

The girl's eyes blaze with that same violet light, her back straightens, and her tone changes immediately. "Welcome, honored guests," she says, radiating respect and happiness. "Please accompany me to the hall of my masters, and allow me to extend you every courtesy on their behalf. We deeply appreciate your patronage."

"What the hell?" Nathan says, blindsided by the change in mood.

She holds out a hand to indicate a doorway leading deeper into the spa. "Fascinating," Sekhmet says, striding forward without hesitation. She glances at me over her shoulder, grinning. "You were right to choose this path, little fighter."

We're brought past lavish suites, down a short side hall, and then to a set of thick wooden doors that part at the receptionist's touch with a crackle of warding magic. They swing open on oiled hinges, bands of iridescent light flashing along their edges as strange spells flex and rumble. Nathan gasps at the beauty they reveal, and I'll admit to a bit of jaw dropping, myself.

Beyond lies what I can only describe as a perfect Grecian bathhouse. High ceilings rise above pools of steaming water, intricate mosaics pass underfoot and crawl along the walls, and marble columns gleam with polish and gold inlays. Private discussion nooks and resting places are littered around the baths, hiding animated conversations and less-savory activities behind delicate purple draperies. Dozens of doors like the one we've entered line the walls, all of them providing guests with a perfect view to the center of the room. There, set on a raised platform and surrounded by attendants, are three beautiful young women.

They seem cast from the same mold, sisters separated only by a handful of years. Each has refined features, a pert, aquiline nose, and curly dark hair done up in a modern style. One dances to the strains of live musicians, bare feet sliding across worn marble that must have seen decades of those lively, elegant steps. Another, the youngest and most strikingly gorgeous of the trio, reclines on a classic Roman couch, head propped on one hand, a Renaissance painting come to life. She chats happily with her sibling, all manner of priceless bracelets, necklaces, and rings flashing in the light as she moves. The third and eldest sister sits on the edge of her own couch, leaning in to listen with a brilliant smile. She lacks the bejeweled finery of her sibling but manages to radiate a sense of warmth, order, and goodness richer than any gems.

They do nothing to indicate they're aware of us, but something tells me our arrival has not gone unnoticed. "Wow," Nathan says, staring at the lavish furnishings. "Didn't mention this on TripAdvisor."

I look behind us at the doorway we used. The receptionist waits on the other side of the threshold, but she appears fuzzy and unfocused, like I'm looking at her through smudged glass. I reach out to the entrance with my divine insight, trying to tease apart the threads of magic there. The wards were easy enough to sense, but now that I know what to look for, I can understand the true nature of the portal we've entered.

"The door's a link between distant places," I say, returning my attention to the room. "Forget the hotel—I'm not even sure we're in California." I point at the center of the ceiling, a half dome opened to the elements. The sky outside is darkened with the fullness of night, while the sun beyond my suite's windows had just finished setting.

Sekhmet, clearly unfazed by the luxury on display, grunts and stalks toward the dais. I hurry to catch up with her, worried. She smiles as I reach her side, whispering, "Do not worry, little fighter. We have been welcomed as guests. I would die before abusing that right."

A bit of my anxiety uncoils. Sekhmet has only a passing acquaintance with the concept of restraint, but she's also a slave to ritual, law, and honor. By invoking the specter of guest right, the receptionist has—knowingly or not—created a contract between her masters and this ancient creature. As long as everyone keeps cool, these mosaics will probably stay blood-free.

"Greetings," the eldest sister says as we approach. "We are humbled to accept the patronage of our peers."

The dancer stops to curtsy, crossing one leg behind the other and smiling as she spreads the folds of her dress. "Too few immortals choose to grace these halls in this untrusting age," she says.

The youngest laughs. "So you'll set them at ease with high-necked platitudes? Bah." She swings her legs off the couch and springs upright, jewelry tinkling. Then she bounces down the steps and sticks out a hand. "Aglaea," she says, grinning. "Soul of splendor and magnificence among the Charites."

I return her smile and shake her hand. "Freya," I say. "Radiant giver of love, life, and beauty. Nice to meet you."

The girl turns to my companions. "Sekhmet," the lioness says, inclining her head. "Guardian of kingdoms."

Aglaea returns the gesture, then looks to my high priest. "Um, Nathan," he says, grimacing. "Really out-of-place Web designer."

The girl laughs, and it sounds like music. "All are welcome, mortal. Please, join us!" She holds out a hand to the dais behind her, where her two sisters wait with bemused expressions.

"Introductions, yes!" the dancer says. "I am Euphrosyne. Elegance, mirth, and merriment."

"Must be a hit at parties," Nathan says, smiling.

"Oh, you have no idea," she replies with a sly grin.

"Don't go scaring him off now," the eldest sister says. "Thalia, may it please. Abundance and cheerful order are my lifeblood. Not to be confused with the Muse of the same name, mind you."

"Olympians, yes?" Sekhmet asks.

She nods. "We are the Charites, though you may know us better as the Graces. Call us that if you prefer. This is our home, and the finest house of health across six continents."

We all pause, doing the math and coming up one landmass short. "We never did get a door in Antarctica," Aglaea explains.

I look at the entrances lining the walls. "So every one of these—"

"Leads to another land," Thalia says. "Usually a spa or retreat of some renown, but always in a place of wealth, happiness, and life. We serve only the most exclusive clientele; those with the connections to know of us, the resources to afford our services, and the good humor to . . . appreciate us."

"Fellow immortals are, of course, always welcome, regardless of personal fortune," Euphrosyne adds, resuming her dance.

"We try to stay neutral," Aglaea says, returning to her couch and beckoning for aid. A delightfully clichéd pair of gauze-clad servants approach, bearing platters of fruit, cheese, and other snacks. A man and a woman, they're both the picture of health, unafraid of showing off their assets, and just the sort of people you'd expect to see serving gods. I arch an eyebrow at them, and Thalia laughs.

"We adore the classic approach. Besides, our guests expect it, and we are nothing if we cannot meet those hopes. Come, join us. We ask for little but time and goodwill, and offer everything within our power."

I smile at that. So this is how these girls have made their way without worshippers—knowingly or not, they gain strength from the healthy spread of delight. Well, no harm in indulging that. I step forward, about to take a treat from the offered tray, when Nathan speaks up.

"Uh, this isn't a pomegranate-stay-forever thing, is it?" he asks, dropping a rather relevant mythological reference to Persephone's most famous mistake. I glance at him, smiling at his dash of paranoia.

All three sisters give him blank looks for a second before breaking out in titters of joy. If Aglaea's laugh was melodious, this is like a symphony, their voices blending together in a wave of warmth. "No, no," Thalia says between giggles. "Nor have we styled ourselves after the lotus-eaters. We hide no peril nor poisons, and offer no temptations beyond that which you see before you."

Euphrosyne waggles her eyebrows at Nathan, adding some splendidly distracting hip switches to her dance. "And aren't those enough?"

He coughs and manages to squeak out, "Very, uh, enough."

I select a fresh-baked cracker topped with fig and cheese from the tray, giving its bearer a wink as I do. The woman smiles back, clearly happy to be of service. The treat is delicious, and her manner relaxes me further. This is no empty-headed slave; she genuinely likes being here, making people happy, just like her masters.

Sekhmet also partakes of one of the offered snacks—something meaty, I notice—and Nathan follows suit. "So, how often do other gods come through that door?" I ask, pointing at the entrance we used.

The trio exchange looks, and a touch of unhappiness finds its way to their faces for the first time. "We can only tell you that, other than yourselves, three gods have entered the doors of Los Angeles in recent memory," Thalia says at last.

"And not necessarily through the CURE Salon," Euphrosyne adds.

"Yet you cannot tell us their identities?" Sekhmet asks, narrowing her eyes.

They all shake their heads. It's kind of eerie to see them do it in unison. "Privacy's important to our clients," Aglaea says. "That makes our policy simple: If you don't specifically tell us it's okay to blab about your visit, we don't."

"I guess that's fair," I say. "Well, keep us secret, too."

Thalia nods. "Of course. Now, please, let us forget such troublesome things and bask in merriment and good cheer. You came for relaxation and pleasure, yes? We are only too happy to serve."

Sekhmet grimaces. "I do not believe we—"

I clear my throat meaningfully. "You promised," I whisper.

She pauses. "Yes. Thank you for your hospitality," she says, looking strained. "Such services would be . . . lovely."

Another cabana boy steps forward, this one holding a silver tray with several handwritten menus stacked in its center. I take one, noting it's a full list of spa services—some of which are probably illegal back in California—as well as potential meals, drinks, and harder substances.

I hold up the menu. "Do I just tell you three, or . . . ?"

Aglaea favors us with her laughter again and waves a hand. A woman wearing (slightly) more clothing approaches, projecting an air of professionalism. "This is Alexandra. She will take your orders and assign servants and suites as needed. Say hello, Alexandra."

"Hello, Alexandra," the woman says, smiling. "If you'll follow me?"

We begin moving after her, saying our good-byes to the Graces as we pull away. "Do visit us any time," Thalia says, waving.

"They seem nice," Nathan says, glancing back.

"Welcoming, yes," Sekhmet mutters. "Pity they cannot be more."

He gives her a questioning look, but she shakes her head with a pointed stare at Alexandra. The woman is a respectful distance ahead, weaving her way around the pools and privacy screens, but it's clear Sekhmet doesn't want to get into details now.

As we follow the girl, a singular doorway in the nearest wall catches my attention. Unlike the dozens of others nearby, it's covered with a dark, heavy cloth. I stop, then veer away from Alexandra's trail, fascinated.

"Miss?" I hear her saying as I draw closer to the cloaked portal. "Lady Freya?"

I reach out a hand, unstoppably curious.

"Um, that door is out of order, mistress!" Alexandra says, sounding panicked. "Please, if you could just—"

I grab a handful of fabric and pull it aside before she can reach me. The door beyond is . . . ruined. Burned, splintered fragments jut out from all angles. Cracked slashes and bullet holes march across its midsection, all exit wounds and outward-facing shards, as if a SWAT team of grizzly bears tried to break through from the other side. I concentrate, and harsh wards of throbbing magic hit me like a wave of fetid trash from a long-sealed Dumpster. The familiar weaves of the Graces and their allies are warring with . . . *something* in that mess, an oddly familiar current of magic I *know* I've felt before.

Glittering chains crisscross the door, adding their own magic to the chaos and sealing the whole affair with indisputable finality. It's like something went wrong, they tried to fix it directly, failed, then threw up their hands and locked it away forever.

Alexandra's there in a flash, hurriedly drawing the curtain back into place. "I'm so sorry, Lady Freya—that portal is no longer in service."

"No kidding," I say, reaching out with my will to fix those strange weaves in my mind. *Where have I seen them before?*

"Now, if you would follow, I can—"

"What happened to the door?" Sekhmet asks, glaring at the dark cloth.

"I—I beg your forgiveness, Lady Sekhmet, but I am unable to say," Alexandra says, looking miserable. "Our v-vow of privacy forbids me."

Sekhmet growls, transferring her gaze from the door to the girl. "A technicality," she says after a moment of study. "You refer to *your* vow, not that of your masters. This is an internal matter, and one of some . . . embarrassment?" Her nostrils flare, and she narrows her eyes in concentration. "No. *Fear.* What do you fear, child?"

Alexandra shuffles back, fidgeting and sweating. "N-not all our guests have been welcome, Lady Sekhmet. Certain creatures wished harm upon my masters and were rebuffed. They corrupted this portal, forcing its closure."

Sekhmet keeps up the stare for another heartbeat, then relents. "Forgive me, child," she says, bowing slightly. "I seek security for myself and my allies, and would stand sentinel against all threats, including those you fear. I will not trouble you further, but if you wish our aid, you need but ask."

Relief blooms on Alexandra's features as Sekhmet backs away. "Thank you, Lady Sekhmet. My masters would feel nothing but honor to count a goddess of your stature among their allies."

I smile at her words—this is clearly a well-trained assistant. "Lead on, then," I say, giving the door another glance before turning back to the bathhouse.

Alexandra brings us to a cushion-filled waiting nook where she takes our orders, committing the various spa treatments and massages we select to memory. I "help" Sekhmet with a few add-ons, then take a moment to watch with amusement as Nathan makes his own choices, uncomfortably skirting the menu's more explicit options. I have to hold back an immature giggle as he stumbles over the section cheerfully titled "Threesomes and More!" Like the rest of the menu, it even comes with painterly illustrations of its most popular items.

I wish he wouldn't worry so. I know his heart; he's not a prude, so this restraint is probably for my benefit. The poor boy *still* doesn't understand just how much I've seen of desire.

As I finish that thought, a whim strikes me, and I reach out to Nathan, seeking his sense of self. I've always respected his privacy, but in this moment the urge to pry is suddenly beyond my meager skills at civility. I feel his nervousness and tease it apart, tracing it back to—*Oh dear*, I think, recognizing that telltale mix of awkwardness, hope, and confusion.

He's in love.

It's a surprisingly hesitant thing, too, like he doesn't know if it's wise to hold such emotions, isn't sure if he can even bear to take a peek and examine them. I can't help smiling; there's nothing wrong with a high priest falling for his goddess, especially if she's built around the concept of such affections. Why would he worry? The last time the issue was raised, we said we'd take our time and see what happens. Have I made such things seem unwelcome since?

Maybe he thinks it might mess with our current relationship, or perhaps he still doesn't realize precisely what "god of love" entails. I'm not some drama-ridden sitcom character, if that's what he fears; I adore this emotion, most especially when it's directed at *me*.

Alexandra beckons to me as another servant approaches, and I realize this is an issue to pursue later. Right now, it's time to enjoy my first massage in far too long. Oh, and let's not forget the manipedi. Or the half-dozen other treatments I picked at random. I don't even know what the hell "reflexology" is, but I'm getting that, along with all manner of aromatic, toxin-purging, relaxation-stuffed indulgences. Ooh, *yes*. Pampering to suit the tastes of the divine, and it's *all mine*. I can't tell you how overjoyed the thought of this is making me.

Even gods can have religious experiences.

GLITZ IN THE SYSTEM

FREYA

I don't care what Thalia says. That place is a trap.

When Nathan and I emerge from the portal to CURE a few hours later, I feel better than I think I ever have. My hair is springy and gorgeous, my nails gleam, and my skin glows. The food was exquisite, the service was perfect, and did I mention my nails? They look *glorious*, expertly coated in a cool, bluish mint shade with a hint of shimmer. It goes flawlessly with my blond locks and fair skin. Everything in there was designed to appease gods, and it *worked*. I swear, leaving caused me physical pain.

In fact, Sekhmet's still inside. I think they're doing her claws as well as her normal nails (I don't know *where* they got the idea she'd like that . . .), so she may end up staying very late. That's just fine, because it gives me a chance to chat with Nathan alone. I glance at him, noticing a stunned look of bliss on his face. I don't think he's ever been in such a place.

"Not bad, eh?" I say, stretching as we leave the spa. The receptionist nods as we pass her desk, giving no sign we're anything more than simple guests.

He groans with happiness. "If that was the only nice thing that ever happened in my life, it would still be worth living."

"And it's not the only thing, is it?"

"Not by a long shot," he says, grinning. "When do we go back?"

"Um, whenever we want? This is LA! We're supposed to enjoy the perks, aren't we?"

"If you insist." He yawns. "That was fantastic, but I am *beat*. Any objections to an early night? I think that flight is finally catching up."

"No, but join me for a few drinks on the patio before you turn in—I have something I want to talk to you about."

"Oh no, drinks with a goddess. I live to serve."

I laugh with him as we make our way to the hotel's poolside retreat. When we're settled in, I decide the time is right.

"I wanted to ask you about your feelings," I say, figuring the direct approach is best.

He frowns. "My . . . huh? About what?"

"I can tell you're in love, Nathan. I'm sorry to intrude, but I can't help it—I'm wired to see that sort of thing."

His eyes pop. "Oh. God. Sorry. No, I should have realized—I just—Look, it's not—I mean, I don't want it to be a problem. It really won't—"

"Shh, hey—why would I mind? It's what I was created to spread. I know the hearts of the world, and I know yours. So don't be afraid. Tell me about it."

"Ugh, I'm sorry, I should have said something earlier," he says, turning an endearing shade of red. "It's just . . . stupid."

"Love is never stupid," I say. "Though it can be inconvenient. But you don't have to worry about that, because I'm here to help."

He nods, seeming reassured by that, though I can tell he still has doubts. He toys with his drink for a moment, then bobs his head again. "Well, okay. So . . . geez, where do I even *begin*?"

"Maybe start by telling me what you want, and what I can do to make things easier?"

"That's just it—I really don't know. It's weird. And it's not like there's a future in it, right?"

"Weird"? Gee, thanks for the compliment, mortal. "It kind of depends on you," I say, trying hard to keep an even tone. This is like pulling teeth. Spit it out already so we can get to the fun stuff! "Gods have all the time in the world, Nathan."

He sighs and rubs his face. "I guess anything's better than waiting and wondering. Okay, let's give it a shot."

That is the worst proposal I've ever heard. "Really?" I say, failing to disguise my scorn.

He seems taken aback by that, bewildered in a way that makes me feel like I'm missing something. "But you just said—I mean, you . . ." He shakes his head, and I sense this isn't going how he expected. "You don't think it can work at all, do you?"

"Oh, for crying out loud! Dammit, Nathan, stop second-guessing yourself, put some steel in your spine, and *say it*," I snap.

I meet his eyes, and watch as the self-doubt fades and resolve begins taking its place. *About time.* "I need your help," he says, blowing out a breath. "I have no idea how to make the first move, and I know this is a stupid thing for a high priest to ask his god, but . . . how do I even *start* with her?"

Say what? "I'm sorry?" I blurt.

"Sekhmet. Do you think she'll—I mean, would she ever—?"

Oh gods. "Y-you're interested in Sekhmet," I say. I think I can feel my eye twitch as the gears of my brain come undone, fly off their cogwheels, and land in a giant heap somewhere unhelpful.

"Well, yes. Who did you think I was talking—" His eyes widen as he plays back our conversation in his head and realizes what's happened. "Oh, *fu*—"

"*THERE YOU ARE!*" a voice thunders, making us both jump in our chairs. We whirl to see Sekhmet storming toward us, an ancient Egyptian steamroller of perfectly toned anger.

She reaches our table in an eyeblink and slams her hands on the surface. Vicious, hooked talons sprout from her fingertips, scoring long lines in the metal with a gut-churning *screeeeech.* "Am I to understand this is *your doing?*" she hisses, leaning in to laser me with her best glare.

My conversation with Nathan hopelessly derailed, I look down at those claws . . . and giggle. I can't help it—they're a bright, beautiful shade of peachy gold, sparkling in the light with pinkish hues. Whoever did this was a master; the tones match her olive complexion beautifully, and it's applied in several coats and layered just right. The fact that someone has done this to the personal weapons of one of the world's greatest engines of death is pretty much the most delicious contradiction I can imagine.

My amusement is *not* the correct reaction, however. Impossibly, Sekhmet's stare gets even more heated, and she growls deeply. "Explain. Yourself," she grates.

I pause, compose my features, then nod. "It's part of the plan," I say, improvising.

She says nothing, though her eyes narrow further. I take that as leave to continue.

"Take a moment to look at them in the light, Sekhmet. Appreciate the time, effort, and craftsmanship. I know how much you care about quality."

Another long stare, and then her eyes dart down to examine those talons a little more closely. The look of intense anger begins to fade.

"This is no different than a masterwork weapon, expertly etched, tooled, and prepared for its wielder."

"Hnh," she grunts, holding up her hand and watching the golden highlights sparkle.

"You say you want to prepare yourself for this battlefield?" I say, getting into it now. "Well, here's how. A new age means new weapons, and around here, that includes sexy, sexy nails. You know you're beautiful—now it's time to flaunt it."

The claws whip back under her skin with a soft *svip!*, and I notice her normal nails have the same polish. She pauses to examine them, too, then smiles. "Wisdom beyond your years," she murmurs. "Oh, we shall *rule* this artificial paradise, little fighter. Yes, I can still rend our foes . . . I shall simply use words and will in place of muscle and claw."

I glance at Nathan as she says this, getting a better sense of his attraction: She's stunning, yes, but also dangerous, supremely confident, and utterly without guile. With her, what you see is what you get, and I can hardly blame a priest of Freya for taking a liking to strong women. So why does the thought of playing matchmaker for these two feel . . . uncomfortable? He's my friend, and—one brainwashed kiss aside—hasn't tried to be anything else. Besides, I *exist* to spread love. Who would I be to stand in the way of such affection?

A jealous god, perhaps?

I cram the thought back down, hoping the Valkyrie in my heart will eat it. No, no, we're not going to play the jilted lover, not now.

There's a war to fight, foes old and new to destroy, and stardom to achieve. I do not have time to become a sitcom character along the way.

"It all starts tonight," I say, standing to clasp her shoulder. "I think I'm ready to make some plans. What do you say?"

"*Finally,*" she says, then barks a laugh. "I live for this!"

"Nathan, you still have enough juice left for a little prep work?" I ask.

"You got it, boss," he says, saluting with his drink. He sounds normal, but his smile looks a little nervous. We're going to have to chat about this later. He needs to know I don't have any problems with his crush, and, well, *I* need to know I don't, too.

Things are already getting complicated and it's only our first day. I sigh, then scooch my chair in so I can huddle around the table with my friends and plot.

One sleepless, plan-filled night, a hearty continental breakfast, and a limo ride later, we're on our way to the first goal in our celebrity strategy. With a twenty-four-hour source of hair and makeup secured (it's important!), we figured the next logical step would be clothes. I'm trying to pass myself off as an up-and-coming star with ties to European royalty, so Nathan will be my personal assistant, while Sekhmet plays bodyguard. All three of us need to look the part.

Now, shopping sprees are fun regardless of where you are in the world, but certain parts of Los Angeles . . . well, they're built for this sort of thing. There are places made to cater to literally every level of fashion mania possible, with styles, prices, and snobbery to make your eyes pop. Let's just say that no matter how much money you have, you can still find something to make you blink and go, "It costs *how much?*"—and in case you haven't guessed, *I love everything about it.* Walking through these shops and specialty boutiques, some of which are appointment-only, wraps me in a warm, exhilarating blanket of vanity. If I weren't dead set on stardom, I think I could empower myself by running a store here and feeding off the wonderfully remorseless pride and self-obsession that fills the air. This is part of my portfolio after all, a defining piece of what I am.

It takes eight days of intensive travel, comparison, and collection before we're finished, and that's just *getting* the clothing. It'll be weeks before all the personal tailoring is done and every last outfit is cut to fit us like a second skin. Sekhmet will rock the alpha business attire with lots of pencil skirts, suit jackets, and low-cut button-downs and blouses, all strong lines and sharp edges. Her palette will be charcoal, pinstripes, and dark patterns, accented by flashes of red and accessorized with severe, compact sunglasses and a "go die" attitude.

Nathan, meanwhile, will focus on the upscale side of business casual with blazers, open-necked dress shirts, and designer jeans in a variety of light browns, blues, and grays intermingled with darker items for a professional-yet-unobtrusive appeal.

As for me . . . well . . .

Okay, look. I'm sorry for this. Really. I have to gush and there's *nobody* around to appreciate all the wonderful, glorious things I've acquired. Nathan would try, but I know he wouldn't get it, and I'm positive Sekhmet still longs for the days of simple pleated dresses, saris, and mountains of heavy jewelry. Since I'm not yet desperate enough to tell the Graces about it, I'm afraid it's falling on you.

My hotel closets are overflowing with outfits for every imaginable location, dress code, and social standing. Overall, I've tried to stick with clean lines, elegant colors and patterns, and cuts that flatter my curvy figure without being (too) indecent. Everything has a modern streak that's often tempered by a handful of vintage touches to make me seem stylish yet approachable.

I've split my fashion strategy into a three-pronged front, starting with low-key streetwear in the form of sleek minis, breezy tops, the occasional tight-fitting pair of light jeans, and casual blazers. My more upscale outfits will focus on snug skirts, knockout dresses, and classy pullovers, and finally, for when things start getting serious and I need to scream "money," I have a diabolically enchanting assortment of dresses and gowns, cutting-edge minis, and perfect tops.

That's not even touching on the tidal wave of sunglasses, purses, handbags, jewelry, and hairclips I've picked up along the way, accessories to enhance my already-immense outfit options, all of which is, of course, accentuated by a jaw-dropping array of flats, pumps, boots, wedges, and sandals.

I'm in my element—this stuff is practically glowing with vanity and splendor, putting a spring in my step and a permanent smile on my face. Glorious outfits aside, my beauty is also a function of my divine strength: The better I feel, the better I look, so having a wardrobe fit for gods transforms my natural loveliness into an echo chamber, rebounding and improving it with every head I turn and eye I catch.

New wars require new armor, and mine comes with designer labels.

In all this, I haven't forgotten about Nathan and the romantic mess I've stumbled upon, but I get the sense he's desperate not to get into it right now, and like I said, my to-do list is already well-stocked. Untangling that web will have to go onto the backburner for the moment, because stardom-wise, we're just getting started.

Now that I'm finally at the point where I know I won't be caught out in something inadequate, it's time for the next phase of our plan: representation. I need a talent agent—a manager to help me get roles and put my name in front of influential producers, directors, and scouts. Doing this on my own isn't an option; not only is time a factor, but everything I know about the movie industry has come from *Wikipedia* pages and "How to Be a Star" guides. I'm hopelessly ignorant about the realities of this business and out of touch as a general rule. Help me, talent agencies, you're my only hope.

As I understand it (at least, as much as Google helps me understand it), when it comes to these organizations, one of the biggest fish is Creative Artists Agency, or CAA. They trade in extremely popular stars and big names, from film and television to sports, music, and even video games, setting up massive deals for major motion pictures, advertising campaigns, television series, and more. In short, they are not the sort of people you go to when you're getting started—they are the power brokers who come to you when you're already famous. Their clientele collect awards like it's a hobby and make headlines simply by walking out of cafés.

Sounds about right for a god, doesn't it?

Once again, I'm going to cheat. My powers of persuasion are without peer in the mortal realm, and I don't care how high and mighty this agency is; all of it is built on the efforts of fallible, too-human staff. CAA's executives would never give me the time of day, but their employees? Another matter entirely.

The sun is high in the sky when we pull into the roundabout in front of their headquarters on the Avenue of the Stars. The building looms above us, two symmetrical towers joined by an expansive glass-walled lobby on the ground floor and distant, imposing offices on upper levels that stretch across its hollowed-out midsection. I can see daylight on the other side of the lobby, making me feel as if the entire compound is sort of floating above the ground. The commission to build this place must have been an architect's dream.

A well-dressed valet in a gray vest dashes up to open my door, and I gingerly make my way out, maneuvering my heels so they don't catch the rented sports car's frame. I feel oddly clumsy; this outfit is beautiful, but I'd hate to try fighting in it. I'm wrapped in a bright turquoise off-the-shoulder bandage dress that ends about two inches above my knees. Gold-and-diamond starburst earrings twinkle as the sun hits me, and my pale gold leather pumps click on the stone of the entryway.

Thick, oblong white columns flank the entrance and march away on both sides. Combined with the imposing, clinically grandiose feel of the place, they give me odd flashbacks to the Greek and Roman pantheons. This feels like a futuristic take on their style, a perfect marriage of wealth and engineering with a touch of religious strength, all set to impress the modern world. As another valet pulls open a door for me and I stride into the lobby, I'm struck again by just how *right* all this feels, how perfectly the pomp of Hollywood fits the needs of the divine.

My heels click on alternating strips of white and slate-gray Carrara marble, the tiles reflecting the stark beauty of this place with a razor shine. Nathan whistles softly as he enters along with Sekhmet. "Hate to be the cleaning crew," he says, bringing a bit of reality to a space that is clearly designed to impress.

"I like it," Sekhmet purrs, keeping her face impassive. "A touch of grandeur is never unwarranted."

I feel eyes on me and notice an assistant taking a not-so-subtle path in our general direction. A handful of undisguised security personnel are paying attention as well. Since I'd rather be the one to start any dialogues here, I strike out for the reception desk, motioning for my friends to keep pace.

A sharp-dressed young man looks up as we approach, smiling warily. "Hello. Do you have an appointment?"

I settle my hands on the cool surface between us and blast his mind with a lance of affection. "No, but I don't need one, do I?" I say, smiling.

His eyes glaze, and he returns my smile, body language relaxing as he leans forward. "Uh, well, it's usually a good idea, but I mean, for you I'm sure they, um . . ." He screws his face up in thought. "Who did you want to see?"

At this point, a few of the other receptionists are looking over, seeming concerned. I wink at them before cutting loose with a wave of power, washing away their hesitations and suspicions before turning back to my new friend. "One of your best rising agents," I say to him. "Not too close to upper management, but—"

I stop at an uncomfortable look on his face. "I'm so sorry, it's just . . . we handle reception for all the businesses here," he explains. "Creative Artists Agency owns the building, but it—they—rent space to—I mean, you'll need to speak to them directly. I don't know enough about their agents to help," he finishes, sounding miserable.

I sigh, getting the feeling there's going to be a lot of bureaucracy to cut through here. "Okay, can you get me in to talk to them?"

"Of course!" he says, brightening. He nods at one of his coworkers, who takes his place as he makes a quick call. After a short discussion, he returns. "If you'll just wait in the reception area by the main CAA entrance, someone should be right out for you," he says, gesturing to one end of the lobby, delighted to help. Then he realizes I'll be leaving. "Please, um, come back anytime!" he blurts, looking hopeful. His friends have similar expressions, and all of them wave and say good-byes as I thank him and head off.

It's not long before someone comes to collect me, a woman in a vastly sharper and more stylish outfit than the receptionist. She pushes through a thick glass door into the lobby proper and looks at us with a very confused expression. She's clearly an assistant of some sort, and desperately trying to place me in her mental catalog of power brokers.

"Hello," she says, holding out a hand. "Irene, Creative Artists Agency. The front said there was an important guest waiting, and, please forgive me, but you are . . . ?"

"Sara Vanadi," I say, completing the handshake and filling her heart with love and adoration. "Your newest client."

Her demeanor changes in an instant. "So glad to meet you, Ms. Vanadi!" she says, giving me the ultimate benefit of the doubt. "Please, follow me. Do you know who you're here to see?"

I walk in behind her, entering the Creative Artists Agency proper. It's a slick, white-walled space with an enormous staircase that stretches up and up, soaring into the central atrium like a sculpture from another time. An enormous light wall parallels it, illuminating the affair with soothing tones. Tasteful, abstract art touches the simple surfaces, adding coordinated splashes of color to draw the eye without overpowering the architecture.

"I need an agent," I say, flashing a bright smile before running through my short list of qualifications. "Know anyone who might fit?"

She seems a bit bewildered by that, but no less eager to please. "Oh, um, clients are usually set up with agents in advance, but I can try to schedule you with one now! Just let me check the planners! If you'll wait here?"

"Of course!" I say. She beams at that and dashes off without another word.

"They always seem so *happy* to help," Nathan says, watching her go. "I'm surprised you don't do it more often."

"What, the whole 'love me' thing?" I say, leaning against a wall. "It *is* nice, but it's not genuine. I'm doing it to reach a goal. Forcing people to worship me just for the heck of it? No, that would feel . . . wrong."

He cocks his head at that, then smiles. "I think I'm glad to hear that."

"Don't want to work for a supervillain?"

"Just seems like something that could get out of hand really fast."

I think about Dionysus and shudder. I can only imagine what he's up to right now. "Promise me you'll speak up if I start getting crazy?" I ask after a moment.

He nods. "You got it, boss."

Sekhmet grins and says, "It would be my honor to stay your hand should corruption find you, little fighter."

It's not hard to figure out what she means by *that*. "Thanks, Sekhmet," I say with just a hint of sarcasm, knowing it'll pass her by.

A few minutes later, Irene returns at a brisk pace, practically running across the marble. She seems pleased as she comes to a stop in front of me, a little breathless. "I've just set you up with one of our rising stars. His name is Mahesh, and he's agreed to meet you. If you'll . . . ?" She gestures deeper into the building.

"Wonderful, thank you," I say, following her lead.

We're brought to a crisp, circular conference room. A large flat-screen TV dominates one wall, and half a dozen expensive-looking chairs ring a glossy white table. The setup makes me feel like I'm standing inside a space-age doughnut. Irene asks if we need any refreshments, then invites us to sit down. Only a handful of minutes have passed when a young man with light olive skin enters the door, shuts it behind him, and fixes us all with a calculating stare.

I return it, giving him a quick once-over. He's dressed in an upscale business outfit similar to Nathan's, but colored to set off his complexion and elevated with a red-patterned silk tie. Clean-shaven, with sharply defined features, a slicked-back haircut, and intelligent hazel eyes, he seems very professional and, at the moment, very apprehensive.

"Hello," he says with a faint British accent, extending a hand. "Mahesh Rao."

I stand and clasp his hand. "Sara Vanadi. Nice to meet you."

I know the name means nothing to him, but he does a good job of pretending I'm still worth his time. He inclines his head at my friends. "And these are . . . ?"

"Nathan Kence," my high priest says as they exchange handshakes.

Sekhmet, features cool and impassive, merely nods and says, "Lady Rashida."

Mahesh arches an eyebrow at that, then sits, gesturing for me to do the same. "Well, Ms. Vanadi, you have me at a loss. You're here, talking to me without an appointment, without *Irene* knowing who you are—quite the feat—and I'm very curious as to *how*."

"Fun, isn't it?" I say, settling back in my chair. "I'm here for an agent. I got through to you because I'm incredibly convincing, and that's entirely due to what I really am."

"All ears, Ms. Vanadi."

I pause to let the anticipation build, then hold out a hand, palm up. "I'm a god, my friend," I say, unleashing an illusion I prepared in advance. There's a warm, glittering flare of light, and a pristine white water lily unfolds, rising from my outstretched palm to float in the air before me. Another flare, and it whirls apart, filling the meeting room around us with dancing white petals and motes of floating gold.

I lean forward, into the heart of the illusion, letting my face push aside those petals until I emerge staring into Mahesh's saucer-sized eyes. "I am Freya, mortal."

His jaw drops, works silently for a few seconds, and then he manages to squeak out, "Is—is this . . . You're pranking me. Right?"

I laugh, flopping back and sweeping a hand through the knot of petals above the table. They scatter as if touched by a gust of wind, taking up an orbit around the walls of the room and clearing the air between us. "I got in here because I'm a god of love, Mahesh. I can make anyone my closest ally. But I'm not going to force that on you, because I need a real friend—someone who knows me for what I truly am and wants to help. Now, are you that person?"

His eyes dart around the room, taking in the illusion, the unimpressed expressions on my friends' faces, and my sweet, imperious good looks. He blows out a breath and shakes his head. "I hope you don't take offense to this, but . . . you have to understand, this is a business of special effects and deception. If I took everything—even this astonishing display—at face value, I'd be a laughingstock. For all I know, this could be a *very* strange joke."

"Such a cynical world," I say, sighing. "All right, you won't trust your eyes? Fair enough. Trust your heart."

Just like I did to convince Nathan to believe in me all those months ago, I reach out to him with my gifts, twisting his feelings toward me. I'm much stronger than I was back then, so I'm able to run him through a wide spectrum of emotions, giving him a taste of happiness, gratitude, hope, pride, and, of course, love. I announce them as they hit, highlighting the impossibility of what I'm doing.

"How—?" he breathes when I finish, seeming appropriately staggered.

I cut the effects, bringing him back to normal. "I'm a god, Mahesh."

He takes a moment to recover, breathing deeply, and I can tell he's thinking it over. Then he purses his lips, drums his fingers on the table, and begins nodding his head. "I'm starting to believe you. I'm not aware of any drug that can do that. At least, not without obvious side effects. But still—a god? Are you—I mean, are there more? It would follow that if there's one . . ."

I turn in my chair and wink at Sekhmet. She nods, and then her human features fall away, ripping apart to reveal the snarling, perfect lioness beneath. "You stand before the Lady of Terror and Life," she rumbles in her lustrous accent. "I am Sekhmet, little son of Karnataka, and the gods watch you still."

He plunges back in his chair, gripping its arms in shock, eyes even bigger than before. "You . . . I'm, ah, pleased—so pleased!—to meet you. Both! Both of you!"

Sekhmet snorts and the illusion returns, snapping across those leonine features and replacing them with the chiseled nobility of the Nile.

Mahesh, panting, puts a hand to his head. Then his eyes dart to Nathan, full of questions. Nathan laughs. "Just a guy, pal. Normal human guy with amazing friends."

That brings a tiny smile to Mahesh, and he sits back in his chair and begins righting himself, trying to reclaim his earlier confidence, when he freezes. I can tell a rather unpleasant thought has struck him. He pauses, narrowing his eyes, then meets mine and says, "All the gods—*all* of them—are real."

I shrug. "For the most part. Some didn't make it this far. The really old ones are probably gone for good. If they still have believers, though, it's a safe bet they're around."

He groans and rolls his eyes. "Do you have *any idea* how many gods we have? My mother will never stop crowing about this if I tell her. 'Mahesh, now you know they really *are* watching, so you'd better—' Aghhh, I can hear her now."

"I'm sorry, do you need a moment?"

"You give a man proof his gods exist and he's supposed to take it in *stride*?"

"Helps if you're a disaffected millennial," Nathan says with a grin.

"Charming." Mahesh rubs his face, straightens his tie, and blows out a breath. He takes another minute to compose himself, steadying his breathing and letting the truth of our reality soak in before he continues. "Fine. Please excuse my surprise at having my world upended."

"Done," I say brightly.

He rolls his eyes and the little smile returns. "And you. Freya. Scandinavia, isn't it? What are you doing here? What would *any* god want with LA?"

I spread my arms. "What any god wants anywhere: believers."

"So you'll just set up a church and expect—Oh." He stops, getting it. "Ohh. Now that *is* clever. You want to be a star. You—Ha, forgive my slowness, Miss Freya. You understand the new gods of this world, and how we worship them."

"Through a screen, not a temple, yes. I want it, Mahesh. To the world, I can be the perfect star. To you, the perfect client."

He drums the tabletop. "Do tell."

"I've had a thousand years to learn how to act. I can speak most of the world's languages, nail any audition, charm every casting director and interviewer, and do it all with a body that, by definition, will never quit."

"All good things. Incredible things, really." He drums his fingers a little more, and I see the gears turning. "All right. I'll admit it: As clients go, you're about as perfect as they come. You want more than a career, though. Much more. You'll have to forgive my avarice, but, well, you understand the town you've entered, yes? Beyond helping to usher in the Age of Freya, what do I get out of it?"

Sekhmet growls. Mahesh tries to hide his reaction, but I see him flinch, just a little.

I smile again. "Besides money?"

He turns rueful. "Five minutes ago, that would have been plenty. But that was before gods walked the world. Money is mortal, and I've just learned there's *much* more to life than that. Let's say I make you a star, set you in the heavens, give you"—his face becomes curious—"power? That's what believers provide?"

I nod.

He bobs his head, seeming pleased. "Makes sense. So you become all-powerful. What can such a being accomplish? What is the worth of a favor from them?"

"Ha," I mutter, grinning. This man, like the city he calls home, is just right for me. "*Name it*, Mahesh Rao."

His eyes dance, and I can see the same wild, imaginative glee descend on his heart as in those who suddenly realize they're holding a genie's lamp. "Immortality . . . ?" he ventures after a moment's thought.

"With certain caveats? Yes. At the very least, a longer life than any of your peers—longer by many times, Mahesh."

He laughs at that, then rises from his chair, reaching a hand across the table. "More than fair. Now is not, I think, the time to be greedy," he finishes as we shake, casting a quick, wary glance at Sekhmet.

"Excellent. How do we get started?"

He sits back down and sighs. "Well, we should probably keep our partnership quiet for the moment—I'd prefer not to have to justify a completely unproven new client to my superiors. Instead, we'll have to go with a more underhanded approach."

"I always enjoy a little trickery," I say, smile widening.

"Couldn't have guessed," he replies, glancing at the petals making a leisurely circuit around the room. "I'm going to take you on as a 'hip pocket' client. Hip pockets are people without official representation from an agency—instead, they get a very shaky agreement with a single agent who thinks they might have potential. In practice, it means the agent may find them an occasional audition on the side. If things work out and they get a part, *then* the agent can pitch that client on better footing. It's certainly not as good as full representation, because the entire agency won't be working to help you get roles."

"And I would want this . . . why?"

"Because I'm going to try to sneak you into the first major audition I can find. You'll pop in, wave your magic wand, and make them love you. Then I go up the ladder and say, 'Look who I found—she's well on her way.' Anyone objects, we have you charm them, too. You'll have the full backing of CAA in no time and the projects will start rolling in."

"Perfect," I say, looking back at Sekhmet. She nods; Mahesh isn't lying. "Make sure it's nothing villainous or overly dramatic. The sooner the better, too. I need roles on the fast track. I don't care about films coming out in five years, and I don't want to be tied to a single sitcom or something like that. I have an endgame in mind, and I want to get there as quickly as possible."

"What is this 'endgame,' if you don't mind my asking?" Mahesh says, seeming eager.

"Stardom is one thing. The love of the people will give me strength, but belief in *Freya*? In my divinity, my existence? *That* is the ultimate goal, and there's only way to achieve it."

Doesn't hurt that I'll get to kill Ares along the way, either.

"I'm sorry, but aside from a very awkward 'coming-out' on *Late Night*, how will you convince the world you're actually a god?"

"That's the beauty of it—I don't need them to believe in me. Just Freya."

"But how—"

"How else? Celebrity status is a means to an end; someday soon, I'll star in the next blockbuster franchise that'll sear itself into the cultural consciousness of the world. Can you see it now, Mahesh? How a new religion can spread in the Information Age?"

He pauses, looking confused. "You can't mean . . ."

"I can," I say, leaning in. "Coming soon to a theater near you: *The Saga of Freya*."

FUN AND GAMES
FREYA

Meet Sara Valen, rising star.

My new stage name is one of the first things we decide on, in part because Vanadi isn't exactly Hollywood, but more importantly, so I can stay off Finemdi's radar. Garen could have shared my former title before I framed him for the destruction of Impulse Station, so attaching it to *major film and television releases* would be suicide. And stupid.

"Now, for your credentials, well . . . we must have something," Mahesh is saying. "Even just a stint in a theater group."

"Please no," I say. "I've seen every variation of *Hamlet* and the others across *four hundred years*. Don't get me wrong, Will wrote some good stuff, but *I'm done*."

He laughs at that and shakes his head. "No, no, of course not. This is something we'll want to spin from whole cloth."

"We're going to fake it?" I say. "How?"

"I have very creative friends," he replies, smiling. "Let's work on putting together a résumé for you, and I'll have them fill in the blanks. They'll toss fake trailers on YouTube for indie films, write blog articles and reviews for theater performances, and so on. Those things will take you only so far, of course, but with your gifts . . . that should be all you need."

"You know, I think I rather like you, Mr. Rao," I say, grinning as my future takes another step closer. "Now let's make ourselves a career."

A lengthy discussion follows, and everyone, even Sekhmet, tosses in ideas for the various under-the-radar roles I could have played. Over the following hour, we compose a list and start making plans for the many consultants, photographers, and star makers I'll need to visit to complete the illusion. That done, we begin saying our good-byes and collecting our things.

There are no contracts or agreements between us beyond words, but I believe my new friend will be true to them, and not just because Sekhmet will eat his skin if he isn't. He seems to have an ideal mix of pragmatism and ambition, and I can always trust that to keep him honest. He stands to gain a great deal here, as well.

Irene walks us to CAA's door, all smiles and chitchat. As I follow, a wave of exhaustion hits, making me sway a little and miss a step; the tricks I've pulled today have taken a lot out of me. I inhale, steadying my stride and promising myself I can relax when we get to the car.

Unfortunately, this hopeful future gets derailed the moment we enter the main lobby, where a very irate young woman suddenly gets in my face. "Is *this* why I've been waiting?" she snaps, staring down her nose at me.

"Uh, what?" I blurt, confused. The girl looks vaguely familiar. In her mid-twenties, she has all the telltale signs of money, inflated self-worth, and just a little too much power. Her perfectly straight blond hair frames sharp, angry, and coldly beautiful features. Her cheekbones look sculpted, her chin is distractingly pointy, and her nose is so symmetrical and precise it can't be the original. A light dusting of freckles accentuates her shadowed green eyes, making her seem like the ultimate cross between "girl next door" and "hateful barista." Bright pink lipstick matches her coral tube dress, and slinky rose-hued heels push her several inches taller than me.

"Mahesh will be happy to see you now, Ms. Riley," Irene says in a hopeful, placating voice.

"Oh, *now* he's happy?" the girl squeaks, transferring her glare. "No-name, dumbass, and bitchface show up and suddenly *I'm* waiting?" She looks back to me. "Go on, tell me you weren't here to see him. I know who's on staff, I know who's on-site, and I know whose time you *wasted*! HARV!"

A middle-aged man in a business suit steps up to join her, adding his glare to hers. He moves with the casual grace of someone who knows how to handle himself in a fight, and his features are almost as sharp and angular as hers. I'd be tempted to call him "pretty" if he were just a little less well-built or his jaw were ever-so-slightly more rounded. "Yes, Kirsten?" he asks in a surprisingly patient tone.

"How late are we?"

"Over twenty minutes. You're going to miss your lunch with the director," he says, seeming genuinely annoyed with us and sympathetic to the girl.

"We're very sorry for the confusion, Ms. Riley," Irene says. "There was a scheduling mix-up and—"

"And who the hell are *you*?" she says, stepping closer to me. "Actually, no, y'know what? You've wasted enough of my time. I see you again"—she fishes in her purse as she talks, pulling out a pure-white smartphone—"god help you." The device clicks as it snaps a photo of us. "There. We're done here. Open the damn door already!"

Irene jumps back, giving us a very apologetic look and holding the door for the woman and her assistant, who march in without another word. She slips in behind them, mouthing "Sorry!" to us before she goes.

There's a moment of silence as we try to process the storm of narcissism we've just experienced. "What the hell was *that*?" I say at last.

"I'm confused—am I 'dumbass' or 'no-name'?" Nathan asks, equally bewildered.

"And you're *absolutely certain* I can't . . . ?" Sekhmet purrs, looking hungrily at the door to CAA.

"Yes. No murdering civilians." I pull my Mim out of my bag, undoing the lock screen and heading for its Web browser. "No matter how *un*civil they are," I mutter as I enter my search terms.

After a moment, the *Wikipedia* page for Kirsten Riley appears on the little touchscreen. "Some sort of entertainment icon," I say, reading. "Had a starring role on a kids' show, turned into a pop star, now she's in movies."

Nathan makes a little sound of recognition. "I think I remember her. Catchy songs." He glances at Sekhmet. "Stupid, though. Horrible person, too."

"Certainly famous," I say, going back to the search and opening a few links. "Lots of licensing deals, fashion shoots, Twitter follow—" I narrow my eyes at the screen. "*Seriously?*"

"What?" Nathan says, leaning in to see. "What's she—Oh."

There's a new tweet on her feed that's only a minute old:

Kirsten Riley
@KrileySmiles

check out the eurotrash thats trying to steal my agent!!! #lol #instafail #nothappenin #bitchplease #stepoff

11:08 AM - 20 Jul 18 · Embed this Tweet

This is followed by a rather unflattering picture of the three of us, looking confused (or, in the case of Sekhmet, homicidal). I lower my phone to stare at the door to CAA, aghast. "Can—can she *do* that?"

"Welcome to show biz," Nathan murmurs.

"I understand your desire to avoid bloodshed . . ." Sekhmet begins with a dangerous grin. "But think of the problems it would solve."

My inner Valkyrie gives a nudge at that, and I grit my teeth. "She's just one jumped-up mortal," I say, jamming the phone back in my bag. "Who cares what she thinks? She gets in our way, we can talk. Until then, we have better things to do."

I stalk out of the building with my friends and signal the valet service to retrieve our car. Mahesh has given us a few to-do items, and I'm glad to have something to take my mind off Kirsten and her wretched manners. I flop in the back of our ride as Nathan takes the wheel, grinning as only a boy with a six-figure sports car can. As he pulls out, following the GPS to our next destination, the fatigue returns in force and I bring a hand to my head.

I hate this. Despite all my schemes, styles, and skills, it doesn't take much to drain my pitiful reserves and remind me how weak I really am.

My recent adventures may have brought me power, but it's not a patch on what I once held. All that manipulation with Mahesh and his teammates at CAA is coming back to bite me. I sigh deeply, massaging my temple. This is infuriating—the limits of my strength are painfully clear, and for a god forged in glory, battle, and adoration, I can think of few things worse.

Sekhmet notices and reaches over to squeeze my shoulder, giving me a sympathetic look. She understands, even if she's managed to hold on to more of her might over the years. At some point, I'm going to need to ask her how she did that. Maybe it's because she never suffered a crisis of confidence like I did.

I lean my head back and breathe, trying to relax and refresh myself. Another spa trip is definitely in the cards for tonight, but that's only going to help get me back to my usual weakling self. Without my regular feed of belief from the theme parks, I'm no longer gaining strength on a daily basis. I have to get in the limelight *soon*.

LA's usual daytime traffic works in our favor for once, giving me plenty of time to recover before we arrive at our next destination. In short order, I'm smiling, posing, and having a ball with one of Mahesh's photographer contacts, setting us up with plenty of high-quality headshots and stills he can use to get me into auditions. After that, it's a strange meeting with a social media consultant who's going to help build my online profile—custom accounts, websites, and even résumés will be crafted from whole cloth in order to make me seem like a legitimate actress looking to break into the big leagues. Getting fans and followers isn't the main goal just yet, so everything is tailored to impress producers and other Hollywood bigwigs who might not even stoop to see me without such pedigrees. Finally, a hair, style, and makeup review session with a fashion consultant—they seriously have consultants for everything here—leaves me feeling a bit better about myself, as the gentleman in charge has only general suggestions and no "critical issues" for me to address.

I end the day feeling like I'm on the right track. If all goes well, auditions will start rolling in and I'll be cheating my way onto a career path only a handful of talented mortals have managed to tread. Pretty great, right? Well, before you start getting jealous, just remember I'm eventually going to need to figure out how to kill a god of war *and* trash a conspiracy that's been around for centuries. You come up with some solutions to *them*, you can start judging me for taking the easy road to the stars.

The evening finds me bone-tired but thrilled. I collapse into bed, close my eyes, and dream of—

Darkness.

The world is the same, as are its people and all their hopes and fears—but the light is gone. Instead of the usual radiance that illuminates my sleep, a cloying blackness eats at the earth, wrapping it in tendrils of malevolence and loss. This isn't personal, either: Every god I've ever known dreams of this, sees the world and understands his or her place in the hearts of its inhabitants. It's all we see when we sleep, and it lets us know where we stand when it comes to the principles from which we were forged.

Something has invaded this place, however, has made itself a beacon of spite in the dreamscape we share. And then it speaks. A voice, echoing and twisting at the edge of my consciousness, reverberates along those midnight threads. It's nothing—just the plea of another dreamer—until I focus my attention and amplify its words.

"I claim your world," it hisses, androgynous and cold. "I claim your cattle, your flocks, your future. You are weak. Bloated with arrogance and made irrelevant by age. I seek your challenge, dare you to show yourself before me. I am *here*"—and the vision sears with darkness, spiraling down, down, from North America, to New York, to the Hudson River, to a rusting set of docks—"and I defy you to test my claim. Come to me. Come see how feeble you have become. I claim your world, I claim—"

And the message repeats, over and over, a constant loop of challenge and malice.

I've never seen anything like this before. Whatever this creature is, it's calling out every god in existence, actually *praying* to us in all our devastating glory, and asking for a *fight*.

The door to my hotel room shudders under someone's fists, jarring me awake. I practically throw myself off the bed, dash over, and wrench it open to reveal Sekhmet standing there, chest heaving with adrenaline. "It's him," she rasps. "Apep. We *cannot* go."

Ah, hell. She's talking about the creature I released when I destroyed Impulse Station—Samantha's mother. Sort of. "I—I wasn't planning—"

She pushes in and begins pacing. Words dribble from her, uncharacteristically subdued and unsure. "He stands astride this world and the Land of the Dead, renewed each night no matter the means of destruction. Made to fight and die, and do so endlessly." She looks at me, eyes wide. "Made in a different age, Freya, as we all were. When night fell, it was believed Apep wished to devour the sun, and so my kin gathered to destroy him, to fight for every dawn. Now those believers are gone and we no longer guard against this creature, but does the sun still rise? Of course. Apep cannot consume it, but—do you see the flaw? Do you see how the cycle has been broken? As long as the sun rises and sets, he *cannot be killed.*"

"I know, Sekhmet," I say, reaching out and trying to get her to slow down. "It's a problem, and one we'll have to face someday soon, but we're *all* kind of immortal by definition. Even if some idiots show up for a battle royal, what can he really do to them?"

She frowns and shakes her head. "I do not know. What does he desire? Has he gained some new knowledge in all these years? Does he wish to face a specific god? Or is he simply bound to pursue conflict at night? I seek vengeance and judgment, you hunger for beauty and war, and Apep . . . is it chaos he craves, or something else? It *burns*, this ignorance of mine."

"Look, we're dealing with something really old and really strange," I say, aiming to calm her down. "I think it's okay not to have a clue what he wants. I mean, how are we supposed to get inside his head? This is a god that isn't *really* a god, right? No prayers, no religion, he's nothing without—Oh."

"What?" Sekhmet says, pacing closer.

"It's just . . . oh, crap," I murmur, thinking it over. "How does a god without a religion get stronger? For us, it means gathering belief where we can and trying to do things that call to our natures, right?"

"Yes . . ."

"So Apep never had a religion to begin with. He just had people who hated him *so much* they made a religion out of *that*. They didn't worship him—they worshipped the hatred *of him*. So what does a god who's made to be hated *do*?"

"He, well, he'd have to find a way to . . ." She pauses, the truth hitting her. "Aah, he *goes looking for it*. He does not yet possess the strength to make mankind hate him, so he chooses us instead. He's trying to return to the old ways, to foster loathing and fight the gods."

"All the more reason to stay put and get stronger, right?"

She nods. "Absolutely. I doubt he possesses the power to taint the dreamlands in this way each night, but whenever he manages it, we must hold fast and resist his vile call."

Something tells me that'll be a *lot* harder for her. "I wonder who's going to take the bait."

She shrugs. "Fools. They will spend themselves and achieve nothing but his empowerment. We must rest, conserve our strength, and draw plans against this creature for another day." She pauses. "You . . . do intend to include Apep in your trials to come, yes?"

I nod, getting the feeling she won't take kindly to any other answer. "He's our responsibility. We let him out, so we'll settle that debt when we can."

So Finemdi, Ares, and now . . . Apep? I think, sighing inside. *Why not?*

"Agreed," she says with a sharp flick of her head. She stands there awkwardly for a moment as her breathing steadies, and I realize she's feeling embarrassed for bursting in here all panicky. Then she sighs, shakes herself, and begins to leave. "Well. Very good. Rest," she says as she reaches the door. "Tomorrow, our battle begins anew."

I smirk at that after she's gone. One day, I'm going to sit her down and figure out why she still talks like a *Star Trek* extra. It's the twenty-first century, sweetheart; nobody will judge you for easing up a notch. A minute after she leaves, there's another knock at my door, this one much lighter and more tentative. I open it to reveal Nathan, wearing boxers, a borrowed hotel bathrobe, and a worried expression.

"Everything okay?" he asks. "I heard—"

"Sort of," I say, motioning for him to enter. He takes a seat on the edge of my bed, and I fill him in on Apep's little invitation. When I'm done, he looks relieved to hear I'm not tearing off on a snake hunt anytime soon.

"Ha, you were worried I was going to drag everyone across the country again, weren't you?" I say, plopping down next to him.

He laughs at that. "You? Impulsive? Never."

I elbow him, grinning. He gives me a playful bump with his shoulder, then yawns and rubs his face. "Gah, sorry," he mutters. "So tired. I swear I'm not bored hanging out with gods in Hollywood."

"Not for another few weeks, at least?"

"Yeah, that sounds about right," he says with a smirk. "Then I'm taking up drinking."

"You'll be a Norseman yet," I say, turning to look at him. "Now we just need to get you facing your fears and staring death in the face."

His smile takes on a rueful cast, and he nods. "Okay, yeah, I've been dodging this one long enough, haven't I?"

I shrug. "It's nice to have a hobby."

"Mm. Well, I'm getting sick of it. I need—I don't know. I can't keep waiting; it's torture. So, yeah. Sekhmet. I'm crushing on the Egyptian goddess of vengeance. How does that even *happen*?"

"Have you *seen* those legs?"

"Right? Astronauts on the ISS are probably staring," he says, pointing upward. "It's not just that, though. She's so damn confident and different and scary and—I *like* her."

"More of a cat person, huh?"

He laughs. "Yeah, I'd rather not think about that part. The whole 'lioness' thing is really freaking weird. Gotta say, though, ever since she started wearing that illusion twenty-four seven, it's been easy to forget. 'Out of sight, out of mind.'"

Huh. That seems a stretch, even for a laid-back guy like Nathan. "Seriously?" I say, trying not to make it sound judgmental. "When did you get so adventurous?"

He opens his mouth, witty answer all ready, when he catches

himself and stops. A puzzled look creeps over him, and he cocks his head to the side, thinking. "I don't . . . really know, Sara," he says at last, frowning. "You're right. It's not me. At least, not the old me. It kinda feels like—y'know, when I wanted in on your whole Finemdi thing? It's like that. I feel . . . different. Like I can *do* things now. Like I *should* do things. And getting caught up on Sekhmet being an ancient cat god when there's all kinds of *really cool* stuff about her just seems weak."

Oh, hell, I think, a wave of cold comprehension rising in my chest.

It's *me*. I'm doing this to him. Gods may be thought given form, but it goes both ways; we kind of "bleed" into the world around us, and that includes the people in it. Confidence, a devil-may-care attitude, and a touch of lust? Sound like anyone you know? Yeah. And now it's happening to Nathan, just because he fell in with a very weird crowd.

But there's no way I'm telling him his crush might be a symptom of divine radiation, because he's in love, dammit, and I was made to fan those flames wherever I find them. So instead of going all Debbie Downer on him, I say, "That's the spirit! So what else do you like about her? What's that 'really cool stuff'?"

Note to self: I'm going to regret this later.

He grins. "Lots. I mean, yeah, she has that whole 'hair-trigger violence' thing, but set that aside and you see she really cares about the people she trusts. Goes adorable whenever she's around animals, funds women's shelters in her free time, and is a total sucker for action movies."

He gets an exasperated look, like he's having trouble putting something into words, then continues with a frustrated sigh. "She's— you know, she's *this close* to being a walking stereotype of some outdated berserker, but those little moments where you realize part of her is having *fun* with it all . . . it's hard *not* to like her, Sara." He groans. "I'm sorry. Idiot mode on. Why am I babbling about her to you like this after what—I mean, those *stupid* things I said on the terrace. Agh! Are you actually okay with this?"

"I—well, yeah," I mumble. *Smooth, Sara.* "Yes, you surprised me a little, but I exist to see love grow wherever it can, Nathan. I want to help. I'm totally okay with this."

All right, so I have no idea if that's a lie or not. This whole situation is messing with my head, but hey, if I say something often enough, maybe that'll settle the issue for me. At the very least, getting some direction here might help me focus on this divine war I'm trying to win. Priorities!

Nathan cracks a genuine smile, saying, "That's great, Sara. Thank you."

Well, at least *he's* convinced. Either I believe in my words a lot more strongly than I thought, or he's way too trusting. Which could it be . . . ?

"Aw, what are gods for?" I say with more cheer than I feel. "So how can I help?"

"Man, I don't even *know.* Where do I start? I mean, could it ever work out? Should I even *try?*"

"Nonsense. No high priest of mine is going to chicken out on a relationship. Love *and* war, remember?"

"Love is a battlefield," he says softly, grinning. "So what do I do? Ask her out for drinks? 'Hey, gut any heretics lately?'"

"I think you should just be upfront and honest with her, Nate. Tell her how you feel, what you're looking for, see if she feels the same. Don't forget, she's literally impossible to lie to, so she won't just appreciate the straightforward approach—she'll know when you're being anything but."

"Good point. Is she—? Um, wait. Now that I think about it, here's a better question to ask first: Is a relationship something she'd actually *want*? Has she ever had a boyfriend before?"

"Ehhhh," I say, wiggling a hand back and forth. "She's had lovers, yes . . . even a husband at one point, but who hasn't? Trouble is, those words could mean something entirely different to her. Think of how relationships have changed in the past century. Huge differences, right? Okay, Sekhmet is over *five thousand years old*, and unlike me, she actually *remembers* most of her past. Trying to second-guess her is impossible. I really think your best bet is just asking and taking it from there."

"Man," he says, rubbing his eyes. "Okay. Fine. Tomorrow night. Get ready, 'cause your high priest is going to make a move."

"Just make sure he fills his god in on all the juicy details afterward, all right?"

He laughs. "Is that your version of a Hail Mary? Romantic gossip?"

"Heck of a lot more interesting, at least," I say with a snort. "You know we actually hear every prayer, right? They're . . . like these soft, wonderful little songs. The faintest music, right in the back of my head, and I can hear the words if I concentrate. Thing is, even the catchiest beat in the world can wear thin; any idea how boring it gets to hear the same tune over and over again?"

"Never thought about it like that," he says, frowning. "Wait, does that mean I can contact you anywhere? Just . . . pray and you'll hear me?"

"Seriously?" I say, genuinely surprised. "You *do* realize that's the deal, right? You pray, we answer? And if the high priest of Freya can't talk to her, who can?"

"No, no, that makes complete sense. It's just . . . you have this image of gods being these distant, all-powerful beings in the clouds, and then you meet one and she's this cool girl who likes chocolate and fashion magazines. I guess I figured being able to hear every prayer was more of the myth, too."

I grunt a negative. "Nope. We hear them. Every. Last. One. It's who we are, Nathan. We were made to hear your hopes, your pleas, and your praise."

"Does it ever get annoying, listening to that all the time?"

"Nah," I say with a shake of my head. "Most of the time it's just background noise, but it's not distracting, not any more than the sound of blood in your veins, the whisper of air in your lungs. Prayer's part of our biology."

He spreads his hands. "My goddess," he says. "Coolest damn thing in my life. A few months ago, my goal was being able to afford a graphics tablet. Now I'm helping Freya land a film career and hoping for a date with her awesome five-thousand-year-old friend."

He reaches out and pulls me into a hug. "Why would I need to pray?" he says over my shoulder, giving me a friendly squeeze. "You've already given me more than I'd have ever known to ask."

"Uh, you're . . . welcome?" I say in a silly voice, hugging him back. He laughs at that, then pulls away and stands up.

"Thank you, Sara," he says, and I can tell this conversation has unburdened him of a rather deep-set stress. "Business as usual tomorrow, and then in the evening . . . well, I'll let you know how it goes!"

"All I ask," I say with a forced giggle, feeling a strange brand of awkward. We hug one more time at the door and then he heads off to sleep, leaving me alone to think about things I'd really prefer to avoid acknowledging in any way, shape, or form.

I groan, throw myself onto the bed, burrow underneath the

covers, and flip off the lights. I spend another minute shuffling my pillows, trying to get the perfect arrangement, then do my best to drift off and leave all this nonsense behind for a few hours.

Then I catch a faint, familiar voice joining the meager chorus in my mind. I focus, pulling it out to listen, and of course it's Nathan, praying to me. Thanking me for all I've done. Praying for success with Sekhmet. Telling me how wonderful I am. Saying all the things we gods love to hear.

And so instead of resting, I lie awake for the next two hours, teasing apart all my recent interactions and feeling like I've done something wrong in every last one of them. What is *with* me? Do I have feelings for this boy? No, not "good friend" feelings—I know we share those. I'm talking about the "let's bounce around naked, then conquer the world" ones. It would be easier if I knew for sure. I could march in there, head this off at the pass, and let the good times roll.

But I could be wrong. This could be jealousy, or confusion, or just the result of a decades-long dry spell for a god of love and . . . *Damn, I'm bad at this.* What if I step in, mess with what's happening, and it turns out all I wanted was to keep Sekhmet away from a toy I hadn't played with first? I could ruin two friendships and potentially even derail my plans for empowerment. I've seen this happen before, seen every imaginable relationship success and failure, and I simply am not sure enough of what I want to make a move.

So I won't. I'll sit back, help Nathan where I can, and focus on the many other problems at hand, no matter how weird it feels.

"I so do not need this right now," I say to my ceiling, which has been a very good listener so far. I send it a quick, snarky prayer of thanks and roll over, hoping sleep will find me at last.

"Boo," Samantha Drass says, sending me thrashing out of bed with a scream.

TAKE ONE
FREYA

"W-what ... H-how did ..." I stutter before composing myself enough to yell, "Samantha, *what are you doing here?*"

She giggles, standing up from the bed, and as she does, I realize she's outlined in pale indigo motes of light, making her easy to see in the darkness of the hotel room.

"Sorry," she says. "But if it helps, I'm not actually here."

I blink, taking a tentative step closer.

"Go on," she says, holding out a hand. "Give it a try."

Still feeling off-balance, I reach out and try to grasp her offered palm. My fingers fall through it with a soft azure flare. "An illusion?" I say, frowning. Beneath the image she's presented, the weaves of magic I can make out don't exactly line up with my guess.

"Close. Modified divination effect from an artifact of mine. Whatever you point it at turns into a reverse scrying window, so instead of showing *me* distant places ..."

"It shows distant places *you*," I finish, smiling. "Neat."

"Really neat," she says. Then her demeanor shifts, a hint of nervousness working its way across her face. "Didn't swing by to show off, though."

"Something happen?"

"Not exactly." She sighs. "It's Ares. I wanted to check in, make sure you got my message."

"I did!" I say, the Valkyrie within stirring at his name. "That's why I'm here in LA—I need a *lot* more strength to take him on, figured a career in show biz might do the trick."

She beams at that. "Excellent idea, Sara." Then her smile falters. "Although . . ."

"What? What's wrong?"

"Do you know why Finemdi brought him on board? Ares?"

"They're Greek fanboys and wanted the full set?"

That gets me a giggle. "Ha, no. It's you."

"Me?"

"Yeah. And Impulse. Oh, they haven't a clue it was *really* you, so don't freak, but losing a station doesn't happen every day. They're taking it seriously, and the current theory is that there might be a rival group of gods working against them."

"Well, they're not wrong," I say, thinking of Sekhmet and my high priest with pride.

"No, but they're assuming something on the scale of a full-blown counteragency. That's where Ares comes in—they've hired him to manage their divine tactics and war plans."

She leans in, turning serious. "They want him to weaponize their gods, Sara."

"That, um, doesn't sound great."

"It's bad for everyone, myself included; he's shifted our belief regimens into overtime and cut research projects, which means I can't work on resurrecting my mom anymore. He's also redoubled our efforts to 'recruit' unaffiliated gods *and* persuade existing prisoners to join us."

She sighs. "He's preparing for war."

"Fantastic," I groan, sitting on the bed. "We have to destroy him, Sam."

She nods. "He wants to use Finemdi to wage a personal crusade against his rivals, and they seem happy to let him. I know it's early days for you, and I'm sorry to push, but . . . try to hurry." A mischievous glint enters her eyes. "And let me know when you're ready to discuss strategies of our own—I might have a trick or two to help even the score."

Her image fuzzes, blurring for a moment before snapping back. "Shoot," she says, looking into the distance at something I can't see. "Almost drained. I'm going to need to cut this short, but just remember: I want him gone, too. Let's make it happen."

"Sam, I—This is music to—" I start to say, but then her image fades away with a dim flicker of violet light.

"Oh," I say to the now-empty room. "Uh, bye?"

Alone and suddenly not quite so tired, I lie back down, mind whirling. So *that's* why Samantha put me on my enemy's trail . . . and apparently she wants to walk that path beside me. Well, damn. This is about as good an end to an evening as I could hope.

Just need to figure out how to step up my schedule, I think. Then I glance at the clock by my bed and groan at the time. *And how I'm ever going to fall asleep.*

My first audition is today.

I woke to my Mim buzzing and Mahesh on the other end, all excited and British. He informed me he'd found a great opportunity, an audition for a major supporting role in a big-budget HBO miniseries called *Switch*. Apparently another actress was a lock for it but dropped out due to an unexpected scheduling conflict, so now the producers are desperate for a replacement. He got me a slot for today, and after a panic-filled tear through my wardrobe for the perfect outfit, I joined my allies at breakfast to give them the good news and indulge in some waffles.

Now I'm pressed to the window of our sports car, watching the scenery roll by as my legs bounce with restless energy. I'm in a bright sundress covered in stylized yellow flowers and accented with pale silver heels, and I've already felt the burning desire to race back to the hotel and replace everything about ten times since we left. I'm just so damn nervous. "This is it," I murmur. "Oh, I hope it's good."

"You'll do great!" Nathan says from the front. "They'll love you. Seriously, I have a hunch."

Sekhmet grins. "I share your excitement, little fighter. With Ms. Drass's assistance, this will be but the first step on the path to vengeance."

I nod at that, still watching the scenery. My friends were very interested to hear about Sam's midnight visit, and just as delighted to discover Samantha was already working the inside track on taking down Ares. *Ah, revenge*, I think, beaming. *You might not be so distant after all.*

"I have always enjoyed these programs," Sekhmet says, interrupting my thoughts. "I must also confess to a great deal of curiosity as to how they are made. Do you think any actors will be there?"

"I'm not sure," I say, turning away from the window. "All Mahesh had for me was a quick synopsis of the show, a time slot, and a location. If I get the part, though, then we're *definitely* meeting some."

"Excellent," she purrs, settling back in her seat with a smirk. "Why so hot to see them?"

"I have . . . admired several of the warriors on these programs from afar and would like very much to see them in the flesh. The centurion, the *khal*, that vampire from your lands, the criminal consultant—"

"Sekhmet, I never knew you were such a fangirl," I say, laughing.

She snorts. "Please. This invention of theirs is the finest entertainment since the Roman blood sports. All too passive, of course, yet far more intimate."

"We'll have to get you to Comic-Con if we have time," Nathan says, grinning. "Tons of actors show up there. You could even go full lioness and they'd love you for it. Might even win a costume contest that way."

"A contest? Delightful," she says, tapping her chin. "I will look into this. Ah, but our destination approaches. Tell me more of it later."

Nathan pulls up outside a nondescript office building in the downtown area. There's no sign to indicate this is the right spot, but the address matches. We head into the lobby and check in with the receptionist, who confirms who we are and sends us upstairs.

We follow some bland taped-up AUDITION signs to a nondescript metal door. I look at Nathan and Sekhmet, then shrug and turn the handle. The room beyond looks like a bare-bones office entrance; a few folding chairs are set against its walls and a secondhand couch sits behind a beat-up wooden coffee table. A handful of magazines are scattered across its surface, along with a few Styrofoam cups of half-drunk coffee. There's a chest-high desk at the back of the room, like you might find at a doctor's office, and a young woman who screams "summer intern" pokes her head above it.

"Ms. Valen?" she asks.

I nod.

"Good," the intern says, setting aside a textbook and marking something with a pen. "Right on time. They're just finishing up with another actress—won't be five minutes. Would you mind waiting?"

"Not at all," I say, pulling one of the chairs over to the coffee table and sitting down so I can peruse the magazines.

"Can I get you any coff—" she begins before the door slaps open, cutting her off.

"Thank you *so much* for this opportunity, Ms. Starling, really!" an oh-so-familiar, sickly sweet voice shouts from the opening, aimed back inside. I slowly turn to its source, a mix of dread and annoyance twirling through me.

Kirsten Riley, spoiled Hollywood cliché that she is, bounces out of the room, saying good-byes over her shoulder. "Please let me know when you can! Day or night, just give me a call! Thanks again! Byeeee!"

Her assistant, Harv, follows her out, shutting the door behind him and almost bumping into her as he turns. Frozen mid-step, Kirsten is staring at me, openmouthed.

"Do you think this is a *joke*?" she spits at me. "I—I swear to *god*, I don't know who you are, but if you—No, that's it. You're not worth the time." She slaps her hands together, wiping them off, then throws them up and strides away with a disgusted noise.

Harv trails after her, giving us all a very lengthy, unnerving examination as he does.

The intern's head rises over the desk when the door slams behind the pair. She shakes it with a snort, then goes back to her reading.

"Wow," Nathan says, looking at the exit. "She's going to tweet your face off in about five seconds."

"Yippee. The child has a megaphone," I say, rolling my eyes. "In my day, she'd be milking cows and gossiping with fishwives."

Sekhmet laughs. "In mine, she'd be stuffed in a sack and drowned in the Nile." I arch an eyebrow at that. "Sacrilege *used* to matter," she explains with a shrug.

"It's this obsession with fame that's gone to her head," I say. "She's no different from all those lovely girls who used to pray to me; it's the world that's changed."

"The difference is that *they* praised you, and she blasphemes without retribution," Sekhmet mutters, a hint of darkness entering her voice. "She doesn't need direction—she needs *fear*."

Part of me nods at that, producing a grim-yet-satisfying set of ideas on how to teach such a lesson to Ms. Riley. "She's a distraction," I say, more to myself. My inner Valkyrie needs to shut up and stop agreeing with Sekhmet—serious trouble lies that way. "Dealing with her gets us nowhere—and what *was* she doing here, anyway? Mahesh is her agent, too, right? He had to know we'd see each other."

"We'll have to ask him," Sekhmet says, smiling. "I like that boy; *he* certainly knows to fear us."

"He also knows who we really are," I mutter.

The inner door swings open, and a tall woman with long hair in black ringlets steps out. "Sara?" she asks, looking at us.

"That's me!" I say, trying to match Kirsten's chipper tone.

She smiles and holds the door open. "So glad you could join us on such short notice. Please, come in."

"No problem! Uh, can I have my friends in there?"

"I'm sorry, auditions are usually closed," she says with a sympathetic look. "But they can wait here!"

I hook a thumb in the direction of the outside door Kirsten and Harv just used to leave. "What about—?"

"Oh," the woman says, a rueful expression appearing. "Her. It, ah, wasn't worth the argument."

I give her a knowing look, then shrug. Well, I was going to ladle on the love anyway—might as well get started now. "Are you sure?" I press, filling her brain with affection and glee. "They won't be a bother."

Her eyes widen as my magic takes hold in her mind, and she breaks into a big grin. "You know, I don't see why not," she says, stepping back. "The more the merrier!"

"Great, thanks!"

"I'm Diane Starling, one of the producers," she says in a friendly voice as we follow her into the room. It's a large, empty office space, devoid of the usual cubicles and furnished instead with a long desk in its center, three chairs behind it, and a table full of snacks and drinks. A little video recorder stands atop a tripod next to the desk, ready to capture my audition.

One of the chairs is occupied by a young man with thick glasses and long brown hair that falls to mid-neck. He has exaggerated, friendly features and sharp blue eyes, all of which come across as vaguely Germanic. Another man is standing in front of the desk, leaning one hip on it and looking over a script. He puts it down the moment we walk in, striding over with a big grin. Unlike the usual pretty boys I've come to expect from LA, he's much older—mid-sixties, at least. An African American gentleman with deep wrinkles and an expressive face, he's the only person I've met in this industry (so far) with a sincere smile. I can tell he's legitimately happy to have a chance to meet new people, and a little thrum of questioning hope in his heart tells me he wants us to return the favor.

"Ah, this is Donovan Gladstone, one of the main supporting actors for the series," Diane says as he approaches. "He'll be reading a few scenes with you."

"Sara Valen," I say, holding out a hand. "Pleasure to meet you."

"All mine, certainly," he replies in a rich, raspy voice as we shake.

"And this is Frederick Mandel," Diane says, gesturing to the seated man. "Our casting director."

"Fred, please," the man says, getting out of his chair and nodding. "So good of you to come." He sets a thin set of pages to one side, and I notice it's my résumé. A large glossy picture from my photo shoot covers the first page. Considering we took those only yesterday, I'd say Mahesh has the skills *and* motivation to make this work. The promise of immortality will do that, I suppose.

"Can I offer you anything to eat? Coffee?" Fred asks after our handshake, nodding at the table of goodies.

I shake my head. "Too nervous," I say with what I hope is a charming giggle.

The three of them smile at that, and Fred says, "Please don't be—we're all friends here, and we'll take as much time as you need. The better your audition, the easier our jobs."

"Thanks, Mr. Mandel," I say. "I think it would be best if we got started, then."

Fred gestures at some of the scripts on the table beside him. "If you'd . . . ? Your parts are marked in yellow. Let me know if you need a little time to study, and we'll take the scenes in order."

"Just a minute should be fine," I say, selecting one and reading it over. The content matches what little I know of this miniseries. Set in San Francisco in the near future, *Switch* is a dramedy intended to chronicle the adventures of a young woman in a world where, thanks to some sci-fi medical advancements, full-body cosmetic alterations have become trivial outpatient affairs. There are a lot of big names attached to the script and production, and it seems like they're aiming to provide some interesting social commentary as well as plenty of delicious relationship confusion, romance, and teary-eyed Emmy Awards bait. Sounds like fun.

"So you've done a lot of theater work and independent films, but nothing major," Diane says, reading over my résumé as I flip through the script.

"No wide releases, no," I say offhandedly. I don't know if Mahesh's media contacts have had enough time to translate my fake credentials into fake trailers and such, but there's no need to worry now: I'm here, and that's all that matters.

"Your accent is excellent," Fred says, smiling. "If I didn't know any better, I'd say you were born in the States."

"*Möchten Sie lieber Deutsch?*" I say in a flawless Bavarian accent. It's only a guess, but I think that's where he's from.

His eyes widen at that, and he glances back at the résumé. "It *does* say 'impressive language skills,'" he murmurs.

I grin, then return to the script. After another minute of study, I nod and lower it. "Okay, I think I'm ready."

"Great! Don will start you off on the first scene," Diane says, walking behind the desk. "Just let me get the camera set up."

"Oh, one more thing before you do that," I say. She stops to look at me, and I return her curious stare with a big smile before igniting a white-hot star of love in their minds.

Don's and Fred's looks change in an eyeblink, going from detached and professional to blissfully pleased, while Diane's already-cheery expression turns downright ecstatic. Of the three, I've spared Don the full force of the effect to save my strength, but even he has a silly smile as he takes his place just off camera.

"Y'know, I'm not even sure why we're taking the trouble to do this," Diane says, fiddling absently with the camera.

Fred nods as if he's in a dream. "I agree. It's obvious you're the right choice, but . . . we have to get a demo reel from everyone. That's . . . okay, right?"

"Of course," I reply, situating myself in front of the camera.

Diane gives a thumbs-up, and Fred nods.

"He's still the person you fell in love with, Karen," Don begins. "Can't you see—"

"*How?!*" I yell, trying to find the perfect place between heartache and fury. "I get it, all right? It's not about the—the whole switch thing! People should be able to have whatever life they want. I am filled with understanding and empathy!"

"So why is this different?"

"You—you seriously don't understand?"

"No, look—all I know is your boy shows up with the face he's always wanted, and suddenly Ms. Acceptance starts sounding like a hypocrite."

I stare at him in shock for a moment, then spit my next lines like they're poison. "He *didn't even tell me*, Gene. Making a switch isn't supposed to be a *surprise*. Flowers? Surprise! Weekend trip? Sure! *New body? ARE YOU FREAKING KIDDING ME?*"

Don pauses for a moment to let the delivery stick, then glances back at Fred and Diane, who nod.

"Okay, that's great, Sara," Fred says. "Ready for the next scene?"

We continue like that for a while, running through a wide range of takes, including monologues, comedic bits, and even a few tearful moments. I'm lucky this show is all about relationships: I can draw on a millennium of them for acting inspiration, to say nothing of my personal experiences. I cry for my brother, Freyr; I laugh as I think of Mozart's jokes; and I feel the endless rage of my time with Ares, all of it pouring out into that room.

After the scenes are finished, there's a short Q&A with the trio, covering the role in very general terms and what they'd need from me if I get the green light. It's pretty standard stuff (I think) and very positive, but I hit Fred and Diane with some extra adoration and pride along the way, trying to make them feel like they have a personal stake in me.

Then we say our good-byes, check out with the intern, and head to the elevators. "That was actually really impressive," Nathan says as he presses the call button.

"What, the audition?"

"Your acting." His expression seems caught between sheepish and proud. "I've never seen you try to be anyone but yourself. It's like you've been doing it for years."

"Centuries," I correct, feeling a faraway tone enter my voice. "I played many, *many* roles across the ages. Honestly, acting is easier than trying to be myself, sometimes."

He gives me a curious look as the elevator opens and we step inside.

I shake my head. "It's complicated. Short answer, being a god means being *someone*. A set, predefined person who always acts in one way, even if they *know* it's a bad idea. Acting is . . . freeing. It's like I'm *allowed* to do something different. I love it."

Nathan smiles vaguely as he nods at that, quiet and thoughtful, and I realize this is one of the few times I've hinted to him just how massively conflicted the lives of gods can be. I wonder if it's leading him to think about Sekhmet, too, but this is hardly the time to ask. There's a brief lull, and then our conversation shifts gears, returning to the usual pleasant banter. We step out of the elevator, cut through the lobby, and make our way to the car . . .

. . . which is where we come to a screeching halt, mouths open.

THIRD WHEEL
FREYA

Someone's trashed our rental. Its tires are slashed, the windshield is cracked, and charming phrases like WHORE, THIEF, and GO BACK TO RUSIA are scrawled over it in black spray paint.

"We *so* lost our deposit on this thing," Nathan deadpans after a moment.

"Anyone here who *doesn't* think Riley did this?" I ask. "Anyone?"

Silence.

"Yeah. Thought so."

Sekhmet gives me a pointed stare and holds up her hand. Peach-gold talons pop out of her fingertips, and she arches an eyebrow as if to say, "Eh?"

"Getting really, *really* tempted here, but no, not yet," I say, pulling out my Mim and searching for the rental agency's number.

She shrugs, and the talons slip back. "I will admit it's a simple solution," she says, admiring her nails for a moment. "But results are results."

"And homicide charges are inconvenient," I mutter, dialing. I glance at the car again. "Not that this isn't," I add under my breath.

"I'm just surprised she spelled *thief* correctly," Nathan says as we settle down to wait.

I lean against the side of a building, feeling the California heat radiate through the brickwork, and place my call for help. The rental lady sounds *deeply* annoyed over the phone, but eventually promises to send someone with a replacement car as soon as possible, as well as a tow truck for our former ride. Funny how a pile of cash can make everything better.

It only takes about five minutes before I get bored with squinting at LA's blazing sunshine and decide to find something else to help me pass the time. A quick search in my Mim tells me there's a café within walking distance that's known for its baked goods.

"Done," I say, clicking the phone off and straightening up. Nathan and Sekhmet both send curious looks my way.

"I'm questing for treats," I explain, pointing in the direction of the nearby street corner. "Anyone want to come with?"

"Our new vehicle may arrive soon," Sekhmet says with a small shake of her head. "Best if at least one of us is here when it does."

"Nathan?"

He pauses, thinking it over, then glances at Sekhmet. "Nah, you go ahead, boss," he says after a moment, then adds a subtle wink. "I'll wait."

"Ah, okay," I say. "Back in a few. Call if you need me."

They nod at that, then return to their vigil. I walk away, turn the corner, and immediately stop, pressing against the side of the building and focusing my hearing to eavesdrop on the pair. Based on last night's conversation, I'm guessing Nathan intends something with Sekhmet, and, nosy goddess that I am, I'd like to know what.

A minute passes, and just as I begin to wonder if I'm zipping right past "involved friend" and into "creepy stalker" territory, my priest speaks up.

"Uh, Sekhmet?" he says in a voice that's a little higher than normal.

"Hm?" she replies, sounding distant. Probably on the lookout for threats, as usual.

He lets out a breath. "Sara—I mean, you— That is, Sara told me you— *Gah*, hang on." I picture him running his hand through his hair, like he does when he's nervous.

"Are you quite all right?" Sekhmet asks.

"Yeah, even worse at this with goddesses, apparently."

"Worse at what?"

"Asking—No, that's not—" He blows out another breath, sounding stressed, and tries again. "Look, I know you're the sort of person who prefers it when things are direct."

"This conversation seems to indicate otherwise."

"*Aheh*, yeah," he says in the sort of way that can only be accompanied by a nervous fidget. "So let me . . . ah, just—" He inhales, steeling himself. "Sekhmet, would you like to go out with me?"

There's a tense pause, and then, in a slightly puzzled voice, she says, "Go? Where?"

"On—on a date?" he says, sounding strained.

An even longer pause follows. Finally, after what seems a rather cruel amount of time, she replies in a *very* puzzled voice with, "You are asking if I wish to have sex with you?"

I clap my hand to my mouth to avoid snorting out loud.

"Wha—*No!*" Nathan sputters. "I mean, I guess technically there's an *implication*—"

"So you do not . . . ?"

"No! I do! Just not—" He gasps, a reactor in his brain seeming to enter meltdown.

"I am trying *very hard* to be patient, as I consider you an honorable ally," Sekhmet says, "but if you do not speak plainly, I will become *upset*."

He replies with an exasperated sound, then seems to steady himself. "I *like* you, Sekhmet," he says. "In that stupid, heartsick, gooey way that kills sleep. I'm asking for a date to see if we *match*, not just because you're an eye-popping Egyptian badass."

There's another uneasy silence, and then he adds, "Gods, Sekhmet. I want to see if you're interested in a relationship."

"A relation— *Oh!*" she says in a shocked voice, sounding more surprised than I think I've ever heard her. "You wish that of *me*? With the—the flowers? You are asking to . . . romance me?"

"I'd kind of want to phrase it nearly any other way, but yeah."

"I've never done that before." She sounds stunned.

"So that's a . . . ?"

"Ah! Yes, of course." She clears her throat, and then, in a very formal voice, says, "Nathan Kence. I, Sekhmet, Eye of Ra, accept your proposal. We shall date." There's a slight scrape as she finishes, and I sigh as I realize she must be sketching a bow or curtsy of some kind.

However awkward I imagine it must look, Nathan doesn't seem to mind. "Great!" he says. "That's . . . wow. I can't tell you how relieved I am."

"You are the first mortal in over five thousand years to express a desire for me beyond this form," she says, something sharp in her voice. "Kings. Priests. Conquerors. Men and women who defined themselves by their love for me, and in this moment, you have chosen, have *dared* to ask for more than any. 'Relieved'? You are a *warrior*, Nathan, and the novelty of your invitation is . . . intoxicating."

"So you're curious?" he asks after a moment. "About us?"

"Thoroughly," Sekhmet croons, and then there's a rustling sound and a startled breath from Nathan.

Overwhelmed by the need to know what's happening, I sneak a peek around the corner and work to stifle a gasp of my own. Sekhmet's thrown her arms over his shoulders, pressing their bodies together so they can make out with passionate ferocity. I can't help staring, nor can the handful of passersby on the street; it's like she's playing lioness and gazelle with his lips.

For his part, he seems to be loving it, tightening his hands on her back the moment he gets over his surprise and giving as good as he gets. I slip around the edge of the building as their kiss continues, a bewildering array of emotions ricocheting through my head, and try to focus myself on the strongest anchor I can imagine right now: cookies. The promise of baked goods shines like a beacon in the storm, leading me down the street and away from the new couple.

As I make my way to the café, my brain keeps trying to unpack how I feel about the whole thing, and I keep trying to shove the whole mess back down. He is my friend and my priest, and she is my friend and my peer. *That's it.*

I'm not going to let this get to me. I was caught off guard, that's all. I mean, damn, my priest moves *fast*. And so does Sekhmet, apparently. Cookies. I'm going to eat so many cookies, going to drown the nonsense in my mind with crispy sweetened bliss, and then get back to the business of conquering Hollywood and crushing my foes.

Priorities. And cookies.

Half an hour and a pile of magnificent chocolate-studded delights later, a shiny new car pulls up beside the wreck of our old rental and a grim-looking man gets out, eyes darting from our vandalized ride to us with an expression that says, *"These people."*

We sign a bunch of forms and scary waivers, exchange some very clipped pleasantries with the rental guy, and pile into the sporty number he's brought us. Nathan gets comfortable in the driver's seat while Sekhmet and I take the back, and we're soon cruising LA's congested streets once more. As Nathan returns us to the hotel, I punch Mahesh's number into my Mim, hoping to distract myself with news about the audition.

He picks up after a single ring. "They love you," he says, and I can hear his grin.

"I've had a bit of practice at that," I reply, smiling, and switch the call to speakerphone so Nathan and Sekhmet can listen in.

"Glowing reviews," he says. "They'll try to fast-track you, so get ready for a flight to San Francisco. There's no way the director and network reps are going to sign off on an unknown without a face-to-face, which is perfect for us."

"That's great to hear, Mahesh." I pause, and try to put a bit of steel into my voice. "Guess you're going to have to give Kirsten the bad news."

"Ah, ran into her again?" he says, sounding very pleased.

"Something tells me that wasn't an accident."

"Not at all." I hear a keyboard clicking on his end. "In fact, let's see—ah, yes, already raving about you on every social network she can find. Perfect."

"She—Wait, back up. She knows who I *am*? *How?*"

"Those media consultants you met yesterday? I've instructed them to use your accounts to start a little feud between the two of you."

"You *what*?" I snap, exchanging glances with Sekhmet and feeling blindsided. I take a breath and try to remind myself that I sought an agent out for a reason, and this one may know what he's doing. "I'd, uh, love an explanation about now, Mahesh."

I think he's picked up on my frustration, because his next words tumble out just a little too quickly. "Nothing to bring you down to her level. I've instructed them to keep your voice level-headed and clever. Kirsten doesn't need much to go off, anyway. The point is getting you exposure and followers. Move you up a bit in the search rankings, give the people who matter the idea that you're established."

"And you're sure messing with *her* is the best way to do it? She trashed my rental, Mahesh!"

"Seriously?" he says, sounding like he's fighting back a laugh. "Did you take any pictures?"

Nathan glances back and nods. "A few, yeah," I say.

"Fantastic. E-mail those to the media team. That's great stuff."

"So you planned for her to hate me?"

"No, just took advantage of it. After she gave me an earful about you, I figured it might be worth trying to overlap your auditions. I'm sorry for not telling you sooner, but I didn't want things to feel forced when you met again."

I think it over and look at Sekhmet. She shrugs. "If it turns her wanton foolishness to our advantage, I can find little fault," she says.

"I'm inclined to agree," I say. "Just keep us in the loop next time, all right?"

"Certainly," Mahesh says. "I'll give her a call, let her down, drop a few hints about who's getting the role. Should be more than enough to fan the flames."

I have to admit to a bit of spiteful satisfaction as I picture her response. "And there's no danger of annoying someone in the industry by doing this?" I ask. "She doesn't have any friends in high places, does she?"

"Matter of fact, she does, and it's her father—a media mogul. Very wealthy, very influential, and thoroughly invested in Kirsten's well-being. That said, it's not all nepotism; his money got her started, but she managed a great deal on her own. For the most part. She's actually a talented girl, if a bit spoiled."

"You don't say. All right, well, as long as you think you can deal with him, you have my blessing; go feed those fires."

"Already on it," he says, keys clacking. "Actually, on that note, do you have any objections to a fling?"

"A what?"

"A trivial relationship with a popular actor. Something to keep the buzz going while you're busy with a shoot. Tabloids adore them."

"Oh, eh, sure," I say. *Not like my current love life is going anywhere,* my brain adds with a helpful, involuntary glance at Nathan.

"Great. I'll find a good candidate, send you the details soon." There's a pause, and then he adds in a musing tone, "I wonder if Kirsten has anyone you could steal . . . ?"

"Now you're talking. Just keep me posted, and let me know how things go with the show."

"Absolutely, Sara. Ciao," he says, and then the phone clicks.

I take another deep breath as I settle the device in my lap, then let out a snort of amusement. A feud? How delightfully lowbrow.

"You can't wait to see what she's saying, can you?" Nathan says in a knowing voice from the front.

"Blasphemy! I'm not some gossip addict!" I say, failing to suppress a giggle. I bypass the phone's lock screen and tap the Twitter app. "I'll have you know this is battlefield research."

"'Know thy enemy'?" he asks, hitting just the right amount of sarcasm.

"Shh, I'm trying to read," I say with a grin, waving my hand. Sekhmet grunts in amusement, and I can see she's trying to hold back a smile as she watches out the window, still on alert for danger.

My eyes widen as I begin digging into the strange little war Mahesh has engineered. There's not much to the exchange yet, but what's there is practically radioactive. Kirsten isn't just self-absorbed, hotheaded, and semiliterate—she's also downright *vicious*. I need some popcorn and a drink with a little umbrella to properly enjoy it all, but the gist of the conversation between her and my media team is this:

> **Kirsten:** This girl is ruining everything that is good in my life.
>
> **Me:** No, I'm not.
>
> **Kirsten:** So you're also a liar. People, take a look at the worst person I've ever met.
>
> **Me:** That seems extreme.
>
> **Kirsten:** You want extreme? I will *literally kill you*.
>
> **Me:** It's nice to feel welcome in Hollywood.
>
> **Kirsten:** *[incoherent raving]*

And so on. As far as I can tell, it's working, too: I've already started gaining followers at a staggering rate, so full credit to Mahesh for this minor coup.

"How's it looking?" Nathan asks.

"Ugly," I say, tearing my eyes from the screen. "I love it. You know what? I might have my first project, and my new show biz nemesis is flipping out. I'd say this calls for a celebration. What do you two say to a fancy dinner?"

I kick myself the moment the words escape—I have a pretty good idea exactly what these two are up to tonight, and would dearly like to avoid discussing it.

Nathan and Sekhmet exchange looks in the rearview mirror. "Um, rain check?" he asks.

"We have a date," Sekhmet explains, savoring the word like a new toy. I swear it comes out with a purr.

"Oh! 'Grats!" I say, trying to act surprised. "When did you, uh, set that up?"

"While we were waiting for the tow truck. Remember when you went for those cookies?"

"Of course," I say, wishing I had more. "They got such nice reviews. Had to see." I shake myself. "Well, that's exciting! I guess I'll see you back at the hotel tonight?"

"Will do," Nathan says. "Got a curfew for us?"

"Just bring her back safe," I say with a laugh.

Sekhmet purses her lips, then chuckles at that. "No promises," she says with a hint of spice.

The rest of the ride passes with an odd touch of awkwardness I can't seem to shake. It might just be me, because Nathan and Sekhmet seem quite happy with the whole situation. I don't know. This *is* the first time a high priest of mine has ever gone on a date with another god, so maybe it's just the novelty. That, or I really am—*la la la NO*. I'm not getting back into this. Let them have their fun, and let me work on murdering Ares. *Priorities. Damn it.*

We pass the afternoon planning, snacking, and enjoying the California sunshine. Most of the time is spent researching San Francisco and the various filmmakers attached to my miniseries, getting a handle on the people I might be working with and the places I'll be visiting. At first it's scouting for points of interest and tourist hot spots, but it quickly degenerates into a long list of top-rated restaurants, cafés, food trucks, cocktail bars, fashion boutiques, and clubs. I start feeling a little shallow before I'm even halfway done, so I add *Visit the Legion of Honor museum* to the top of the page. There, now I'm all cultured.

As the sunlight slips away, Nathan and Sekhmet begin packing up, intent on following it into the night. I wave good-bye from my poolside lounge chair, figuring I'll make friends with a few more cocktails before I do the same. Sekhmet says her farewells before heading inside, but Nathan hangs back. He makes sure his new crush is gone, then practically dances over to me. "I can't believe I actually asked her out!" he gushes. "And she's actually *into* me! This is amazing!"

Despite my general uncertainty about the whole thing, that level of glee can't be anything but infectious. "You did great, my priest," I say, returning a grin of my own. "Were you honestly worried she'd turn you down?"

He laughs. "To *start*. I had a whole list of terrible crap I was stressing over. 'Gutted for his insolence' was pretty high on there."

"Well, the night *is* young."

His smile gets a little shaky. "Yeah, I— Geez, I was going nuts over *asking* for a date, and now I have to actually *do it*."

"Oh, I'm just joking—you'll be fine," I say, swatting him on the leg. "Remember, no matter what, you're a high priest of Freya, and your god is never wrong."

"Never ever," he agrees, grin returning. "All right. All right, I can do this. I'm gonna do this."

He wavers for a second, no doubt adding some new worries to

that mental list of his, and I groan. "So do it already!" I say, giving him another encouraging swat.

"Hey! Okay! Yes. Sorry, right." He shakes his head ruefully, then starts moving to leave. "G'night, Sara!" he says as he goes.

I give him a parting wave, then return to my research on San Francisco's hot spots. With a drink in hand and the air still warm from the fading sun, it seems like a great way to spend the night, but only a few mojitos later, I find myself getting bored and decide to pack up. There are some popular clubs nearby I've been meaning to visit, and Mahesh tells me I should start baiting the paparazzi when I get the chance. Having my face on a tabloid magazine is apparently one more rite of passage I'll need to hit sooner or later, and my feud with Kirsten will probably escalate that timing.

Various potential outfits make their way through my mind as I head upstairs. I'm debating between a miniskirt and top or a dress as I unlock my room and head inside. I toss my laptop on the closest convenient surface and reach to turn on the lights when the skyline beyond catches my eye.

I pad across the carpet and slip out onto the veranda to watch night fall over the city, clutching the railing and letting the warm breeze play with my hair. A handful of stars have made an appearance, twinkling dimly through Los Angeles's light pollution, and a sad smile tugs my lips as I settle my arms on the balcony and watch them. A deep, unexpected longing hits me in that moment, an impossible craving to wind back the clock, to watch those same stars shine on my ancient kingdoms and return to a time of steel, superstition, and strength.

I think of the clubs, the music, the storm of camera flashes this evening promises, and shake my head. Not tonight. I spare a last glance for the heavens, then go back inside, shower, and throw on some nice jeans and a simple top before heading for the lobby. I hail a cab at the hotel's taxi stand and ask him to take me to Griffith Observatory. I'd been meaning to visit, and tonight's as good as any to spend with the heavens.

My driver tells me it'll be near closing time, but the thought of having a mountaintop refuge all to myself just makes the idea more enticing. A little over half an hour later, we arrive in the observatory's parking lot on the slope of Mount Hollywood. There are still a good number of tourists and locals alike wandering the grounds as we pull into the roundabout in front of the building. I pay the driver and strike out across the entrance lawn. The concrete Astronomers Monument looms above me, its art deco renderings of six of the field's most famous figures turning my head before I continue to the main building.

It's a beautiful place, tastefully lit at night, and the cool wind here helps banish the summer heat rising from the city below. I've heard wonderful things about the facilities inside, but I only have eyes for the view beyond. Los Angeles sprawls before me, a garden of light greater than anything my medieval heart could imagine. I linger on the etched towers of finance and success that frame its downtown before turning to the distant glimmer of moonlight on the waters off Santa Monica's shores. I can't tell you the last time I took an evening off to watch the stars. A touch of liquid gold begins to gather at the corners of my eyes from the unending splendor of it all.

I beeline for the curved ramps that lead to the observatory's terrace and make my way to the iconic arches that encircle its planetarium. The tourists' ranks thin as closing time approaches, and security guards start hustling the stragglers away, breaking the serenity of the place with loud calls of "Park is closed!" and annoying sweeps of their flashlights.

A handful approach my post on the promenade's wall, aiming to escort me off the hill alongside the rest of the visitors, but I send them away with a touch of my magic, encouraging them to pick a cozy spot for a long nap. Soon, it's just me, an empty walkway, and the sky above.

I can almost imagine I'm back in my homelands, watching the heavens spin above the farmlands of my flock. I put a hand on the railing, intending to lever myself onto it so I can lie down and immerse myself in the night sky, when a soft *click* stops me. I freeze, recognizing it in an instant.

It's the sound of a gun being readied.

"Evening, miss," a deep, professional voice says from the shadows of one nearby arch. "A moment of your time, if that's all right."

I sigh and turn away from the magnificent view. Why can't *I* be the one on a date?

10

STARRY-EYED

NATHAN

Nathan drums his fingers on the tablecloth and hopes for death. Sekhmet stares at him.

Nathan checks the menu again, finding its contents unchanged from the last six times he's looked, which sadly implies that "Deadly Fast-acting Poison" is not among them.

Sekhmet continues to stare at him.

"Do you still need a few minutes?" their waitress asks, startling him. "Anything I can bring you while you decide?"

"A gun, please."

"Pardon?" she says, clearly thinking she's misheard.

Nathan blows out a sigh. "Nothing. Few more minutes, yeah."

Ah, well, he thinks as she leaves. *Not the worst date I've ever been on. At least Dionysus hasn't shown up to this one.* He looks around for a moment, worried. *Yet.*

Sekhmet watches the waitress go. Then she turns her beautiful dark eyes back to Nathan and . . . continues to stare at him.

Things had started off so well, too.

They'd both been perfectly chatty on the drive to the restaurant, swapping stories and complaining about the traffic. They'd even had an excited conversation about an upcoming superhero movie they wanted to see, while waiting for the hostess. Then they'd sat down, gotten menus, and everything had gone to hell.

Nathan wasn't even sure what had happened. One minute they'd been talking and laughing, and the next, he found himself in the middle of a choking silence that had, by this point, stretched to soul-crushing lengths.

He'd tried to lift it, of course, but every topic he tossed to Sekhmet was batted aside by precision grunts or monosyllabic dismissals. It was as if he'd sat down with a completely different person. Once, a lifetime ago and a restaurant away, he could remember being very eager to see where the evening went.

Now he prays for an earthquake to consume it.

"All right, I give up," he says after a few more seconds tick by. No point in pretending this was anything other than a complete failure, and as long as he was going down in flames, he might as well learn what started the fire. "What'd I do?"

To his immense surprise, Sekhmet releases a throaty laugh and preens like she's just won a race. "Ha, wonderful," she says. "This is better now, yes? More . . . romantic?"

"Wha—?"

"Our date. I ignored you, you capitulated, you like me more now."

"I—I *do*?"

A tiny frown makes an appearance. "That . . . is how it works, yes? Just a moment, perhaps I missed a step."

She leans over and begins rooting through her purse. After a moment's search, she retrieves a marked-up fashion magazine coated in handwritten notes, circles, and hieroglyphics. "Let's see . . ." she murmurs, paging through the dog-eared periodical. "'Play hard to get,'" she reads. "'Be clear,' and 'don't send mixed messages,' of course. See, I was very consistent, wasn't I? 'Wear something sexy, so he'll know what he's missing.'" She looks at her short wine-colored mini, then back at him, concerned. "This is attractive?"

"Uh. Very. Sekhmet, what are you—?"

"So the apparel is correct, then. What else?" More riffling through the magazine. "Did I ignore enough of your jokes? You stopped making them rather quickly, so I thought—"

"Sekhmet?" he tries. "Sekhmet, look at me."

"Hm?" she says, pausing her search.

"Is that a magazine for teenagers?"

She holds it up, and Nathan's heart drops when he sees the brightly colored cover. "Yes, well, few pieces of comparable literature are targeted at women of my age," Sekhmet says. "So I chose something closer to yours."

"Gotcha. Um . . . *why*?"

Her lips twist and she lowers the magazine. "I am . . . oh, this is difficult."

Nathan watches her, feeling it would go better if he didn't press. After a few seconds of hand-wringing, Sekhmet sighs and says, "I have not done this before. Your world, its society and culture . . . you must understand how impossibly *distant* it is from what I know. I want for this to go well, this outing you proposed, yet I *do not know* how such things are done. I—I feel I am missing so many pieces!"

"But that's not—"

She picks up the magazine again and shakes it at him. "Look at all these!" she says, sounding distraught. "I do not have any friends with which to 'dish' about you, nor do I understand how to speak

137

'guy.' I am unsure what *LOL* is, or how to make you do it, and we—"
She groans, slapping another note-coated article. "Oh, we have not
even *texted*!"

"There's, uh, a lot about texting in there, I take it?" Nathan asks,
unsure how to correct her without laughing.

"*Pages*," she says, morose.

"So . . . look," he says, trying to find the right words. "All that
stuff we were talking about on the ride over? And the lobby?"

"Yes . . . ?"

"*That* was already the start of our date."

She freezes at that, eyes going wide. "Oh no, then I have
already—"

"Made a great first impression," Nathan says, trying out his most
placating smile. "Seriously, you don't need to be something you're
not. I don't want a relationship with plain Jane. I asked *you* out."

"Then y-you're aware?" she says, sounding hopeful. "Of this
distance? It is not a, ah, 'downer'?"

"Sekhmet, you're a multimillennia-old cat goddess from ancient
Egypt. I think distance is assumed."

That gets him a wan smile. "It is more than time or place,
Nathan," she says. "The hearts and minds of your kin . . . they have
changed. I haven't."

"So what?" he says immediately. "Who says you need to?"

Her eyes slide to the magazine.

Nathan lets out a small groan. "Screw that noise. *I like you.*
Wouldn't have asked you out if I didn't, and—here, let me just . . .'"

Wanting to make a point about how unlike a typical date *he*
was, too, Nathan begins focusing on his link to Freya, drawing
threads of spellcraft to himself through that celestial keyhole.

There's an endless pool of the stuff, a font hidden beneath reality just *waiting* to be tapped . . . if you can reach it. Nathan's connection to his goddess is his ticket in, the foundation for every trick in his growing spellbook. It took a *lot* of practice to do anything with it, of course, but he'd hit the jackpot when it came to teachers. Freya, Sekhmet, and all the other gods seem born from and to the stuff, and they wielded its reality-warping might as reflexively as a heartbeat.

It isn't so simple for Nathan, but the flipside, Freya had explained, was that he wasn't bound by belief in what he could do with it. Enough time and effort, and he could stand among the gods themselves, could surpass even them in the variety and breadth of his designs. And so, to prove to Sekhmet how neither of them needed to be bound by convention, he tries something new.

Carefully, Nathan teases threads of force into existence, looping the invisible strands of energy around the magazine to form a hardened barrier. He frowns as he does it, trying to remember his lessons with Freya and build on the principles she taught.

"It's all about the rift," she'd told him, "the breach between your soul and our magic. Widen it, give it a reason to help you, and *it will*. Don't obsess over *what* you're doing—focus on where you're getting it *from*."

He wraps the magazine a few more times, just to be safe, and then, with a mental twitch that feels a bit like yanking the leg out from under a chair, wrenches them together.

Instantly, the magazine crumples into a quarter-sized lump of smashed paper, sucking into itself as all those strands burst under the pressure he's applied. The compressed ball spins once, rolls to the side of the table, and teeters on the edge for a moment before falling off.

Sekhmet watches the death of her magazine with amusement, and once it's gone, returns her attention to Nathan.

"Well put," she says after a moment. She stretches, laughing to herself, and fixes him with a very different look when she's done. "So all their advice about letting *you* make the first move, those prudish tips to restrain oneself and 'see what develops' . . . ?"

Nathan feels an overjoyed smile begin to make its way onto his face. "Y'know what?" he says. "Might just want to listen to your heart, there."

"Mm, that is *not* what speaks to me at this time," Sekhmet says, and before Nathan can reply, she lunges across the table, wrapping her arms around him and smashing her lips against his as they topple backward onto the floor.

A chorus of gasps from the other diners follows their descent, but Nathan can't really bring himself to care, busy as he is with an armful of writhing, smooching Sekhmet.

"Sir? Ma'am?" their waitress says as she dashes over, shocked. "Do you, um, need any help?"

Sekhmet breaks away for a moment to give her an amused look. "I think we are prepared to order our meals," she says, then turns back to Nathan. "I find myself rather . . . hungry."

"We could get it to go," he suggests, hopeful.

She barks a laugh at that, grabs Nathan's chair with both hands, and springs upward, wrenching them from the floor with inhuman strength and agility. The waitress backpedals as Sekhmet, Nathan, and his chair come off the ground and smack upright with a clatter. Sekhmet picks herself off of Nathan's lap, traces a finger beneath his chin, and saunters back to her own seat. As she does, he notices she didn't even knock over the wineglasses in her leap.

"The porterhouse," Sekhmet says after a glance at her menu. "With the lobster mashed potatoes."

"Uh, very good," the waitress says. "For you, sir?"

"I'll try the Alaskan king crab black truffle gnocchi," Nathan says, reciting the choice he'd picked out around his third pass at the menu.

The waitress takes their wine orders, exchanges some quick pleasantries, and then moves away as quickly as decorum allows. Nathan has a feeling she won't be all that broken up when they leave.

"No steak for you?" Sekhmet asks after she'd left. "Are they not famed for them?"

"I'd feel bad," Nathan says, shrugging.

"For the cow?"

"Ha, no. Well, a little. But mainly for Freya. She's kind of obsessed with high-end steaks, and I already got the impression she'll be feeling lonely tonight. Didn't want to rub it in."

"Lonely?" Sekhmet repeats, taken aback. "She seemed perfectly supportive."

"Well, yeah, but she'd never want us to feel bad for going out. I think—eh, it's hard to explain."

Sekhmet gives him a look of patient interest, making it clear she'd be happy to hear the long version.

"Okay, you . . . know how gods influence people, right?" he says after a moment.

"Of course. We are primal—keystones in the foundations of existence. It is only natural we should have an impact on those around us."

"Right. Sure. Freya's worried it's getting to me, affecting my judgment. I-I'm not entirely sure if that's true, but I *do* know I'm starting to get a really good sense of how she's feeling these days, maybe even better than she knows herself."

"And how is that?"

"Frustrated. She knows Finemdi's the real threat, but part of her thinks taking Ares out will make everything better since he's working

141

for them, so she's bending over backward to focus on that." He blows out a sigh, feeling a little frustration of his own at the thought. He might have agreed to help, but that didn't mean it sat right with him.

He's devoted to Freya—maybe even to a fault—but silly concepts like "sanity" still keep him from applying that same loyalty to her current mission.

"And you disagree with this course?" Sekhmet asks, picking up on it.

"Well, yeah!" he says, straightening in his chair. "C'mon, they just recruited the guy. He can't be that important to them yet, no matter what Samantha says. If anything, the focus should be on Finemdi as a whole, because as long as they exist, we'll always be looking over our shoulders. Freya's letting anger blind her. Nine hundred years of it, sure, and that sucks, but it's not like bad ideas suddenly get validated once they hit a certain number of centuries."

"You speak with great authority on such spans of time," Sekhmet says, a tiny smile tugging at her mouth, "for one who has seen so little of them."

Nathan pauses. His first reaction is to apologize and back down, but then he notes his date's bemused expression and realizes that if anyone might appreciate a touch of conviction, it's her. "I know I haven't been around very long," he begins, "but you did say that the world has changed—maybe those old vendettas deserve a fresh pair of eyes?"

"And hers are not quite so . . . 'fresh'?" Sekhmet asks, still seeming entertained.

"Sometimes!" Nathan says, sticking to his guns. "I mean, you're a god"—Sekhmet smirks at that and feigns surprise, like it's news to her—"so tell me: Is it better to have a mindless follower who goes

142

along with everything you want, or someone who's willing to challenge you?"

"A challenge is, of course, always preferable," Sekhmet says. "Though I believe you have crafted your question knowing my fondness for such things."

"Ha, maybe. I think Freya's the same way, though. Open to disagreement, as long as it comes from the right place."

"You *do* have a free-spiritedness in you," Sekhmet says, her tone approving. "A fact she has surely marked, as it is rare for even the most rebellious to question their gods. How, I wonder, did you come to embrace such a trait so thoroughly?"

Nathan thinks it over for a moment. "Probably being a military brat," he says. "Loved my dad, hated his rules. I'm not sure you can grow up in that world and *not* want to question authority."

"Indeed," Sekhmet purrs. "A fine instinct—if, as you said, it comes from a place of support."

"It does, honest. I'm not trying to be a wet blanket for *fun*. I just want to make sure she's aware of the dangers. I mean, Ares . . . he beat her once, right?"

"Profoundly."

"And since then, he's gotten stronger and she . . . well . . ."

"Hasn't," Sekhmet finishes.

"So how is going after him not a horrible idea? I'm not crazy, right?"

"It is . . . tactically flawed, yes."

Nathan frowns. "Then why—I mean, *you* seem totally on board with this whole plan. I get that you live for vengeance, *and* to help women, *AND* you vowed to see this whole thing through, but I—I know how smart you are, how much you care about her. **All that** stuff is good, but is it enough?"

"No, it is not," she says, thoughtful.

"So help me understand."

Sekhmet looks at him for a moment, her face unreadable. Finally, she inclines her head and says, "I would like to tell you a story. May I?"

Nathan blinks at that. "Hit me," he says after a pause.

"I found myself in India, once," Sekhmet says, her gaze distant. "Lush, thriving land. So much life and splendor, and their gods, ah . . . they are *power*, Nathan. Like nothing you've seen. The worship they receive . . ." She trails off for a moment, caught up in longing, then shakes herself and continues.

"I came into conflict with one not unlike myself. Her name was Kāli. A goddess of change, of destruction and life. I do not recall her offense, but my attempts to 'rectify' it were . . . ill-conceived. I was defeated." She gives him a wry look. "Quickly."

"Hard to picture," Nathan says.

"Imagine my surprise," she says, smiling. "But then something curious happened. She healed me. Honored me as a guest. Told me if I still desired retribution, that was logical, but she bore me no ill will for my actions and would treat me as a friend until I chose otherwise."

She chuckles and fiddles with her napkin. "I was astounded, of course. Asked her why she would accept a foe so readily. I have never forgotten her reply. Would you like to hear it?"

Nathan nods.

"She said, 'You are of vengeance. I am of destruction. Of these realms, perhaps you believe mine a means to your ends.' She shook her head and laughed, and to my ears, it was sad.

"'To quest for vengeance is to be unchanged,' she continued. 'It is a state, a desire—not an act. The needs of vengeance can stretch

144

for an eternity, always as fresh, as painful as the day they were forged. Destruction, then, is an answer, because destruction promises change. In your mind, you may desire one, but in truth, you long for the other.'"

Sekhmet stops, watching Nathan. "What . . . does that mean, exactly?" he says, fidgeting under her attention.

"I asked as much," she replies. "And she did, in fact, explain, but allow me to answer in a different way. Consider your god's quest. Think of where it began, and where it led. Think of the choices she made, the journeys from the Old World to the New, from despair to apathy and now revival. Without it, would her path have crossed yours, or mine once more? Would we be here now, enjoying each other's company, if she had not chosen this course?"

"I . . . no. Probably not," he says, getting it.

"I do not support Freya's cause because I believe it wise, Nathan. Nor even because I vowed I would. I do it because it holds, as Kāli said, the promise of *change*, and after nine hundred years, I am eager to see it find my dear friend."

"Huh," Nathan says, turning Sekhmet's words over in his head. "You think more good will come out of all this? Really?"

"Has it not already?" Sekhmet says, reaching out to entwine her fingers in his. "If the path you walk has brought you joy, then you must accept it may hold more, no matter how much you fear its end."

"You know," Nathan says, heart pounding at the caress of her hands, "for someone who claims to be a few thousand years out of date, you're sounding pretty on top of things."

She smiles at that. "Tell me more of my qualities, mortal," she says, and her laughter mixes with his, and Nathan realizes he'd hunt a thousand monsters like Ares if it meant he got to hear that music every day.

Their meals arrive, and as they eat, their conversation turns to simpler things, though with someone like Sekhmet, that still means tales of war and wonder. For Nathan's part, he tries to stick to stories from a mortal perspective, focusing on things she might find interesting or surprising about the future in which she lives.

"These are great," he says after she finishes describing an escapade in New Orleans. "I could listen to you all night. Still up for that cocktail bar afterward?"

"Absolutely," she replies, caressing one of his legs under the table with her foot. "And I must add that your experiences are just as fascinating. I find this"—she waves a hand at the restaurant around them, then at him—"*important*. You are my window to a world."

A bit of Nathan's glee fades at that. "Always happy to play tour guide," he says, trying to make it sound upbeat. He really *is* glad she finds him interesting, but "cultural ambassador" isn't quite what he's going for.

Sekhmet's foot pauses, and she leans in to peer at him with wide, wondering eyes. "You seek to hide pain from me," she says, tilting her head. "I have caused you hurt."

Nathan tries to play it off, smiling and shaking his head. "No, no, really, everything's—"

"Yes, you—Aah, you fear my interest is self-serving," she says, concentrating. "You dread a hollow pairing, a relationship of give and take and little else."

Nathan looks at her, his smile slipping. "Kind of, yeah," he says at last. "I've had a great night, and I really like you. I think we could—I mean, I just want—"

"Fine, foolish creature," she says before darting out a hand to snatch one of his. "I am a *god*," she says, capturing him in those deliciously intense eyes of hers as she runs her fingers across his palm.

146

"The world is mine by rights. You cannot offer me riches I cannot take. You cannot offer me information I cannot learn. You cannot even offer me your faith, as that already belongs to another."

He stares at her, distracted by what she's doing to his hand, but also feeling pinned by the power of her scrutiny.

"And yet I delight in your presence," she says. "You represent something I have never had: a *partner*, a mate with no illusions, no ulterior motives, no influences beyond desire and the hope to experience this world at my side." She drops his hand and stabs a finger at him, the speed and violence of the motion undercut by the silly smile she wears. "You have more to offer me than any. Never doubt the power of that."

Nathan leans back, understanding. Now *this* is a promise he can lose himself to, can love her for. He grins and draws closer. "I'm confused," he says. "Are you saying you like me just because I like *you*, or . . . ?"

Her eyes glitter. "Mm, is *that* what you heard? You are suggesting I seek another, then? One I do not find quite so enjoyable?"

"It's probably for the best," he says with mock resignation. "I mean, a relationship built on desire? The betrayal!"

"If only there were some way to make it slip your mind," Sekhmet muses.

"Shame, right? I really thought— Wait!" He snaps his fingers. "Quick, kiss me and I might forget your treachery."

Sekhmet laughs, says, "Mortal, *nothing* about me is forgettable," and then, to their waitress's dismay, sweeps across the table once more to press her lips to his.

11

SEE THE LIGHT

FREYA

"Garen?" I whisper into the night air, feeling little flutters of panic.

"Who? No," the voice says. "I'm here to talk about your . . . career."

I breathe a sigh of relief. A random mortal with a gun, I can handle. In fact, my evening just got a whole lot more interesting.

"What do you want?" I ask, leaning a hip on the promenade's outer wall.

"Nothing drastic. Just turn down the job with HBO."

I laugh. "Or you'll shoot me? Seriously? Okay, where are the cameras?"

"This is not a joke, Ms. Valen," the voice snaps, all steely and grim. I notice he's positioned himself so the lights of the city are in my face, but he's in total darkness. Nice setup. "Find another show."

"Aw, but I like this one," I pout, really starting to enjoy this.

"I don't want to have to kill you, sugar, but—"

"Chicken," I say.

"I'm sorry, did you—"

"Where are you from?" I ask, trying to place the voice. He sounds familiar. "I'm guessing Kirsten sent you, so—*Harv?*" I gasp. "Oh, Harveykins, is that you? Personal assistant *and* gun for hire! Love the flexibility."

There's an exasperated sigh from the shadows. "What is *wrong* with you? Do you want to die?" Harv asks. I stifle another laugh. Hearing frustration strain those deep tones of his tickles me to no end.

"Oh, because I know who you are? Pfft, whatever. I'm not leaving the show. Tell Kirsten she can cram her inflated sense of self-importance up her ass and, while she's at it, kiss mine."

Stunned silence follows. "Can you go now?" I ask after a few seconds. "I'm kind of having a moment here."

"You're not—I have a *gun!*" he stammers, moving out of the shadows so I can see it—and him—more clearly. Those well-defined, almost-but-not-quite beautiful features of his are deadlocked between unexpected fury and stunned disbelief. The weapon in his hand is comically large, a high-caliber bear stopper probably chosen for its intimidation factor. Obviously, I'm not following the script.

"And I have . . . *this!*" I reply, giving him the finger. "Scram."

His jaw drops. "I'm warning you, I *will*—"

"Shoot me?" I say with a sarcastic twang. "Go on! Make sure you double-tap! I'm worth two bullets, aren't I?"

Rage cascades from him in waves, but despite the strength of that anger, I can tell he never actually intended me harm. He's probably so used to dealing with spineless socialites that even the barest hint of defiance would've thrown him for a loop, to say nothing

149

of my brazen replies. To be fair, I'm sure he's very threatening if you don't happen to be immortal.

"You're insane," he says. "I'm giving you one final chance—drop the gig or I *will*—"

I cut him off by sticking out my tongue and blowing a raspberry at him, then closing the distance between us in two quick strides, clasping his upraised hand in mine and pushing the gun barrel against my heart. "Do it. Dare ya," I hiss, moving with him as he tries to back away.

"Get away from me, you stupid—!"

"Shoot me. C'mon. Coward," I snap, pushing him back a step with every word.

"Let go of my damn hand!" he shouts. His back legs hit the promenade's wall, and I start leaning into him, forcing him to bend backward over the edge.

"Stop!" he yells, eyes widening as he realizes how close he is to the void. It's not a terribly huge drop to the mountainside below, but it's probably more than enough to kill or seriously injure someone unlucky enough to take it.

"Bye, Harv!" I say, grinning as I add just a little more pressure. I don't actually intend to go through with it, but putting the fear of, well, *me* into this bruiser seems a just comeuppance for the stunt he attempted tonight.

Unfortunately, Harv doesn't quite see the humor in it.

"No!" he screams, panicking. He drops his weapon, twists his body, and uses one knee and both hands to lever me up and over his head, tossing me off the observatory in one unexpectedly fluid motion.

I yelp in surprise as I pinwheel into open air.

For a moment, it's just that once-peaceful breeze whooshing

around me. Then the slope of Mount Hollywood zooms up impossibly fast and I smash into it face-first with all the agonizing momentum of a four-story drop. My body bounces once and my shoes fly off as the impact rumbles through me with all manner of snaps, crackles, and pops. I roll down the cliff face, the world a blur of sky and sand. I'm a tangle of flailing limbs and pain for a good hundred feet before a nice, scratchy patch of scrub brush halts my momentum.

I lie there hurting for a moment, wishing I were in Sekhmet's nonairborne shoes for the second time tonight, then get to work righting myself.

"Freaking *ow*," I say with a groan, rolling over onto my back. My limbs don't exactly have all the usual joints or angles one would normally prefer, making every movement difficult. At least my bag stayed with me—even if the shoulder it's on isn't seated quite right.

I wait for my body to reshape itself according to the vision of its long-dead designers. It's not particularly fun; I find myself wincing every so often as something important clicks back into place. The view *is* nice, though. Finally, when everything's roughly where it should be, I get myself to my feet, stumble out of the scrub, and begin dusting off my clothes.

"Note to self: Do not taunt hit men," I mutter, batting briars from my jeans.

I'm picking some scraggly twigs out of my hair when a noise draws my attention. There's a steady crunch of footsteps approaching, accompanied by occasional glimmers of light; someone's picking their way down the hill toward me, using a flashlight to guide their way. I can make out snatches of conversation as they approach.

"—was I supposed to know she's crazy?" Harv is saying. "I just . . . *Yes*, I know she's Hollywood. Haven't met one with a *death wish*, have I?"

He sighs, listening to someone I can't hear. I'm guessing he's on the phone.

"Look, I know it's a mess. Either way, your daughter gets what she wants, right? Isn't that my job?"

Another pause. When he speaks up, it's in a frustrated grumble. "Gene and Vitty never come to you with this crap because *this crap isn't their job!*"

His footsteps stop as he listens to whoever's on the other end, and I sneak to one side, crouching behind a nearby tree.

"Uh-huh. Yes, Mr. Riley. . . . No, Mr. Riley." He lets out another sigh. "All right. Yes. Yes, I'll try to think next time! Right *now*, I've got a dead or hurt girl to . . . *No*, I haven't found her yet."

He groans, and I can almost hear him grit his teeth from here. "*That's what I'm doing!*" he snaps, picking up his pace with big, angry strides. "Now, if she's still alive, what do you . . . Yes, *if*. It's a slope, she might've—look, I don't know! What should I do if she *is*?"

I hear him whistle. "Cold. I mean . . . Yeah, I understand, it's just . . . Right, but she didn't . . . Fine," he says, drawing close to my hiding spot.

"Yeah, thanks, boss. Yeah, I'll call when I—"

I lunge as he pulls even with me, knocking away his flashlight with one hand and grabbing a fistful of his shirt with the other. I know how fast he is, so it's no surprise when he drops his phone and manages to magic a gun out of his jacket. He swings the weapon in a tight outward arc, trying to pistol-whip me in the jaw. I lean back, dodging the blow and smirking as its momentum leaves him wide open for a split second.

I tighten my grip on his button-up, tense my neck muscles, and bring my forehead smashing into his face with one staggering *crack*.

His knees buckle and he tumbles to the dirt, dazed but not out. I take the opportunity to relieve him of his firearm. It's much smaller than the hand cannon he used to menace me, and probably his actual weapon of choice.

He moans, holding a hand to his head, and curses softly. "Weird night?" I ask, frisking him for more weapons. "Aw, poor baby. We're just getting started."

"How——?" he mumbles, trying to get his eyes to focus on me as I root through his clothes.

A moment later, I sit on the ground in front of him, cradling the bigger gun I saw earlier, a folding knife, and a collapsible baton in my lap. "For me? On the first date?" I say, shaking my head before tossing everything but the blade downslope. "Just not that kind of girl, sorry."

"I saw— *Ohh.*" He tries to get up as he speaks, but a wave of dizziness sends him back onto the slope, where he clutches at his head. "I saw you hit," he says in a weak voice after a few seconds. "Your neck. Think I heard it. Arms, legs, everything twisted on the way down. You can't be walking, can't be——"

"Kicking your butt?" I suggest. "You're right, of course. I shouldn't be alive." I lean over him, smiling down. "Wanna guess how I managed it?"

He just stares at me, still disoriented.

"Hmm . . . maybe it's the part where I can't be killed," I say, flicking open his knife and drawing it across my arm.

"You crazy——!" he gasps, trying to scramble away as my blood starts dripping onto him.

"Oh, would you look at that," I say, ditching the blade and giving the gash in my arm a pointed stare.

The wound's already begun to close, and I'm delighted to see it's going a lot faster than the last time I did this to prove my divinity to

153

Nathan. *I really have been getting stronger these past months.* I glance at Harv when it's halfway done, smiling to see him hopelessly focused on my limb, fascination and horror mingling on his face.

"And gone!" I say after it's healed, turning my arm so he can see there's no trace of the injury. "Got another theory?"

His hand twitches behind his back and he brings out *another* gun I missed, aiming it right between my eyes. "Stay back," he says. "Just—just stay right there."

"Oh, like that worked *so well* before."

"I mean it! I'll—"

"Kill me? Ooh, scary!" I say, wiggling my fingers. "Now hand me that thing, little man, before you hurt yourself."

He hesitates, eyes darting from me to the pistol like he's torn between obedience and assault. "I said *now*," I snap in the voice of the Valkyrie.

His fingers seem to move on their own, dropping the weapon into my waiting hand. He looks at them like he's wondering how that happened, then stares at me with a face full of fear. "What are you going to do?" he asks in a croak.

I step away and snatch up his flashlight from where it fell, shining it over myself. "Ugh. Find a cleaning service, to start," I mutter, surveying the damage. My clothes are a mess of grime and blood. "So, you're Kirsten's Mr. Fix-It, I gather?"

He nods dumbly. "What *are* you?" he asks.

I give him a level stare, then draw myself up. "I'm a god, you moron."

"A . . . god?"

"Yeah. Rar, smite thee and all that. You just tried to snuff an immortal. Bad call."

"I'm sorry, you're *what*?"

"I swear, I need to put all this on a business card," I say to myself. I lean down and stare at him. "Hey. Look at the birdie," I whisper, then hold up my hand and trigger another illusion. A tongue of gold-tinted fire blazes from my fingers, bathing the hillside in a cheerful glow. Harv leaps back, pressing himself against the earth.

"We have a lot to discuss," I say, and toss the illusion at the tree above us, where it erupts and flows to cover it like a lazy, living carpet. I creep closer, bearing down on Harv as golden sparks rain around us.

"And you're going to tell me everything."

The sight of the city below is intoxicating. I could stare at it for hours.

"Strangest thing, learning there are gods from one who wants her name in lights," Harv says from beside me. We're still on the hill, sitting side by side and enjoying the view.

"Let's just say we're both having odd evenings," I say with a faint smile.

He nods at that, and we watch for another minute in silence. We've just wrapped up a delightful conversation about my future, some mutual concerns, and whether I'd be throwing him down a mountain for his insolence. Fortunately for Harv, he chose a highly cooperative approach, involving a bit of behind-the-scenes help for me and the hope of a few extra years of life for him. It seems some good might come out of this evening for us both.

"Sorry again about the, um, high dive," he says out of the blue, oddly awkward for such an imposing man.

"As long as you can get Kirsten's dad on my side, we're square," I say. "Well, that and a ride home."

"Fair enough," he says. "She won't like this, you know."

"And that's just the icing on top," I say, grinning. He chuckles at that, probably imagining her reaction.

"So a goddess, huh?" he says after another pause.

"That's me."

"I never believed in God."

"And now you have your pick," I say, sweeping out a hand at the stars above us. "We're all listening. Though it's in your best interest if I'm the one you worship—only way I can guarantee you those extra years."

"Worship?" he repeats, raising his eyebrows. "How does that work? Find a Church of Sara?"

"Freya," I correct, gesturing at myself. "You pray to her, believe in her—in me—and *never* stray from that conviction, you're pretty much set."

"Freya? Wait, I *think* I've heard of you . . ." he says. Then his brow furrows in concentration.

I'm confused for a moment, wondering what he's thinking, until that vicious little mind of his sends a twitch of curiosity my way. Ah, he's trying it now—not a man to waste time, I see. The curiosity becomes commitment, reaching out as a delicious pulse of hopeful faith. It finds me, and the connection strengthens, rebounds, and grows. A whisper echoes from his mind to mine: *Can you be real?*

I smile and give him a slow nod. "In the flesh," I say, and send a thought back to him, a divine vision of me as I once was; ancient, armored, unstoppable. Freya the goddess, the warrior, the lover. My past and, one day soon, future.

He laughs. For a moment, there's a bit of childlike giddiness there, a sense of joy completely at odds with the shark of a man he presents to the world. "You're her. You—I didn't realize it could feel so reassuring. To know there's someone listening." His faith flares, and that hopeful curiosity solidifies into belief. Just like that, one more worshipper adds himself to my paltry flock.

It's almost a cheat, sitting here—true believers shouldn't need to see their god to know she exists—but I work with what I'm given.

"Whatever I can do, it's yours," he says. "A good word? Sure. But if things get rough, you need more than that, give me a call. My services are just the beginning of the pain I can bring."

"Deal," I say, unlocking my Mim and handing it to him. "I'll add you as 'Professional Pain.'"

He laughs, punching in his digits. "My number. Unless you do the 'voices in your head' trick . . . ?"

"Not my thing," I lie. Truth is, I'm not yet strong enough to hold full conversations with my worshippers, especially long-distance. The best I can do is send visions, emotions, and symbolic imagery, and even then, they have something of a range limit. These days, as long as I'm in the same city as a follower I want to contact, I'm pretty sure I can get through, but any farther than that and even the simplest sensation or image will probably fall apart.

Strangely enough, I can hear prayers clear as crystal, no matter the source. Perks of the job, I guess.

"Well, glad you pissed off the boss's daughter," he says. "Go easy on her, all right? She's not so bad."

He says it casually enough, but there's a sudden wariness in his stance that makes me think this man actually cares about her. It may be oddly placed, but that capacity for concern moves him up another notch in my book. "She's safe," I say, making a mental note to go over things with Sekhmet as soon as I get back. "Though it's strange seeing anyone worry about her. She's kind of terrible. No offense."

"Stockholm syndrome," he says, smiling. "But seriously, she's a teenager stuck under a microscope, trying to impress the world while dealing with all the usual static girls her age endure. My job is making sure a lot of the *unusual* static that comes with the spotlight never touches her."

"Like me?"

He grins. "Don't like my chances there."

"Someone's learning." I stretch and pat him on the back. "Well, this has been fun and all, but I'd kind of like to get going. Any chance you brought an ATV?"

He shakes his head. "Sedan, sorry. Bit of a hike uphill, *and* I parked pretty far back, too. Tell you what, though—we're almost halfway down. I'll head up, grab the car, and meet you at the bottom. I'll text when I'm at my car so you know when to start."

"That works," I say, examining the hillside neighborhood below us.

"Great," he says, getting to his feet. Then he smiles. "Oh, and most of my tools seem to have gone missing. If you happen to come across any on your way down, mind picking them up for me? They aren't cheap."

"No promises," I say, laughing.

He waves and begins trudging uphill. I snort again, then lean back on my palms and return my gaze to the city. All those teeming millions, each with their own hopes and hazards to navigate. Somewhere out there—at least, according to the Graces—three other gods are having adventures of their own, and I haven't the faintest idea who they might be. Mahesh is probably burning the midnight oil trying to keep me in the lead for *Switch*, while Kirsten waits impatiently to hear about Harv's success in getting me to drop it. Socialites writhe on pulsing dance floors, waiters bus tables and talk shop as their restaurants close for the night, and moms and dads prepare lunches for the next day.

My eyes settle once more on the stars, and I wonder who else they might be shining on. Somewhere far from here, Ares spins new schemes of war and violence for Finemdi, Apep hungers to kill all life and light, and Garen seethes and plots vengeance against me. Actually, I'm just guessing on that last one—he might have decided to open a taco truck, for all I know. Something tells me he's about as likely to let go of a vendetta as Sekhmet, though.

Speaking of, I wonder how she and Nathan are doing . . . ?

A little twist of anxious, seething curiosity settles in my chest at the thought. I drum my fingers in the dirt, trying to relax, to return to the stars and city lights, but rather involuntarily, my gaze twitches to the spray of grit-caked blood I left nearby. *Plenty of uses for the red stuff,* I think, a pack of scrying spells marching through my mind. It's not like I'd even need one of my preprepared contingencies, either. This is child's play.

No, no, we're not spying on our friends. I shake my head and deepen my breathing, desperately hoping my flighty hindbrain will fixate on something else.

My restless fingers start kicking up sprays of sand.

They could be in trouble, a little voice whispers helpfully. *Might be worth checking in, just in case.*

I wince, trying to resist.

Just a quick check?

"Ugh," I say, getting to my feet. "Meddlesome goddess."

I walk over to where I ditched Harv's knife, spend a few seconds searching through the loose dirt, and bend down to pick it up. Dropping to my knees, I use it to gouge a rough, bowl-shaped furrow in the earth, then pack down the sand with the flat of my hand. I stare at the depression for a moment, feeling disgusted with myself, then sigh and dig the knife into my wrist. I grimace as blood flows from the wound, glinting dully in the starlight and pooling in the hollow I've created.

I hold the knife in place, using it to keep the injury open until there's a thick puddle of the stuff before me. Then I set the weapon aside, let my arm heal, and begin to focus on the fluid.

If I were trying to peek at anyone besides Nathan, I'd be completely out of luck. Scrying isn't particularly hard, but for a weakened little witch like myself, viewing someone out of the blue—especially without a lock of hair or some other personal effect—would be like trying to climb Everest in a bikini. Nathan, however, is bound to me through his faith *and* my magic. All those spells I've been teaching him? Each is like a piece of myself, embedded in his soul, and tracing that is as easy as staring into a mirror.

Sad little weaves of magic drip from my fingers, sinking into the blood and turning its surface smooth as glass. The pool thrashes once, erupting for a split second in a crimson frenzy of runes and gnarled spikes. Then it flattens, glistens, *reflects*, and suddenly I'm looking through a tiny window into somewhere else.

Strains of jazz, laughter, and idle chatter reach my ears first, followed by a warm, orange-tinted glow. The scene sharpens, resolving into a beautiful room of wood panels, rough brickwork, and tasteful tile. Exposed beams stretch overhead, bathed in light from antique chandeliers. Beneath them, cheerful clientele exchange lively chatter over mixed drinks.

A saloon, I realize, noting the period decor.

I twiddle my fingers, pulling at the weaves like a puppeteer, and the view snaps back, shudders, searches. An impressive bar comes into focus, a liquor-stuffed centerpiece crafted from an old apothecary's cabinet. Smiling bartenders mix cocktails and chat with customers seated on swiveling stools. My view blurs, swinging left to show me a wall riddled with cubbyholes and accented by thirteen old-fashioned umbrellas. There, seated across from each other in carved benches set just below a candle-lit shelf, Nathan and Sekhmet chat happily.

There they are, safe and sound, I think, giving my friends a wistful smile. *Satisfied?*

"So here she is, surrounded by *twenty* cats and kittens, all gifts for the new couple, and she *knows* most of these creatures will never survive the trip home," Sekhmet is saying, eyes flashing with glee. "So she decides to rescue them."

"You're kidding," Nathan says, hanging on her every word. "But she's lost almost all—"

"Of her clothing, yes!" Sekhmet laughs.

"Really?" I shout at the scrying pool as I recognize the tale. She's gossiping? About *me?*

"So how did—?" Nathan asks, heedless of my outburst.

"Well, she's trapped in the bridal suite, yes? Climbing gear lost. Clothes destroyed. Surrounded by gifts of all kinds, cages of prized cats, and . . . the wedding dress."

"No," Nathan says.

"Yes!" Sekhmet slaps the table. "She *steals* this priceless thing, *squeezes* herself into it, hides her face with the veil, grabs the damn talisman, and bewitches *all twenty cats* to follow her out the door *beneath the dress!*"

The pair burst into crippling laughter, rocking on their benches. I pull back, crossing my arms. *Hmph. What, was I supposed to* leave *the cats?*

Eventually, the merriment fades to soft chuckles as Sekhmet finishes the story. She even includes the part about the stained glass window and the drunken monks, the traitor.

Nathan wipes tears from his eyes when it's over, and stares into Sekhmet's. They don't say anything else, but the goofy grins on both of their faces speak volumes.

Okay, that's enough. I cut the flow of magic and scatter a dash of sand into the pool. The vision freezes, rips, and fades, leaving me on my lonely hillside with all kinds of fun thoughts.

Damn it all. Those two are cute as hell. Seriously, take it from a goddess who knows: There's some real chemistry there, the kind I was built to celebrate. If they were *anyone else*, I'd be drooling to find out more about their relationship. As it is . . . well, I *still* don't know how to feel. I think my best bet is ignoring them as much as I'm able. This whole affair remains a diversion I can't afford, not when so much is at stake.

My phone buzzes, providing a much-needed distraction. I pull it out and read the text; Harv's reached his car. Groaning for effect, I haul myself to my feet, flip on the flashlight, and begin making my way down the hill, keeping an eye out for the rest of his arsenal as I do. Harv's right about it being a fairly short hike. Before long, I'm standing in front of a tall fence that separates some wealthy family's backyard from the untamed wilderness of Mount Hollywood. I skirt the obstacle, walking beside the property until I emerge in a secluded roundabout.

I pull out my phone again, look at the map, and head down the little offshoot of a road for a hundred feet until it connects with Nottingham Avenue. I text Harv to let him know where I am, and it's barely another minute before his dark sedan pulls alongside me.

"Where to?" he asks as I get in.

"My hotel," I say, then frown in thought. "I'm guessing you already know where it is."

"Wouldn't be very good at my job if I didn't," he says with a smirk.

"Great. Time to abuse their cleaning services," I say, looking myself over with a grimace.

"Try not to get any blood on the upholstery before we get there," he says.

I immediately stomp my bare, dirty feet on his floor mat, firing an insolent stare at him as I do.

"Happen to find anything that belongs to me on the way down?" he asks, still smiling.

"Kirsten's good practice for dealing with me, isn't she?" I say, digging through my bag and pulling out some of his toys. I couldn't find the baton but managed to locate the rest in my trek downhill.

"You're a cakewalk in comparison," he says, pocketing his goodies one by one.

"Am I? Well, Harv, I—"

Rippling, screaming, bewildering *chaos* wells up in my head, cutting me off as it shudders through me with ecstatic wonderment and weirdness.

You know that screeching feedback you get when a microphone gets too close to a speaker? It's like that, only inside my mind, and instead of noise, it's a mottled, thrashing wave of imagery and emotion, uplifting and overpowering in the extreme. I find my hand slapping against the car dashboard in front of me as I struggle to remain upright.

"You okay there?" Harv asks, leaning in with a look of concern.

"Totes," I snap, trying to shake the sublime strangeness from behind my eyes. "Mind stepping on it? I have some, uh, odd prayers I need to answer."

He nods at that, and mashes the accelerator.

I spend the return trip to the hotel in anxious silence, trying to tease apart just what's going on in my mind. I've never felt anything like this—it's like a prayer gone squirrelly. There's a strange sense of madcap joy mixed in with uneven helpings of confusion, delight, and pain. The warmth of familiarity blends with unmistakable hints of exotic splendor, all of it ricocheting through me from a source that's at once achingly close yet impossibly odd.

I need to hurry, to know what's going on. I have no idea what it could mean, but little hints and nuances in this sea of strange are leaving me with the sneaking suspicion my high priest is somehow involved. I think Harv is picking up on my anxiety, because he makes the drive with reckless speed. Those bizarre sensations increase as we near the hotel, and I find myself dreading and hotly anticipating what I'll find there in equal measure. I thank Harv when he drops me off, then dash upstairs to our rooms, racing to locate the hive that's spawning these visions.

My heart hammers in my chest as the elevator doors open and I tear down the hall, visions of crackling peril electrifying my mind. I fear the worst, and every footfall seems to come just a second too late to prevent it.

I think Nathan's in tremendous trouble.

SWEET DREAMS

FREYA

Looking back, I'm not sure why I'm so surprised by what I discover. Let's call it denial.

I skid around a corner, weather a tempest of *weird*, and blast through the door to Nathan's room, wrenching the solid wood from its hinges with a burst of inhuman strength, all to find something I'd been planning to ignore forever.

Yeah, Nathan and Sekhmet's date went *great*. If you want to measure "fun times" in terms of property damage, then this place is glee ground zero. It looks like a whirlwind of love and claws went to *town*. Feathers waft through the air, courtesy of several exploded pillows and a bed that looks like it's been opened up for surgery. The walls are dented with enough force to assume you could measure the cause with a Richter scale, and sad flaps of carpet have been flayed from the room's floor in odd, crawling patterns.

I stare, jaw dropped in sheer amazement, at the carnage before me. I haven't a clue how even half of this is possible without construction equipment. The sources of the devastation, currently scrambling in panic, were entwined on one shattered balcony door and some torn chunks of the room's sofa before I made my dramatic entrance.

Nathan hurriedly wraps himself in whatever scraps of clothing and bedsheets he can get his hands on, while Sekhmet lies perched in a hunter's crouch, ready to spring at any threats. She relaxes as soon as she recognizes me, sliding into a leisurely pose that reminds me of the Graces.

"You startled me, little fighter," she says with a throaty sigh.

I blink, and close my mouth.

"Um, hi, boss," Nathan rasps, still trying to cobble together an outfit from the shreds around him. That draws my attention a little more closely to my high priest. Nathan looks—how do I put this? Imagine someone who's just run a marathon, gotten dunked in an ice bath, then finished things off with a visit to a sauna and a bottle of the world's finest champagne. My high priest is *beat*, and besides his general state of exhaustion, he also looks . . . happy.

As I stare, a cut over his left bicep closes and heals. His other nicks, bruises, and scratches are all fading away in slow motion, as well. I'm confused for a moment until I remember Sekhmet is, among other things, a goddess of healing and medicine.

Huh. Well, I guess if you're going to sleep with the Egyptian embodiment of vengeance, femininity, and war, it helps if she's willing—and able—to patch you up afterward.

And during, come to think.

"I'm—I'm going to *go*," I say, jabbing a thumb behind me. "Just . . . uh . . . got some news, but how about you swing by later and we'll discuss?" I take a quick breath, letting the spectacle of the room and its steamy demolitionists sink in a bit more. "In the morning? Cool?"

"Not urgent?" Sekhmet says, stretching like a cat.

"Not . . . at *all*, no." Short of a Finemdi raid, I can't imagine what *could* be critical enough to keep me here, basking in the awkward. A light fixture detaches from one wall with a clatter, and I take that as my cue to leave.

"Bye!" I say, stepping out and trying to jam the door back in place. Nathan provides a very uncertain wave, while Sekhmet gives me a lazy nod. I force a smile as I wedge the door upright, then move into the hallway.

There are even scratches around the lock, my mind cheerfully provides.

I shake my head, then bury it in my hands, gritting my teeth as I clench my fists in my hair. An all-too-familiar emotion runs through me, stronger than ever, and it's finally sharpened to a point where I can recognize its unsettling nuances for what they really are.

I'm jealous.

There! I admit it! Are you *happy*, world? It's alllll clear to me now, thanks to how I felt about that delightful tableau. I know things weren't awkward because I interrupted two lovers who are *also* close friends of mine. I'm a *fertility goddess*, remember? All the fun stuff they were doing? Part of me deeply approves. Even more maddening is the fact that I'm *not* hung up on the guy! I'd been wondering if maybe I wanted a try at a relationship, but no. This is something far deeper and divinely primal: *Thou shalt have no other gods before me.*

That's right, we're not talking about a simple love triangle. No, this is next-level relationship stupidity, because I'm apparently a territorial Old World psychopath who doesn't want her high priest getting close to any other god but her, and it took that charming moment to prove it to me.

Oh, there are so many happy experiences ahead. As a god of love, I've seen a million romances, from star-crossed to sublime. This may be a slight twist on the classics, but at the end of the day, we have two lovers and a third party who's upset about it. I know the playbook forward and backward, and this particular scenario has all *sorts* of gems to look forward to, like:

- Pretending to be happy for friends when you're screaming/dying inside
- Listening to relationship successes and wishing they were failures
- Listening to relationship failures and hoping a breakup is imminent
- Hating yourself for feeling this way about people you care for

And so on. Even better, this is a relationship I dare not upset, because doing so could push away my two closest allies and derail my dreams of glory and vengeance alike. Between my personal feelings and the resurgence of my faith, there's no contest: I am literally incapable of choosing any other option.

So where does that leave me? Sucking it up and dealing, that's where. I *will* be supportive, happy, and upbeat, keep the whining to a minimum, and my eyes on the prize. There's simply no other choice. Moping around is for people without religions to rekindle. I straighten my back, take a deep breath, and fix my hair. Yes, this is stupid and it's all my fault. Yes, I probably shoved Nathan in this direction when I meddled with his mind back when he got cold feet about attacking Impulse Station. Yes, I—

ALL RIGHT, I GET IT. I roll my eyes, then punch the wall.

My fist smashes through the paneling with a meaty *crunch*, and I draw it out of the new hole, astonished. The hell?

I put my angst on hold for a moment, bending down to poke at the damaged wall. I'm *not* this strong. I mean, I used to be, but it's been centuries now. This is a high-quality place, and that is not cheap construction I just shredded. I look over my hand. A few minor scratches, but no broken bones or gushing wounds. This wasn't angry strength—I'm legitimately mightier than I was a few hours ago. What just happened?

I look at the mutilated door to Nathan's room. I shouldn't have been able to do that either, I realize. You always see people smashing through doors in movies like they're made of cardboard, but real ones take true effort to savage, especially solid things like this. This is something Sekhmet could pull off, but not—

Hmm.

I think back to that bizarre surge of energy that filled me when—when my two friends were together. Familiar and exotic all at once, right? Okay, let's add it up: I'm a god of love. Nathan is my high priest. He shares a portion of my power and can draw on it for strength and spell-casting. In return, he provides a stronger and purer foundation of belief than any ordinary follower. What he did with Sekhmet was an act of love, which you could honestly look at as either an offering in my name or a sanctified deed on my behalf, through a mortal proxy. Either way, for a very brief, very weird moment, he forged a link between Sekhmet and me, sending a little of her sheer might my way. It can't be permanent, but it's certainly real, and will remain so as long as they continue their relationship.

So what did I send to her?

My head pounds, and I lean against the wall with a frustrated sigh. This is awesome, unprecedented stuff here, and I know *something* must have transferred to my bloodthirsty friend, but I'm really not feeling up to a theological audit: It's late and I've had a very long day. When you land a major television role and that's the *least* interesting life event to happen in a twelve-hour period, something's wrong. I shelve my thoughts and questions and head for my room, suddenly feeling exhausted. Forget taking a shower—I barely manage to strip off my dirtied shirt and pants, find my favorite pink pajamas (covered in little hearts), and tumble into bed.

I stare at the ceiling for a few minutes before letting slumber take me, sending out a little prayer of my own: Please let tomorrow be saner. I close my eyes, take some deep breaths, and try to will myself to let go of all the tension and stress of the day.

It takes another fifteen minutes, but I finally begin drifting off.

Then the delightful couple next door starts again.

Nathan and Sekhmet seem far more shocked by the whole "brush with a hit man" thing than I was. Nathan, I sort of get, since assassins lurking in shadows are a lot more threatening when you can actually die. Sekhmet, though, surprises me—she seems to feel this lapse in security is somehow her fault.

"I should have been with you," she says, eyes ablaze. She thumps the seat beside her, drawing a glance from the limo driver up front. "This is a grave—"

"It's fine, Sekhmet," I say, waving a hand and giving our chauffeur a reassuring look. "It's not like he could've actually hurt me. Besides, I think you have enough to worry about with the hotel people."

She snorts. "Oh, their faces. You should have seen it, little fighter. As if these walls had never seen a night of passion before."

"Considering they were still standing when we checked in, probably not."

"Hmm," she purrs. "They do not build them as they used to, I suppose." She puts a hand on Nathan's knee. "I wish I could still take you to my temples. Now *those* were sturdy enough for gods."

"We'll find a replacement," he says, grinning. "Like a bed-and-breakfast . . . bomb shelter."

"Certainly," she says, eyes flashing with a very different emotion. She wiggles her fingers at him. "Do your little computer searches, and I will follow."

I clear my throat. "So that's my news, anyway."

We're on our way to some sort of premiere event at Mahesh's behest, enjoying a limo ride and basking in the rays of morning light that stream through the open sunroof. Mahesh wants to build on my stellar audition with some red carpet time, making sure I continue to be seen as the rising star we've started presenting to the world. My goal is to get in front of cameras, look pretty, and charm anyone who looks halfway important. Piece of cake.

The sounds of a waking city are mixed with angry honks and screeches as our driver navigates the already-congested streets to our destination. Though the early start of this event put me off at first, it's actually good timing to get us out of the hotel and away from the reconstruction efforts. The staff were *highly displeased* when they went in to survey the wreckage from Nathan and Sekhmet's bout of late-night property damage (the shouting actually woke me up). I think we might have gotten kicked out if it weren't for my gifts—love and money, as usual, managed to make everything all better.

"A new ally—especially this criminal warrior you describe—could be a boon to our efforts," Sekhmet muses, tapping her jaw. "But only if you are certain he can be trusted."

"If he were following me for money, I might be worried," I say, looking out the window and trying to guess how far we are from the premiere. "Nobody's going to beat a life-extension policy like mine, though."

"Marvelous. How easily swayed you precious creatures can be," she says, reaching out to ruffle Nathan's hair. Is it just me, or is she *way* more laid-back today?

"Hey!" he says, ducking. "Death is the one thing we *all* have to come to terms with—putting that off sounds like the best deal you could find."

"Ah, then you'll be happy to know how far away I've placed yours," I say, grinning.

He gives me a curious frown. "Say what now?"

"Stay faithful and you will see *centuries* pass, my friend."

"Cen— Wait, you can really *do* that? I'm not going to die?" He looks equal parts shocked and elated. It makes my smile even wider. *Beat that, Sekhmet.*

"Not of natural causes, at least. You're not going to age, either. Enjoy."

He seems so grateful, I actually feel a little embarrassed. "How?" he asks after a moment. "Can all gods do this?"

"No," Sekhmet says. "My realms are many, but the afterlife is not among them."

I nod at her. "I get top billing for love, war, and beauty, but I'm also a goddess of death," I say. "It's part of why I can claim half of all those who die in battle, and it lets me meddle with fate."

"So you just say, 'Hands off—this one's mine!' and don't collect?"

"Basically. Only works if you worship me, though. It's not like I literally get priority over *everyone* who goes down fighting. You have to *believe* I do." I laugh. "I guess that means I could technically give you the same deal if you followed someone else from my pantheon. I'd just prefer it be me."

"Absolutely fantastic," he says. "You know, you're still the best thing that's ever happened to me, Sara."

Sekhmet shoots him a look, clearly feeling a little possessiveness of her own. "Well, she brought us together!" Nathan says, sounding defensive.

She laughs at that, then pops a claw out of her index finger and holds it up, pretending to examine it. She gives him a sly smile as its peach-gold polish glimmers in the sunlight.

He glances at me as if to say, "I'm in over my head." I just smile and focus on the city beyond my window. See? No bitterness! I'm doing good!

A few minutes later, we pull up to the event, which looks to be set in an upscale theater. There's a decent amount of press here, including some of the major TV outlets, and even a medium-sized crowd of fans. It's nothing on the scale of, say, the Academy Awards, but there's clearly enough star power on the invite list to warrant a bit of a show.

I wait for a valet to open the limo door, scooching forward with a big smile I can't wait to show off to the cheering crowds. The door swings wide, I straighten the folds of my dress, and—

"*Move it!*" a shrill voice explodes. A bony bundle of hate shoves aside the valet, barrels into the limo, and plops herself down on the seat beside me, slamming the door closed behind her.

Kirsten Riley pushes her face up against mine, shadowed green eyes glaring like emerald suns. "Did you sleep with him?" she snaps at me.

Out of the corner of my eye, I see Nathan holding out an arm, trying to calm Sekhmet, who looks like she's about three seconds from gutting our new passenger. "Hi, Kirsten," I say, trying out my celebrity smile. "Lovely day."

"*DID YOU SLEEP WITH HIM?*" she shrieks, the red glow of rage exploding across her cheeks and washing out those perfect freckles of hers.

"Gonna need to narrow it down."

"RRRGH!" she growls. "HARV! *Didyousleepwithhim?*"

"Much as I'd like to see if you can turn redder, no," I say, smile never faltering. "We just had a little chat, he realized I could get you in a *lot* of trouble if he tried to pressure me into dropping *Switch*, and we left it at that."

"What?"

"*Extorrrrtion,*" I say, drawing it out like I'm talking to a child. "I know it's a big word, but it can still get you arrested."

She sputters for a moment. "I wouldn't— Harv . . . Daddy would *never* let that happen!"

"Test me, bitch."

Her eyes go wide, and she works her mouth for a moment before yelling, "Give me that *part, you stupid Euroslut!*"

"No. Now get out of my limo before I have Rashida here *throw* you out," I say, jerking a thumb at my friend.

Kirsten looks at Sekhmet, who provides her best slasher smile and adds a meaningful crack of her knuckles. The little starlet goggles for a split second like she can't believe anyone would *dare* threaten her, then snarls at me as the fury returns.

"Gah! This—this *isn't over!*" she yells, fingers scrabbling at the latch behind her. "You think you're *sooo* clever with your— How does this even— *Open this door!*"

The valet outside complies immediately, hauling it open and

offering a hand. Kirsten slaps it out of the way and tears out of the limo. As soon as she's upright, she sticks her head back in and says, "You're going to *wish* you'd stayed in Siberia. By the time I'm done, the only way your fat ass will be on a shoot is if you're bringing the *bagels* to it!"

With that, she smashes the door shut and storms away.

The three of us in the car exchange bemused expressions. "Could totally go for a bagel," I say at last.

"Ooh, me too," Nathan pipes up. "Think they'll have any inside?"

"One way to find out," I say, heading out of the car at last.

The rest of the event is actually quite lovely, but in terms of pure entertainment, nothing can really top Kirsten's ineffectual fit. Part of me wonders if there's anything she really *can* do to mess with my plans, but without her little scare tactics, what else could she possibly have to threaten a *god*? I decide to brush her from my thoughts, focusing instead on networking with the glitterati.

After a few delightful hours spent soaking in camera flashes, random reporter questions, and the offerings of craft services, we all agree it's time to head back. The Sunset Tower's repair efforts are still under way when we return, so Nathan and Sekhmet have to wait for another room to open up in the evening. I offer to let them hang out in mine, but Nathan suggests going on the zoo trip she'd been asking about earlier, and that's the end of that. You should see how she perks up the instant someone mentions the z-word.

I wave as they go, and a small part of me can't help feeling amused at how oddly well they work together. I mean, I'm still conflicted about our little triangle, but the part of me obsessed with love and relationships (a very, very big part, in case you've forgotten) is intrigued.

Most of the time, dalliances with celestials like Sekhmet don't end well for mortals. If some cruel twist of myth doesn't end the relationship, another jealous god usually shows up to do something horrible. Time and again, history has shown there's little but pain in pairing the earthly with the eternal. Thing is, all these tales of romantic woe come from the mists of the past. I don't know of a single liaison like this happening in modern times, let alone involving a high priest with an extended lease on life. Nathan really isn't like most mortals—not anymore.

I mean, something strange is clearly happening to the guy. Proximity to the divine can twist people, and he's been my priest, roommate to five goddesses for over a month, and, as of last night, *extra* close to one of them. We're literal forces of nature, and part of that includes placing something of a personal stamp on whatever bit of nature we happen to be near. That means somewhere inside of Nathan, a PROPERTY OF FREYA tag is clashing with a PLAYTHING OF SEKHMET poster and a bunch of HAWAII ROCKS! graffiti. What that could mean for the poor guy's state of mind is anyone's guess. As far as I know, this is fairly new ground he's treading, and I have to admit I'm curious to see where his path is headed.

You know what? Clubbing can wait. Those two are doing interesting stuff, and now I'm gripped by a sudden desire for something equally exciting. I haul out my laptop, root through my suitcase for a particular note card, and set myself up on the balcony.

It's time to advance the cause.

I open my e-mail account and begin drafting a new message to Samantha. Even if everything goes my way on the screen, it'll be years before I can *think* about going toe-to-toe with Ares. Fortunately, Samantha's promise of aid might just tip that timetable, because if anyone can help me kill this scumbag sooner, it's her. At the very least, maybe she can give me some clues about the trinkets I stole from Finemdi and what they can do. I haven't forgotten those baubles, but they're going to stay in their suitcase until I'm sure I can use them without blowing my head off.

Actually . . . maybe I *should* at least take them out for this. I head back inside and haul out the hard-side case packed with our share of the loot. I take each piece out carefully, arranging them on the bed in neat rows, then snap a picture with my Mim. Carefully, I pack everything back up, send the image to myself, and return to the laptop, where it's waiting for me. Ah, technology—what marvelous conveniences you bring.

I add the picture to my new e-mail, write a short and to-the-point message, and hit the Send button with a thrill of satisfaction. That done, I lean back in my chair to enjoy the setting sun.

Not ten minutes later, a reply comes in. I sit up, surprised by the speed of Samantha's response:

Info request (and hello!)

2 messages

Samantha Drass <samantha.e.drass@gmail.com>
Sun, Jul 22, 2018 at 10:37 AM
To: Sara Valen <saraseesyou@gmail.com>

Hello Sara,

I miss you, too! So glad you got in touch—*and* that you managed to get away with that many relics. I had a feeling this request might be coming, so I took the liberty of performing additional research and forming a basic plan of attack. The following is just a suggestion, but I believe it may be a good foundation for your eventual encounter with Ares. Here is what I propose:

- Incapacitate Ares with halāhala. You are familiar with this: It is the standard poison Finemdi uses to subdue deities. Its potency degrades over time, so to be effective on a being of his strength, you'll need a fresh dose. I'll do what I can to sneak one to you, but if I'm not able to do it in time, you'll have to get it from one of our facilities or agents.
- The spherical device studded with small copper spikes in the image you sent (second row, third from the left) is a dogmatic lance. It is essentially a focused version of the leveler I gave you—aim it at Ares while he is insensate and will it to activate. Combined with the halāhala, it should be enough to disrupt the ties between his physical form and the morphogenetic substrate that fuels it.
- Immediately damage—*but do not destroy*—Ares to the point where he can no longer function.
- When the effect of the lance wears off, the Rule of Form will attempt to reassert itself, repairing and re-empowering Ares to match his believers' image. At this point, your knowledge of "magic" becomes pivotal. The energy restoring Ares will manifest as transmutative threads that you can manipulate. Redirect the flow to yourself as if you were rewriting a persistent spell and you will subvert his regeneration, effectively "stealing" his strength for yourself.

Now, bear in mind that there are limits to the amount of power you will be able to consume, and that this will not fully eliminate Ares. That said, I'm certain these actions will leave you in a highly advantageous position, and once you're there, well, the choice of how to deal with your foe is yours. I hope this is helpful. If you require further clarification or advice, please do not hesitate to ask—I'm happy to assist!

Sincerely,
Samantha

On Sun, Jul 22, 2018 at 10:28 AM, Sara Valen <saraseesyou@gmail.com> wrote:

Samantha!
Hello again! How is everything? Are you doing okay? Is this even an e-mail I should use to just, like, chat? Or is it all official? Anyway, let's stick to business for now. I've been thinking about our mutual friend Ares, and I'd really like to get your thoughts on what I could start working on to knock him down a peg or twenty. He is BAD NEWS and I need help.

Hope things are going well—miss ya!

Best,
Sara

P.S.: I've attached a pic of the artifacts I stole from Impulse—do you think one of these could be useful?

I'm giddy. *This is it!* I think, vibrating with glee as I see for the first time a clear and plausible path to vengeance.

More than vengeance, actually—if Samantha is right, I'll be taking his power as well as his life. What delicious justice. Sure, there's the little matter of stealing some of Finemdi's poison and actually getting close enough to Ares to *use* it, but this is all far better than that vague plan of "Get stronger; kill, kill, kill" I had going before.

I reply with a quick e-mail of overjoyed thanks, close the laptop with a snap, and get up to start my day with a megawatt smile. I'm not going to tear off for the first Finemdi site I can reach, obviously. I'll stay the course for now, focus on my career and the power it will bring, but everything I do from here on out will be with Samantha's advice in mind. This is exactly the breath of fresh air I needed. Centuries of waiting, and now my revenge is a sweet, tangible thing, suddenly real and close at hand. As I start going through my wardrobe and selecting the perfect outfit for the evening, I wonder if Samantha knows just how happy she's made me, and just how badly I needed to hear such a plan.

The answer, of course, is that she did, because someone told her. Someone who knows how gods work and precisely what *I* want. She believes the moment of joy I'm experiencing now will, in part, balance the pain she intends to inflict upon me later.

It won't.

13

IN A FOG

FREYA

I got the role!

It took more doing than I expected, though. Even with glowing recommendations and a top-tier audition tape, it turns out getting a major part on a cable miniseries as an unknown is incredibly hard. The show's head writer and another producer grill me in LA in a meeting overseen by Diane Starling, and then there's a flight to San Francisco for a sit-down with two HBO execs and the show's director. I send out love taps left and right, feeling like I'm battling some sort of production hydra—charm one gatekeeper, and two others step up to take their place.

Still, however rocky the path, in the end I stand triumphant, backed by green lights and thumbs up across the board. They pay for our tickets to San Francisco, book us rooms at the Fairmont for the duration of the shoot, and we're on our way. Filming will take place in apartments and offices across the city, as well as key streets, scenic spots, and soundstages. There's a hefty amount of green-screen work planned, too, though I guess that's not surprising considering the show's near-future setting. I can't wait to see how it all looks in the end.

We're given a handful of lighter days to start, and it's a nice ramp-up for what's sure to be a demanding experience. Meet-and-greets with cast and crew, makeup tests, script readings, wardrobe fittings, and other trivialities leave us plenty of free time, and though some of it gets eaten up in passing Nathan back and forth for mystic training sessions and sexy-fun dates (I'll let you guess which of us gets which), most of that freedom goes to exploring the Bay Area.

For two major cities set so close together, I'm shocked by how different San Francisco and Los Angeles are from each other. While the latter feels unrestrained, even wanton, the City by the Bay has an odd sense of pride that sets it apart. Coming from a land where people just plain don't care what you think (for good and ill alike, granted), there's a strange undercurrent of *judgment* here you wouldn't have expected at first glance.

That first glance is remarkable, too. The city rolls up and around hills, embracing the land at the mouth of this beautiful bay like an old friend. There's so much splendor here, yet so much defiance. It's as if its people are afraid the slightest touch will change everything, jostle the house of cards and ruin the good things they have going. There's light and darkness in every city, every person, but here, it seems there's a deep ache to embrace the former and deny the latter.

How perfectly puzzling.

I think my heart will always belong to Los Angeles, but perhaps San Francisco can claim my mind. At the very least, it's stolen my stomach. I feel like it takes only a handful of weeks before I'm on a first-name basis with most of the city's food trucks, to say nothing of its taco shops, bakeries, gastro pubs, and, well, you get the idea. I'm glad for those first days we spent exploring the area, because after the cameras start rolling, there's little time for much else besides the job.

Do you have a picture in your head of what filmmaking is like? Maybe it's a lot like mine was: pampered stars relaxing in luxurious trailers, days spent nibbling at the offerings of craft services like the emperors of old, then sweeping out for a few tantalizing moments to feed their talent into waiting cameras and boom mikes.

Yeah, no.

Let's be clear: Stardom is *work*. If you're even halfway near this industry, then I don't care who you are or what role you play—I have newfound respect for you. From A-listers to reality TV laughingstocks, everyone is doing a job, and it is *hard*. Don't even get me started on the crew members. Those camera guys and lighting specialists will sometimes spend *hours* making sure a scene is lit and the angles are perfect while you twiddle your thumbs by the craft table, then keep on doing their job as you step up for a zillion separate takes. This is a career, and like most things in life, success really only comes to those who work for it. That's right, even the idiots you love to hate are working hard every day to broadcast that image to the world. This is not a place for those who think they can coast. At least, not for very long.

I throw myself into it. It's exhausting like I'd never have guessed, but working on *Switch* is also probably the most fun I've had in . . . well, *ever*. The cast and crew become more than coworkers almost immediately, igniting friendships that feel like they could last for years. These are people you hang around for days, weeks, *months* and get to know like family. It quickly becomes apparent that the best productions come from a place of camaraderie and joy.

It helps that *Switch* is also good. It's well written, balancing comedy and tragedy as deftly as any modern miniseries. It has a strong hook but never loses sight of its cast or their connections to one another while it explores its near-future setting. Karen, my character, is a fun-loving, multilayered firebrand, and I delight in giving her life.

Nathan and Sekhmet begin all helpful and interested, but their involvement starts to wane as my days get longer, and I can't blame them. Being on a set is really cool the first few times, but after the novelty wears off, it just starts feeling like a strange office space. Once Sekhmet becomes convinced I'm safe with my new friends, she and Nathan start disappearing for longer stretches of time. They tell me they're off exploring the city, wining and dining, playing tourist, and just having fun, but the frequent jabs of sexy feedback in my brain tell me that's not all they're doing. I do my best to ignore it when it happens.

Which is a lot.

Mahesh still manages my presence online and off, making sure I answer tweets (including Kirsten's, which have gotten even *more* enraged, if that's possible), smile for the paparazzi, and keep my name in circulation. Every now and then, he has me zip back to Los Angeles for a little more exposure and visibility among Hollywood's elite, too.

I'm not sure when it happens, but at some point, I realize I could get used to this life.

Days slip into weeks, and I start to let my guard down. I try not to, actually making a bit of an effort to stay paranoid, but with the show gobbling up all my attention and a startling lack of Finemdi assault teams breaking down my door, I can't help relaxing. Apep doesn't even make a peep in my dreams. I still make sure to run Nathan through at least a few lessons in wielding my mystic gifts every night, but even that's low stress; I can tell he loves every second of those training sessions, and he's definitely getting a little better at it every day. Honestly, the only real problem I've had so far came at the beginning, and that was in makeup and styling.

Karen's a brunette, which is fine (my hair actually takes to dye really well, since it never grows; no ugly roots!), but she also wears her hair short. It's a cute style—a layered pixie cut that matches her personality to a tee—but it's *short*.

See, it's impossible to cut my hair.

You can style it all day long, set it in curls, whatever, but the moment you try to *remove* it, it'll grow back in seconds. It's as much a part of my image as, say, my arms, so it's not going anywhere. A high-end tailored wig might work, of course, but then I'd need to answer some uncomfortable questions about why they can't just do it the easy way, especially when hair and makeup changes are in my contract.

Once again, I had to lean on my gifts to fix things. After some experimenting, I managed to create a tailored illusion of the proper hair. The deceptions *look* real enough, and they show up on camera just fine, but the catch is that I have to befuddle my stylist every time she tries to make changes and keep up the masquerade off set, as well. I can't let any of the crew suddenly see me with long hair after I've spent weeks with them otherwise. Still, it means the image I present to the world is very different from the Freya my foes know and loathe, so I try to think of it as one more layer of security.

That's it—literally the only major roadblock I've hit since filming started. It's almost too easy, to the point where I'm getting a little paranoid about how awesome it feels. It's as if I really *am* the up-and-coming star I'm pretending to be and not some goddess who attracts unwanted adventures like a misfortune magnet. Weeks turn to months, I start to relax, falling back into the lifestyle of a minor Hollywood celebrity and loving every second of it. There's just the bay, the shoot, and the joy of seeing my star rise.

It's wonderful.

Completed episodes pile up, reshoots come and go, the press junket rumbles to life, and my schedule starts getting dotted with promotional interviews and marketing meet-ups. Mahesh stays true to his word, making sure I get good exposure alongside the show's more famous cast members. Advance press is strong, there's good word of mouth online, and I'm getting buzz as a surprising new starlet.

When something strange *does* happen, I'm almost relieved—I'd been waiting for another shoe of some sort to drop.

It happens while I'm on one of those press endurance runs, the kind where they sit you in a nice camera-ready room and send a gauntlet of interviewers at you to save time. Basically, it means you spend several hours answering the same questions asked a zillion different ways until your brain starts leaking out of your ears. If you've ever seen an interview with a celebrity who looked out of it, annoyed, or like they just plain did *not* want to be there, it probably happened on the tail end of one of these days.

Somewhere between *Entertainment Weekly* and *Ain't It Cool News*, an assistant tells me my next interviewer is Sebastian Gallows, from something called *Eye on the Stars*. I give him a nod, and they send in my new nemesis.

Sebastian is a slim man in a crisply tailored pinstripe gray suit, which already sets him apart from my other interviewers. They all dressed nicely, sure, but this guy belongs in a boardroom, not writing cable TV puff pieces. He plops down in front of me, sending over a faint smile as the camera guy makes adjustments. It doesn't come close to reaching his eyes, which sparkle with a dark blue sheen that carries vague hints of violet.

"Hi, Ms. Valen," he says, crossing a leg and lacing his fingers on his knee. I notice he has no notes, no recorder, nothing. Also a first.

"Hi," I echo, feeling a little taken aback. "Sebastian, was it?"

"Mm," he says, raising his chin.

"A pleasure."

"Mm."

I frown, and that smile of his seems to widen, just a little. The camera guy gives a thumbs-up and says, "Ready whenever you are."

"Fantastic," Sebastian says, bouncing his leg. "Ms. Valen, just a few questions, if I may."

"That's why I'm here!" I say, feeling an odd sense of déjà vu as I play up my lively, cheerful image.

"Delightful," he murmurs, then leans in. "*Switch* airs in three weeks, and I understand the majority of your work is done. Commentary tracks and press meetings aside, what will you do next?"

Huh. Most interviewers start by focusing on the show itself or my status as a newcomer before heading to future plans. "I have a few potential projects lined up, but nothing's finalized," I say, going with my stock answer, which isn't far from the truth. Nothing's set in stone, but Mahesh has already brought up the possibility of guest roles on a few criminal and medical dramas, as those apparently chew through actors thanks to their "case of the week" plot structures.

"Honestly, it's hard to shift gears after working with such a passionate team. I wouldn't mind a few weeks to decompress before starting on something new."

"Would you say you're tired?" he asks, and something in the way his eyes flicker makes me feel like he's watching me more for my reaction than what I'll actually say.

"Uh, no, not at all."

"Mm," he murmurs. "Why show biz, Ms. Valen?" he asks after an awkward pause.

"I love it," I say, adapting another easy answer. "Working with incredibly talented people, making new friends, and entertaining fans? This is a dream come true."

"Was it always your dream?"

"Ever since I was little."

"When was that?"

What? "Uh, late nineties?"

"There have been some rumors about your age, Ms. Valen," he says, flicking invisible lint off his trousers. "Advance reviews are noting your performance as 'surprisingly mature' and 'deeply nuanced'—high praise for . . . was it twenty?"

"Twenty-one," I say, feeling tense. That's the age we decided on, since it lets me drink at all the fancy parties without worrying about any camera snaps dinging my reputation.

"Mm. Yes. You look rather young, is all."

"Totally twenty-one."

Another pause stretches. "Norwegian," he says at last. "Born in Tønsberg, yes?"

My eyebrows raise. It's not that he has this information—we put it out there to make sure my new identity would stand up to scrutiny—but he's actually pronounced the place correctly ("tuns-bahr"). "That's right."

"Oldest town in Norway."

"Really rich history," I say, sliding back to bubbly to hide my sudden nervousness. We picked it for just that reason, but now I'm worrying our little inside joke might have had some unforeseen consequences.

"You don't have a trace of an accent," he says.

"Thank you!" I say. "Lot of coaching, believe me."

"Mm."

I want to frown, but resist when I remember the camera's still rolling. It's hard—those little grunts of his are really starting to tick me off.

There's another pause as he watches me carefully. Then his gaze sharpens, he sets his leg down, and he whispers, "You're a slack-faced vomit guzzler," in Old Gutnish.

Several things race through my mind. First, that's a variant of Old Norse he's speaking, and there's practically no chance a starlet—even a Scandinavian one—would know the first thing about it. Second, he's pitched his voice so low, the odds are just as slim that any normal girl in my seat could hear clearly enough to make it out, let alone translate it.

Third . . . *what did he just call me?*

I *know* I'm being tested, taunted for some dire purpose, but it's so hard to resist smacking him down with the fury of the heavens. He's clearly watching to see what I'll do, and unleashing the Valkyrie is precisely the wrong move, no matter how badly I want it. I clamp on to her, holding tight as she flashes up in a surge of heat, and instead try to favor the surprise I'm also feeling, to twist it into something that could be mistaken for curiosity.

"Sorry, didn't quite catch that," I say, desperately hoping my voice sounds light.

He watches me for a few more seconds. "Mm," he says at last, and stands. "Those are all my questions, Ms. Valen. Thank you for everything."

"That's all? I feel like you barely got to ask anything."

"Aren't you sweet?" he asks with a dark smile. "Just a doll." He nods at my assistant, who steps up to lead him out.

Once I'm sure he's out of the room, I turn to the cameraman. "Can I get a copy of that?" I ask.

"Sure," he says. "Weird one, wasn't he?"

"Very," I murmur, mind rattling with worries.

That night, back at our hotel, I review the unedited footage of Sebastian's interview on my laptop with my friends. "If he is a god, I do not recognize him," Sekhmet says, frowning her way through a third replay of the conversation.

"And he's insulting you there at the end?" Nathan says, looking deeply offended on my behalf.

"Absolutely. In a way only a god could possibly understand."

"Clever," Sekhmet says, examining the man with obvious hunger. "He wishes to expose you, and chooses a personal blasphemy as his means."

"It almost worked, too," I say, running a hand through my hair. "I barely hung on."

"You can see a bit of it on your face," Nathan says, reversing the footage and playing the pivotal moment again.

"Is it obvious?" I ask, anxiety ratcheting higher.

"I don't know," he says after another repetition. "Maybe only if you know what you're looking for."

"Does he?" Sekhmet asks.

I give her a helpless shrug.

"Who is he, then? What are his goals; who are his masters?"

"Well, there's the obvious," Nathan says, and we turn from the laptop to look at him. "Finemdi."

I grimace. "I'd really like that to not be the case."

"It makes sense, though."

"Not entirely—if he *is* working for them, why the whole interview song and dance? I mean, something about me tripped their radar, right? If they're suspicious, why not just take me down and be done with it?"

"Maybe this is just something they do regularly," he says. "Show biz seems like a great way for gods to get power, after all. You might not be the first to think of it."

Damn. He could be right about that. Once you realize gods aren't picky about where they get their belief, making the leap to the entertainment industry isn't exactly rocket science. I've made the mistake of assuming I was the only one with a hot idea before, and I will *not* repeat it. "Okay, that sort of follows," I say, nodding. "But still— can't they detect gods? Playing twenty questions seems redundant."

"Can they? I mean, I know *you* can sense when they're around, but do they really have some sort of godly Geiger counter for the mortals to use?"

I frown and turn to Sekhmet. She shakes her head. "Somehow, I never received a tour of their armory."

"I guess I didn't see anything like that, either. Garen never gave any sign."

191

"So maybe they can't wave a tricorder and figure out who you are," Nathan says, "but sending an actual god out to verify a hunch would probably be seen as a waste of resources."

"And beneath that god, depending on who they are," I add.

"Right, so they send Mr. Personality to tick you off and sound the alarm if it works."

I blow out a breath. "And he didn't. At least, not yet."

"You are certain?" Sekhmet asks.

"Nobody's breaking down the door," I say. A very loud silence follows. Familiar as we are with the universe's cruel sense of causality, there's a pregnant pause as we all turn to look at the entrance to my hotel room.

A few seconds pass without any "hilarious" coincidences ruining our lives. "So we're good, right?" I say at last.

"For the moment," Sekhmet says, still watching the door. "I would advise caution . . . and restraint."

"Restraint? From you?" I laugh, surprised.

She grins, finally turning back to me. "You did say things would need to be different."

"I didn't expect it to stick," I reply, still smiling. "Okay. So act normal and stay the course? Assume assault squads aren't waiting around the corner?"

They glance at each other, then nod. "Running could be even more suspicious," Sekhmet adds.

"Yeah, true. Well, that works for me. I have a few more press events to finish, and Mahesh wants me back in LA afterward for some new auditions. I'm getting buzz, guys! Buzz!"

"Fitting for the queen bee," Nathan says. "Just be careful, okay?"

"Oh, I'll be the most paranoid little goddess you ever saw," I say, tweaking his nose. "Now don't you two have a date or something?"

Nathan snaps his fingers. "House of Prime Rib. Yes. You're going to love this place, Sekhmet. Hunks of meat the size of your head."

Her eyes glitter. "Oh! Lead on, lovely mortal," she says in a thick voice. I think she's five seconds from drooling.

"Happy to! You good for now, Sara?" Nathan asks, getting up and offering Sekhmet a hand. She rolls her eyes with a smirk and stands on her own.

"Completely," I say, giving a quick wave and turning back to the screen.

I grimace when they leave, hoping that didn't come off as too dismissive. I've been trying really hard to act like everything's awesome when it comes to their lovey-dovey dealings, but this whole Sebastian thing has me distracted.

I guess it's gotten better. A little. I mean, filming this show has helped me shove their relationship to the back of my mind (unless they happen to be "playing tourist"), but things still feel weird. Basically, I'm caught between wanting it to end and crippled by curiosity about how it's going.

Their love—oh, and it's love, believe me—is something new, which is kind of a big deal for a goddess who thought she'd seen it all. I mean, yes, gods have romanced mortals since the dawn of time, but the link Nathan's priestly nature has forged is downright astonishing.

It's a blast, let me tell you.

At least Nathan's doing well. Even with everything that's been going on, I haven't let up on his priestly training. There's no way I'm letting him go unprepared into whatever conflict awaits, so I've been focusing on combat and utility magic, expanding his repertoire of spells so he won't get flambéed the second he steps in the ring with the supernatural.

He's getting great at shields in particular, which is almost entirely on him. I'm more of a *"Die!"* girl, so my spell-casting efforts tend toward nearly the exact opposite of Nathan's new area of expertise, but I know enough to recognize talent when I see it. His leaning elsewhere isn't terribly surprising, either. That's the thing about mortal magic—unlike gods, they have *choice.*

Give someone the gift of spellcraft, and you get a window into who they are, as if all those webs and weaves can't wait to match themselves to their new wielder's heart. Nathan, it seems, is a protector, someone who wants to deflect pain from those he loves.

It's possible he fancies himself a knight in shining armor, but I think it unlikely. People like that tend to romanticize themselves, to approach chivalry from a selfish place. No, I believe those who truly wish to shield others from loss do so because they understand all too well the hurt they wish to halt.

And Nathan's lost plenty.

After we get to the point where I can't dent his barriers (which doesn't take long, sadly), we bring in Sekhmet, which becomes a rather humbling experience for us both.

"A fine thing," she says after he forms a shield between them, splitting his hotel room with a wall of gleaming force. She smiles vaguely, then hauls her fist back and sends a lazy punch blasting through it.

Thrashing, severed threads of spellcraft twitch and unravel around the impact site, unmaking the wall in moments, and as Nathan winces from the feedback, she walks through the remains of his spell and kisses him.

"Yet I am finer still," she whispers.

Nathan shakes his head, then grins and says, "If I get a kiss every time I lose, why win?"

Sekhmet laughs, and gives him a knowing look. "Because until you succeed, kisses are all you'll get."

His next shield is much, much stronger.

Punches and inspiration aren't Sekhmet's only contribution, either: She also takes it upon herself to begin training Nathan in physical skills and techniques. Between the two of us, he makes great strides over the months, getting stronger, faster, and deadlier in the ways of battle both mystical and mundane. He was never pasty, but now he's actually approaching "fit." It's great to see, though still kind of annoying when you combine it with the fact that he's getting aid from another goddess.

Besides Spell-slinging 101 with Nathan, my only other encounters with the supernatural are the dozens of preset contingency spells I have to reapply to myself each month. I'm getting better at really basic things—especially magic that's closely tied to my portfolio, like scrying—but unless I want to risk draining myself when danger nears, these triggered spells remain my best bet. Most of them are variants of illusions like the ones I used to impress Harv and Mahesh, though there are a few showstoppers, too.

I hope I won't have to use them anytime soon, but better safe than sorry.

Another week of last-minute requests and interviews passes in a blur, and then it's just a short flight home. I'm not sure when we'll be back in San Francisco, but I already have a checklist of must-eat specialties for us to hit when we do return. For now, though, my new hometown calls.

I grin as we step out of LAX and into the warm sun of SoCal. Being here is a relief. Don't get me wrong, I enjoyed the shoot, but these past months have been pushing me to my limits. Even so, I can tell things are improving; I'm not much mightier, but there's a peculiar sense of support growing behind my eyes.

Setting aside the odd influx of power Nathan and Sekhmet's relationship has been sending me, everything I've been doing in service to this new career has definitely helped. The press, the Twitter warfare, the high-end clothes and trigger-happy paparazzi— it's all feeding the call of vanity, and that means something. It's like the pool of strength I draw from hasn't gotten any deeper, but the months I've spent playing starlet *have* widened it. Still can't call lightning from the skies or raise the dead, but hey—progress!

Public perception of Sara Valen seems fairly good, too. Just as we were leaving the airport, I noticed my face on a celebrity magazine at a tabloid stand, a very bright headline shouting, SARA'S SKIN SECRETS! (TWO WORDS: IN. SANE!). I've been popping up a lot in gossip rags and periodical spreads, and with HBO's hype machine running full bore, there's a good number of articles about me and the rest of the show's cast. The fact that I'm a relative newcomer is an added bonus, as there's nothing like a mystery actress without a past to set tongues wagging. Of course, some bloggers have less-than-flattering theories for how I landed such a sweet role, and the number of times I've run into paparazzi hoping for a candid photo op is verging on ludicrous (seems there's always an unmarked sedan following us, these days), but on the whole, I'm quite satisfied with how the spotlight's been treating me.

We settle into our rental car and Nathan begins driving us back to the Sunset Tower Hotel. I pull out my Mim a half second after my seat belt clicks, intent on catching up with my growing fan base and checking my e-mails.

I'm soon engrossed in the unrelenting chatter of social media and the latest round of volleys from Kirsten Riley's camp. Stars above,

I love this. I'm not sure it's ever getting old, either—I mean, how could it? Take a sprawling world of info about everything from celebrity cats to your favorite actress's hair product, smash a tidal wave of raw emotion and opinions onto it, and I'm *in*. For a god of passion and war, mainlining that sea of memetic madness is absurdly addictive.

Somewhat later, I'll realize this compulsion of mine has a nasty side effect: tunnel vision. While I take another dip in my favorite digital waters, what I don't know is that it's causing me to miss Nathan's constant glances at his own phone, or the knowing looks he's exchanging with Sekhmet through the rearview mirror.

My high priest is up to something, you see, and I'm too wrapped up in the distractions of fame to notice.

EXHIBITIONISM

NATHAN

"Is this cheating?" Nathan asks Sekhmet.

"On whom? Freya?" she replies, looking up from her museum guide.

Nathan shakes his head. "Oh, no—I don't think she'd *really* mind us sneaking off to New York for a night on the town."

"Then why the secrecy?" Sekhmet says with a sly smile.

"Because I wanted to surprise you, and that's already hard enough when it's just me with something to hide," he says. "You're *very* good at killing mysteries, you know."

"I'm good at killing *everything*," she says with a wink, and gives her map a shake. "Now, why have you brought me here? Or is that another enigma I must slay?"

Nathan smiles at that. In lieu of an answer, he nods at the soaring entryway of domed arches and stately columns around them. Hordes of tourists stream in all directions, eager to experience the treasures of New York's Metropolitan Museum of Art. It's nice,

Nathan feels, to be part of that crowd, to take a day off from gods and glamour and just . . . hang out.

"My dad took me to the Met a long time ago," he says, feeling unexpectedly wistful. "Awesome experience for young Nate, and a big part of why I went into art and design. There's this one painting of a girl here—*Lady with the Rose*, I think. She had this incredible *smirk*, and I remember wanting *so badly* to be able to make something like that."

Sekhmet holds up her map to Nathan and taps the section labeled EGYPTIAN ART. "I am reasonably certain you brought me here for more than mere reminiscence," she says in a knowing tone.

Nathan can't help laughing at that. For a five-thousand-year-old cat goddess, she does a remarkable job of keeping him grounded. "Well, sort of," he says, holding out a hand. "It wasn't *my* past I brought you here to see."

Sekhmet's smile widens, and those stunningly dark eyes of hers seem to pull at him with passion and delight. "You know, I believe I quite enjoy being surprised," she says, entwining her fingers in his and letting him lead her into the museum.

"So what *did* you mean by 'cheating'?" she asks as they approach the Egyptian wing.

"Oh, right—how I got us here," Nathan says. "I mean, using the Graces' spa portals to skip across the country? Feels a little easy, y'know?"

"Magic is, by definition, a cheat," Sekhmet murmurs, pocketing her map. "It is almost always used to defy natural laws."

"Does that mean you have a problem with it?"

She scoffs at that. "One must pick their battles, love. My responsibilities concern the laws of Ma'at and the rights of women. So long as it does not violate them, magic is simply another tool to be used in their service . . . just as you have so cleverly used the Graces' spells in mine."

"Well, that's—"

Sekhmet cuts off his reply with an elated gasp as they move into the following room. "How *delightful*!" she says, clasping a fist to her mouth as her head twitches in what seems an attempt to look in all directions at once.

They've entered the first gallery of the Egyptian wing, an elegant space dotted with freestanding podiums and plinths, glass cases, and wall-mounted displays, all containing beautiful relics from the ancient world. "Look, Nathan!" Sekhmet cries, dragging him to stand before an imposing lion carved from lightly speckled granite. "Why—but this is from Henen-nesut, I'm sure of it!"

She kneels down to view the stately creature head-on. "Over four and a half thousand years gone, and here you sit," she whispers, eyes wide.

"Friend of yours?" Nathan asks.

"An homage, more like," Sekhmet says, getting back up. "I was *quite* the subject for statues and carvings, I'll have you know."

"Yeah, about that—there's a room just down the hall to the left I think you'll enjoy."

Sekhmet's smile grows eerily wide at that, and for a heartbeat Nathan imagines he could catch a flash of the lioness's fangs beneath the illusion. It's in these moments he feels most terrified by and drawn to the woman before him. Dating Sekhmet is like trying to romance an inferno, to clasp a creature of ancient aggression so close you either smothered its flames of carnage or were consumed by them. Either way, it's all or nothing, a conflict at turns brutal and brilliant, subtle and shocking. As real as any war, theirs is a relationship with its own particular feints, charges, tactics, and stratagems, each deployed in the hopes of winning another inch of territory in the other's heart.

Nathan loves her for it.

Exploring the Egyptian wing with Sekhmet is like stepping back in time with the finest, most self-centered tour guide imaginable. Every scrap of pottery seems a springboard for another story, usually tinted in some way by scandals, sleights, or slaughters directed at or committed by the goddess herself. By the time they pass beneath a doorway titled EGYPT UNDER ROMAN RULE, Nathan feels he already knows more about the secret lives of the pharaohs than any other mortal on the planet.

Sekhmet begins edging her way around a tightly bound sarcophagus on the floor, a tale about its occupant already on her lips, when she freezes, her attention drawn to the hall beyond. Her mouth drops open and her whole body seems to tense, and then she springs forward, clapping her hands rapidly as she practically dances into the next room.

"It's me! Nathan, it's me!" she exclaims, drawing a few curious glances from other patrons. She skids to a halt in the center of the room, pointing at two seated statues set before a wall of preserved Egyptian murals and hieroglyphics. Twins carved from dark granite, each sculpture depicts a well-dressed woman with the head of a lioness, her intense eyes staring straight ahead.

"Amenhotep made these for me—the Magnificent, they called him," she says, releasing a very happy, high-pitched noise. "Just imagine: temples *filled* with my likeness, over *seven hundred* seated and standing graven tributes to my name, each an entreaty for health, protection, and long life."

She whirls to look at Nathan, eyes aflame. "I must have them."

Nathan blinks at that. "Wait, what?" he says, hoping he's misunderstood her.

"The statues. They are mine," she says, leaning in to examine the right-most carving. "The headpiece on this one is the more damaged of the two, but the body seems in fairer condition. We shall secure it first."

"You're joking," Nathan says, already knowing the truth with sinking certainty.

"Oh, take heart," she says, giving him what's probably supposed to be a reassuring smile. "I will perform this labor. Now, do you think they have attached it in some way?"

"No, Sekhmet, hang on, you can't steal a statue from the—"

"*Steal?*" she repeats, incredulous. "I am no thief! I am the rightful owner of these pieces, exercising my *divine right* to reclaim them."

"Um, okay, but that was *four thousand years ago*! Isn't that—"

"Three thousand, four hundred years."

"Fine! Point is, people don't care about *Star Wars* spoilers anymore and that's barely *forty* years old. Somehow, I don't think anyone's still taking receipts on statues from the Twelfth Dynasty."

"Eighteenth," Sekhmet says absently, listening with only half an ear as she examines her ancient likeness. "How much could this weigh? No more than . . . fifteen hundred kilos, surely?"

Nathan fingers the phone in his pocket, wondering if he should cancel their dinner reservation now or try to remain optimistic. "Sekhmet, please, let's—"

"Oh wow, hey there!" a familiar voice says from the entrance behind them.

Startled, Sekhmet and Nathan turn to meet their unexpected greeter. Walking up to them with a bounce in her step is, oddly enough, Samantha Drass, daughter of Finemdi's former CEO and teenage science superstar. She's dressed in a well-cut lab coat and light indigo button-up (an odd choice for a museum, Nathan reflects), her pale green eyes are wide with delight, and her young, freckly features seem to radiate glee. Something tickles the back of Nathan's thoughts at that, a hazy question he can't quite resolve. If he knew her better, he might be able to narrow down precisely what's bothering him. As it is, he's never had many opportunities to interact with the girl.

It's something a part of him has always lamented, as out of all the people he knows, she's the closest in age (by several orders of magnitude, in some cases). If there's anyone who would understand the craziness of his life, it's her. He doesn't regret palling around with gods, not for a *second*, but doing it with a friend? Someone to commiserate with when, say, your girlfriend started plotting *grand theft idol?*

Would've been nice.

"A pleasure as always, Ms. Drass," Sekhmet says, straightening. "What brings you to this place?"

"I come here all the time," she says with a wave. "Lovely museum; great for gathering your thoughts after, um, work."

"Ah, of course," Sekhmet says, something cold in her eyes. "And what have you done for your masters today?"

Samantha gives her head a rueful shake. "You know I'm not in it for them."

"Yes . . ." Sekhmet says softly, eyes narrowing as she focuses on the girl. "You speak truthfully, yet while I trust Freya's judgment, I would prefer knowing your aims for myself."

"It's a personal matter," Samantha says, hesitation in her voice. "But not one that will aid Finemdi in any way, I assure you."

Sekhmet nods at that, affirming that Samantha has passed

another lie detector test. Nathan relaxes a little. It's not that he doesn't trust Samantha. In fact, he rather desperately *wants* to trust her, to have that mortal connection he's been missing. Of course, she *did* encourage Freya to hunt Ares and happens to work for a global god-killing conspiracy, but Sekhmet seems to believe her, which means Nathan can do the same.

The lovely thing about his girlfriend's powers of truth telling *isn't* that she can spot falsehoods—anyone with half a brain can twist their words around that kind of limitation—it's that she can tease apart lies of omission and half-truths, too. If you want a prayer of sneaking something under her radar, you have to word things *very* carefully, and it only gets worse when she has reason to be suspicious.

So far so good, Sam, Nathan thinks with a little smile. Then, noticing the lull in conversation has begun to stretch to awkward lengths, he decides to speak up.

"How *are* things going at the office, anyway?" he asks. "We've barely heard a peep since Orlando."

"Great for me," she says, grin returning. "Besides a ton more work—Meridian *is* our headquarters—they've been keeping me busy trying to recatalog everything from Impulse Station."

"Any interesting developments?" Nathan asks, legitimately curious about a day in the life of a Finemdi worker bee.

"Well, let's see," she says, looking toward the ceiling as she thinks. "We got another lead on a precursor in Greenland, so we've been poring over data from the teams they scrambled there. There was an artifact from one of the Greek primordials—we think Nyx—that popped up in the Namib Desert, too. We had to figure out how to get it here without triggering another eclipse."

She makes a *hmm* noise, then snaps her fingers. "Oh! Some

rookies hauled in another Coyote clone last week. *That* was fun—took them the better part of the weekend to find all the scorpions."

Nathan exchanges a look with Sekhmet, who gives him a bemused shrug. *At least she's just as lost.* Samantha doesn't seem to notice, however, continuing to discuss her evidently insane workplace.

"We got the green light on a proposal to build a new base in the Dreamtime," she says, looking proud. "Now we just need to work out the logistics with ArchEng so the whole thing doesn't turn into colored sand again. Oh, and on that note, I need to submit my review of the rangers' idea to test if Otherworld extends off planet."

She leans in as if sharing a secret. "They want to build a rocket there, see if it'll be a more efficient way to enter LEO or even selenocentric orbit." She rolls her eyes and gives her head a shake. "I think the scale's all wrong, and that's even *if* the methane/LOX admixture follows the same physical laws over there."

Sekhmet blinks at that. "You . . . certainly seem to be helping them with a wide variety of tasks," she says after a moment, seeming unsure if she's confused or annoyed by it all.

Samantha sighs, clearly assuming it to be the latter. "I remain your ally, Lady Sekhmet—I may be in the employ of your sworn foes, but I *do* wish to aid you and Freya in your struggle. However unpleasant you find it, I hope you'll agree this relationship is in your best interests."

Sekhmet's lips twist, but from the way her posture relaxes, Nathan knows she's already decided to trust the girl. "I cannot deny the appeal of this facility," she says at last, directing her gaze at the room around them. "The presentation of these collections is both attractive and respectful."

Nathan smiles at the sudden change of subject. Sekhmet may

have decided to let the subject of Samantha's allegiance drop, but she certainly isn't about to admit it.

"Right?" Samantha says, her smile returning. "So what about you? Doing a bit of sightseeing?"

"At first," Sekhmet says, looking back at her statue. "Now we are discussing the best means of removing this sculpture."

"Whoa, no! *We* are not discussing anything," Nathan says, wanting to set the record straight. "*You're* the one telling me you want to steal—sorry, *remove*—a gigantic stone Sekhmet from the Met! Where would you even put it?"

"I have storage facilities," Sekhmet says, shrugging.

"And it wouldn't be better here, where people can appreciate it, *and you?*"

Sekhmet purses her lips at that, tapping a finger against them as she considers his argument. "Please do not mistake me," she says after a moment. "I am quite grateful to the proprietors of this establishment for taking care of my possessions, but they *are* mine. I am not content to view them as simply another *tourist*."

"But—"

"Um, Nathan's probably right, Sekhmet," Samantha says, piping up.

"Excuse me?" she says in a flat voice.

"It's just . . . there's a lot of security here, and they'd be on you in seconds!" Samantha says, fidgeting. "You both could get in a lot of trouble."

Sekhmet says nothing, but the look on her face begins to darken.

"And, um, Finemdi keeps a pretty close eye on this museum, too," Samantha says, fingers twisting. "You don't want to get them on your case, do you?"

Sekhmet watches in silence for a handful of seconds, then growls. "Liar," she spits. "Your cowardice is repugnant. Finemdi does not

206

watch this place, and you are well aware the 'security' that *does* is beneath me."

"I-I'm sorry, Lady Sekhmet," Samantha says, suddenly meek. "I was just— I mean—"

"Spare me," Sekhmet says with an imperious sniff, turning back to the statue. "If you will not help, then away with you."

Samantha sighs and gives Nathan a crestfallen look.

At least you tried, Nathan thinks, returning a sad shrug. *Should've known better than to straight-up* lie *to her, though* . . .

Without waiting for more arguments against it, Sekhmet steps up to her chosen statue, bends down, and wraps both arms around its legs. As she tightens her grip, digging her fingertips into the stone, a nearby guard begins heading toward her, saying, "Miss, do *not* touch—"

With a heave, Sekhmet wrenches the statue from the floor, swaying back a step as she swings the absurd weight above her in one impossible motion. A thin crack shoots across the polished stone beneath her heel, the result of a metric ton suddenly slamming into one precarious place.

I guess even goddesses know to lift with their knees, Nathan thinks, eyebrows rising at the sight of his girlfriend hefting a massive seven-foot granite idol onto one shoulder.

Samantha backs away, clearing a path to the door, and motions for Nathan to do the same. The guard, meanwhile, has stopped mid-sentence, mouth stuck open at the sight of Sekhmet's unimaginable deadlift. The handful of museum patrons lingering in the room all wear similar expressions of shock, and some begin fumbling for their smartphones.

Then the alarm sounds, a siren cutting through the astonishment, and everything starts moving at what seems like double speed. First, the museum guests panic, nearly all of them making a mad dash for the entrance. At the same time, the guard, regaining his composure, hauls out his Taser, levels it at Sekhmet, and fires. Trailing conductive wires, two darts leap across the room and embed themselves in her left side.

Nathan grimaces as his girlfriend's muscles twitch beneath her dress, electricity dancing across her obliques with a chattering sizzle, but other than that, she gives no sign of discomfort. In full defiance of mortal biology, she merely tilts her head to stare at the guard and favor him with a cruel smile.

"Surely you jest," she says, and shifts her grip on the statue, freeing one hand. She reaches down, plucks the electrodes from her skin, and casts them to the floor with a snort.

Superiority established, she begins moving toward the exit, the weight on her shoulders transforming every step into a ponderous thud.

The guard, clearly unsure what to do next, stares at the useless device in his hands, then drops it and begins speaking rapidly into his earpiece.

By the time Sekhmet reaches the entrance to the Egyptian wing, a full squad of six security guards await her, several with real guns drawn. Most of the museum patrons scattered at the sound of the alarms, and the staff are ushering the last stragglers to the emergency exits.

"Place the statue on the ground, lie down, and put your hands on your head!" barks one of the gun-toting guards.

Sekhmet merely giggles at that and begins *running* straight at him, the enormous weight bouncing with every booming footfall. Half the guards scatter at the sight, desperate to get out of the way of what's basically a very small oncoming train. The leader and his friends, however, stand their ground and open fire.

Nathan pulls Samantha behind a doorway as the gunfire starts, the little scientist releasing an adorable squeak of surprise as he grabs her. His chest pounds, adrenaline and worry for Sekhmet sending his heart rate into overdrive. He chances a peek around the stone of the entryway, fearing the worst.

His eyes widen as he catches a glimpse of the final moments of his girlfriend's charge. He's heard stories from Freya, of course, tales of their escape from Finemdi's Impulse Station that featured the two goddesses fighting side by side against teams of mercenaries wielding military assault rifles, but he's never really been able to picture it . . . until now.

Sekhmet is cackling, laughter lost amid the gunfire as she practically *skips* into that stream of lead like a toddler splashing through a summer rainstorm. The guards' bullets might as well be packing peanuts for all the good they do. Despite plenty of solid hits on her legs and torso, her pace barely wavers.

Sekhmet blasts through the bewildered guards, bowling several of them over with her unstoppable momentum and clipping one of the columns beyond with the statue. Exiting into the museum lobby in a spray of cement chips, she stops to realign herself, checking her idol as she does. A look of regret crosses her face as she brushes a hand over some new gouges and bullet holes. She casts her gaze back to the room she's taken it from, then down to the museum's entrance, and sighs.

"I think she feels bad it got damaged," Nathan says, watching.

A moment later, as more guards begin arriving, Sekhmet proves him right by gingerly placing her statue on the ground beside her. She gives it a friendly pat, then shouts, "Apologies! All these years unspoiled, and now look what's happened."

A nearby guard yells for her to step away from the statue and lie down. Sekhmet laughs at that and says, "I am not unwilling to admit gratitude at the care you have taken."

Another shout for compliance, and more raised weapons follow her words.

"I . . . have been a poor guest, have I not?" she says, ignoring the commands. "Perhaps she *is* better off in your hands." She frowns, and her gaze zips back, looking in Nathan's direction. "Again I obsess over what is past, to the detriment of my present."

"Lady, what the *hell* is wrong with you?" a guard snaps, edging closer.

She smiles at that, then sketches a quick bow at the man. "Do take good care of her!" she replies, and before he has a chance to react, she darts away at a blistering pace, racing for the exit at rally car speeds.

Samantha's phone dings in her pocket, and Nathan turns to give her an incredulous look when she takes it out and begins typing a reply.

"Is this *boring* for you?" he says, listening to the sound of glass shattering in the distance as Sekhmet barrels through the double doors at the entrance ahead of a swarm of security.

"Sorry, no, it's just work," Samantha says, sounding distant. "We got a live one—live *ones*, actually. Three new gods, very powerful—and guess who's on intake duty!"

She sends her text, puts away the phone, and smiles at Nathan. "Looks like I'm pulling overtime tonight. This was nice, though! Hope to see you again!"

"Er, yeaaaah . . ." Nathan says, starting to feel this girl might not exactly be the "relatable mortal pal" he envisioned. "You, uh, want me to walk you out?"

"Nah, I'll be right behind ya. Just need to send a few e-mails."

"Ah, all right," Nathan says, backing away. "I'd . . . better catch up with Sekhmet before she, like, tries to hail a cab with a security guard's arm or something."

"Good luck!" Samantha says, giving him a happy wave.

Nathan returns the gesture, takes a moment to lament the loss of the date night he had planned, then gets up from his shelter and begins following the trail of destruction to the exit.

From behind the doorway, Samantha watches Nathan go, waits a breath, and then stands. Her expression changes as she surveys the emptied room, silly smile refining into a look of amused satisfaction. She begins padding forward, pulling up the sleeve of her lab coat as she does. She checks the pale web of spellcraft there, watching as the threads of magic that represent Sekhmet and Freya's high priest move away. Confident they've left for good, she reaches into a pocket and squeezes the etched lodestone that lies within.

Instantly, the lights die and the nearest alarm boxes go silent, their last wails hushed in strangled screeches. Samantha spares a glance for the lifeless camera blister mounted high above, then makes her way to one of the display cases.

As she moves, she brings a humming porcelain flower out of another pocket and, in one smooth motion, sweeps it forward to give the security glass a dainty tap. Instantly, the screen shatters, thick chunks of safety glass clattering to the floor. Samantha reaches in, withdraws the object she spent the better part of a month putting a *far* more elaborate scheme into acquiring, and slips it into the lining of her coat with a grin. Sekhmet's antics made things much simpler, and all the goddess had needed was the barest push.

Her work complete, Samantha tosses a panicked look onto her face, clutches her arms to her chest in mock dismay, and begins running for the exits.

TRICK SHOT

FREYA

I'm awoken from my late-afternoon nap by the faint sounds of conversation from next door. Groggily, I check the bedside clock, wondering if I've overslept. *Weren't they supposed to be back a lot later?*

At first I'm worried something's gone wrong, but their chatter sounds unconcerned. Maybe they changed their plans.

Shaking my head, I lean over and grab my laptop, telling myself there's never a bad time to tend my social networks. I've just started reading my latest e-mails when there's a knock on my door.

"Come in!" I yell, shifting the computer so I can sit upright in my bed.

The door swings open and my friends enter. "Hey, guys!" I say absently, still reading entries as they approach. "How was— *What?*"

One of the e-mails has caught my eye, its subject line tearing a surprised gasp from my throat. It's from Samantha, and I bolt out of bed in shock as its full meaning smashes home.

Sekhmet registers my concern and rushes to my side. "Little fighter . . . ?" she prompts.

Wordlessly, I hold the laptop out to her, thumb on the e-mail, and her eyes widen as they flick across its title.

"Guys?" Nathan says, looking between us. "Clue a lowly mortal in?"

"'Urgent,'" Sekhmet reads. She pauses as she takes in the rest of the message, and her voice hardens when she reads it aloud: "'Hawaiian friends captured by Finemdi.'"

"Oh," Nathan says, deflating.

"They're in New York," Sekhmet says, scanning the e-mail. "That's how she knows—she just performed their intake evaluation."

"*That* was—" Nathan begins, then shakes his head. "How the hell did they catch them? I mean, after all these years, you'd think they'd have learned a thing or two about staying hidden."

"Ares," I explain, arms crossed and lips twisted. "It must be part of his new drive to expand Finemdi's 'stockpile.' He's trying to weaponize us, remember? Looks like our friends just got recruited."

"We must rescue them," Sekhmet says. "We cannot allow our allies to remain imprisoned, much less provide further resources to our foes should their wills be broken."

"I agree, but it's not like they stashed them in a cardboard box under the overpass—those girls are at their *headquarters*," I say, miserable. "Getting to them will mean dealing with crazy defenses, *multiple pantheons* of brainwashed gods, *and* Ares."

"We must do so eventually," Sekhmet persists. "Can we not—"

"No!" I snap. "We have a plan for a *reason*! We're not strong enough to deal with Ares by *himself*, let alone fight through him *and* the rest of Finemdi for a rescue! This—oh, this *sucks*."

There's a tense silence as I stew. Several unhappy minutes pass,

Sekhmet pacing, me glaring at the city from the balcony, and Nathan fidgeting awkwardly. "Well, at least they're all in the same place now," he pipes up, clearly uncomfortable with the mood. "I mean, you were going to be taking down Finemdi and Ares anyway, right? Grab the sisters on the way out? Three birds, one stone?"

"Not the time to start digging for silver linings, Nate," I mutter.

"Right, got it," he says. Another awkward pause threatens to stretch, and I notice him squirm at the thought. He *really* hates a bad mood.

"Anything I can—I mean, want anything?" he says, sounding a little desperate. "That cookie shop you like isn't far."

My lips twist. I *do* appreciate his efforts to lighten the mood, but part of me wants to sulk a little longer. Then again, I think this offer is more for him, not us.

Besides . . . cookies.

"Fine," I say in a stubborn voice. "And a brownie."

Nathan nods with a relieved grin and takes out his phone, hunting down directions for the store. I hide a smile of my own. Lovable little mortal, always hoping for the best. We head out together once he has the route mapped, Nathan driving and adding idle chitchat to plaster over the pain left in the wake of Samantha's message. It helps—for a time.

I polish off the last of the cookies just before we return to the hotel, and my mood darkens with their passing. The treats help, but I have a serious problem to consider: I was a registered god at Impulse Station once, just like the Hawaiian sisters. If Ares is dead-set on reclaiming everything they lost and then some, how long before he picks up *my* trail?

And who's to say he hasn't *already started*?

I try to relax after we get back to our rooms, to lose myself in online shopping and advance reviews of *Switch*, but it's no use. My goals might be completely unachievable at this point. I mean, I still can hope for enough success in Hollywood to let me challenge Finemdi and Ares before they hunt me down, but that could be years, even decades away, if it's possible at all. Bleh.

It's my only option, though. No sense in abandoning everything until I know for sure. I sigh and give Mahesh a call. He's full of news about *Switch* and potential auditions, as well as a few high-profile clubs he'd like me to visit so I'll stay in the spotlight. I smile as we chat; his enthusiasm is infectious. I let his suggestions and schedules wash over me, making notes and adding ideas where I can, determined to keep myself from getting lost in self-pity. There's a war on, and this is merely a setback. I *will* win.

Phone calls and inner turmoil eventually land me poolside, relaxing in one of the deck chairs and soaking up some sun (no, I can't tan, if you're wondering). I'm watching cat videos on my phone and sipping a cocktail when Nathan sits down beside me with a sigh. "Hey, Nate," I say, toasting him with the drink.

"Hey," he says, settling in. "Bad time?"

I shrug. "Frustrating. I'll be okay. How about you?"

"Good." He pauses. "Weird."

I sit up, setting phone and mojito aside. *Ooh, what have we here?* "Sekhmet?"

"Sort of. It's mostly me." He frowns, thinking. "Have you—I mean, you've dated a god before, right?"

"Nathan, I had a *husband* at one point."

"Oh. Right . . ." he says after a moment of confusion. "I remember reading that. 'Otter'?"

That gets him a snort of amusement. "Óðr," I say. Then my smile fades. "The perpetually misplaced. Spent *centuries* getting over his heedless, wanderlusting hide. Thank the Fates his part in my myths was minor. I loved him, wept for him, and, well, can you imagine what that's like? To have part of who you are *defined* as a devoted wife to an absent husband?"

He gives me an odd look.

"You're running into something like that right now, aren't you?" I ask, watching him.

He's silent a little longer, then nods. "I think so. Look, I love the girl—I really do. It's just . . . she's never going to be able to change, is she?"

Ah. I think he's finally starting to understand one of the major downsides to being a god. *You think it's hard on relationships, just try being one of us, kid.*

"What happened?" I ask.

"Nothing, really. Things are great. But . . . I worry about her. She still has problems with the world, her place in it. More than you, I think, and more than she lets on."

"She always did try to hide any sign of weakness. Predator thing."

"I figured. I just hate seeing her lose control of herself." He pauses. "Shoot, we never told you about our date, did we?"

"No . . . ?"

Nathan laughs. "Okay, buckle up." With that, he proceeds to unload a lively tale of museum theft in New York, and at turns, I find myself impressed at his cleverness in using the Graces' portal network, amused by Sekhmet's attempted larceny, and deeply interested in Samantha's guest appearance.

"I can see how that might get you thinking about the . . . complications in dating a god," I say when he finishes.

"Eh." He shrugs. "More than anything, it makes me feel bad for her. She has fun in the moment, but when it fades, I know she's left worrying if she'll ever be able to fit in."

"I never realized that was something she wanted."

"It's not really about taking statues of herself out of museums," he explains. "It's about trying to live in a society that doesn't want to *let her*."

"Ah."

"The world gets her down in general. I mean, she's not wrong— we *do* accept a lot of bad stuff like it's nothing—but I think she really stews in it."

"Anything else in particular . . . ?"

"Few days ago," he says. "She was reading about an attack on a girls' school. I could see her getting furious, twitching, like she wanted to personally tear apart the guys who did it. Then she closed her eyes, shook her head, and went for her phone."

"Calling one of her organizations?"

He nods. "Any idea how many she has?"

"Dozens, I think. She's crazy-rich—centuries of investments will do that—and I know she sinks most of it into protecting women. Probably how she's managed to stay so strong, too." I've put a bit of thought into that one, and it's the best explanation I've managed to find. Seriously, that girl has *power*.

"Probably," he repeats, sounding distant. "Point is, I can see she's hurting. Her whole purpose is stopping stuff like that, and the best she can do is try to send the right people to the right place. She *knows* it's better like this, that she can get more done this way, but I don't think she feels it."

I shake my head. "She won't."

"Sucks."

"Sucks," I agree. I stare at him for a moment, then frown. "So that's really it?"

"What?"

"You wish you could cheer her up when she's feeling down? You're dating a cat goddess who's older than the pyramids and *that's* the only thing that's weird? C'mon, give me *something*."

He laughs. "Okay, okay, there *might* be other things."

"Tell! Or confess." I flutter my hands at him. "Whatever."

"She's obsessed with anything from her past. Gets *super* possessive about it, too."

"Preach it," I say, thinking of her ritual knife, the dumbest airplane carry-on choice of all time.

"Oh, bonus: no sense of shame. A waiter spilled a glass of wine on her, so she stripped out of her dress in the *middle of the restaurant* and took it to the kitchen to clean it."

"Yes!" I say, giggling. "Try getting her to remember to use the changing rooms when she's clothes-shopping."

"And privacy?" he says, getting into it now. "What's that? To her, 'locked door' means 'push slightly harder.' I mean, it's not like I can mislead her or keep secrets since she eats deceit for breakfast—"

"Can't fool her with illusions, either," I interrupt. "I've tried! Nothing."

"I don't mind that part, but *man*, there are some things you don't want your lady friend walking in on. Ever."

I think about that one, then snap my fingers when I realize what he's talking about. "Oh! Yeah . . . gods don't really go to the bathroom. I kind of forget you mortals use it for more than showers and makeup."

"Her too," he says with a little groan. "Also, adrenaline junkie with *complete* disregard for personal safety. Skydiving, BASE jump-

218

ing, free climbing, cliff diving, you name it. So glad she can heal people, because she takes *me* with her, too."

"Did she at least quit it with the UFC fights?"

"Yeah, but only after the organizers started getting suspicious," he says, shaking his head. "Though I think she just replaced it with the bar crawling."

"What, she join an underground fighting ring?"

"No, she goes out to nightclubs, lounges, whatever; waits for creeps to stalk her. Bonus points if they try to slip her roofies. Wanna guess what comes next?"

"Beats the ever-living snot out of 'em?"

He touches his nose. "She says she's making sure they can't hurt other women, but I think part of her just wants to pound scumbags into the dirt."

"Can't it be both?"

He sighs, and it's a contented one. "It's all about perspective, I guess. I think you have to expect some strangeness when you're dating an undying, unchanging badass from ancient Egypt. And what was I expecting? Bickering over IKEA furniture?"

"Not much precedent for your relationship, I'll give you that."

"No, and I love it," he says, beaming. "So . . . *refreshing*. For both of us."

"You *do* make her happy," I say, a bittersweet smile on my lips.

"He does at that," Sekhmet says, walking up to join us. She's wearing a bikini, sunglasses, and enormous floppy hat.

"We were just gossiping about you," I say, waving at a nearby chair.

She tosses down a hotel towel and leans back, enjoying the sun. "Good things, I trust?" she asks, smiling.

"I told her you don't cook or clean, but you *do* mix a mean cocktail," Nathan says, watching her recline with a silly grin.

"The proper priorities, as I've explained," she says, settling into her chair. "In ancient times, only heavy drinking could stay my wrath. Surely that tradition deserves remembrance."

"Surely," I say, laughing and taking a pointed sip of my mojito.

I glance at Sekhmet, who's looking at Nathan with happy, far-away eyes, and suddenly another image flashes at me: Sekhmet in the car when we first arrived in LA, straight-backed and alert, fingers flexing, eyes darting out the window. She's changed. My smile slips as a rather obvious truth slaps me. Her upbeat attitude? All that joy and restraint? *It's him. And me.* Hell, even her speech has gotten more casual.

I guess I've been too distracted these past few months to notice. Such a poor excuse, too. I'm not sure how I missed the degree to which their relationship has warped her. Sure, Sekhmet might be imposing a bit of herself on Nathan, but because he's a conduit for my will in this world, there's a whole lot more Freya flowing in the other direction.

I wonder how far this can go. I mean, gods are a product of their believers, but it's not like either of us has many of those. In the absence of man's prayer, what keeps us so single-minded? Can we change our stripes? I was able to ignore the call of my mantle for years by burying myself in apathy, but is that the only way?

What happens when a god invites another into their heart? If this continues, where will it leave Sekhmet? Some unprecedented stuff is happening here, and I don't have any answers. I find myself hungry to uncover those truths, and there's nothing I can do except watch from the sidelines.

I sigh and take another sip of my drink. Toss it on the pile, I suppose. One more thing to keep an eye on.

We chat for a few hours by the pool, skirting all topics that might bring down the mood, and for a while, it actually works. Friends can be the best medicine, and that goes double when you're a god of love. Eventually, however, the sky begins to darken and guests start leaving the deck, each intent on adding their own spice to Hollywood's nightlife. Like all good things, even this fine moment cannot last, and we soon follow suit, making our way indoors with the setting of the sun.

Nathan and Sekhmet start making plans for the evening, and I'm quick to shoo them out on another date night, letting me follow Mahesh's advice and enjoy a club without the two of them getting frisky nearby. Distance helps, and with enough pounding music, alcohol, and dance partners, I can ignore the tickling in the back of my head from the pair. Boulevard3 is my chosen place of peace, and while it's not exactly going to inspire meditation and oneness, it does have free tacos and chocolate strawberries. Practically the same thing.

I arrive and dance my way into a blur of lights, booze, and bodies for several hours. It's a mind-smashing event of the sort Dionysus would enjoy—not one of those things you do to feel better about yourself, but to keep from feeling worse.

At some godsforsaken hour when more-responsible people are starting to awaken, I finally stumble out into the warm Los Angeles night, pawing at my phone to call a cab. I squint at the too-bright screen, swaying a little as I flee the crowds. Maybe I'll walk. Camera flashes pop nearby, but I can't tell if they're directed at me or some other train wreck of a celebrity. I'm certain I make a wonderfully disheveled sight: lipstick smeared, hair in disarray, dress wrinkled and twisted, tottering on mile-high Louboutins into the darkness.

I'm not actually sure how it's possible for me to get drunk, but

I've had a lot of practice at it over the ages. My pantheon has more than its fair share of professionals when it comes to adult beverages, and for some reason, we can all get hammered. Discussion question for the class: If it's nigh impossible to poison a god, how the *hell* does that work? Well, whatever—I'm way too out of it to care.

"Ms. Valen?" a high, smirking voice calls out of the black. "Stupid freak?" it adds in Old West Norse.

I sigh and turn around, trying to plaster on a cheerful smile. "Mr. Gallows! What a surprise!" I chirp messily.

Sebastian steps into the little pool of light in this wonderful deserted lot I've managed to find. He's wearing the same suit and joyless smile as before. "A pleasant one, I hope?" he says, sidling closer.

"Always happy to meet a member of the Fourth Estate," I say, forcing myself not to stand up straight.

"Mm. So well spoken," he says. "For a festering pisstub," he tacks on in Old East Norse.

"Why thank you," I say, doing my best to ignore the insult. This is bad. Battle may be the ultimate tool for sobering up and I can already feel the haze lifting, but I still have a long way to go before it's situation normal upstairs.

"I just had a few follow-up questions, hope you don't mind," Sebastian says.

I give him a lazy blink. "Not at all. Fire away."

"Who led the Norman conquest of England and became its first Norman king?" he asks in a smooth, friendly tone.

Oh! William the Conqueror! That's an easy— Gah! Stupid drunken goddess! I barely stop myself from blurting out the correct answer, screwing my face into confusion as quickly as I can.

"Sorry, I've got noooo idea," I say, putting some extra slur into it.

"No worries," he says, adding, "Idiot leech," under his breath in Proto-Norse.

Honestly, that one just impresses me—I haven't heard that tongue in well over a millennia. I think he might have consulted some linguistics experts for this.

He waits a moment, searching for a reaction, then moves on. "Do you believe in God?"

I'm about to ask, "Which one?" before I realize what he's doing and stop myself. Thankfully, this is another answer Mahesh gave me, so I don't need to spin something on the spot. I'm a good Christian girl, with just a touch of doubt to appease the less religious portions of this country.

"I do," I say, nodding eagerly. "I mean, I don't know for sure, but I feel like there just *has* to be someone out there, y'know?"

"Mm," he says, watching me very carefully with that one. "I'm curious; how did you ace your audition for *Switch*, anyway?"

"Showed up, said my lines, did it well," I say, trying to hide my increasing frustration. "How else would I do it?"

"Great question," he says, eyes boring into mine. "Because I have it on good authority that you should have never gotten the role; that someone *else* was a lock for it until you showed up. Heard it from that someone *herself* in another interview, actually."

I freeze. *Kirsten.*

"It's why I came to see you in the first place, actually," he continues. "When my bosses caught wind of such a . . . unique talent, well, they just had to know more."

It was her, I think, staggered by the consequences of our silly feud. Kirsten probably complained to anyone and everyone who would listen about my sudden rise to fame, and one way or another, those whispers found their way to Finemdi.

All that squabbling for exposure, and I never once thought it might actually draw a different kind of attention.

I'm an idiot.

"So, any comment?" Sebastian prompts, seeming to drink in my hesitation.

"I don't know what to tell you," I say at last, trying to quash my latest round of self-doubt. "Success can rub people the wrong way. Do well enough, and even complete strangers will try to tear you down."

"Rotting coward," he says in quiet Dalecarlian, before continuing in English with, "I know just what you mean."

"Hey, sorry, didn't quite catch that first part," I say, rubbing my head and playing up the "drunken socialite" angle. "Guess I'm a little out of it."

He keeps staring at me for another few seconds, and it looks like he's wrestling with some internal decision. Then his expression softens, and I'm shocked to see a mix of remorse and relief surface there. "No, no, it's my fault," he says in a very different tone. It's no longer smarmy and over the top, and I see his whole posture has changed, relaxing and pulling back. "Just a little game I like to play with stars—see if they can catch different languages. Please don't think anything of it."

"Oh," I say. "Did I win?"

He chuckles, and it actually sounds genuine. "Big-time. Hey, y'know, this was really unprofessional of me, cornering you here on your off hours. I'm sorry. Don't know what I was thinking. Can I get you a lift home? Call you a cab or something?"

Is he . . . ? I pause, frowning, and he laughs and jerks a thumb behind him. "Or I can just shut up and leave you alone. Seriously, you didn't have to answer all those questions. I really appreciate the help."

He is! He bought it! Holy crap, I'm in the clear. He must have decided I'm just a normal human after all, and since he's no longer trying to get a rise out of me, getting me home safe is the least he can do. Hey, go me.

"Nah, I'm good. Thanks, Sebastian. Write somethin' nice about me," I say with a wave.

"Count on it," he says with a charming wink and a wave of his own. "Good night, Ms.—"

A dull streak howls out of the night, smashing through the back of his skull and continuing on through my chest with the force of a nuclear sledgehammer. I'm picked off my feet as the thing plows through me in a welter of red, sending me sailing onto my back. The booming echo of a high-powered rifle reaches me around the same time I hit the asphalt.

My hands twitch and curl, clutching at the air as my body short-circuits. I don't need a spine to control my limbs, but this kind of trauma is more than enough to play havoc with their movement. My vision swims, fading in and out as I try to get ahold of what's left of myself. It's like lifting a boulder, but I finally manage to crane my neck up to get a good look at the wound in my chest.

Actually, calling it a "chest" at this point is being charitable—there's a comically large hole in me, and while it's mending slowly, the sheer size of the thing is going to take a while to heal. My lip curls in sadness and disgust as I notice what's left of Sebastian; he's all kinds of dead, headed for a funeral that will be firmly closed-casket.

I let my head slide back to the pavement, staring at the harsh sodium lights of the barren lot and wondering what the hell just happened. A minute later, footsteps reach my ears, sharp and confident. There's a *crunch-crunch* as they cross the gravel at the edge of the lot, lighter taps as they whisk over the pavement, and finally slow scrapes as they edge around the obstacle course of blood and unmentionable bits surrounding the two of us.

My eyes widen, shining in the dark as a figure emerges from the night to lean over me with a dangerous, disgusting leer. Dark brown eyes twitch with glee, and whatever blood I have left runs cold.

"Hello, sweetheart," Garen says.

16

CRASH

FREYA

"A promise kept," he adds.

"Reliable men are so hard to find," I say. I notice the distinct shape of a massive rifle sticking out of a rucksack on his back. "Is that a fifty cal in your pocket, or are you just happy to see me?"

He kneels, looking me over. "Considering how much those bullets cost, I'm just pleased it only took one."

"Are you calling me a cheap date?"

He laughs at that, then flicks me between the eyes. "Stalling, aren't you? How far are you from putting up a real fight? Or messing with my head?"

"Hours, probably," I lie with a smile. In truth, it'll probably be another few minutes before I can really move, and then a handful more before the wound vanishes. At least my drunkenness has fled; nothing like a ten-inch exit wound to sober you up.

"Forgive me my trust issues," he says, reaching for a sheath at his side. He undoes a buttoned loop of fabric and pulls out a stainless steel knife with an odd notch near its tip and a small metal button where the blade joins the handle. "This is a WASP knife," he says, holding it up so I can see it clearly. "Stab, press, and it shoots a burst of freezing, compressed air into the wound. Expands to the size of a basketball inside of you. Divers carry these to defend against *sharks*. You try something, I *will* use it on you."

I pause, staring at him. "Call that flirting?" I say after a moment.

"Hey!" he says, pricking me lightly in one shoulder with the knife. "Pay attention! That's a dead Finemdi agent over there. So he has a piece of the God Ahriman in his pocket. You remember what that does, don't you? In a few seconds, it is going to figure out its friend is gone and teleport the body home. Once it arrives, they're going to ID it, look up its owner's location, and come hunting for the goddess he was supposed to check on." He leans closer. "That's you."

I glare at him. "I followed, thank you."

He favors me with that awful, smug grin of his. Gods, I did *not* miss it. "Now you can either play nice with me, or I use this and *maybe* you'll have half a torso to work with when their assault teams show up." He pauses. "Thoughts?"

"What do you want?" I snap.

He takes a deep breath, looking around. "Nice night, isn't it?"

"Really? You tracked me down and turned me into a colander for a *chat*?"

"Tracked—? Oh, that's rich!" he barks, eyes alight. "I've been watching you since you landed here. The first time."

"What?"

"Don't use magic at airports," he says, keeping an eye on my re-forming wound. "Finemdi has sensors installed at most of them. I just swung by Orlando International every other day to check on the results, then wiped the logs after I found you."

"Thanks for the tip," I say, wincing as a few ribs shuffle into place. "So you've been playing private eye the whole adventure?"

He shrugs. "Easier than ever these days. Most of the time, all I had to do was monitor the bugs in your suites. Directional mics picked up the slack."

"You've been listening to us? All these months?"

He gives me a pitying look. "Who do you think leaked the Hawaiians?"

"*You—?*"

"Oh, save it," he scoffs. "Capricious nature spirits surrounded by theme parks full of *tourists*? It would've been irresponsible *not* to report them. Only reason it took so long is I had to make sure I couldn't be traced for it."

"So why not narc on me while you were at it?"

That gets me an incredulous smirk. "Because they wouldn't consider you a threat, and the same nonsense that ended with Impulse at the bottom of a lava lake might happen all over again."

"So you figured I'd cross paths with Finemdi eventually, and all it would take to ratchet up their response was your sacrificial lamb over there?" I ask. "Cold, Garen."

"Sacrifice," he repeats, and his face flickers with a touch of regret. "Sort of assumed when gods get involved, isn't it?"

"Hey, he is all on *you*, buddy."

"I suppose." He shrugs. "Better one now than hundreds more when you pull your 'wolf in sheep's clothing' cutie act," he says with no shortage of bitterness.

"Sweet excuse. Presto, you're a saint."

He glares at me.

"Well, what did you expect?" I snap. "Actually, what do you *want*, Garen?"

"Just this," he says, holding out a hand to indicate me and Sebastian. "See, *I* can't kill or capture a god on my own, but Finemdi *can*, and since I'm pretty high on their target list"—he flicks me again, and it's a lot harder this time—"that meant playing the long game."

"Got a point? I have places to be."

"And here I thought you liked to banter," he says, feigning a hurt expression. Then his features harden. "You destroyed Impulse Station, killed hundreds, and framed *me* for it. My mother died because of *you*."

"Seemed like her choice to me," I say.

He brings the tip of the knife closer. "I could have saved her. You took that from me. Forget the job, the people, even the fact that my friends are *trying to kill me*; I'm not one for regrets. But my mother? You—you arrogant, heartless—"

"I gave her a *choice*!" I spit back. "All those years, did she ever *ask* to be saved? *Did she?* When I talked to her, do you know what she made me promise her?"

"I don't care!" he yells. "You found a soul trapped in hell and gave it a way out. What did you *think* would happen? She needed time, needed *hope*, and you—"

"Two things," I say, ignoring him. "End her suffering, and spare you. I managed both. Your mother's last requests, and look where it got me."

He rolls his eyes. "Oh, yes, let's all shed a tear for the sad little star." Then he pauses for a moment, thinking. A few awkward seconds pass before he shakes his head. "But fine. In gratitude for 'sparing' me, and in the spirit of sportsmanship, a peace offering: one head start."

"Sorry?"

"They're coming, and there's enough of your blood here for them to track you for hours. I can either leave you in chunks, or let you make a run for it. Another *glorious* 'choice,' if you will."

"So generous." I sigh. "Yes, I'll take it."

"Great. Have fun with them."

"Can't wait!" I snap, then lever myself into a sitting position with a groan. He sways back but keeps a firm grip on the blade. "So what, you just going to walk away?" I ask. "Not even a little gloat before you go?"

He blinks at that. "I don't know what that would get me. This isn't me winning, Freya—this is just making sure you don't, either."

"Yeah, it's a real mystery, you not having any friends." I gesture at the knife in his hands. "You done trying to scare me?"

That gets me a long stare.

A few seconds pass, then he stands up and steps away, sheathing the weapon. I push myself to my feet, catch my balance, and look down to assess the situation. "Couldn't have picked a T-shirt night?" I mutter, dismayed at the ruin of my designer wardrobe.

What's left of my dress belongs in a war museum. Everything else, including my bag, is coated with a liberal dose of blood, and just about the only part of me that *isn't* wrecked is the ragged circle of clean skin on my chest.

I point at the mess. "If you didn't like the outfit, you could have just said so."

He snorts. "You've got about ten minutes before they're all over you," he says, stepping away. "Happy trails, Freya. It's probably too much to hope they'll decide to kill you, but I'll settle for a prison sentence."

"Thanks for the date, Garen," I say, flipping him off. "You're a great guy and all, but I think we should see other people."

"You and me both, sweetheart," he says, backing away into the night.

His footsteps crunch on the gravel again, and then he's gone, leaving me with Sebastian's corpse and a mountain of worry. Damn that man. He's making a habit of destroying my false lives, and I'm starting to suspect he might be smarter than me, too. I glance back at what's left of Sebastian. Well, maybe not *entirely* smarter.

I crouch beside the dead agent and begin searching him. Rolling back his sleeves reveals armbands similar to the ones Garen used to shoot me through a steakhouse, near the start of all this. There's a bit of deflated silk in one pocket that can only be where he was keeping his chunk of Ahriman, and some dangerous-looking trinkets in the others. A concealed carry holster provides me with a large revolver loaded with a selection of hollow-point bullets covered in runes. Cool. An ammo belt tucked underneath his vest yields more of the strange ammunition, as well. There's also a cell phone, which I leave, a wallet with nothing of interest save a few crisp twenties and a gift card to Cold Stone Creamery, which I steal, and a set of car keys. I take those as well, figuring I want to be in control if Finemdi gets to me on the road, rather than trapped in some poor guy's cab.

I find the real prize near the end. Concealed in a hidden pocket on the inside lining of his jacket is a familiar-looking syringe filled with a milky white fluid: halāhala. The good stuff, straight from whatever Shiva replacement they've managed to concoct (I've done my research; there's no way they have the genuine article, not when you're talking about a god that powerful and widely worshipped—not yet, at least). I still haven't a clue how I'm going to get close enough to Ares to use it, but at least this is one piece of the plan checked off.

I strap on the holster and ammo belt, shove the syringe and as many of his mystic doodads as I can into my bag, then put on the bracers. It's dangerous, wearing strange artifacts like these, but I can't fit anything else into my bag, and I'm not leaving the things. Once I'm ready, I straighten up, kick off my heels, and head back in the direction of Boulevard3, clicking Sebastian's key fob and following the chirps until I reach his ride.

It's an enormous black SUV, one of those things that screams "visiting dignitary," or perhaps "overcompensating." I unlock the doors, haul open the driver's side, and throw myself in. The car starts with a satisfying roar, and I gun it onto the streets, dialing Nathan's cell as I swerve around early-morning traffic.

He picks up on the fourth ring. "Whazzit?" he murmurs, clearly not quite awake.

"Hi!" I say brightly. "Just thought I'd check in on my favorite priest, see how he's doing, let him know *Finemdi is on my ass GET UP GET UP GET UP!*"

"Wh-*what?* Crap! Sekhmet? Hey!" he yells. There's a fumbling noise, then: "Okay, you're on speaker. What's happening? Are you okay?"

"Sebastian showed up after I left the club," I say, jerking the wheel around some stopped cars and running a red light. "Then Garen—freaking *Garen*—blew his brains out and pinned it on me so Finemdi hunts me down *and* treats me like an actual threat when they do."

I pause for a moment, realizing that was basically the exact same thing I did to him at Impulse. I'm briefly impressed at his planning, and then the anger and fear take over again. "I'm heading for the hotel. We need to get the hell out of town, at least until they can't track me."

"Understood—I will gather our things and prepare," Sekhmet says, all ferocity and focus.

"How *are* they tracking you?" Nathan asks.

"Garen said they'll use my blood, that it'll let them find me for hours after it's spilled," I say, glaring at the thought of some Finemdi seer crouched over the crime scene, directing his allies to me. "I didn't have a mop and bucket handy."

"Okay, should we come to you?"

"No, get packed and meet me downstairs. It's a straight shot to the hotel down Sunset Boulevard. I'm like five minutes away."

"Got it, boss," he says, then pauses. "Be okay, Sara," he adds, worried. "I don't know who to pray to when my god's the one in trouble."

I smile, glad to hear his concern. "Pray to me anyway! Buck's gotta stop somewhere. See you soon, Nate!" I say, then hang up.

I yelp and slam on the brakes, bringing the SUV to a halt. There's a red light ahead and a mix of delivery trucks and taxis are blocking me. With oncoming cars, I'm stuck until it changes. "*Seriously?*" I scream, slapping the steering wheel. The sun isn't even up yet and already there's traffic? What is *with* this city?

Sighing, I pick up my phone again and find another number in the contacts page. This time, it rings only once before someone picks up.

"Sara?" a wary voice says on the other end.

"Harv! Hey!" I say. "How's legitimate business?"

"Uh. Great. Is this an emergency, or . . . ?"

"Yes, actually," I say, revving the engine with a nervous twitch of my foot. The light refuses to change. How long has this thing been red? Come on!

"Oh. Oh! Sorry, you didn't sound . . . imperiled," he says. "How can I help?"

"Yeah, it's this thing I do where I don't act like really important things are—never mind. Bad dudes are on my tail and I need trigger-happy friends. Know anyone who feels like shooting up the Sunset Strip?"

"Only half of LA," he says with a chuckle. "Where are you and what's the situation?"

I give him a quick rundown of where I'm headed, what I'm planning, and what to expect (doom, and lots of it). Somewhere near the end of that, the light changes and I crush the gas pedal, wondering just how much sand is left in my hourglass.

Then the driver's side window shatters in a storm of glass, and I realize it's already gone.

A dark-suited man on a tricked-out motorcycle (seriously, the thing has neon wheels—this can't be standard issue) is riding along-side me, holstering a pistol and examining me intently. I'm con-fused until I realize how deeply tinted the SUV's windows are. He wasn't trying to hit me; just see who was driving.

"What was that?" Harv asks.

"Your god getting into a car chase! Hurry or you'll miss the fun," I say, and toss the phone onto the passenger seat.

I turn back to see the man on the bike consulting a smartphone embedded in the inside lining of his jacket's left sleeve. It's hard to make out while keeping one eye on the road, but I think it's display-ing a picture of me. He nods, then reaches into his jacket and begins rummaging around. I jerk the steering wheel to the left, trying to smash him while he's distracted, but he simply hits the brakes and lets me zoom in front of him, into oncoming traffic. I yell as cars barrel at me and swerve to avoid a head-on collision.

When I return to my lane, I glance in my rearview mirror and notice my pursuer is holding a new weapon now, something that looks like a tuning fork made of swirling air and mist. He points it at the SUV and the device solidifies, sharpening to a metallic black. I realize it looks exactly like the color and texture of the car I'm driving a split second before he gives me a little smirk and jerks his arm up.

The entire SUV launches off the road and straight into the air, following the arc of his hand. He spins it over and around, and the car follows suit, slamming me against its roof. There's a moment of stomach-churning weightlessness as my descent begins, and then a thunderous crunch as the vehicle completes its spin. Glass fills the air, a thousand twinkling razor stars rattling against the sound of squealing metal as the SUV smashes back onto the road, upside down. The car connects and seems to stick for a heartbeat, and then physics reasserts itself, suddenly remembering that this vehicle and everything inside of it—including me—should be going about forty miles an hour.

Kids, always wear your seat belts.

The inertia rips me out of my seat and sends me through the windshield in an eyeblink. Over the course of seventy feet and several bone-jarring bounces, I become extremely well acquainted with gravity and how poorly the body mixes with it and asphalt at high speed. I spin to a halt far beyond the tumbling ruin of Sebastian's ride, looking like I lost a fight with a coal separator.

Coughing, I lever myself up on shredded hands and scream in fury. "Am I just NOT ALLOWED to wear nice clothes?" I yell, throwing myself to my feet as pedestrians scream and scatter in all directions. "Is *that* the message?"

"Miss, we'd like you to come with us," the motorcycle rider says, edging around the obliterated SUV. He has what looks like a tranquilizer gun trained on me. "We'll even throw in a new dress," he adds with another smirk.

I wipe blood from my face with a sigh. I have a pretty good idea what's loaded in his weapon. If they manage to tag me with it, my escape is going to come to a swift and poisonous end. "Any chance I can convince you I'm just a trendsetter enjoying a night out?" I ask, readying myself.

He looks surprised, then laughs. "Sorry, lady. Nobody walks away from a crash like that." He takes one hand off his gun and taps his right shoulder.

I glance at mine. There's a big piece of the windshield sticking out of it. I make an irritated noise, pull the glass out with a grunt, and throw it at my feet. "Well, fine. But I'm still passing on the invite. Beat it."

He just smirks again, readies his gun, and nods.

I cross my arms over my chest, just like Garen did when I came at him in the restaurant, and channel a hint of my strength into the bracers I took from Sebastian, willing them to activate. They come to life with a hum, a baleful crimson glow highlighting their runes. The motorcycle agent fires his gun at me, sending a little dart jetting out with a sharp hiss of pressurized gas, right on track for my neck.

Then things get messy. What I didn't know was that motorcycle man had two friends with him, both of them sneaking up from either side with syringes of their own. The three move in perfect coordination, knowing that if I dodge or block the dart, they'll still have two trained agents tackling me from opposite directions. The antique syringes they carry are probably enchanted to cut through even the toughest skin or armor, making them an excellent backup plan.

What comes next is wholly unexpected and, if you pretend I

knew it was going to happen, makes me look unbelievably badass. As the dart sails forward and those two agents leap at me, the bracers ignite with a hellish flare of lightning. I had been hoping these things were defensive, like Garen's, but their purpose is about as far from that as you can get. Lances of caustic, shuddering energy leap from each, firing off to my left and right just as the two agents swoop in for the takedown. Both are caught mid-air by the ferocious red beams, sheared in half and tossed away like newspapers swirling through a bonfire.

I'm untouched by the storm of energy, which carves out pieces of the road and incinerates the dart the moment it gets close. The ruby blaze flickers and builds, creating a deadly bubble around me as those lances obliterate the buildings on either side of the street. Then there's a sputtering electric cough and the whirlwind flickers before dying out. The shops and storefronts around me spark and burn, fires playing through the great swooping gashes I've torn into them. I look around in awe, feeling a slight pang of embarrassment for such unintended destruction. My SUV's crash drew a few onlookers and stopped what passes for traffic at this hour, but after this little light show, everyone with half a brain and the means to leave is making a panicked dash in the direction of *anywhere else*.

Their energy spent, the bracers crumble and detach, falling from my forearms with a clatter. "Oh!" I say, stepping back from their remains. "Sebastian, I like your style."

The remaining agent looks shell-shocked, gun shaking as his eyes rove from the bodies of his friends to the postapocalyptic meltdown of the street around us. Then he pulls out another dart and starts fumbling with his weapon, feverishly trying to reload it.

I haul my new revolver out of its holster and point it at him. "Hey! Drop it!"

He freezes, new dart still in one hand, then slowly lowers it and the gun to the ground before backing away, hands up. I focus on his mind as I walk forward, searching not for love or affection, but despair. There's a good amount of it in there already, and I build upon it, ratcheting it to unbearable levels of pain and self-doubt. The change in his demeanor is instant. Tears shimmer in his eyes as his knees hit the ground, and he flops over to one side, sobbing.

I miss a step as I approach, dizziness bubbling in my head and fuzzing my vision. Inspiring love is part of who I am, which makes its destruction that much harder. I hate this, not only because it's far more draining, but also because it makes me feel that same loss, if only for a moment. I stop, breathing deeply until the disorientation passes, then move to stand beside the miserable agent.

I scoop up his gun and load it with the dart, pausing to examine it in the light before I begin searching the man. He continues crying, oblivious to the pat-down, and I grimace—I did this to him, and it's precisely the opposite of what I'm made to cherish. I try to ignore those regrets, telling myself it's a better fate than his friends got, but even after I pull away with the loot, I can't help feeling a little down.

Sighing, I strap on his holster and slot the tranquilizer gun into it. He has two extra darts, which I also take. The man didn't have a pair of bracers, but I *did* find his crazy tuning fork, a piece of Ahriman—which I leave—and the keys to his bike, which I throw down the street. I have no clue how to ride a motorcycle, and now is not the time to learn. Besides, plenty of people went running and ditched their cars when I torched the block; I'll just steal one of those rides. Before I leave, I strip the man of his jacket and toss it on, covering the laughably ineffective scraps of my dress.

I glance at the tattered remains of the other two agents and shake my head. Much as I'd like to load up on more weapons, I have a feeling the next Finemdi assault is already on its way. I spend a precious minute hunting for my bag, finally tracking it down in the wreck of the SUV. Of my phone, there is no sign. I loop the bag over my head, adding the extra darts and the tuning fork to it, then head for the nearest intact vehicle.

It's a minivan, and the keys are missing. The next car is equally unhelpful, but the third, another gigantic black SUV like Sebastian's, is actually still running. I do a double take, eyes darting between it and my ruined ride, and realize this is probably how the motorcycle agent's friends got here. How nice of them, bringing me a replacement. I hop in, clip on my seat belt (this time), and take off in the direction of the hotel. Once I've skirted the rest of the abandoned cars and begin picking up speed, I allow myself a small breath of relief. Three agents, and I survived! Granted, it was through more dumb luck than I would've liked, but I can't argue with the result.

. . . *though that could have gone horribly if I'd been with my friends*, a nasty voice reminds me. I grimace as I imagine what might've happened if I'd been trying to "shield" Nathan with those bracers. This is why you have to be *incredibly careful* with unknown artifacts. Instead of protecting everything in a bubble around me, like I'd been expecting, those things would have melted my closest allies like butter in a blast furnace.

Two police cars flash past, sirens blaring. A few seconds later, an ambulance follows. I notice thick streamers of smoke rising into the lightening sky in my rearview mirror, and start counting seconds in my head until I see fire trucks. At least the streets were fairly empty—dawn isn't exactly a happening time, even for a place as popular as Sunset Boulevard. I hope that means those buildings I roasted were unoccupied, too.

I look myself over and sigh. It's not like I got out of there unscathed, either. My magical tour of Asphalt World left long, gruesome, soot-streaked scars in all kinds of fun places, and underneath the agent's jacket, what's left of my clubwear would raise eyebrows at a bikini contest. I'm going to need a change of clothes if I want to blend in, and enough time without getting injured to look like I belong somewhere other than the emergency ward. At least I'm healing faster than ever these days. My budding career, combined with the feedback from Nathan and Sekhmet's bond, is doing wonders for my powers of self-repair.

A screech of tires snaps my attention back to the road. Another big SUV, almost identical to Sebastian's and mine, tears onto the street behind me, trailing smoke from its wheels as it struggles to make the turn off Fairfax Avenue at high speed. I catch a glimpse of five grim men and women readying weapons and feel my hands freeze on the steering wheel. There's no sign of mirth there, no sense of excitement like I got from the motorcycle rider—these agents are ready for war, and judging by the arsenal they're training on my car, I doubt they're going to start with anything as neighborly as tranquilizer darts.

Then I feel the Valkyrie rising in my chest, banishing those thoughts of fear. *Did someone say "war"?* Oh, if it's a fight they want, I'll give them a showdown that'll bring this city to a standstill. Screw the plan, screw the danger, and screw these carbon-copy creeps for thinking they could intimidate a girl like me. I stamp the gas, wondering if my struggling car is ready for the fight of its life.

Because I am.

THUNDERSTRUCK

FREYA

I didn't even need to psych myself up.

As one of the Finemdi agents stands through the SUV's sunroof, aiming gods-know-what at my car, salvation sideswipes them. Harv's sedan zooms up on their left, pulls away for a moment, then barrels in to crunch against their side. The impact jars the weapon out of the agent's hands, sending it clattering to the road below, and the man falls back into the SUV's interior, shaken. There's a roar of automatic gunfire as two of Harv's friends unload on the big car from the passenger side and backseat. The barrage punctures the tires, rips through the doors and windows, and sends the SUV careening off the road and into a liquor store.

For a moment I'm stunned, doing little more than following the curve of the road and watching the wreck vanish behind me. Then I stick my hand out the window and wave happily at Harv, who just nods at me from behind the steering wheel like this is another day at the office. He escorts me the last few blocks to our hotel, pulling into its roundabout a moment after I do. Nathan and Sekhmet are waiting beside the main entrance, framed by two planters and several suitcases. They're both wearing casual clothes and worried expressions.

I lean out the window as I pull up and shout, "Get in!"

The two grab their things. They're just starting to move toward me when there's an odd *crack* in the air and my car dies. I lean back in and fumble with the keys, trying to restart it, but it's no good—the engine doesn't even give a hint of turning over. Confused, I get out and turn to Harv just in time to see him slamming his own door with a displeased look on his face. He raps the roof of his car and his two friends get out, carrying automatic rifles low and close to their bodies, fingers off the triggers. They're both meaty guys in nice suits. One's tall and top-heavy; the other's average but built like a pug—muscled, barrel-like, and furry.

"I think you'd better get ready to make a stand," Harv says, walking up to me. He gestures at one of his pals, and the man hands him another rifle. "Ms. Valen, this is Gene and Vitty. Guys, this is our new best friend."

They both nod at me, then go back to watching the street.

"Nathan and Rashida," I say, pointing at my friends as they join us.

"Hey," Harv says. "You have any idea what's coming? All the lights are off in the buildings, too."

I glance around and realize he's right—every lamp, window, and car in sight is dark. Nothing's moving on the street. This can't be good.

"Bad news," I say.

"Sara, you look . . . okay, no offense, but you look like a truck hit you," Nathan says, voice thick with concern and a hint of nausea.

"Not far off," I say. "It's been a rough night. Really glad to see you both."

"You had us worried, little fighter," Sekhmet says, putting a hand on my shoulder, then pulling me in for a hug. She doesn't seem to mind the dirt and blood this gesture leaves on her clothes. Even with everything going on, part of me is just present enough to note this as another change—she was never the hugging type.

"Those storm clouds?" Harv asks.

I look up. He's right—the predawn sky has just gotten a lot darker in the half minute since our cars died. "That narrows it down," I say. "Boys, unless you want to tangle with another god, I'd think about getting back to your beds. I called for help with mortals, not my kin."

Harv glances at his friends, then shrugs. "Eh. We were already on duty. Ms. Riley's place isn't far."

"You pulled daughter dearest's security for me? I'm flattered."

He smirks at that. "You should be."

There's a distant thrum of thunder, and we all look up again. "Seriously," I say. "That little voice in the back of your head telling you this isn't your fight? You should listen to it."

Harv snorts and gives me another shrug. Thunder booms again, a lot closer this time, and I turn to Nathan and Sekhmet. "I don't suppose I have a hope of getting you two to save your skins?"

Nathan shakes his head, and I feel a little stirring in the back of my mind as he draws some priestly juice, readying himself for a fight. Sekhmet just rolls her eyes and sets her suitcase against the car.

Lightning cracks in the sky directly above us, and the thunder that follows is like a deep, booming laugh. The pressure starts dropping as a wind kicks up, sweeping a charge of ozone through the air. The sky is almost black now, filled with roiling, angry thunderheads. More lightning flashes, ripping in and out of those storm clouds, and pieces of paper dance across the street on sharp gusts. There aren't many people out at this hour to begin with, and the few who are begin picking up the pace and moving indoors, seeking shelter from the unnatural weather.

Honestly, I wish I could join them.

The storm builds, and a misting rain begins to fall, obscuring the block and dampening the sounds of a waking city with the ceaseless *hiss* of water. Then a bright, blinding slap of light cuts through the haze. A heartbeat later, a fork of electricity touches down in the middle of the street, shaking the ground and washing out the world in a flare of white.

I blink rapidly, trying to clear the afterimage of the bolt, and when my vision returns, there's a man standing in front of us, sandal-wrapped feet astride a new rift in the asphalt. A spotless white toga snaps in the wind, cinched at the waist with a golden belt. Long slate-gray hair streams from his head, and a luxurious white beard rolls down his barrel chest. Electric eyes set in a face of staggering strength regard us with merriment and disdain.

Have you ever watched a gnat settle on a window beside you and decided to destroy it? How much effort and planning did you put into that moment, that impulse to end a life? You could crush it from the world with the barest twitch of your hand.

That's how he looks at us: with eyes of thoughtless death.

Marble lips crack into a grin, sending laugh lines sweeping across that immortal face. "Ah, a beauty," he says in a voice of thunder and mirth. "I assume I require no introduction?"

"I'm sorry," I say, knowing full well who this is. "You meet so many gods in this business, it's hard to keep track."

He chuckles, and the sky seems to pulse in time to his glee. "Is that so? I must strive to be more memorable, then."

Lightning builds behind his eyes. Without warning, he raises an arm, gives a casual flick of the wrist, and sends a wall of electricity lancing through the air to fry me and my friends. I barely have time to grit my teeth before the attack tears into me. I feel muscles clench and rip as the voltage picks me up and launches me off my feet, smashing me against the side of the hotel in a spastic heap of twitching limbs. I'm momentarily thankful the assault didn't knock me unconscious, but that gratitude flips to sorrow as I watch Harv and his two pals go down. Arcs of energy bubble through their bodies, crackling and ricocheting between them and the car they were using for cover—they're dead before they hit the ground.

Sekhmet is the only one who's prepared. In one absurdly fast motion, she seizes Nathan with both hands, clutches him to her chest, and spins to put her body between him and the lightning. It shouldn't work—flesh is an excellent conductor of electricity—but Sekhmet is a goddess of protection and healing, a creature of boundless magic and rage, and if she says Nathan isn't going to get hurt, then the laws of physics can pound sand. The energy splashes against her back like a breaking wave, standing her hair on end and doing little else.

I draw a shuddering breath, berating myself for giving in to my rebellious side and getting Harv killed. So damn senseless. "Zeus," I choke out. "Yes. I—I know you."

"Ha. Jogged your memory, did I?" he says in a happy rumble. "Funny, that. Now be a good girl and come along. I so dislike these errands."

"Busywork for the Father of the Gods?" I say, managing to reach a sitting position. I notice Sekhmet has uncurled herself from Nathan, but she's keeping him close. Good. "How unbecoming."

"My, but you are a glutton for punishment," he says, then tilts his head. "Or a fool. I find myself uninterested in learning which. Hermes. Bring our friends to collect this nuisance."

For a moment, there's just the sound of rain and distant thunder. Then a blur, and a Finemdi agent appears a few feet away from Zeus, looking windblown and disoriented. As he rights himself, the blur returns, depositing another agent. This happens twice more, and after the fourth agent pops onto the street, Zeus nods and holds out a hand, summoning an orb of crackling electricity above its palm.

"Now submit to these fine men and women, or suffer," he says, sounding bored.

"I am no match for you," I say, swaying to my feet.

"Wisdom at last," he says. "Though you have little—"

"Much as I respect her," I say, interrupting, "I doubt Sekhmet could defy you for long, as well."

He nods. "You are little more than distractions. Yet I sense some doomed attempt at trickery approaches. Tell me, sweetling—what miracle do you hope to produce?"

I smile and sketch an unstable bow. "A young girl such as myself should not have to face the Father of the Gods. That, I think, is best left to Mother."

He arches an eyebrow and opens his mouth to reply, but I cut him off with a shout. "Izanami!" I scream, channeling the name into a prayer. "Queen of the Yomi, She-Who-Invites, goddess of creation and destruction, I call upon you! By my hand you were made free, and now I request the same of you! Izanami! I desire life and death in equal measure! Izana—"

247

Zeus's face darkens as I speak, and the agents begin readying their weapons, stepping forward. The lightning in his hand builds and my hair begins to stand on end, but before he has a chance to fire, before I even finish my prayer, the odds change in spectacular fashion.

It's nothing at first—a trick of the light, a flicker out of the corner of the eye. Then a patch of the street *lifts*, pulling up into a wave of shadows, a curving tentacle of utter midnight. The arc snaps through the air, silent as the grave, and connects with the Master of Olympus in a killing blow so careless, it could have come from him. The shadow whips across Zeus's chest with blinding speed, carving it in half and sending him toppling to the street in two directions.

There's an awkward silence as the Finemdi agents stare at the bisected god thrashing on the asphalt beside them. Then the shadows expand, seeking new victims. Shuddering filaments grow from the road, trailing hands and talons of pitiless void. They twist and elongate, stretching into inhuman arms and sprouting grotesque joints as they lunge through the air to snare agents. The men and women barely have a chance to scream before they're gone, dragged beneath the street as if into silky black quicksand.

Zeus levers himself up on one arm, lower half already re-forming like a candle melting in reverse. A half-dozen spheres of lightning snap to life around him, bathing the area in a flickering blue glare and banishing the nearest shadows. At the same time, the blur returns, bringing more agents to the fight. Even as the first wave succumbs to hungry shades, their friends start arriving in seemingly unending numbers.

A pale white face looms into sight just inches from my own, startling me. "A favor owed," Izanami whispers, unblinking black eyes boring into mine as her shadows do battle behind her. She looks unchanged from when I mistakenly set her free back at Impulse Station, a rotting porcelain doll with a superiority complex nearly as big as Zeus's. Her neck twists, turning her head unnaturally to watch the carnage. "The bearded one offends me," she says in an absent tone. "He resists. Such hubris is discourteous."

There's a twitch, and she's staring at me again with no sign of having moved to turn her head. "I will deal with him. Your servants will deal with his. And you will consider my debt repaid."

I nod. "By your will," I manage to say.

The edges of her lips curve just slightly, producing the vaguest of smiles, and then she whips away, flowing toward the bodies of Harv and his friends on dozens of shadowy hands like a spider with the abdomen of a dead girl. Carefully, she reaches out and touches them, allowing hundreds of tiny threads to seep from her fingers into their corpses. As the tendrils dig into Harv's body, there's a momentary pause and something like a voice echoes in the back of my head, asking for permission to take him. I jerk in surprise as I realize what she intends, and that for Harv, I need to *allow* her to do it—he died believing in me, and that gives me authority over his remains.

I grant the request, releasing my claim like a sigh into those waiting shadows. Izanami clutches her hands over the corpses, and suddenly all three men are yanked to their feet, the breath of life crammed back into dead flesh through shadow and magic. I gasp and grin, thrilled by this unnatural rebirth. She's opened the gates to the afterlife, called them forth to live and fight anew in a highly practical demonstration of the perks of being a death goddess. Wounds closing, eyes trailing streamers of darkness, the men collect their weapons. Moving with inhuman speed, they pop over the car and begin picking off the Finemdi agents with quick, tightly controlled bursts. Harv bares shadow-wrapped teeth as he mows down my foes, happily trading lives for the new one he's been granted.

Sekhmet, meanwhile, is in full blender mode, tearing through the nearest pack of opponents with bloodthirsty delight. She cackles with horrible glee as she fights, exulting in the brawl like a kid at a birthday party surrounded by hostile piñatas. Nathan is putting his talents of aegis to the test, deflecting gunfire with a rippling half-dome shield of pure spellcraft. Whenever he spots an opening, he channels a spike of fire magic into the air around unsuspecting agents, engulfing them in hungry, instantaneous bonfires that Zeus's rainstorm does little to douse.

As for our savior, the moment she finishes her resurrections, Izanami lets herself sink into the ground, disappearing into a pool of gloom. A split second later, she explodes out of the street behind Zeus, who's currently distracted by the sport of destroying her shadow creatures with bolts of lightning. She strikes with a hand cloaked in blades of endless night, shoving her arm through his back all the way up to her elbow. He gasps in shock as those void-wrapped fingers pop out of his chest, then tumbles to the ground as she wrenches her arm up and takes his head with it.

Then the blur slams into her, hitting so hard I can actually see the concussive shock wave. The hotel windows rattle and raindrops dance as she's picked bodily from the ground and launched a good eighty feet down the street.

Damn, Hermes, I think, watching as the blur zips after her and catches up before she can even hit the pavement. It leaps, snatches her from the air and pile-drives her into the blacktop with a hundred deadly blows, the entire barrage a ghostly afterimage caught in an eyeblink.

The shadows race to her aid, leaving a field of torn bodies and maybe five remaining agents. As I watch, another goes down, unable to avoid the supernatural precision of Harv, Gene, and Vitty, our new undying shadow men. Then Sekhmet grabs my arm, wrenching my attention from the bizarre tableau. "Do we stand?" she hisses.

The question jolts my brain back into gear. This is massively interesting, but we can't stay—Izanami has bought me the time I needed, and I'd be a fool to waste it. Zeus is already regenerating, we need to escape, and my options have narrowed to a single choice.

"Not this time," I say. "Gather our things. Back inside. We're getting out of here."

She nods and dashes over to snag her suitcase—I notice it's the hard-sided one with our stolen artifacts—before grabbing Nathan by the hand and bringing him safely back to me. I pause for a last look at the insane brawl, then shake my head and run for the doors to the hotel. As I go, I catch Harv's eye. He gives me a wolfish smile and a thumbs-up, then returns to his gunfight. Despite it all, I laugh at the fun he's clearly having with his new empowered lease on life.

Two staffers are just inside the main door, watching the action with eyes the size of dinner plates. They barely take notice of us as we sprint past them and into the lobby. Quickly, I lead us through the hotel, listening to the cracks of gunfire and ominous rumbles of lightning fade as we run deeper into the building. Confused guests and worried managers are littered throughout the halls, all seemingly unsure if they're caught in the middle of a war or some madcap viral marketing campaign. I ignore them, racing for the one place I know I'll be safe.

The doors to the CURE Salon & Spa smack open under Sekhmet's bloody hands, and we stride through the entrance to the sound of tinkling glass. The place is deserted and won't be staffed

251

for hours, but I don't need help—I know the way. I retrace the route to the thick wooden doors that guard the portal to the Graces' domain, then reach out with my will. They're designed to open for the appropriate staff members of the spa, but the magic behind them isn't hard to hack. There are a handful of weaves here: one to ward the doors, another to open them in the presence of the proper individuals, and a third to verify those people are legit. I just tickle the second spell, telling it the third has already done its job, and the doors swing open with a hum of magic.

I walk through the portal, wondering if I should tell the Graces to hire a network security consultant. Even though these are spells, not software, the principles are fairly similar.

Bright afternoon light streams through the domed roof, but other than that, the palatial spa is unchanged from our previous visits. The Graces lounge on their raised dais, overseeing a field of relaxation and debauchery while scantily clad servants whisk over the marble paths, eagerly carrying out their masters' mandate of generosity.

The three goddesses look at us with great interest as we approach, Sekhmet's suitcase heralding our arrival as it clicks across the mosaics. "You are troubled," Aglaea, the youngest, says with a frown as we come to a stop before them. A rare note of tension throbs in the air between us.

"Or just trouble," Thalia, the eldest sister, says unhappily.

"What is this?" Euphrosyne asks, halting her dance. "You bring discord to our home, and not of the sort we claim to soothe."

"I'm being hunted," I say, opening my jacket to reveal a surgeon's nightmare of still-healing wounds. "I have time, but not much. I humbly ask for clothes and cleansing before I take my leave."

The three sisters exchange a worried look. "We do not take sides," Thalia says. "You know this."

"Refusing to aid me *is* taking a side," I say.

"Inaction is not the same as opposition," she says, and the tension ramps. "Please, do not seek to turn us against our purpose."

"Your purpose is hospitality," Sekhmet says, stabbing a finger at them. "Such an aim implies the protection of your guests."

A long pause follows, and the sisters exchange another look, somehow communicating in silence. "Friends you shall always be, but guest rights are reserved for those who enter our domain legitimately," Thalia says at last. "You did not."

"A technicality," I say.

"And yet," she says, inclining her head.

"Oh, this is stupid," Nathan says. "Look, you opened your doors to us. You said we were always welcome. Well, CURE was closed and there wasn't any 'legitimate' way to enter here. Now, were you *lying* about that twenty-four-seven invite, or does your *super-important* hospitality end with the operating hours of a Los Angeles spa?"

Aglaea snorts at that and shakes her head. "He's got ya there, sis," she says to Thalia.

"But . . . we can't—I mean—" Thalia sputters. Euphrosyne sighs, then resumes her dance, already seeming resigned to the inevitable.

Thalia's lip twists, and she looks at her feet. "Hurry, please," she says in a small voice. "We *cannot* endanger our guests."

"I'll be fast," I say. "I promise. And thank you—I understand what I'm asking."

She nods and twitches her hand. Alexandra appears a moment later, bearing some clean towels. "If you'll accompany me?" she asks.

All three of us are bathed, scrubbed, and swathed in fuzzy cotton. The whole process is a frenzy of soap, water, and oils, taking only a handful of minutes. We each have something like a half-dozen servants assigned, and they move us through the process like a Formula One pit stop crew. My pathetic rags are removed and replaced with a flowing dress of white silk hemmed in crawling cobalt designs that remind me of the mosaics in the main chamber. Sekhmet's bloodied clothes are also taken away and exchanged with a similar outfit. Nathan, who made it through the chaos without a scratch, returns from his spa trip in the same jeans and button-up he put on after my wake-up call, a world away.

I emerge feeling halfway decent, certain I've left behind about forty pounds of dirt, dried blood, and shrapnel after the servants are finished. Just about all of my injuries have healed, and the remaining ones are hidden by my clothes. Sekhmet collects her suitcase as we leave the baths, looking for all the world like a supermodel valet. "Now what?" she asks as we begin our walk back to the main room. "I assume we choose another portal? How long until they lose your scent?"

I shake my head. "It could be hours. We take any of those gates, they'll be on us."

"Then we must ensure that occurs at a battleground of our choosing."

"No. We'll still lose. I don't know what they'll send after Zeus and Hermes, but you can bet we won't be able to beat them—and there's no glorious death waiting, either. We'll be captured and locked up. How many years did you spend behind glass at Impulse?"

The fire gutters in her eyes. "Too long," she says in a weak voice.

"So that's it, then?" Nathan says, looking between us. "Game over, we lose?"

I give him a wan smile. "No. There *is* an out, but it's crazy-dangerous and it'll mean pissing off the Graces. We'll probably never be able to come back here."

"Does it require us to violate guest rights?" Sekhmet asks, deadly serious.

"I don't think so. We won't be harming them or their charges, we'll be leaving this place as requested, and we won't be breaking any rules. Well, explicitly."

"A technicality, then?" she asks with a snort.

I grin. "Something like that."

"I'm in," Nathan says. "How?"

"There *are* places in the world with enough spells, wards, and defenses to block the tracking magic they're using," I say. "Places we can hide."

"Where?" Sekhmet asks. "And how can we reach them from here?"

"Well . . . that's the problem," I say, shifting nervously and picking at my dress. "We've been somewhere like that before. All of us."

Nathan frowns. "I don't—*Oh*," he squeaks, the light dawning.

Sekhmet's eyes widen and she stares at me, shock and pride on her face. "Bold," she says.

"Desperate," I correct. "Come on, follow me."

Alexandra is waiting for us at the entrance to the baths. Smiling, she holds out an arm to direct us to the main hall. We follow at first, but when she turns to lead us back to the central dais, I veer to the left, picking up the pace. By the time she realizes we've gone off script, I'm already standing in front of the curtain-shrouded gateway, whipping the drapes to the side.

The door is just as I remember it: wounded, chained, and throbbing with angry magic. Magic I remember. These weaves tickled my memory for good reason, and now we're going to follow them back to their source. "Miss!" Alexandra calls, hurrying to catch up. "Why are you—?"

I press my hands against the scarred wood, immersing myself in that haze of warring spells. Breaking permanent wards like these is child's play for a spell-caster like myself; part of the reason Impulse Station ended up taking a lava bath is because I shattered all of their mystic defenses in one go. The challenge here is that I have to be *selective* in what I destroy. I don't know precisely where the attack on the Graces began, and even if I wanted to travel there, the actual destination is probably covered in traps and cameras and other unpleasant crap.

Instead, I need to break the Graces' spells to reestablish the connection, but also tweak the link to send us somewhere *similar* to the original target. As for the chains and physical barricades . . . well, Sekhmet can handle those.

"Miss?" Alexandra repeats, sounding panicked. "Please, step away from the door! *Miss Freya!*"

There's a *twang* behind my eyes as I snap the first ward. The wood shimmers, the door seeming to bulge in its frame as though it's just taken a deep breath.

"No! Stop!" Alexandra yells, then turns and begins running. "Help! Send help!"

"Better hurry," Nathan says, watching her go.

"Impatient boy. Let a lady work," I mutter, closing my eyes to concentrate. Another spell crumbles, and the door shudders in response.

More shouts reach my ears, followed by the sound of stamping feet and lots of movement. "Sekhmet, the chains," I say, breaking the Graces' penultimate ward.

"Happily." Peach-gold claws slide from her fingertips, and she smiles at me before launching herself at the door with a battle cry. Silver links rattle to the floor as she tears into the barriers.

The commotion behind us gets closer, all angry yells and commands to stop what we're doing. There's a stirring in the back of my head as Nathan pulls on my gifts, then shouts of surprise and the sounds of tumbling bodies. I spare a glance over my shoulder to see a pack of heavyset security guards not ten feet away. Some are picking themselves off the ground, while others are pounding their fists against the air between us, making weird hollow sounds as they rebound off an invisible shield.

Nathan gives me a wink. "Just inspiring patience," he says.

I smile, then return my attention to the mess of spells before me, trying to mangle them into something helpful. As I work, I realize why the Graces could never safely destroy this gate: The source of the invading magic is in some distant land, impossible to sever from afar. The best they could do is draw their own spells against it and seal things off. Luckily, I have no intention of breaking those energies—just altering them.

Imagine the spells here are threads of silk, looming over this refuge from some vile place far above. Every person, possession, and gust of air that moves between these portals is like a drop of water sliding along one of those strands, and thanks to magic, they can travel up as well as down. Instead of passengers, however, I'm sending a little spell of my own up the line. The Graces are powerful, true, but what they wield in mystic might, I more than make up with talent.

My spell reaches the top of the line, latching on to its source and ripping it out by the roots. I send new orders into the void, and in response, my magic begins to graft additions to the hostile spell like a spider remaking a web. The thread twitches in my mind's eye, hungering for a new home, and for the briefest of moments, a global sense of awareness builds in my mind, dozens of compatible targets across the world offering themselves to me. This magic is made to anchor itself to certain places, certain strongholds, and it badly wants to be reunited with one.

I frown, trying to decide where to go, then settle on the one place I *know* might hold a friend. There's a moment of reaching, an expectant pause as the magic streaks out to its new target, and then the link catches, holds, solidifies. This thread has all the appropriate credentials and weaves needed to pierce the intimidating wall of defenses around my choice, and as it burrows in and sets up shop, I try to direct it to a random place deep within those walls.

"Uh, Sara?" Nathan says, sounding worried.

I turn back to see the three Graces approaching his barrier, looking furious.

"Sekhmet?" I ask.

"The way is clear," she says, opening her hand and letting pieces of wood and metal drop to the floor.

I shatter the final ward. Immediately, the doors fly open, knocking aside the small pile of debris Sekhmet created. A rippling portal beckons, showing me a hazy, unfocused view of what looks like a cramped room full of machinery and pipes.

"*What have you done?*" Thalia rages, smashing a fist against Nathan's wall. The barrier *melts* from the force of her blow, fibers of magic tearing, fraying, drifting to the floor like cotton candy in a downpour. Nathan gasps, stumbling backward from the strength of the hit.

"I'm sorry!" I shout, pulling him toward the gate. "Truly!"

"You've put us all in danger!" Aglaea yells, youthful features twisted in anger. "We trusted you!"

"No! No, it's going to be fine!" I say, backing up. "We're using this to leave and then I'm breaking it from that end. You won't have to worry about this portal ever again!"

That gets me some skeptical looks.

"I hope you can forgive me," I say as the three of us reach the threshold. I crack a smile. "And honestly, do you think I'd knowingly endanger the greatest mani-pedis on earth?"

I take a step back through the swirling gateway before they can reply. My friends move with me, Sekhmet pulling the suitcase behind her. My new sandals scrape on grime-coated concrete as I back into the room, and as soon I'm certain we're all through, I sever the threads of spellcraft that brought us here with a thought. The portal vanishes instantly, leaving us in vague darkness. The air is warm and carries a hint of sewage. I blink in the dimly lit gloom, trying to make out my surroundings as fear begins to rise in my chest.

Oh, Sara, you brilliant idiot. You actually got us here.

I knew the risk in going to any of these strongholds was extreme, but I've chosen perhaps the most dire destination possible, all on the chance we'll find a trusted friend within.

We've arrived in the bowels of Meridian One, Finemdi's world headquarters in New York, and I've just destroyed our only way out.

18

HOME, SWEET HOME

NATHAN

The weight of calamity presses on Nathan like a physical force. His awareness of all things mystical might be a hazy, far-flung thing, but even he can tell the place they've entered is practically *rippling* with spells, an overbearing riot of lethal defenses, curiosities, and utilitarian magicks lapping at the shores of reality like a rising tide. There's more than enough here to protect and empower a hundred Impulse Stations, backups and countermeasures stacked so thickly it's hard to tell where one layer of fortification ends and another begins.

It's clear Finemdi learned a great deal from its past mistakes. Nathan's goddess wasn't taking this place down the same way she had the last. In fact, with this much crap in the way, he isn't sure how you'd even go about *denting* it.

"Sara?" he says, calling into the shadows. A few dully glowing switches and readouts are the only source of light.

"Hey, Nate," her voice says from somewhere to his left. "How's it going?"

"I missed breakfast."

She laughs at that. "And here I thought I was having a bad day."

There's a whisper of movement and then a *click* from the far side of the room. Fluorescents snap to life above them, illuminating some sort of maintenance stronghold. Metal pipes snake through the walls, ceiling, and floor from all angles, terminating in various control and monitoring stations. A handful of circular grates dot the poured concrete floor. Sekhmet is by the only door, her hand on the light switch.

"Somewhat less imposing than I imagined," she says.

"I tried to aim the spell deep and out of the way," Freya says, looking around. "I'm guessing we're on a random sublevel."

"In a Finemdi outpost, right?" Nathan says, hopeful. The dire touch to the magic in the air seems to promise otherwise.

"Worse—their headquarters," she says, confirming his fears.

"What—? *Why?*" he asks with a horrified gasp. "Were we not in enough trouble?"

"Samantha's here," she replies. "Way things are going, I thought we might need a friend."

"That's *it?*" Nathan says, appalled. "This place feels like they dug it out of Mount Killdoom and you think *she's* going to turn it around? Don't get me wrong, Sam's great and all, but if this place is a hurricane, she's an umbrella."

"I didn't have a ton of time *or* options," Freya says, sounding a little huffy. "It's not like everything else was a bed of roses. At least this hole had *something* in its favor."

Nathan looks at her, getting the impression that whatever magic she pulled to get them here was complicated, and she feels a little unappreciated.

"That *was* some pretty fancy spellwork," he says, trying to placate his goddess. "Barely got a hint of what you were doing, and I . . . guess I should be grateful we got out of there at all—I certainly wouldn't have been able to do it."

She holds her frown a little longer, then relents. "Thanks," she says with a half smile, reaching out to touch his shoulder. "You weren't so bad, yourself. And sorry. I should've talked it over with you both."

"Things were kinda rushed back there," Nathan admits. "And Samantha *is* the sort of girl I'd want on our side. Probably would've ended up here anyway."

"Allies *are* welcome," Sekhmet says, walking back to them. "But is that the only reason?"

"What do you mean?" Nathan asks.

"Ares is here, as well," she says, then turns Freya. "Do you intend to take your revenge?"

Freya blinks, and Nathan feels a stab of anxiety. Did some part of her actually pick this place for *that*? They weren't even *close* to ready.

She shakes her head. "I'm not strong enough yet," Freya says, though Nathan wonders if he can catch a hint of uncertainty in her voice. "If he recognizes me, it'll go badly for all of us. We need to focus on finding a way out."

"What are our options?" Nathan asks, hoping there's a plan. Back at Impulse, her goal had been destroying the place, not escaping it . . . which became something of an issue once the lava started rising.

"Asking nicely?" Freya says with a helpless shrug.

Sekhmet winces, and Nathan palms his face. "So we're trapped at Evil Inc.," he says in a weary voice. "You can't, like, teleport us out?"

She grimaces. "The gateway's completely gone. I could probably whip up a spell to pull us somewhere with a day or two of preparation, but there's no way it would ever get through their wards."

"Can we break those?" Sekhmet asks.

"Not this time," Freya says. "There are multiple sources and dozens of redundancies. The second I snap one, they'll be on alert."

"What about just punching a hole in the side of the building?" Nathan offers, hoping the Norse cure-all of "hit things, and *hard*" might work here.

Freya considers that for a moment, then sighs. "Maybe, but that's dangerous—this place is hardened against assault, and even if we could weaken the wards enough in one spot to make an exit, that brings us right back to the whole 'alarms go off, goons come running' scenario."

Nathan throws up his hands. "So . . . front door?"

She makes an *errrt!* noise, like he's guessed wrong on a game show. "You remember how crazy Impulse's security was? Even on the way out? We'll be flagged and tackled the second we get within thirty feet of that gauntlet."

"Geez, yeah," he says, running a hand through his hair. Then an idea hits him, and he snaps his fingers. "Hang on, there's gotta be another way. Think about those agents they kept piling on back in LA—wherever they started, I'll bet they didn't get out and walk. They need some sort of teleporter or slingshot or *something* to get people in place that fast."

"That . . . isn't bad, Nathan," Freya says, and he feels his spirits start to lift at the glint of hope in his god's eyes. "You're right—they must have some kind of emergency exit for critical ops or disasters."

"So we find this . . . 'slingshot' and use it to escape?" Sekhmet says. "That has merit. Though you will still be hunted."

Freya groans. "Yeah, they won't be able to pinpoint me after my blood craps out or whatever, but I'm still on their list." She thinks it over for a moment, then nods. "Okay, two goals: Find their records and mess with them, *then* take the back door out."

"Oh, good, our plan was sounding too easy at first," Nathan says.

"Just keeping you on your toes."

He sighs. "I'm not disagreeing: Even if we escape, we're not getting far if they've got your number. The second your face pops up on a camera or the news or something . . . bam, it's raining agents."

Sekhmet nods, giving them both an undaunted look. "Great deeds are never easy," she says, cool and eager, like she does this sort of thing all the time. Nathan finds himself grinning at his girlfriend, wishing he had anything close to that level of self-assurance. She gives him a sly look in return.

Freya turns to him, interrupting the moment. "We're going to need Samantha for this. Can you work on finding her?"

"Sure, I'll—Wait," he says, stopping himself as he realizes what she's just implied. "Are you saying we should *split up*?"

"Yeah. I need to track down servers and slingshots, and you and Sekhmet are going to find our friend. Why?"

"That's pretty much how all horror movies start, is all."

"Well, pretend we're in an action comedy."

"Oh!" he says, tapping the side of his head. "How obvious. It's all better now, thanks!"

"Great!" she says, giving him an exaggerated smile. "Speaking of film, let's make sure some random security camera doesn't ruin my new career." She closes her eyes and concentrates, letting the illusion of Sara Valen drip away to reveal her glossy golden hair.

"There," she says, fluffing those tresses. "They shouldn't have a reason to suspect me, even on tape, but if they *do*, I'd much rather they pin something on Freya. *She* can hide. Stars can't."

"Think we'll need a similar treatment?" Nathan asks, wondering if she has enough mystic juice on hand to craft illusions for them both.

Freya considers it, then shakes her head. "I'd rather not risk them picking up on magic like that, especially if I'm not around to mask it. Besides, I'm the only one who should be doing something obviously wrong here. You're just going to be hanging out with Sam, remember?"

She slips her bag off her shoulder and starts rummaging through it. "Sekhmet can stash the luggage here, but I have a few . . . party favors to hand out. Who wants a weird revolver with rune bullets?"

Nathan raises a hand. "Ooh!" He's been joining Sekhmet on her trips to the shooting range for a few months now—this seems as good a time as any to put that into practice.

Freya gives him the holster and ammo belt. "Next up, god-poisoning syringe," she says.

Sekhmet nods and walks over. Freya places the hypodermic in her hand, taking care to keep the needle's tip away from her skin. "And that leaves me with the tranquilizer gun and a freaky tuning fork. Great. Everyone ready?"

"Will these artifacts be safe?" Sekhmet asks, pointing at the suitcase.

"Doesn't seem like anyone comes here very often," Nathan says, wiping a thick layer of grime from an old console.

"I don't blame them," Freya says, sniffing. "This place reeks."

"Very well, then," Sekhmet says, wheeling the case behind a pipe-covered conduit.

"Okay," Freya says, adjusting her dress to hide the tranquilizer gun beneath its folds. "Hopefully this place will be like Impulse: death coming and going, but relatively safe once you're inside. We won't have keycards, so if you're stopped by a locked door, try to get someone else to open it for you."

"No problem," Nathan says, smiling. "I'll just show a little leg."

"Depending on the god, that might work," she replies with a wink. "If what Samantha said is true, this place is going to be gigantic—take your time, try to find a map, and act like you belong. Let's agree to meet back here in . . . shoot, anyone have a watch?"

Nathan and Sekhmet pull out their phones. "Seriously? Nothing else?" Freya says with a sigh. "Dammit, I lost my Mim. Okay, what time is it now?"

Nathan glances at his gadget. "It's . . . aw, man. Dead," he says, fiddling with the blank display. "Zeus can suck it." He looks at Sekhmet, who shakes her head. "Well, you woke us around five on the West Coast, so if we're in New York now, I'm guessing it's sometime after eight in the morning."

"All right, let's all try to find a clock or whatever while we're out, then meet back here after lunch. One to two in the afternoon sound good? If someone misses that window, whoever's here should wait another hour, then start looking."

"Lunch? You're actually going to stop for a meal?" Nathan asks.

"Are you kidding?" she replies, and to Nathan, she looks like she might have already started to drool. "I'm going for breakfast, too. It'll be a great way to mingle and pick up details about the place. Might even be able to find some allies here!"

Nathan smirks at that. "And the fact that Impulse's meals were incredible has *nothing* to do with this?"

She pauses, then holds up her fingers in a pinch as if to say, "Maybe a tiny bit."

"Gods," Nathan says, amused. It was a good thing, really, to be around friends he could joke with even here, in the belly of the beast. "Fine. Fiveish hours to explore and get back. Anything else?"

"Stay safe; don't trust anything?" Freya says.

"Words to live by," Sekhmet says, shouldering her bag and straightening herself.

Freya looks down at her own accessory with a scowl. "Somehow I doubt blood spatters are in season here," she says to herself. She fishes out her tuning fork and straps it onto the holster under her dress, then tosses the ruined bag behind a console.

"Good luck, guys," Freya says once she's done, sounding a little nervous. "I'll head out first. Wait a few minutes, then follow?"

Nathan and Sekhmet nod. Freya sighs, then turns to leave, and Nathan's heart jumps in his chest at the thought of her heading into whatever hell awaited.

"Hey, Sara?" he says before she can go farther. "Try not to get into trouble, all right?"

She turns back with a questioning smile.

"You've got a lousy track record, is all," he adds, fidgeting.

"You're not the boss of me," she replies, grinning.

"I just don't want to have to find another god to follow," he says with a halfhearted laugh, trying to stay positive. "Such a hassle."

"Well, as a favor to you, then," she says, walking back to give him a hug. "You keep yourself in one piece, too, all right?" she says over his shoulder. "Finding a good high priest isn't much easier."

"I *guess*," Nathan says as they part, adding a lighthearted touch of sarcasm to mask his mounting worry.

Freya winks at him, then looks to Sekhmet. "I don't have to tell you how much I'd miss you, do I?"

"No," Sekhmet answers with a laugh. Then she holds out her arms. "But such sentiments . . . never hurt."

Freya gives her a hug, too, tight and fierce, then bobs her head as they part. "Cheer up, guys," she says. "New York pizza is waiting for us."

Nathan's stomach grumbles at the thought. "Finally, a goal worth the trouble," he says.

She laughs with him, an awkward chuckle shared on the precipice of disaster, it seems to Nathan. They stand there for a moment, both seeming equally displeased with the idea of facing what lies beyond. At last, Freya shakes her head and moves for the door. She takes a deep breath when she reaches it, pausing with her hand on the knob.

"What joys do you hide?" she mutters at it.

Part of Nathan hopes she'll decide to go back for more jokes and good-byes, but he knows that would just be delaying the inevitable.

A moment later, Freya squares her shoulders, seeming to reach the same conclusion, and opens the door. A long, familiar-looking hallway lies beyond, its sealed concrete floor coated in ribbons of color, intended to direct maintenance staff. Nathan can make out another nondescript door opposite theirs, incomprehensible numbers etched into the wall beside it.

His god turns back for one more look, then slips into the depths of Meridian One.

Nathan and Sekhmet both let out little breaths they'd been holding as the door snaps shut behind her. "Few more minutes, then follow?" he asks in an uneven tone.

"Indeed," she says. There's a pause. "Are you afraid, my love?" she asks after a moment, wide eyes shining in the dull light.

He snorts. "I'd be an idiot not to be."

She nods at that. "Then we are both wise."

"I really—" he begins, then cuts himself off, shaking his head. "*Really* hope we'll be okay, Sekhmet," he finishes in a much smaller voice.

She remains quiet, looking at him, before her expression crumples. She wraps her arms around him and holds him close. "As do I," she says, soft and tense.

He hugs her just as fiercely. "Just stick with me, all right?" he says, still holding her.

She pulls back and looks at him, features laced with concern, and he manages a smile. With mock gravity, he says, "Long as we're together, the world can't touch us."

That gets him a touch of laughter. "And what is the source of such confidence?" she asks.

His smile widens. "Because if anyone hurt you, I'd move heaven and earth to get them, and I'm betting you're no different."

"Oh, Nathan," she says with a dark chuckle, hugging him again. "I . . . cannot say."

He blinks at that, confused.

"If you are to come to harm," she says, something dire in her voice, "I honestly do not know what I will do."

Nathan stares at her, at the odd mix of conviction and uncertainty on her face, and smiles again. "Then let's make sure we never find out," he says, and kisses her.

19

FRIENDS IN HIGH PLACES

FREYA

It's even worse than I remember.

This place is a sprawling nightmare of tunnels and enchantments, a ludicrous hive of the magical, malicious, and mundane. I commit the name tag of our maintenance room to memory and do my best to fix its location in my head as I start picking my way through the halls, but part of me is deeply worried I'll never find it again. I have a few spells that can help, preset triggers to find lost items and people, but I'd rather save those contingencies for something more important than my own personal GodNav system.

My heart skips a beat when I stumble across an elevator. At last, a way to populated floors and, just maybe, someone who knows their way around this maze. I press the call button, idly clean my nails while I wait for the car to arrive, then board a few seconds later. My jaw drops when I see the selection of floors: Counting basements, this building has more than *eighty levels*, putting it on even footing with some of the tallest buildings in the world.

Considering the sheer size of each of those floors, it may beat them all in terms of footprint.

If they weren't cheating, that is. Wherever Meridian One is located, I'm willing to bet it looks nothing like its true self on the outside. Finemdi seems to adore space-warping magic, and if Impulse Station was anything to go by, this place could very well be hidden in a utility shed behind some bushes in Central Park.

I review my options with a sour look, then sigh and press the button for Level 69. Immaturity, be my guide. The elevator fires off with a smooth hiss, reaching my juvenile choice in less than a minute. The doors open on what's clearly some sort of corporate office space. Thick carpeting compresses underfoot as I take a wary tour of extremely stylish business spaces that would fit right in alongside the high-tech grandeur of the Creative Artists Agency. I pause at the thought, realizing that a few short, carnage-filled hours ago, I was happily playing the starlet on the dance floor.

This is not *how I saw the rest of that night going.*

I can't figure out exactly what the purpose of this floor is, but going by door labels, stray documents, and the occasional staffer, I'm guessing it's some sort of accounting department. Oh, *glee.*

I'm trudging through a recreational space filled with televisions, expensive-looking chairs, and enormous windows that look out on the New York skyline when someone finally takes notice of me. It's a young woman in conservative business dress who catches my eye as I maneuver around a table with built-in gaming consoles and headsets. Her eyes grow wide when she spots me, then dart to either side as if she's trying to figure out how to make herself scarce.

"G-good morning, Mistress Freya!" she stammers as she draws near, clearly frightened.

"Morning!" I say in a bright voice, continuing past.

271

It's only after I've gone five steps that I stop and realize what's happened. I make a slow turn, confused, and catch a glimpse of the intern as she hurries away at a power walk that's just shy of a run. Her shoulders are hunched and she's moving like there's a tiger stalking her from behind one of the nearby laptop nooks. Then she sneaks a quick look over her shoulder, sees me watching her, and literally *squeaks* and picks up the pace. She's gone in a few seconds, anxiety streaming in her wake.

"What the *hell*?" I say to the empty air.

She *recognized* me. How is that even *possible*?

That girl knew my name, felt familiar enough that she had to say something . . . and was utterly terrified of the consequences of doing so. I just got here, didn't I? How could she possibly have a clue who I was? And know enough to have that sort of reaction?

This makes no sense. Even *if* she knew me and what I did at Impulse Station, she should be setting off alarms and releasing the hounds, not acting like she's just passed the schoolyard bully in the hallway. I-I'm at a total loss. What's going on here?

I stand there nearly a minute, trying to puzzle out an answer and waiting to see if she'll be back with the Jerk Squad, but neither makes an appearance. No alarms, nothing. I shake my head, deeply troubled, and continue my search. Over the next half hour, as the office begins to fill with early-morning workers, I have another dozen encounters that all go pretty much the same way. These people clearly know me, and their general response always seems to boil down to, "Oh god oh god please don't hurt me I'm too young to *die*," before they make their escape.

Finally, I manage to corner a clerk in a break room as he waits for a pot of coffee. He's in his mid-twenties, probably fresh out of college or grad school, with black hair and sleepy-looking eyes. The way he's watching the coffeepot fill gives me the impression that this is his favorite part of the morning. "Hi there!" I say, planting myself in the doorway.

He spins, a smile on his face. Then his eyes lock on me, and the joy curdles on his lips as he turns an ashen shade of despair. "Mistress Freya," he whispers. "H-how can I— That is, if you *would* need help, is there, uh, I just—"

Okay, this is ridiculous. I blast his mind with affection, smashing aside the terror and dismay like cobwebs before a fire hose, and close the distance between us. "There, not so scary now, am I?" I say as I walk up.

"What? Oh, ha, no, no—I don't know what I was thinking, sorry. Um, coffee?" he says, holding up his mug with sheepish, puppy dog affection. I notice it reads FINEMDI EUROPEAN FINANCES in block letters above the company logo, which is drawn in red and green and covered in little ornaments. CHRISTMAS 2016 is written beneath in a holiday-themed font.

"No, thanks," I say. "What's your name?"

"Clark!" he says brightly. "I—I know we've never spoken, but it's just so good to meet you, Mistress Freya. Would you like to, um, maybe see a movie or something? Get to know each other better?"

"That would be great, Clark," I say, wondering if I've overdone it on the love. "Next week? Until then, can you tell me how you know me?"

"Oh, sure," he says, clearly tickled by the idea of our upcoming date. "You started working on the executive level a few months ago as HR coordinator and head assistant to the chairman." He leans in, lowering his voice as if sharing a secret. "They say you've increased productivity in the business office and reduced tardiness by, like, a ridiculous amount, but you're"—he fidgets, like this is something he wishes he didn't have to say—"very mean. 'Force of nature' mean. Most everyone tries to stay out of your way. They've sent your picture around in e-mail chains and everything. 'Don't piss her off!' and all that."

He frowns. "But you seem really cool!" he finishes in a bright voice.

"Yeah, thanks," I mutter, mind whirling. *I work here?* But—but I can't work here! I have *very distinct* memories of *never* being here. Unless . . . did they make a Freya of their own? I mean, I know Finemdi has the hideous power to forge its own deities, but why in the world would they want *me*? And how would they even do it? Samantha said you need all kinds of info to make it stick! And why is *this* me apparently a colossal bitch? I'm nice! It's my thing!

"Listen, Clark, this is really important," I say, putting my hands on his shoulders and looking him the eyes. "I need to know where you'd go to look up a god's records. Whatever Finemdi knows about them."

"Well, it's all digital," he says, fiddling with the milk and sugar. "Not like there's some special server room or, y'know, file cabinet. Use the right credentials and any computer in the building will get you what you need."

"Do *you* have those credentials?" I ask, feeling exasperated.

"Course. Have to be able to check on gods for filing, see who contributes what, how important they are for each assigned team so we can help payroll calculate bonuses, that sort of thing." He takes a sip and closes his eyes in satisfaction.

"And can you *edit* those records?"

"Absolutely," he says, stirring in more sugar. "We have to fill in fiscal impacts, remember? Some gods contribute more than others, but we track everyone. Like, Hestia basically gets a fully dedicated analyst, but the others vary depending on time of year, what ops they're running, the—"

"Great! Fine!" I say. "Can you help me edit my file? I'm in a hurry, and this can't wait."

"Sure! Here, follow me," he says, and sets off at a brisk pace.

I follow him a few doors down to a cookie-cutter office with C. HARRISON stenciled on the nameplate. I've noticed there are no cubicle farms here—everyone has an office, or at least an open working environment behind closed doors. I guess unlimited space and money means they can do away with some of the sadder business clichés of the twentieth century.

Clark sits behind his desk and gestures for me to pull up one of the guest chairs set against a wall. I grab one and wheel it over, settling in as he finishes booting up his machine. "Just a quick edit, right?" he says, navigating the desktop.

"Right," I say. "Then I'm gonna make your mind overflow and forget we ever did this."

"Hmm?" he says as he loads up a website.

"Nothing."

"All right, let's see," he says, typing. "F-R-E-Y-A, right? Or is there a *J*? Oh, there you are. Okay, looks like you have two records: one for a pseudo-Freya and one for the original. Which do you want?"

I narrow my eyes. I'll be damned. They *did* make another me. "Both."

"Can do. Original first, then," he says, clicking on the link. The page loads up with my dossier, including the headshot they took back at Impulse Station. I scan the page, noting they have my old alias and last known addresses as well as my relationship with Nathan, but nothing on Sekhmet or the Hawaiian sisters, or anything after

Orlando. The last place they have for me is the false address I had Nāmaka submit before she flooded their server room, and it looks like she remembered to delete my real apartment details at the time, too. Way to go, Hawaii.

"And the fake?" I ask.

He clicks the other page, and my double is suddenly staring back at me. It's uncanny. The girl shown here is a strange mirror, my physical copy, and yet . . . the differences are plain. There's a hardness around her eyes, a cruel hint to her smile, a pinched haughtiness in her cheeks. This god is not your friend.

Ty kráva. *I have an evil twin.*

I scan the page, but there's a lot to process, and I really should hurry. "Can you print this?"

"Sure," he says, sending a command to his team's printer. "We can pick it up from the printer when we're done here."

"Okay, good. Now go back," I say. "New search. Find Sara Valen. S-A-R-A . . . yeah, V-A- There it is." I point as the auto-complete fills in his search field.

He opens the link. It's filed under "Unidentified Gods" with an "Active Operation" marker on it. Someone's attached one of Sara Valen's short-haired publicity stills for *Switch* to the top of the page. The most recent update describes my antics in Los Angeles, the cleanup team, and the heartening news that they lost my trail shortly after an encounter with Izanami, who managed to escape after much death and mayhem. A new agent will be assigned to the case after a briefing scheduled for later today, and they've moved back into monitoring mode while they wait for me to reappear. Perfect.

"Right, this whole file," I say, pointing at the screen. "Delete everything. The picture, all the stuff about her TV career, known addresses, all of it."

He hesitates, fingers poised over the keys. "Really? I mean, look at this op—it just came back. This got edited, like, half an hour ago."

"Yeah, that's why I'm here," I say, feeding him another pulse of love. "Whole thing was a bust. Got the wrong girl. Can you undo it?"

"Oh, of course!" he says, resistance fading beneath my onslaught of affection. I watch as he clears the various fields, unlinks my IMDb page and headshot, and basically turns the file into a blank slate. In a few minutes, all that's left are the operation expenses, the links to the—good gods, *twenty-three* agents who were killed or injured a few hours ago—the follow-up plans . . . everything but the girl they were targeting.

I have Clark craft some edits out of whole cloth, explaining how Sebastian was attacked out of the blue, the search for the unknown deity is ongoing, stuff like that. "Is there a code name for blank gods?" I ask as we finish. The entry still needs a name.

"John God or Jane God," he says, filling in the latter.

"Obviously. Now, is there a record of what we just did? Any kind of history?"

"Sure," he says, and scrolls to the top of the page, clicks on Tools and then selects Page History from the drop-down menu. Hyperlinked version numbers appear, each followed by the date of the changes, a Changed By field (the first lists Sebastian Gallows, while the most recent shows Clark Harrison), and a Restore This Version link.

"How do you delete these?" I ask.

"You need to be an admin, like me," he says. "Every space has its own permissions."

"So you can do it?"

"Yeah. Me and a few others on the floor, the folks in IT, upper management, my supervisor—"

"Please stop talking."

I'll spare you the *utterly fascinating* details of wiki navigation, but ten minutes later, after some awkward discussion, emotional manipulation, and page edits, Sara Valen has a clean slate and all records of my actions have been purged from the system. Clark tells me it'll still be possible to recover the original versions, but that requires a server rollback and a lot of red tape. Without probable cause, he doubts it'll be an issue. My timing is excellent, because according to the wiki, the operation won't have a replacement for Sebastian until later today, and an assigned agent familiar with the file is the only person who might wonder why "Sara Valen" is no longer a person of interest.

After we're done, I crank the love and affection for Clark into overdrive, blasting memory from his mind and replacing it with a hazy soup of warmth and fuzziness. He'll be back to normal in a few minutes but won't remember the past few hours beyond a sneaking suspicion that something really, really nice happened.

It's an effective way of covering my tracks, but not a trick I enjoy using. In part, it's because drop-kicking someone's brain into a love haze is a minor abuse of my gifts, not far from applying the acid of regret instead, like I did to that Finemdi motorcyclist. The other, more important reason is that it's incredibly draining. I wait until I'm a few halls away, then find one of those relaxation rooms and collapse onto a beanbag chair, breathing heavily.

I spend a few minutes there, watching the shadows of the nearby skyscrapers shift in the morning light and feeling pretty good about myself. Sure, I'm still a meager gnat of a goddess, but I've just stolen my career back from under Finemdi's nose. How many other gods can lay claim to such deeds? Now there's just the question of escape . . . and this "other" Freya. I snagged her file from the printer on the way out; now might be a good time to review it. I lean over and pull it out of the commemorative Finemdi tote (I'm not kidding) Clark was kind enough to let me borrow. It's no Kate Spade, of course, but I was feeling naked without a bag of some sort, and who knows what else I'll need to carry?

Flipping through "Mistress Freya's" file gives me chills.

This girl was apparently made by direct request from the highest levels of the organization. She's worked for the chairman since she "reached cohesion" shortly after the destruction of Impulse Station, doing all sorts of busywork and staff coordination for upper management. She was built with those skills in mind using *my* intake profile and . . . orientation quiz?

"Oh come *on!*" I yell at the paper. Of all the poor decisions I've made, *this* is what comes back to bite me? I remember that test—it was meant to help Finemdi focus their efforts on "empowering" me, but I caught it for the trap it truly was. My answers for that thing were half joke, half misdirection, intended to keep from being targeted with their poisoned belief. Now I find they've used them after all, bundled them with brainwashed faith to forge a hateful copy of me, and for *what?* Do they do this with every god who slips through their fingers? Impossible. And she's the chairman's *assistant?*

"I'm a goddamn *secretary?*" I snap, working myself up.

There's more, but I'm too annoyed. I stuff the papers back into the tote and fume for a few minutes, thinking it over. Part of me advises caution, tells me there's a lot at stake, that bizarro Freya is, however enticing, simply a distraction. A much angrier part, on the other hand, demands I hunt this walking blasphemy down and beat the answers out of her. I mean, it's just *weird*, right? I don't pretend to understand Finemdi's inner workings, but *this*— No, I have to find out what's going on. The whole affair makes precisely *zero* sense. Sure, escape may still be my primary goal, but if I can get answers while I'm at it, then all the better.

First things first, though: I really need something to eat.

I get out of the beanbag with a groan, tilting myself onto the floor before staggering upright. For the zillionth time, I find myself yearning for the power of my glory days. *Gods*, did I take it for granted. Forget tweaking the minds of mortals like Clark; with my full suite of spells, I could've given *Zeus* a run for his money. At least things have gotten better. A year ago, this kind of effort would've put me down for hours. Now it just means I'm going to be a little wobbly for a few minutes.

Suitably reassured of my growing strength, I head in the general direction of the nearest elevator. I'm definitely shaky, but I'll manage—especially after some breakfast. According to Clark, most gods hang out around the thirtieth floor, so that's my destination. I figure I stand a better chance of enjoying my meal and overhearing something juicy about potential escape routes if I manage to lose myself in a crowd.

A few minutes later, I exit the elevator and begin navigating some rather lovely tiled corridors. Large marble planters full of flowers, carved columns, and tasteful art installations keep pace with me as I follow luxurious strips of malachite to what I hope is the lunchroom (one of the few tips I retained from my time at Impulse was that green lines lead to food and recreation). I soon pass through a bejeweled archway and step openmouthed into a landscape of mind-warping regality and wealth. I thought the retreat of the Graces was something special, but it's a third-world flea market compared to this place.

I've entered a vast atrium, easily the size of several football stadiums. Rolling hills of fresh green grasses are dotted with soaring temples, sculptures, and mansions. Oaks, sycamores, willows, and more spread their leaves over sun-drenched ponds, while fish dart in the shallows, brilliant sunlight reflecting off their scales in sharp, beautiful flashes. Clear streams connect these glittering pools, filling the air with the sound of babbling water and giving purpose to several delicate bridges of hand-carved wood that join the wandering footpaths.

This serene park is surrounded by terraced hills of earth and steel. Outlandish homes and castles sprawl across the layers, their lawns intercut with gardens and waterfalls. Massive illusions coat the distant walls and ceiling, providing the artificial sun that crawls lazily through a bright blue sky and drawing the eye to far-off mountains and fertile meadowlands. Songbirds flit through the air on brightly colored wings, while exotic animals and creatures of myth stroll the grounds alongside their divine masters. Grecian temples sit beside Slavic fortresses, Shinto shrines, and more, each pantheon seeming to have carved a uniquely beautiful fiefdom for itself into the verdant landscape.

Our world has many gods. I know this intellectually, have studied the history of my kin as much as any scholar, and despite centuries of fog and befuddlement, I can still remember the names of hundreds. Even so, I have always considered us a rarity, jewels cast among the sands of an endless beach, and treat every encounter with one of my peers as a singular, remarkable event. It is this mindset that makes the tableau before me all the more striking.

There are gods everywhere, dozens of living legends enjoying the riches of this artificial paradise. Dressed as I am by the Graces, I fit right in alongside what's clearly a slim Greek majority. Most of their pantheon seems to have a place here, followed by a hearty assortment of European, Slavic, and Eastern gods, as well as scattered pockets from the Americas, Africa, and the Pacific. I even recognize a few transplants from Impulse Station, and—

"First time?" a voice asks in a friendly, rumbling Irish brogue.

I turn to take in my greeter. Leaning against a nearby column is a tall, well-muscled man. Unlike most of the style-impaired deities here (togas are *so* last millennium), he's wearing a navy-blue tartan suit, which hangs open to reveal an ever-so-lightly rumpled white shirt and dark blue tie. His hair, shining golden locks kissed by a touch of fire, falls to shoulder length and frames a face of gleeful confidence and irresistible amusement. Piercing green eyes glow with strength and assurance, and his smile promises good-natured mischief and friendship.

"Lugh," he says, springing off the column and approaching me with an outstretched hand. He pronounces it *Lú* in those rich Irish tones, and I feel a touch of pink creep into my cheeks as he clasps my hand in his. "Of the Tuatha Dé Danann. God of skill, mostly. Wee bit of the sun, touch of war, you get the idea."

Oh, *yes*, I do.

"Freya," I say, cranking my smile into the megawatt range. "Of the Vanir. Goddess of love, beauty"—he smirks at that and tilts his head, like it's obvious—"war, magic, sex . . . you know, the good stuff."

"That I do. So what brings you to our haven, sweet girl?"

"Is it so obvious?"

"What, that you're new?" He laughs, and mimes a wide-eyed look of awe. "Everyone makes that face, the first time."

"I was at Impulse," I say, deciding to go with half-truths in case he's good at picking out liars. "Finemdi caught up with me again, and here we are."

"I was there!" he says, laughing. As he moves, I notice the flash of an ID badge clipped to his belt; looks like even gods get carded here. Something to keep in mind. "A very dramatic end. We're all still wondering what really happened."

" 'We'?"

"My kin and I. Banded together after Impulse collapsed, made our way here. Didn't you—" He frowns. "Forgive me—I talk of my people, yet I'm not sure Finemdi has welcomed a scion of Yggdrasil before you."

Wait, what? They've never had a Norse god here? I may have a high opinion of my pantheon, but that's just odd.

Ragnarök, the Twilight of the Gods, may be playing a part here, of course, even if it didn't *precisely* happen. As the foretold end of my pantheon, it's supposed to come with all kinds of apocalyptic nonsense—a serpent rising, our sun devoured, armies of darkness, and swords brighter than stars searing all life from the world—but the only real outcome of that prophecy was the deaths of my most prominent peers, including my beloved brother, Freyr. As near as I can tell, the sheer strength of humanity's conviction that Ragnarök *had already happened* erased my allies from existence . . . but that doesn't account for all of us. Many went unmentioned in that tale, myself included, so I *can't* be the first Finemdi's found.

Either Lugh's simply mistaken, or something strange is going on. "I'm sorry?" I say.

"At least that I've seen," he explains. His frown softens. "You must miss your peers. I have my doubts, entrusting our fates and faiths to Finemdi, but at least I can share them with kin." There's a ripple of sympathy and embarrassment in him, and his features turn sheepish. "I make a poor greeter, do I not? Please, join us, Freya. A guest at our hearth, a voice in our halls, a friend in our hearts."

He holds out a hand, and I want so badly to take it. I mean, I *do*, reaching out with a smile and letting him guide me to the nearest sights, but I want it to be more than a gesture. In that moment I feel a tremendous sense of loneliness, of distance, because I know it's only temporary. I can't stay here, can't let myself succumb to its tempting promises, but oh, how I wish for the freedom ignorance would bring. This place is *nothing* like Impulse. Do you have any idea how long it's been since I traveled with my peers, felt the joy of *belonging*, not just to friends and allies, but a pantheon? I could have a life here, could watch days drip into decades, relaxing in the shade of temples and men of marble.

And all I have to do is forget.

Since that's impossible, I resign myself to playing the awestruck tourist, following Lugh to nearby sights of magic and miracle. I'm not going to lie—it's amazing. There are stands of utopia trees, branches heavy with protean fruits of endless flavors, each promising a taste of joy from a new corner of the world. Pools of ambrosia ripple with iridescent immortality. Soul forges twinkle and pulse, creating, unmaking, and fusing all manner of birds and beasts for the curiosity and amusement of their masters. Miniature worlds twirl above manicured lawns, little globes of life growing, dying, and colliding in an endless waltz, eons washing over them in the blink of an eye.

There are temples greater than any man could build; impossible columns of forged light support diamond statues, plinths of typhoon stone hum with hurricanes of faith, curved fractal towers promise lifetimes of exploration, and more. These are not tricks, not illusions from petty charlatans like myself. They are the playthings of pantheons, the works and wonders of centuries, and I am humbled by their very existence. This is true power, the stuff of legend and myth made real, and I—

Stars above, I *want* it. This is everything we've been designed to desire, a literal heaven on earth, and it could be mine. Easily.

And I have to burn it, burn all of it with the single-minded fury of the Valkyrie. It's built on a lie, one I cannot swallow, will *never* accept. Despite the joy I feel, the sense of purpose and community I've missed for centuries, I cannot open my heart to it, cannot *allow it to exist*, because war does not discriminate. I said I would torch the world if I knew Ares could be found among its ashes, and the same is true for Finemdi. I am sworn to their destruction, and if achieving that end means bringing down the walls of heaven, so be it.

Doesn't mean I'm not broken up about it, though.

Honestly, I'm close to tears by the time brunch rolls around. The food here is heartrendingly good, a marvel on par with everything else I've seen today. Impulse's offerings were basically three-star Michelin fare, but imagine what the greatest chefs in history can do when "magic" is an ingredient on their shelves. Zao Jun, the Chinese god of cooking, rubs shoulders with Hestia, Greek goddess of the hearth, the pair forging dishes of surpassing skill and spectacle from within a cavernous kitchen realm of their own design.

There are mimosas that taste of orange-tinted sunshine and starlight, sparkling in a glass. Juices that conjure images of summers without end, water chilled in the hearts of glaciers, cocktails infused with essences of desire and celebration. Actual cornucopias spill their contents across tables of living wood, impossible foodstuffs masquerading as mortal fare like it's a continental breakfast on Mount Olympus. There are crepes as light as air stuffed with berries that ripen on your tongue, miniature loaves of filled bread, each ingredient the ideal temperature, meats crisped in ovens of eternal flame, their skins forever crackling with juices and memories of the hearth.

If food were music, this is the master symphony of an angelic choir.

"Not bad?" Lugh asks as I stuff my face.

"*S'amazing*," I moan through a mouthful of pancake clusters, each a tiny cake elegantly layered with bands of syrup and preserved fruit.

"One of the reasons we stay, honestly," he says, taking a sip of something fizzy that churns with hypnotic swirls of purple and aquamarine. "The belief *is* nice, as is the chance to do some good in the world after all these years, but we are made for nature and the open road. The Tuatha Dé Danann do not require this . . . congress. We prefer lives of sharp pleasures and pains; solitude, battle, romance . . ." His twinkling green eyes flash to me. "They are better fierce, quick. Not muddled and drawn-out, like this."

That gives me pause, and I grab a crème brûlée pig while I try to think of a proper reply. It trots across my palm, oinking happily, and I pretend to examine it with glee. Lugh's words have the ring of truth to them, but I know Finemdi's the real reason he and his kin can't bring themselves to leave. That belief he mentioned? It comes with all kinds of strings attached. Finemdi's masters know it shapes us, so they lace their offerings of faith with a compulsion to stay, to obey, to avoid rocking the boat.

Lugh is trapped, and he doesn't even know it.

"So where do you go when wanderlust gets the better of you?" I finally ask, popping the pig into my mouth. It melts into a blanket of warm sugar and scorched custard, and for once I don't feel bad about eating one of my beloved swine.

"Where else?" he says, surprised. "The Otherworld."

I frown. Did I miss something in the employee orientation packet? "And that is . . . where, exactly?"

He laughs, happily and without malice, a joyous bark that makes me feel my confusion was more than worth it, if only to bring this charming man a moment of glee. "Here!" he says, sweeping out an arm. "There, everywhere. The Otherworld sits beside us, a bright mirror to these mortal lands. Tír na nÓg, our home, is but a part."

Now that *one, I know.* "Oh! Like our Valhalla."

"A touch. Ah, but you're a little close to the afterlife for my liking. The Otherworld isn't what follows death—it's what escapes it. A place of undying summer and joy, of youth and beauty and—" He pauses. "Oh, but why not simply show you?"

"What, now?"

"No better time," he says, getting up and offering a hand.

He leads me away from the feast, toward the Celtic portion of the grounds, where the hills begin to twist into whimsical shapes and the openings of burial mounds and caves loom like watchful eyes. Lugh walks up to the mouth of one of the smaller tombs, an unassuming gateway of earth and stone, and gestures at it proudly. "A step beyond, a world beside," he says, grinning.

I move forward slowly, sandals crunching on dirt. The moment I pass the threshold, my vision *snaps* and suddenly the tunnel doesn't seem so close and dark. It's wide and inviting, well lit by a warm light I can't quite place, and the air smells sweeter, of morning rain and flowers. I thought this passage went deep into the ground, but just around the bend, I see it curves up toward a circle of sunlight.

I approach it, almost in a trance, and when I reach the entrance, I find myself surrounded by endless fields of soft green grasses, a fertile ocean uplifted by a riot of wildflowers, all of it rustling peacefully in gentle breezes beneath a summer sky. Otherworld, Mag Mell, Tír na nÓg—whatever you want to call it . . . it's real.

A rush of delight fills me at the realization. I have distant memories of Valhalla, Yggdrasil, and, of course, my own realm of Fólkvangr, but a part of me had begun to wonder if they truly existed, or if I was simply made to *believe they had*. I know gods can summon creatures, can warp the world around them and, if they're powerful enough, edit reality to suit their whims. Logically, that implies the places, people, treasures, and terrors of myth all exist *somewhere*, but I've lacked the might to reach my own for so long, I'd begun to doubt I ever had it.

This proves otherwise. With enough strength, the realms of the gods *can* be touched, our seats of power unlocked and explored. I *must* remember this, must try to return to my home when I have the mystic muscle to do so. If I could look on my meadows again, could once more lay claim to the fallen who gather there, well, I might have an army made to order.

As I stand at the entrance to paradise, soaking in the warmth of summer and dreaming of conquest, my brain finally sputters to life and reminds me I've missed something devastatingly important. *What did Lugh just say about the Otherworld? It parallels our own, right? Put it together, Sara.*

I lay a hand on the tunnel wall, feeling giddy as the implications of this little trip hit home. These lands are lovely, to be certain, but the laughter and cheers that explode from me as I look on them are for another reason entirely:

I've found a way out.

20

FORK IN THE ROAD

FREYA

"Splendid," Lugh says, taking in a lungful of summer air as he stops beside me.

"Without question," I say, then turn to him and begin digging for answers. "So is this the only entrance?"

"No, just the most convenient," he says, bending down to pick a flower. "We forged the link after our arrival, but there are passages without number. Some open at the promise of adventure, others for worthy souls or those who hold the keys, but any will admit the divine."

He places the flower in my hair, taking care to thread its stem around my locks. "You need only know the Otherworld is waiting."

"And the same is true for exits?" I say, smiling at his gesture. "I mean, do I have to use this one?"

"Well, should you wander far and find yourself pining for the mortal realm, there are certainly others—though they would probably return you far afield. Distances mean less here than there."

Perfect.

I touch the flower, feeling a mischievous grin make its way onto my face. *While we're at it* . . . "Lugh, I—" I draw closer. "How do I begin to thank you for this?"

His eyes twinkle. A mix of jest and playful hunger stirs beyond, but all he says is, "A meager tour is hardly deserving of debt. Your delight is payment enough."

"If you knew how long it had been since I stood before such wonders—"

"You owe me nothing," he says. "Come, step away from the pangs of favor and politics. Tarry beneath the sun of my lands, flee to your own adventures . . . I care not, save that you are pleased."

I arch an eyebrow at that, a knowing smile on my lips. The hell with it. He's been nothing but helpful, without guile or expectations, and there are hours to go before I'm supposed to meet my friends. "What was it you said of 'sharp pleasures'?" I walk my fingers up his shirt. "'Fierce'? 'Quick'?"

Those fingers curl around his collar. "How quick?"

His grin turns wanton and he moves to press our bodies together. "I care not . . ." he repeats, and the rest of the line hangs silently between us, an unspoken promise.

I shift my hand up, sliding it against his neck, feeling his muscles, the warmth of his skin. "Not very, then," I say, pulling his lips to mine . . . and sneaking his ID badge off his belt.

I walk out of the atrium an hour later, a bounce in my step and a few extra flowers in my hair. That was everything I'd been missing. I know stopping in the middle of a life-or-death struggle to indulge one's passions probably isn't the best idea, but I'm fairly sure the little party favor I snagged more than makes up for it. That, and there are far worse places and partners. Sweet summer skies and enchantingly soft grasses in a realm of youth and happiness beat just about any mundane bedroom, after all.

I check my pocket as I get into the elevator and punch in my new destination, making sure Lugh's number is still on the scrap of paper tucked in there. We exchanged digits before parting ways, because, well, sure he's gorgeous and ruggedly pleasant, but more important, he's *nice*. When it comes to gods, it pains me to admit how rare that quality can be.

I giggle, remembering a few choice moments. Add those delights to the devious glee of what our mini date has enabled me to do next, and you get one happy goddess. That's not even touching on the fact that I've completed both of my high-stakes, nigh-impossible goals (Identity? Check. Exit? Check!) before noon. Honestly, this place isn't nearly as bad as I feared.

The elevator slows as my destination approaches, and I straighten my shoulders and try to tamp down my enthusiasm. Riding high on unmitigated success and an unhealthy supply of confidence, I've decided there's no harm in taking on just one more quest: the mystery of fake Freya.

The distant voice of reason tries to tell me how terrible this idea actually is, but the fires of curiosity, outrage, and pride drown her out. The Valkyrie's being given free rein when what I *should* be doing is finding my friends and getting the hell out of this viper's den. This can't be the first time I've made the mistake of asking questions best left unanswered, but who's counting? It's hard to deny your nature.

The elevator doors open on a marble-tiled executive suite straight out of *Obscenely Wealthy Businessman's Quarterly*. Unlike most of the other levels, getting here actually required me to swipe a keycard reader next to the floor buttons. I'd expected an obstacle like this would eventually get in my way, so stealing Lugh's ID was for more than mischief's sake, if you can believe it.

On that note, I'm not a total idiot. I know the goal is getting out of here without Finemdi realizing I was ever on-site, and if somebody gets wise and starts checking security tapes, they'll figure out what I've done. That's why I stole more than Lugh's badge—with one of my preset illusions running, I've also taken his appearance.

Fiery golden hair frames my new face, replacing my usual wide-eyed glee with suavely confident features of lightheartedness and strength. On me, his vague sense of ready camaraderie comes through a lot more strongly, a clear undercurrent of delight replacing the faint contentment of the genuine article, but I doubt anyone will look that deeply.

Besides the expensive stonework, there's a set of double doors on the far side of the room, the usual high-end chairs and coffee tables, and a bit of a security presence, as well. A glassed-in guard station sits to the left of the elevator doors, while two intimidating sentry guns hang from the ceiling, barrels tracking me as I walk forward. Three guards wait behind the bulletproof shielding, all of them heavily armored and glowing with mystic devices. They watch my approach with aggressive disinterest.

"Gentlemen," I say, nodding.

There's a click and the ornate wooden doors ahead swing outward. I beeline for them, trying to keep my pace even. The whole setup is massively intimidating, and the awkward silence of my walk across the anteroom, guns and guards shifting to follow my every step, makes for a nerve-racking experience. I start imagining all kinds of terrible things happening in my short journey but manage to reach the exit without any of them turning real. I breathe a sigh of relief as I enter the next room, the doors swinging closed the moment I pass their threshold.

I'm left in a long, richly appointed hallway. It looks sort of like Versailles got stretched through a Scandinavian design studio. There's a playful sense of rococo in the asymmetrical scrollwork and gold leafing that skips along the walls and ceiling, but it's more hinted at than anything else, peeled apart in the pursuit of minimalism and modernist streamlining. Large and inviting doors await me at the end of the corridor, while a dozen smaller ones offer exits to either side. I glance at the hand-etched nameplates set beside each one, looking for—Ah, here we are: SUPPLIES, my old friend.

I try the handle and find it unlocked. Lights flick on as the door swings inward, revealing a large utilities closet. It's a well-organized space full of cleaning kits, vacuums, trash bags, tools, spare reams of paper, and other office necessities. I walk into it with a grin, stopping just inside the doorway. These rooms are a gift to underhanded goddesses like myself, and I'm pretty sure I've seen more of them in my travels than labs, prisons, torture suites, or any other supervillain headquarters cliché you can imagine.

There's nobody wandering the hall now, but I'm not sure how long that will last. "Tamworth," I whisper, naming one more fine breed of pig in order to unleash another preprepared spell.

An illusory bubble whirls into place around me, projecting a copy of the corridor in all directions. If anyone were watching, it would look like I just vanished. In truth, I'm hidden by a small sphere of doubled images, a curved panorama taken from the hall and closet entrance as they appeared when I triggered the spell. Just like the hair I wore for *Switch*, this is simply altered light, meaning it'll show up perfectly fine on video.

That done, I settle against the doorframe and wait. I've resigned myself to skipping lunch, so that leaves me around two hours before I'm supposed to meet Nathan and Sekhmet downstairs. If my quarry doesn't put in an appearance before then, I'll have to try again later. Still, I like my odds: I know she works on this floor, I'm *fairly sure* this is the only elevator down from this level, and if she's at all like me, she's not missing lunch if she can help it. Add it all up, and I don't look so stupid now, do I?

The minutes crawl. Without my Mim at hand, my go-to choice of killing time with games and websites is lost. I start bouncing my back against the hall, boredom growing. Trying to focus on the task to come, I take my doppelgänger's file out of my tote and start flipping through it again.

A handful of well-heeled staffers and managers come and go as I read, spotless dress shoes and pumps clicking across the marble. I notice they always enter the corridor from one of the side doors—never the big pair at the end. They don't smell of divinity, making them either high-ranking mortals or half-breeds. None are my prey, so I let them pass with little more than a glance. My bubble is off-center, pushed up against the wall to cover the door to the supply closet, which lowers the chance they'll stumble into it by mistake.

Finally, at almost precisely noon, the doors at the far end of the hall smack open. Hard blue eyes stare dead ahead as she enters the passage with powerful strides, severe black pumps snapping against the tiles, every footfall a fancy gunshot. Her golden-blond hair is straightened and sleek, whispering across her shoulders like something out of a shampoo commercial. She's clad in a stunning outfit of tightly fitted black pants and matching designer smoking jacket. It doesn't look like she's wearing anything underneath, and the jacket is cinched mid-torso, creating an eye-popping neckline. The effect is somehow malevolent, businesslike, and scandalous.

Even without the piercing barb of deviant confidence she radiates, there's no mistaking this girl. I'm staring at my clone, Finemdi's "pseudo-Freya," and she's every bit as beautiful and terrible as promised. I raise my hand as she approaches, fingers wrapped tightly around the grip of the tranquilizer gun. She frowns as she nears, clearly sensing *something's* off, but her pace never wavers. I wait until she draws even with my bubble, then fire the dart directly into her neck.

She slaps a hand at the injury, stride faltering. She manages a little squeak of surprise before her eyes roll up in her head and she faints. I'm already leaping forward, reaching out to stop her fall and drag her into my illusion. She collapses into my arms, and I take a moment to steady us both before turning to the closet and shoving her in. She lands on the tiles in an unconscious heap.

Smiling in triumph, I kick her legs out of the way and shut the door behind us. If there *are* cameras in that hall, then someone reviewing the tapes will probably be able to figure out what happened, but considering how fast it all went down, I doubt I have anything to worry about until the alarm is raised. By then, I should be long gone.

The first thing I do is drop my Lugh disguise. Then I pick my twin's pockets, taking her keycard, cell phone, and—*Geez, really?* Holstered at the small of her back is a tiny holdout pistol, loaded with a single rune-covered bullet that looks just like the ones I stole from Sebastian. *I should figure out what those do at some point.*

I spend a few seconds studying her after I finish, wondering what it would be like if she weren't brainwashed and evil. *Wouldn't it be fun, having another me around?*

I shake my head, filing the thought for another time, and strip her completely, even stealing her shoes before putting on every last piece of clothing and accessory she had. It's not a switch—I'm not about to give her my clothes so she can toss them to bloodhounds—so I fold my dress and stuff it into my tote. I stand up straight, thankful for the recent months of practice wearing heels, and look myself over. Sleek black pants, cleavage for miles, and killer pumps. *Hey, I'm scary-hot.*

I complete the look with one last illusion; the same I use for *Switch.* This time, instead of making myself a short-haired brunette, I flatten my hair and give it the proper gloss to match. I use the camera on her phone to look myself over when I'm done. Perfect. You'd never know I wasn't her.

Finally, I bind my twin to some storage racks with a mishmash of extension cords, zip ties, and a couple of rolls of duct tape. By the time I'm done, she's so covered in restraints you can barely see skin. It may be overkill, but I'm not about to take any chances. More tape to seal her mouth and fix some printer paper over her eyes, and I'm ready to go. I give the room a final check to make sure I haven't missed anything, then straighten my shoulders, kill the illusion at the door, and walk back into the hall.

Knowing how strong the halāhala in those darts can be, she'll probably be out for at least a few hours, and even when she wakes, I'm pretty sure she's going nowhere fast. This gives me plenty of time to tour Finemdi as Freya, mighty and dreadful administrative assistant.

Part of me really wants to go back in there and wait until she wakes up so I can interrogate her. I'm fascinated and disgusted by her existence, and I'm pretty sure "banter with evil version of yourself" belongs on everyone's supernatural bucket list. All the same, I know it'll be a dead end. What's she going to tell me? At best, she'll be tight-lipped and snarky, and at worst, she'll recognize me. Either way, I'm not getting anything good out of her—certainly not more than I could find out *as* her.

I stride down the hall, retracing my clone's steps and trying to put anger and confidence into every *clack* of her heels. I reach the double doors at the far end and throw them open with what I hope is the proper degree of irritation. The room beyond is definitely her office. The general style is a continuation of the corridor's minimalist grandeur, but the walls on my left and right are floor-to-ceiling windows that look out on the Manhattan skyline.

More cheating, I think with a smirk, looking from one side to the other. There's no way this building is that thin—they've warped space somehow, allowing her to have an impossibly choice view.

There's another set of doors directly ahead of me. To their right, a long, sleek desk hangs from the ceiling on golden chains, its surface lowered to thigh height. An overstuffed office chair sits behind it, and a slim computer monitor, keyboard, and mouse are the only objects on its surface.

Three couches of surpassing comfort surround an etched glass coffee table to my left, its top branded with the Finemdi logo in threads of gold. There's a silver platter waiting for me here, a glass dome covering what appears to be someone's lunch. Always keen to explore foodstuffs, I bend down to examine it further.

The meal is extravagant, clearly the product of the same hands that prepared my brunch. A goblet of rich red wine sits beside a plate with a perfectly scaled roast pig in its center, psychedelic swirls of sauces and jams radiating from it. It even has a tiny apple in its mouth and looks like it just came out of the oven, its surface glistening with heat and oils. Then I look closer and realize the wisps of steam above it are frozen, halted in their ascent like gauzy banners in a dead wind.

Confused, I reach out to the platter with my divine senses and realize it's actually a powerful artifact: The weaves here are designed to halt time the moment the lid is closed. It's delightfully irresponsible; a massive amount of power and resources were probably needed to create this, and it's being used to keep someone's food fresh.

But who?

I turn to look at my double's desk. She might be my darker half, but even at my worst, I doubt I'd ever order pork. It must have been delivered here while I was busy tying her up. I glance at the big doors beside the desk. They're beautiful, carved from ancient wood, polished to a sleek, waxy shimmer, and etched with spiraling runes and scrollwork.

I look down at the lunch, then nod and wrap my fingers around the edges of the platter, carefully lifting it off the table. It's time to meet my boss.

The doors shimmer as I approach, wards reaching out to examine their new guest. They flicker and vanish an instant later, seeming to find me acceptable, and admit me to the private office of Finemdi's chairman.

A massive window takes up the entire back wall, silhouetting a high-backed chair and an equally enormous stone desk. The monolith's a strange black-and-gray mix of minerals—slate, granite, sandstone, obsidian, and more—tumbled together with a beautifully raw and unfinished feel. Ragged, splintered edges and asymmetrical outcroppings make it seem like it belongs on a mountaintop, not an executive office. Only a large portion in its center is smoothed, a flattened surface with room for a computer and other office accessories, yet something tells me it was sanded down over centuries, not by craftsmen in a workshop.

A spiral staircase of bronze and gold cuts through the room to the right of the desk, an immaculately tooled column leading to unseen levels above and below. Heavy shelves and display cases are set against the walls, full of odd trinkets and artifacts. Just beside the desk is a large platinum birdcage, every line of its cylindrical shape stamped with runes. It, like the rest of the office, is bizarrely unoccupied.

I frown, looking for this lunch's owner. Something buzzes in my ears, an odd hum with a familiar cadence, but I can't find the source. I'm not even sure I actually heard it. Have you ever walked into a room and forgotten why? Standing here feels like that, like I'm missing something I once knew. There's a strange twitch to the air around that cage and behind the desk, a barely there shimmer I can't quite bring into focus. I take a few more steps into the room and the buzz sounds again, this time a little clearer. That flicker at the desk is more pronounced, and I feel like I can remember more of it.

It's like I'm seeing and hearing something, then immediately forgetting it.

This is giving me a headache. I turn away from the desk, letting my attention drift to the items set against the wall. They're . . . eclectic. Some cases and spaces on the shelves are empty, yet trembling with the same uneasy amnesia I get from the desk and cage. I try to ignore these, focusing on the contents I *can* see.

Many of them are your expected arcane doodads and priceless baubles. You know, the standard incomprehensible gadgets and legendary items from antiquity. Puzzle boxes, rune stones, grimoires, swords and shields, jewelry and armor, you get the idea. Mixed in with these relics, however, are odd collectibles. There are signed copies of several novels, including *Eight Days of Luke* and *American Gods*, a few *Sandman* and *Journey into Mystery* comics, framed posters from a weird mix of movies, including *The Mask* and most of the recent Marvel films, and all sorts of action figures, busts, comiquette statues, and film props, all of—

"Yuz wa plaaaz wifsomzng?" The buzz returns, almost clear enough to tease apart. My eyes dart away from the collection, returning to focus on the desk again. The blur, sitting behind it. Staring at me. It's—I can almost—Dammit, I *know* there's something—

The masquerade shatters.

"Freya?" the man behind the desk asks, but I'm too busy getting my mind blown to reply. It's like something's broken in my head, a dam I never knew existed, memories and knowledge bursting, rushing, waters tearing away cobwebs of deceit. Snakes and skin changers dying, their colors running, pooling to form the shape of a myth, a foe, a face.

There's a man in that chair. He's been sitting there since I entered the room. There's a raven in that cage. It's been watching me the entire time.

"She tires of you already," the bird says in a deep, heavily accented baritone, cawing happily.

The man sighs and flicks a pen at the cage. "Impossible," he says, smiling as the raven flaps its wings and glares at him. "I'm naturally distracting."

Midnight hair falls in ringlets, framing erratic eyes. One moment, they're a warm, welcoming brown. Then the light shifts and they gleam with indigo highlights and malicious glee. Another twitch, and they're a deep, alluring red, treacherous and unhinged. His face is long and fair, graced with a sharp nose and an eternally amused half smile, yet touched by a ghost of pain, even torture. He wears a gloriously dark business suit, its tie patterned in alternating loops of black and gold, a nest of silken snakes.

I remember him. Can't help but remember. *He should be dead. How is he not dead?*

This is the man who destroyed my people, who slaughtered our most beloved son. Trickster, liar, murderer, shape-shifter, freak. *This* is the creature at Finemdi's heart, the architect of blasphemy and perversion, and my sworn foe? Oh, how the fates must laugh.

I hold out the tray, smiling, and speak to him for the first time in centuries.

"Your lunch, Loki."

21

FOOL'S ERRAND

FREYA

"Something on your mind?" he asks, leaning back in his chair and nodding at a bare spot on his desk.

I saunter over and place the tray there. *Something on my mind? Something on my MIND? Why aren't you DEAD? How's THAT for a question, you backstabbing coward?*

Gah, this is *bad*. I need every wit about me, and right now my thoughts are a storm of shock and outrage. How is this possible? How is he alive? Why him and not Freyr? Why not *any* of my friends? The Valkyrie thrashes and rages in my breast, telling me to kill him, kill him now, don't wait to listen, to chat, to do the *stupid dance* you're going to—

CRAM IT, I think back, forcing that voice down through sheer will, telling her vengeance will come, that I need answers first. "Just wondering the real reason you made me," I say aloud, trying to pick a question that will get him talking without revealing my deception.

"I could've sworn I told you. Ages ago," he says, eyes bouncing down at my chest, then back up again.

Oh, EW!

"You always have another motive," I say, desperate to stay a step ahead. "Another plan. You don't need to go to this kind of trouble for a familiar face."

"No, I didn't," he says, tilting his head. "And yes, I do." A shrug. "What's it to you?"

"Can't a girl be curious?"

"Ah. I'm not the only one with secrets today, am I?" His eyes glitter, flicking from green to blue. "You have a trade in mind?"

Oh, I'm so screwed. This charade's not going to last. The creature in that chair is a literal god of lies, a living font of plots and twisted machinations. I'm not even an apprentice in this field, and here sits the grandmaster.

How is this EVEN A DEBATE? the Valkyrie screams. *Lying tongues matter little after YOU CUT THEM OUT.*

"I *do* happen to have a secret or two saved. For a rainy day," I say, pleading with her to *shut up*.

"Really?" he says, suddenly eager. "I feel a drop."

"I asked first."

He laughs, eyes alight. I glance at the raven as he does. The bird's gone deathly quiet, examining me with unnerving directness. "I'm not used to giving things away for free," he says at last.

I put my hands on his desk and lean toward him. Judging by the way he's been staring and the lust that drips from his mind, I think I have the proper—and appalling—idea about the nature of "our" relationship. "Did you think *I'm* any different?" I say in a fierce, knowing tone.

His eyes flicker rapidly as he stares at me. Then he scoffs. "Oh, that's enough," he says, chuckling. "Please, don't take offense—you're honestly not bad. Time was, I would have indulged you further, but at some point you're going to embarrass yourself, and who wants that?"

Crap. "Excuse me?" I say, hoping I've misheard.

"You're not her." He draws a curvy silhouette in the air with two fingers. "Freya. Full points for getting in here, though. What are you after?"

He points at the display cases. "Trinkets? Take two—they're small!" He spins his chair and strikes an imperious pose. "Or is it me? Are you a hilariously deluded assassin? Haven't had one of those in ages."

Ugh. That fell apart even faster than I feared. I sigh, pushing away from his desk and flopping into one of the chairs in front of it. "What's it matter?" I say. "Game's over."

"Game's just beginning," he says. "Who sent you? I just *love* the idea there's someone left to challenge."

"Don't you care who I am?"

He waves a hand. "Only if you don't play. Then you tell me after all kinds of horribly tedious unpleasantness. So play. Who are you here for? Why?"

He'll see through any lie I tell, I think, feeling hopeless. I'm about to say, "Me," and bring it all crashing down. The word's on my lips when I realize there's one more option: the truth, again.

"Ares," I say, throwing the name before me like a shield.

His smile widens. "Fascinating. And Freya?"

"I have a personal interest in her."

"*So* close to wanting to ask who you are," he says, grinning with far too many teeth. There's an odd tic to his mouth, and for a moment he wears the curving fangs of a wolf. They're gone in a flash, a ghost of animal hunger. "But no, I have a better idea. You and I are taking a little trip."

"What? Where?"

"You came for Ares, didn't you? Well, I happen to know precisely where he is. So come. We'll meet him, have a nice chat, and discover what your future holds."

No, no, no, I think, feeling my stomach seize. This is *not* how I wanted a face-to-face with my old enemy. I can't just *tell* Loki that, though, so how on earth do I get out of this without dropping my true identity *or* walking into a deeply dangerous reunion?

"Just like that?" I ask, mind racing and heart hammering. "How do you know I don't have some evil plan to kill him or something?"

That gets me a high-pitched titter, and something in his neck seems to vibrate. "Maybe you do. But how else can this end? Locking you away? Letting you go? How dreary. You have business with Ares, that much is clear, and I'd prefer not to draw it out—I'm a very busy man, you know."

"Don't let me keep you," I say, holding up my hands. "Wanna pencil me in for next week? How's your Thursday looking?"

"Packed, m'fraid," he deadpans, drumming his fingers on the desk. "Got an opening around *right the hell now*, though."

He pauses, waiting to see how I'll react, and I stay quiet, trying not to let him know how frightened I am.

"Terrible things happen if you don't accept," he adds after a moment. One of his eyes elongates, its pupil turning reptilian, and I have to work to repress a shudder.

"Do any nice things happen if I *do*?"

"Sure, why not? I'll . . . uh . . ." He looks around, seeming to care little for the terms. "Give you something from here. And tell you why I made that Freya."

"Surprisingly reasonable," I say. "I, uh, accept." *Not that I had a choice.* At least I'll get something out of this, and buy myself a few more minutes to think of a plan.

"Shocking," he says. "Treasure first? Or secrets?"

"Why her?" I ask.

"Secrets, then," he says, suddenly grinning with the jumbled jaw of an anglerfish. He nods at the office around me. "What do you see?"

I look around, trying to understand what he's getting at.

"Big office? Trophies?" he suggests, teeth shivering.

"Victory, I suppose."

That gets me a little frown. "Meaningless. Oh, I understand it might not seem it to you—you're quite naive, after all—but wait a few centuries, and even a seat of power such as this can become a hollow place."

"I don't know," I say, nodding at the cage. "You have your little friend."

He snorts. "Muninn is hardly a gracious companion."

The bird huffs.

"So you were lonely?" I say. "That's it? How disappointing."

The frown returns, deepening. "I cannot deny my lack of peers, but it's hard to feel neglected when *none* are your equal. 'Lonely'? Please. *That is assumed.* No, my poison is simpler: boredom."

"So she's just . . . ?"

"Novel. An experiment. I mean, I've won, haven't I? Finemdi culls the gods, and with trickery as the centerpiece of my mantle, the lie at its heart ensures I grow in strength for every moment of its existence. The only beings who might guess the truth are convinced I'm dead, and the greatest among *them* think *they're* dead, too."

He gets out of his chair and begins walking toward a large section of the display cases, and I realize the same veil that screened him from my mind has lifted there, as well. My jaw drops as I realize what was hidden: Thor's hammer and belt, Odin's spear, Sigurd's sword, Fenrir's chain. Bottomless drinking horns, a kettle shimmering with the mead of poetry, my—oh, oh—my cloak of feathers, my *necklace*—

"Brísingamen," I whisper, throat rough with desire. *Mine*, a greedy voice inside me hisses, drowning out my rage with the strength of her longing.

"Took some doing, of course," Loki says, running a hand over a case containing an assortment of magical rings. "But considering how often the Fates used Thor and the rest to upend my designs, well, let's call my little mock Ragnarök an investment in privacy."

He flicks the glass of the display case. "Want to know how I knew you weren't her?"

"I'm just dying to," I say, trying to hide my awe with sarcasm. I can't stop staring at my necklace, following its priceless lines as my mind whirls. If what he says is true . . . it's all a *lie*? My brother, Freyr, lives? Odin, Thor? If the Twilight of the Gods never happened, if it's all smoke and mirrors and we were *forced* to believe . . .

But HOW? And where are they?

"There's no need to be snide," he says, looking at his collection. He walks over and points at my necklace. "She looks at this every time she walks in. Don't think she even realizes. Can't help herself." He turns back to me. "You didn't. First time that's ever happened."

I scowl. Such a simple thing. Not that I knew my treasure was here, of course.

"I'll admit I was curious about more than companionship," he says, then tilts his head and looks at me with the golden eyes of a lion. "I'm curious about so many things."

"Get used to it," I say, determined to keep as much from him as possible.

He smiles, teeth quivering into serrated wedges for a heartbeat, giving him the mouth of a shark. "I've tried not to edit myself too heavily," he says. "I've seen gods fall apart under the weight of conflicting beliefs. Faking Ragnarök was enough—meddling further would have tempted fate—so I left well enough alone."

There's a pause as he watches me again, and then he leers. "Including the desires," he adds.

I return what I hope is an indulgent smile. It's tremendously difficult, considering all I want is to smash his head against my necklace's display case and clasp it around my neck as I grind his skull to powder.

"The legends never made a pairing of Loki and Freya," he continues, sauntering back toward me. "But they *did* say she was the most beautiful of us all. However distasteful I find it, I *am* a part of those myths, of that pantheon, and the belief that she is the loveliest woman in the world is, by definition, a part of me."

He shrugs. "I had to see if it was true."

"And you could never risk using the *real* Freya, 'cause besides the fact she'd sooner spike your head on a flagpole than show you affection . . ."

"Yes, yes," he says, giving an irritated wave. "She'd know I was alive. Might start looking for the lost ones, might manage to break the spell."

Well. This explains why Lugh never saw another Norse god: Finemdi's actively *avoiding us*. Loki would have done everything in his power to avoid bringing a single member of the Æsir into the fold on the off chance they'd manage a peek behind the curtain. It's almost hilarious. Thousands of years of playing the villain, and now the ultimate thorn in our side *can't* mess with his favorite marks if he wants to maintain the masquerade.

Delicious irony aside, this ranks among the best news I've heard in my long life, because aside from imperiled ol' me, the rest of my kin remain beyond Finemdi's grasp. They're all out there somewhere, even the lost ones, the ones I thought Ragnarök had claimed. I feel something trill in my heart at the thought, at the sudden realization of what this really means: *My pantheon is not dead.* For centuries, I've fought for myself, lived with the expectation that I was the last of a shattered faith . . . and I'm not.

Death does not separate us, only magic—and *that* happens to be my area of expertise.

Despite the heart-stopping danger, I'm abruptly elated to have come to this snake's lair. I can do more than restore myself to glory now; I can restore *everything*, rip my peers from the history books and splash them across the stars once more, set the Norse atop the world and reclaim our rightful place as the greatest gods to walk the earth.

All because Loki let slip a secret to the one goddess he really shouldn't have.

"Then, despite your best efforts, she shows up after all," I say, filling in the blanks and trying to keep a smile off my face.

"It *was* a surprise to see her at Impulse," he says, giving no sign he's noticed my delight. "But ultimately a pleasant one. Running into her was the spark."

"Running—?" I repeat, confused. *When did I ever see him before?*

"Then she vanished with the rest of the station and, well . . ."

"The idea remained," I finish for him. "And a rather enticing profile."

"Couldn't resist," he says with a bounce of his eyebrows, drawing close and placing his hands on my hips.

THAT. IS. IT! Before I can stop myself, I haul back and slap him across the face, sending him reeling against the edge of his desk.

Oh, that felt GOOD, I think, taking in the damage as he staggers upright. It appears months of "offerings" from Nathan and Sekhmet have made me a potent little goddess—the blow was enough to dislocate his jaw, snap his neck, and crush his cheek.

"Did I say you could touch me?" I shout, not caring what might come.

He rolls his shoulders, clicking his spine back together. The wound on his face is already gone, healed with intimidating speed. *How powerful* is *he?* I think, eyes widening.

"So delightfully *angry*," he says, using his tie to mop up the blood on his jaw. He stuffs it back into his suit and waves a finger. "But I already have a violent consort, I'm afraid."

"How did you do it, Loki?" I ask. "How'd you fake the end-time *and* get the Æsir to believe it?"

"Sorry, you already got your secret," he says, and holds out a hand. "Shall we?"

"B-but—you said I could have—" I stutter, trying not to stare at my necklace.

"Hmm, did I?" he says, stroking his chin. "I'm fairly sure I never said *when*. Let's see how things go with Ares, first. Come along."

He spins and starts heading for his office doors. I'm moving to catch up when he glances over his shoulder, a sly smile on his lips. "Oh, and bring my lunch. If it's not too much trouble."

I look at the serving tray, then back at him with a sour expression. "You're asking me to wait on you? This is just to be a dick, isn't it?"

"Who said anything about 'asking'?" he says, smile turning cruel. "And yes."

I glare at his back as he leaves, knowing this is probably just the tip of the egomaniac iceberg. I'm hardly in a position to protest, however, especially if I want a shot at that necklace, so I sullenly return to his desk, snatch the tray from it, and hurry to catch up. I dash into the outer office just in time to see his form twist and warp. In a handful of steps, his suit blanches and extends, unfolding into a spotless white lab coat. Streaks of gray zip through his hair as it fades and fuzzes, becoming endearingly disheveled before turning pale as bone. Those spiteful, superior features soften and age, giving him a round, cheerful face. He turns to me as the transformation completes, looking for all the world like your classic absentminded professor . . .

. . . whom I've seen before.

My eyes grow wide as I recognize the mask he's donned. He reaches into a pocket and pulls out an ID badge, clipping it to his coat with a grin. I don't even need to read it to know it identifies him as GOODSON, BARNABY. The man I ran into as he was coming out of Corrections, back at Impulse. So that's how Loki met me. Where he got the idea to create my twin.

"Can't just go for a stroll in my own skin," he explains in Barnaby's kind, distant voice. "Must have a bit of mystery for the rank and file."

"Careful," I say, catching up and following him out. "Keep making that face, it'll get stuck that way."

"Not a god of comedy, then," he says with a sigh.

I give him an irritated look, then follow as he heads for the exit. A quick elevator ride takes us to one of the building's subbasements, even lower than the utilities wing where I arrived. The security here is heavy, an underground fortress stocked with grim guards and menacing weapons, but "Barnaby's" badge gets us through without incident. We pass through three sets of progressively thicker blast doors, thread around what appears to be a laboratory complex, and enter a sprawling prison.

"Are you *holding* him here?" I ask, trying not to gawk at the security.

Loki snorts at that. "Of course not. This is where he works."

"Figures," I mutter, realizing how well the setting matches what I know of the man.

There's no whimsy to this place—no spires of rock, ghoulish gargoyles, or other villainous accessories—just sharp, no-nonsense barriers, catwalks, and cells. Sterile efficiency is the order of the day here, leaving no room for escape routes or schemes. I'm guessing they have every air duct sealed, every pipe miniaturized, and every inch watched by cameras and patrolled by guards. Even on the accountants' floor, there was a touch of humanity, a sense someone had a bit of fun with the design. Here, the message is clear: Abandon hope, ye who enter.

I'm getting an *incredibly* bad feeling about this. Sure, fine, going after my twin and sneaking into her boss's office was risky, but this is a brand-new level of *doomed*. What's going to happen when we meet up with Ares? How is this going to go any way but poorly? Oh, I've really stepped in it now.

Gods and mythical creatures of all shapes and sizes watch us as we pass. A sinuous, ever-moving man with three heads paces one cell, all six eyes burning with flat, reptilian disgust. Another imprisoned god is enormous, yet emaciated and hunched, sitting cross-legged in a freezing, rime-coated suite. The walls around him are covered in crawling Aztec runes and pictograms. He smiles at us with a too-wide mouth, and my breath becomes a chilled fog in the few moments his gaze settles on me.

Others seem less sinister, likely having been locked away for the crime of not following Finemdi. A dark-skinned man reclines in an enormous leather chair, surrounded by fine furnishings, collectibles, and knickknacks. Bone-thin and scarecrowish, he's dressed in a tuxedo suit and top hat. Glossy sunglasses hide his eyes, his lips wrap around a fine cigar, and he raises a tumbler of clear liquid to toast me as we pass. I notice he returns his attention to an adult magazine as soon as it's clear we're not stopping. A little farther on, a bright red girl—

I halt outside her cell, surprised and confused. Loki turns and laughs when he notices who's captured my attention. Completely naked but for garlands of skulls, bones, and lotus flowers, she'd be utterly gorgeous—if her head weren't missing. The woman's neck terminates in a clean stump, blood streaming from it at a startling rate to splash on the cell floor. I notice large metal grills are spaced evenly to drain the mess. Aside from the bloodstains, several packed bookshelves, and a few simple pieces of furniture, the room is bare. Wreathed in unkempt black hair, the girl's detached head watches us from a nearby end table, her attention momentarily diverted from a book her body holds for her.

"Chhinnamasta," Loki says, tapping on the glass. "Hindu goddess of self-sacrifice, sexual energy, and restraint. One of the few Indian gods we've managed to capture."

He leans closer. "Not many believers for a bloodthirsty, haunted freak, are there?"

The girl's body lowers her book, and her head purses its lips. "Life is messy," she says in crisp, brittle tones. "A panting, hungry search to perpetuate itself. To escape death, we serve it. I offer the truth of this, the sacrifice that is our blood and fluid. Unsurprising few are brave enough to embrace it."

"I'm more a fan of 'no strings attached,'" Loki says before resuming his walk. I watch as the girl returns to her reading, then follow him, eyes darting between a seemingly endless parade of sealed gods and muzzled beasts as we continue our tour.

My worries ratchet with every step; I'm going to need help if I want to avoid joining their ranks. As I trail Loki, I start sending symbols and imagery to Nathan, using our bond between god and worshipper to cheat some rather pertinent knowledge into his head. I've never sent visions to him—or pretty much *anyone* in centuries, aside from Harv—but I've become rather desperate. Hopefully he'll get their meaning, and hopefully I haven't gotten rusty. Communicating actual information is *really hard* when all you have to work with are vague, myth-approved flashes of prophecy. Stupid visions.

I send him towering mountains carved with the floor number, hedge mazes outlining the security setup, a trail of blood to show the route we've taken . . . everything my high priest might need to reach me. As clearly as I can, I wreath these symbols with the pounding sentiment that things are about to get deadly serious.

A handful of seconds later, I receive a prayer in return: *Hang on, Sara; we're coming, and Samantha's going to help.*

I allow myself a tiny sigh of relief. He got it. Not only that, but he's bringing exactly who I'd want. With Samantha at their side, my friends should be able to get anywhere, and if she's coming along, she may be what's needed to tip the odds. That makes me feel a *lot* better. I send back a burst of gratitude, then return my attention to the tour.

"So many," I say, eyes darting from cell to cell.

"Well, this *is* the scenic route," Loki says.

"Why do it?" I ask, drawing even with him. "Why start a war on the gods? What do you get out of this?"

"I don't know," he says, smiling. "Maybe I should start a YouTube channel."

"I'm serious."

"Hi, Serious, I'm Loki."

I make an exasperated noise, and he laughs. "I didn't start Finemdi. They'd been going for over a century before I found them."

Huh. That's interesting—makes me wonder who *did* create this place. "And you thought it was a good idea?"

"What, do I look stupid?" he says, feigning insult. "Terrible. Had to be stopped. Most of these idiots"—he gestures at the rows of prisoners—"probably felt the same. Only reason I'm not on *that* side of the glass with them is because I know you can't kill ideas."

He pauses, staring at a stern-looking god. The man has flowing hair of gold and radiates light like a living sun, throwing our shadows behind us as we pass his cell. "But you *can* poison them," Loki says as we move on. "And so."

"You snuck in, put yourself in charge, and didn't change a thing?" I say, confused. "I mean, what's the difference?"

"Besides the incredible irony? I don't want a world without gods, girl—I want a world with *one*."

I give him a skeptical look. "You never struck me as a monotheist."

"Pfft. Religion. Keep it. I have a theory I'm testing."

"And that is?"

He turns his head, a hint of amber glowing in his eyes. "All you're getting," he says, falling silent.

315

I sigh, looking at the poor pig on the tray in front of me, and feel a bit of empathy for this trapped, roasted creature. That feeling is multiplied as we pass a larger-than-usual cell, this one home to a trio of very familiar goddesses.

My pulse quickens, but I try not to let my stride falter or give away much of a reaction as I take in the new home of Hi'iaka, Nāmaka, and Pele. Samantha was right: My friends are being held here, and in what appear to be Hawaiian-themed confines. Several lovely pieces of koa wood furniture sit on floors coated in woven mats, and there's even a fountain made from golden bamboo in one corner. The three nature spirits are all sitting on a couch pointed at the back wall, chatting among themselves. They don't even look up as we pass, their attention captured by an old episode of *Desperate Housewives* playing on a large flat-screen TV. As prisons go, it looks surprisingly comfortable.

"—don't understand what *any* of them see in Susan," Nāmaka is saying. "She's not worth the trouble."

"You're such a Bree," Hi'iaka says, dismissing her opinion with a snort.

I smile at the banter, hoping it means they're being treated well, and make note of where they're located. If I somehow get out of this, I'm beelining it to them. For now, though . . . my future's not looking quite so hopeful. At least Loki doesn't seem interested in chatting further, making the rest of our journey blessedly quiet. A few minutes later, we reach our destination.

My tour guide turns and twitches a hand, gesturing at an upcoming intersection. "Ladies first," he says. I send Nathan a final vision of where we are, take a deep breath, then turn the corner.

My blood freezes.

Standing in the hall before us, staring at a clipboard and dressed in a US military uniform, is Ares. Even from behind, he radiates violent authority, his pale skin seeming stretched taut with power. His coarse black hair is slicked down with gel, and his posture is utterly straight. A pen twiddles between marble fingertips as he jots notes. He's facing a cell at the end of the hall, apparently oblivious to our arrival. I feel a trill of adrenaline as I stare at him, the centuries falling away to place me on a green hill in a distant land, watching those twitching hands swing a blade toward my neck. I shudder at the memory, not quite believing this insane scenario is actually real. All these years, and he's *right there.*

For his part, Ares seems distracted, attention captured by the notes he's taking and the contents of the cell before him. It certainly seems important, looming a little larger and brighter than the others near it. A hazy, rippling spike of magic surrounds this chamber, its weaves intense and intricate. There's a large crystal-studded control panel of sorts set into the wall beside it, and most of those strange energies seem tied to its dials and switches. Beyond the usual sheet of warded acrylic glass, a darkly familiar creature waits.

And waits.

I recognize him almost as quickly as I did Ares, but my association with this deviant is far more recent. Ahriman, the Zoroastrian god of destruction and wrath, stands within the cell, dressed in unkempt rags. His body is rigid and unmoving, frozen mid-tirade, eyes locked on the air directly in front of the control panel. Flecks of spittle surround snarling lips, and curses lie trapped behind clenched teeth. His face is a map of rage and unstoppable hatred, red-tinted eyes burning with promises of extinction.

I take an involuntary step back, remembering the brutal visions the merest *piece* of him seared into my mind at Inward Care Center. Garen used it as part of his introduction—proof he dealt with gods.

I later learned those disgusting trinkets are standard-issue for Finemdi agents, the chunks functioning as a bizarre escape plan, a means to drag their hosts out of danger when mortal threats loom.

Of course, if you're fast enough, there's only so much they can do. *Just look at Sebastian Gallows.*

"Look familiar?" Loki asks, lowering his voice.

How did he—? I'm about to admit the truth of what I'm seeing, of who I am and why I've come, when I realize he's pointing at the tray in my hands.

"Same concept," he says. "Just costlier. Keeps food and gods fresh!"

Ares stops writing at the words, then continues a few seconds later. He's clearly aware others are in the hall now, but seems content to ignore the interruption. I choose to focus on Loki's statement, completely fine with putting off our inevitable introduction for a few more seconds to puzzle out what they've done to Ahriman.

It hits me. "He's stuck in time," I say.

Loki shakes his head. "No, no, that's a little unnecessary. He's just very, *very* slow. Might manage to spit whatever insult's on his mind in a few decades."

"Why not do this with all of them?" I ask.

He turns to stare at me with the piercing slate-gray eyes of a hawk. "It's expensive. This cell ties up a *lot* of resources, and when I say 'a lot,' that's like saying 'it took a lot of bricks to build New York.'"

"If you don't mind," Ares says at last, a touch of temper electrifying the words as he lowers his clipboard. "I'm rather—"

He stops as he turns to stare at us both. "Oh. You two," he says at last, mistaking me for my twin. "Rare to see management descend so far. Why are you here?"

"I've brought you a surprise," Loki says, chuckling as he lets Barnaby's features melt away.

"And e-mail was unavailable?" Ares says, annoyed. "I'm on a schedule."

"Ah, of course," Loki says, nodding at the cell. "How's it going?"

Ares sighs. "I am attempting to expedite the process. The time lock is effective, but its long-term costs are, as you're aware, extreme. His demeanor is not helping matters, either. Responses to cajoling *and* torture are equally poor. He is . . . obstinate."

"Aren't they all."

Ares clears his throat, clasping his clipboard behind his back and giving Loki a meaningful look. "Ah, yes," Loki says, rolling his eyes. "Always a hurry. Well, this won't take long." He snaps his fingers at me. "Sweetums?"

I sigh, walking up. *Here it comes.*

"Who do you see, Ares?" Loki asks.

Ares glowers at him. "Your secretary."

"Correction," Loki says. "*Your* secretary."

"Pardon?" Ares says as my mouth goes dry. *Son of a* bitch.

"You get a Freya, I get a Freya. Everybody gets a Freya!" Loki says, tossing up his arms before turning to me. "Isn't that right . . . Freya?"

"*What?*" I snap in unison with Ares.

"The wards on my office door," Loki explains, straightening his suit. "They're quite picky. So picky, in fact, that if they let you in and you *weren't* my new beau, you almost had to be the genuine article. When you couldn't see me *or* your necklace, that clinched it."

Well, that's just great. "And you've been . . . what? Toying with me since?"

"Pretty much," Loki says, dusk-red eyes gleaming. He turns

back to Ares. "It's really her, Ares, so whaddya say? Need an assistant?"

My nemesis stares at me, ancient recognition cascading through burning eyes. "Pathetic girl," he barks with vile mirth. "Miss my shelf?"

And I'm gone. The Valkyrie rips control from me the second she hears those spiteful, grating tones. "Your end is *here!*" I shout at him, watching as if from a distance as I toss Loki's lunch tray to the floor with a clatter and stab a finger at Ares's chest. "The conquest, the bloodshed, the victories . . . ? *No more.*"

Behind the fury, my heart sinks with the sudden realization that I've been manipulated into coming here . . . by myself. That brief moment when my spell crept through the portal at the Graces' and I had my choice of Finemdi facilities? Well, Sekhmet was right all along: I didn't pick this place because Samantha was here—I did it for *Ares.* The Valkyrie's hungered for this reunion ever since she learned it might be possible, and with one subconscious push, she got it.

"I swore I'd see your fall," I continue to shout, getting spit on his medals. "Now, my ven—"

Ares snorts, places a hand on my chest, and gives a little shove. What follows is a deeply humbling experience, because for such a simple motion, he's able to put an absurd amount of force into it. The air blasts out of my lungs as I rocket backward from his touch, skidding down the hall and tumbling painfully until I come to a stop over fifty feet away.

"It's certainly her," I hear Ares say over the sound of blood rushing in my ears. "Hard to forget such pitiful *whining.*" He pauses, and as I struggle to regain my footing, I see a hint of amusement touch his features. "You know, I do believe I actually *missed* it."

"Wonderful!" Loki says, clapping his hands. "Freya? You still with us?"

"Go to hell," I spit, staggering upright.

"Been there, done that, got the desk," he says. "Now cheer up: Do you know how many girls would die for this job?"

"I'll kill you. Both of you," I seethe.

"You'll never get a promotion with that attitude," Loki says, snickering.

Ares grins, eyes aflame with cruel delight. "Welcome to Finemdi, love."

BEST SERVED COLD
FREYA

"You can't—" I sputter.

"Just did," Loki says, giving me an irritated wave. "Unless you'd rather rot in a cell for a few centuries." He turns to Ares. "You play nice, now."

"Have I ever?" he says with a laugh.

"*Excuse me?*" I shout. "If you think I'll just go along with this without a fight—"

Loki's hand elongates, sprouting extra fingers and flattening before shooting forward on an elastic arm to wrap around my body and lift me from the floor. I'm caught, a crane of flesh hoisting me off the ground and pinning my arms to my sides. His arm is a messy, jagged thing now, far too many joints zigzagging through the air to connect the web of fingers around me with Loki's shoulder. He laughs, and I bounce in the air in time with his mirth.

"Of course not," he says. "There. Gotten it out of your system?"

There's a sudden *click*, and Loki's chest explodes in a blast of orange-tinted sparks. I tumble to the floor as he staggers to one side, dropping me. He's re-forming before the gunshot even stops echoing, but those flares of tangerine energy aren't dissipating; they stay embedded in his torso, burning like chunks of mystic napalm.

"Gettin' a little handsy there, pal," Nathan says, rune revolver smoking in his grip. Sekhmet and Samantha are with him, the latter carrying what looks like an opal cattle prod and dragging our hard-sided case of artifacts behind her. "Where do you find these guys, Sara?"

Ares's eyes widen at the development, but rather than leap to Loki's aid, he simply crosses his arms over his chest and leans against Ahriman's cell, seeming content to watch.

I get to my feet. "Tinder addiction," I say. "You mind shooting him a few more times?"

"No!" Loki gasps, eyes whipping to Nathan. "I order you to—!"

My friend cuts him off by unloading another three rounds into his blazing body. Each impacts in a new burst of color, taking enormous cartoon chunks out of him with sizzling pops.

"Love the timing," I say, running up to Nathan and giving him a big hug.

"We actually ran part of the way," he says, and I note the sweat beading his forehead. "Started sensing *major* stress from you, figured time wasn't our friend."

"Still isn't," Ares says, unmoved by Loki's writhing plight. "Minions of hers, I presume?"

"It *is* you," Sekhmet says, claws extending from her fingertips. "How convenient. Almost disappointingly so, but then, every hunt must end."

"As will *you*," Loki gasps. With a ghastly *squelch*, his head rips free from his burning body, separating him from the effect of the rune bullets. It rolls a few feet before compact, grasshopper-like legs sprout from its stump. His mouth splits and deepens, yawning open like a frog's, and dagger-sharp teeth branch between his lips. Those insectile legs coil beneath him, and he launches himself at Nathan, maw wide.

For a decapitated head, he moves *fast*. From disgusting start to finish, the whole thing takes maybe two seconds. By the time Loki's teeth are on course for my priest's face, all I've managed to do is blurt out a retching noise; Nathan has no chance to get out of the way.

Fortunately, he has Sekhmet for a girlfriend.

The cat goddess flows around him, darting to intercept Loki. Dozens of needle-sharp fangs clamp onto her upraised arm, sinking deeply into her skin, but she's already bringing the pain. Peach-gold talons shred Loki's distorted face, and he warbles in agony before shoving away from her.

He hits the floor on thick, hairless feet, body bloating and expanding with muscle as his form balloons into an enormous gorilla. Sekhmet ducks a ponderous blow, striking under one shaggy arm and tearing through his abdomen. He roars and brings another fist down, but she simply slides around it, embeds two handfuls of claws into his flesh, and climbs him like a tree.

Ares raises his eyebrows with mild interest as Sekhmet twirls in the air above Loki, but makes no move to help his supposed ally. My friend crashes onto the ape's back, reaching down to attack his eyes, and his form deflates immediately, splashing into a pool of skin beneath her before exploding into a thrashing nest of tentacles. Sekhmet adapts her strategy, ducking low and severing the rubbery columns at their base, and the duel shifts gears again, becoming a strange back-and-forth dance as Loki keeps changing his shape to counter her assault.

I'm really not getting across the speed on display here. Each phase of this battle lasts mere seconds. Sekhmet moves like lightning, but Loki's shape-shifting and healing are more than a match. For a moment, I wonder why he hasn't fallen back on his beloved illusions, but then I realize Sekhmet defies that sort of thing, and he probably knows it.

"Magnificent," Ares says, sounding like he'd love a bucket of popcorn right now.

I glare at him, enraged by the notion he's found my friend's life-or-death struggle *entertaining*. "Samantha, mind if I borrow that toy of yours?" I ask, leaning over to whisper to her.

She passes it to me quietly, saying, "Touch tip to target, add willpower."

I take it, give her a tight smile, and begin walking toward Ares, keeping an eye on Sekhmet's ever-shifting battle as I do. I get two steps before Samantha puts a hand on my shoulder.

"The cell," she whispers. "There's a teleport failsafe for Ahriman. It'll move him off-site if he's out for more than thirty seconds."

I turn back to her, frowning.

"Just in case," she says with a wink, and I finally get what she's hinting at: a potential assist for the bout to come.

Beside her, Nathan winces as Sekhmet and Loki slam against a wall, then looks to me, seeming to come to an internal decision.

"Let's kick his ass," he says, moving to follow. Samantha, fantastically enough, pulls out a rune-covered rod with a diamond cap and does the same, intent on involving herself in Ares's downfall.

I actually feel myself start to tear up a little at that, dearly touched by their support. I mean, okay, I *am* Nathan's god and all, but it's staggering to see Samantha in my corner. This is a shy, pragmatic scientist we're talking about; I had no idea she felt that deeply for me, or would care enough about Ares to risk her young life against him. I grin at them both, incredibly grateful, and start walking again, examining my foe and the cell behind him as I do. My pace quickens as I realize what Samantha meant about Ahriman. Even against this overpowered meathead, victory might be possible.

"What's this?" Ares says as we approach. "Come for another lesson in your inadequacy?"

"Centuries, I've waited," I say, brandishing Samantha's cattle prod.

"They were not kind to you," he says, voice dripping with disdain. "Now be away. Allow me to observe this fine duel."

"Oh, am I *distracting* you?" I ask, venomous. "Deepest apologies, *dick*."

"You are feebler now than when we first met," he says, getting progressively angrier. "Do not embarrass yourself."

"You're right," I say, and he rolls his eyes and huffs at my continued intrusion. "I'm weaker, you're stronger, and it's going to make victory all the sweeter."

"*Fine*," he spits, shoving off the wall and turning to face me. "When I grind your smirking face beneath my heel, perhaps it will at last afford me a measure of peace."

With that, he lashes out, sending a backhand of titanic power soaring toward my left temple. I barely duck beneath it, flinching at the suction of air that follows in its wake, then jam the cattle prod into his hip and will it to fire.

There's a shrieking *zzap!* and Ares seizes as paralytic, rainbow lightning engulfs his torso. He staggers back, smacking into the glass of Ahriman's cell, and I follow with him, keeping the prod buried in his side. At the same moment, a flattened, vertical beam of pure white light rips into him from over my left shoulder, and I almost drop my weapon in surprise. The lance of brilliant energy slices up and outward, leaving a cauterized canyon in Ares's chest, and I dart a glance back to see its source: Samantha and her diamond rod.

"Not . . . *enough*," Ares grits, and I whip around to watch as the god of war moves his head in painful, stuttering twitches to stare down at me.

Baleful black weaves of destruction practically *ooze* from his skin, and I yelp in shock as the cattle prod disintegrates at their touch. Large hunks of the thickened glass behind him slough away into dust, and even the concrete tiles at his feet splinter and sag at the barest caress of his might.

Free from the lightning's effect, Ares pulls himself up and swings a fist down to crush me. Samantha sends another beam through his chest, but he barely seems to notice. I try to throw myself back, out of his range, but my feet slip in powdered cement, and I feel myself falling onto my back, watching as if in slow motion as he swings toward me with a blow strong enough to snap a redwood.

Then the air turns to shimmering jelly, and instead of converting me into floor pizza, Ares's fist connects with a half dome of force, courtesy of Nathan. The field crumbles and snaps under the impact, but it's enough of a delay to let me roll to one side and spring away.

Samantha carves chunks out of his body and Nathan lashes him with tongues of coruscating fire, but Ares ignores the damage to follow me, wounds regenerating almost as quickly as my allies can inflict them. I back up another step, considering my next move, and my eyes fall on the crystal panel beside the cell. It's completely unlabeled, but to someone who can see the threads of magic it manipulates, its functions are clear as day—including *OFF*.

"Tag!" I say, slapping a hand on the Deactivate Everything trigger.

Ares's eyes widen as the remains of the glass partition slide away beside him.

"—ing whore of—!" Ahriman bursts out, suddenly returned to motion and cutting himself off when he realizes the situation has changed. He spares but a moment's glance for me, the raging battle between Loki and Sekhmet, and my friends. It's only when his gaze stops on Ares, the man responsible for his recent suffering, that he reacts.

A cold, slow smile reveals pointed teeth, and Ahriman launches himself at my foe with an inhuman cry of brutal delight.

"*Subire septem,*" Ares coughs at the oncoming predator, voice choked by fire and light.

Ahriman, dirty arms outstretched, vanishes mid-leap in a whorl of twisted air. My eyes pop at the sudden disappearance, and I wonder for a moment if Ares has learned some measure of spellcraft, as well.

A trigger phrase, I realize, though the understanding brings me no relief. Samantha said there were teleport contingencies for Ahriman—those words must have set them off.

Ares winces as another beam from Samantha shears off the back of his head and then he turns to me. "No tricks," he grates. "Only death."

"Spoilsport," I say, edging away.

Ares darts for me, and even with Nathan firing off a concussive blast to break one of his legs mid-sprint, there's no stopping that momentum. He smashes into me like a seven-foot bullet, and I feel something go *crack* in my chest as we both slam to the floor.

"Cute," I wheeze. "Jeju Black."

My contingency spell triggers instantly, a hammer of sheer force centered on Ares's suffocating mass. He's wrenched away in an eyeblink, hauled across the room by a rocket's worth of thrust to collide with the far cell in a booming quake of flesh and cement.

I roll to a sitting position, and my heart drops as I watch my foe right himself, wounds already stitching themselves shut. *I really can't win this*, I think, hopes flagging as he starts pounding toward me again.

Nathan and Samantha pour on the firepower, but it's barely enough to make a dent in this ridiculous creature, an unrelenting engine of battle in the shape of a man. Despite the constant stream of damage, he's already made it halfway back to me, and there's not a thing I can do to keep him from closing that gap. Despair grips me in those final seconds, a sense of terrible truth settling on my shoulders: I never stood a *chance*. Why did I let my arrogance win out over reason, over the logic and caution of my friend? Stars above, why didn't I *listen*? He was right, my priest, at least until my pride and a blind desire for conformity crushed that spark of dissent.

I'm a god of love, I berate myself, *and I thought I could win a war, could defeat its champion at his—*

Wait, I realize, stiffening.

I'm a god of love.

Ares wraps a hand around my neck, sweeping me from the tiles in one vicious motion to hang, kicking, in the air above him. Fingers capable of twisting steel tighten slowly, their owner savoring every ounce of pressure ratcheting against my throat.

"Pathetic girl," he sighs, barely audible above the screams and assaults from my desperate friends.

"*Love me*," I gasp, unleashing every scrap of passion, adoration, and affection in my soul and driving it into his like a freight train.

I couldn't do this to just anyone. Against the other villains of my life, misery is the weapon of choice, the only emotion I can bear to bring them, but for Ares . . . ? Centuries of scheming, of striving for his fall have made him more than a man to me—he's also a *goal*.

And you can love to hate a goal.

So I gather it all, days and weeks and *lifetimes* of focus and commitment, nine hundred years of unflagging *devotion*, and focus that epic sum into a single searing burst of mind-shattering revelation.

Bloodshot pupils dilate, and Ares seems to lock in place, that nasty grin slipping into frozen stupor. I hang there limply for a moment, watching patches of blackness creep into the corners of my vision, and wonder if there's any room left in this living weapon for love.

Then I collapse to the floor, dropped by nerveless fingers, and get my answer.

"What am I—?" Ares mumbles, staring at nothing.

I hold up a hand to my friends, ordering a brief cease-fire. Ares looks down at the movement, and concern crinkles his eyes. "Freya!" he says, seeming aghast. "My apologies, I didn't—Here, let me help you up."

Those brutal hands reach down to gently grasp my sides, and Ares lifts me from the floor, setting me upright as gingerly as if I were cast from porcelain. He reaches up to brush some wayward hairs from my face, a goofy grin drifting across once-barbarous features. "That . . . got out of hand, sorry," he says. "Complete misunderstanding on my part, I assure you."

Battle roars from Sekhmet and Loki, the latter currently in the form of an acid-spitting hydra, draw our attention before I can reply. "Want me to deal with him?" Ares asks, frowning at the ongoing brawl.

"Uh, no, thanks," I say. Loki probably knows enough about magic to be able to rip my webs of compulsion out of Ares's mind the second he realizes what's happened. "But if you could step into that cell, I'd be grateful."

"Of course, sweet thing," Ares says, still grinning. I glance at Samantha and Nathan as the god of war sheepishly pads into Ahriman's former accommodations. Panting, exhausted by their efforts, they look completely bewildered by this turn of events. Those expressions only get better as I walk over to the controls and flick a switch to seal our former adversary inside.

The damaged glass slides shut, and he simply waits behind it, seeming content to know he's done my bidding. I give myself a moment to sigh in relief, then turn my attention to the other battle raging beside us. From start to finish, my scrap with Ares has lasted *maybe* a minute, but in that time, Sekhmet and Loki have transformed the rest of the hallway into a blood-spattered, ichor-smeared war zone. Clearly, neither of the two has been able to gain the upper hand.

Then a razored wingtip scores a line across Sekhmet's upper shoulder, and I realize it's only one of many injuries she's still trying to heal. Loki can't react as quickly as her, but he's realized he doesn't need to—his regeneration appears just as unstoppable as Ares's, and in a war of attrition, that alone will grant him victory.

Sekhmet, thankfully, seems to have reached the same conclusion.

As she dodges the claws and stinger of a nightmarish scorpion-wasp hybrid, she laughs—*laughs*—in the aberration's twitching face, then reaches behind her back, around the folds of her Grecian dress, and—

It happens far too quickly to register. I thought this contest was hard to keep track of before, but the instant her fingers close on whatever's buried in that cloth, it becomes all but impossible. I can only make out a flash of light from something long and sharp before a blur of slicing, tearing, scraping annihilation replaces my friend. Loki might be a shape-shifting speed demon and an even faster regenerator, but against this new development, even he has no hope of keeping up. Long slashes score his hide and chunks of armored carapace slough away as if by magic, his form shattering and dwindling as Sekhmet obliterates him with terrible swiftness.

He flops to the ground, seeming unable to control his many limbs. Unwanted skin and chitin crumbles, his form dwindling as he fights to escape the blur of devastation. As more and more of him dissipates, I realize he's had enough, that he's winnowing his shape down to something small and quick. He'll make his getaway, send in his legions, and live to fight another day.

It's infuriating.

I ransack my mind as Loki's body cracks and contracts, realizing we're almost out of time. Who cares if we've won this battle? If he gets away, I don't like our chances of survival, and my hold on Ares will last only so long as it takes Loki to catch on that it's there. Problem is, I can't think of a damn thing in my meager arsenal that could so much as scratch him. Groaning in frustration, I hang my head and . . .

. . . stare wide-eyed at the tray on the ground beside me.

"Sekhmet!" I yell, snatching it from the floor. The blur halts, and

I see my friend again as she snaps to attention, one hand holding a quivering chunk of Loki's unwanted form and the other plunging a very long, very familiar dagger into his side. *The ritual knife,* I realize, having almost forgotten the blade she tried to pack in her carry-on, ages ago.

I wrench my body and send the tray and its domed lid sailing toward her. "Seize him!"

A housefly pops out of Loki's splintering carcass as she drops the knife and snatches the serving set from the air. The tiny black dot zips straight up, seeking escape. Sekhmet coils her legs underneath her, does that little prepounce butt shimmy all cats adore, and launches herself skyward.

I watch in awe as she ascends, arms held wide with the tray and its lid, a mad cymbalist in flight. She reaches out as she nears her prey, curving both hands through the air, and there's a glorious *clang!* as she brings the glass top and serving platter together around the fly. She spins as she falls back, slapping onto the concrete floor with a perfect three-point landing, the tray clutched to her chest in one hand.

The remains of Loki's lunch touch down nearby with an abrupt splatter.

I dash up, skipping around the pools of bleeding monster, and reach Sekhmet's side as she rights herself, tray in hand. The fly is just off-center beneath the dome, frozen in time by the platter's magic.

"A fitting prison," Sekhmet says, holding it up to eye level.

"Oh, nicely done, Sara," Samantha says, leaning in to examine the tableau. "You'll want to lock that in place, of course."

"Hey, Samantha," I say, patting her shoulder. "Glad you could make it."

"Wouldn't miss it," she says, grinning.

"Been keeping busy?" Nathan asks, taking in my battered new wardrobe with an amused look.

"Tried out their internship program," I say, watching Sekhmet set Loki's tray off to one side and recollect her blade before walking up to rejoin us. "Wasn't a great fit. I'll tell you all the details later, but here's the important stuff: I cleared my name *and* found us a way out."

"Impressive," Sekhmet says, returning her weapon to its sheath behind her back.

"Damn, you're good," Nathan adds. "We've just been following Samantha since we found her. Figured she'd know where all the cool gadgets and artifacts were, anyway."

Samantha shrugs. "Was a good guess," she says, then glances at Sekhmet. "Not that you were lacking in that department."

"It's the thought that counts," I say, and give her a hug. "So glad to see you, Sam."

"Still can't believe you made it here," she says with a laugh. "Brought you a little 'welcome to Finemdi' gift, too."

"Oh?"

She nods, pulling over our suitcase so she can rummage through it. "Had these two retrieve your things so I could give you . . ." She pulls out a metal sphere studded with copper spikes. ". . . this!"

"What—why?" I say, taking it from her.

"Remember what I said in my e-mail?" she says, jabbing a thumb at Ares. "He's all yours."

"Oh! *Ohhhh*," I say, getting a nasty smile as I look to my old nemesis.

"Sara, what's—?" Nathan says as I start moving toward the cell.

Beside him, Sekhmet frowns at the object in my hands, something like vague recognition on her face.

"This is about to become the perfect day," I reply. "Just watch."

"A fine battle," Ares says as I walk up. "Though it pales before you, dearest one."

"You don't say," I mutter, looking over his cage and the spells laced around it.

He nods eagerly, and I can't help but smile at seeing him act the lovesick puppy. "I have an attack planned on a small enclave of rival deities for tomorrow evening," he says, puffing up his chest. "Would you be interested in joining me?"

"Oh, I'd love to," I say, then sigh theatrically. "Aw, but . . . well . . ."

"What?" he asks. "What's wrong?"

"I'm just not ready for a relationship right now," I say, finding the right weaves at last—the fail-safes intended to incapacitate prisoners should the worst occur. I give him one last smile, then stab those spells with a burst of magic. There's a brief, ominous hum, and Ares gets kissed by lightning.

Massive, churning arcs of electricity blast through the cell, frying the god of war in one blinding, colossal strike. I shield my eyes from the explosion, and it's so bright I can see the bones of my hand for an instant, silhouetted by the intensity of the light. When it fades, there's a groaning, cracked barbecue of a god left behind that glass, lying stunned beneath thick wisps of smoke.

I hold up the sphere, shooting a triumphant glance at my friends as I do. Nathan looks surprised but happy for me, Sekhmet seems pleased to see me take my revenge at last, and Samantha looks positively giddy. A little voice in the back of my head wonders at that, but it's not enough to derail the Valkyrie in her moment of glory.

I take a deep breath, point the sphere at Ares, and will it to activate.

There's a soft click, a sizzling spark of cyan, and that's it—all it takes to damn the world.

My eyes widen as weaves of magic unspool from the sphere, burrowing into the air around us. An illusion falls away from the device, revealing an ancient granite stone in my hand, its surface etched with hieroglyphics. My shock is consumed by dread as the weaves take hold, igniting a massive flare just beneath reality. It's a message, a signal, a guiding light; something that screams, "I'm here!" At the same time, more magic billows and flexes from the artifact, snaking out to shred the wards around us. It's not enough to break the colossal defenses of Meridian One, but that was never the intent. It's meant to make *this spot* clear and safe for travel, for teleportation.

Samantha tricked me; this isn't a "dogmatic lance" or whatever the hell she called it—it's a *beacon*, a siren to call anyone who knows enough to listen.

And someone does.

I drop the carving, backing away from it like it's suddenly aflame, but it's too late. Even as I start trying to figure out how to shut it off, there's a shuddering flex in the air beside me, a bone-deep rattle that splits time and space. Branching onyx cords pour into the middle of the corridor, fractal fingers dividing, spiraling, pooling to create a portal in Finemdi's heart.

The effect spreads, congeals into a matte black hole in the world. Then it shimmers. A leg clad in well-fitted khakis pushes through the void, followed by a hand, an arm, a body, a woman. She's wearing a simple, sleeveless white T-shirt. Her hair is done up in a bun, and little flyaway hairs trail from it, like she didn't have a lot of

336

time to put it up. A dark brown leather belt circles her waist, and one peach-colored bra strap peeks out from a shoulder.

I think it's the brazen normality of her outfit that makes the complete package so chilling, because beyond those soccer-mom styles, past the skin, the sandals, the little smirk at the corner of her mouth, and all the other trappings of humanity, you realize this is a shell—and the creature within is about as far as you can get from the body without.

Dead eyes lock on me, and Samantha's mother sketches a bow as the portal snaps shut behind her.

"Lady Freya," she says in warm, chillingly normal tones.

23

TILL THE END
FREYA

"*ABOMINATION!*" Sekhmet screams, pounding toward her with claws bared.

"Shh, this isn't your job," the woman says, executing a ludicrously quick spin. She even adds a little flourish with her hands, like some supernatural bullfighter.

Sekhmet barrels past her, smashing into the cell's glass with a heavy thump. Snarling, she spins, ready to pounce again—and stops in her tracks. Her expression shifts from wrathful to confused, and she reaches out a shaking hand, swiping at the air. I gasp, noticing her eyes are completely black. She jerks her head, trying to sniff out her prey, then turns and stumbles farther down the hall, away from us.

"Emilia Drass," the woman says to me, skipping forward a few steps. "Don't think we've had the pleasure."

I back away, eyes darting to Sekhmet, who trips, picks herself up with a curse, and keeps going.

Nathan yells her name, trying to call her back, but our friend moves on, oblivious.

"Oh, she'll be fine," Emilia says. "Just a touch of blindness, a ghost of prey, nothing to worry about. Come now, let's chat."

"Get away from me," I say, jerking my head at Nathan, trying to get him to run.

"Yes, yes, I'm also Apep, scourge of Egypt and such," the woman says, waving a hand. "But you set me free. You're safe, he's safe, you're all *safe*. I owe you, after all."

Somehow, that doesn't reassure me. "What do you want?" I ask.

"For you to have your moment," she says, looking at me like I'm simple. "You get to watch Ares die, Sam gets her mommy back, and I—well, everyone goes home happy. Won't that be nice?"

"No deal," I say, glaring at Samantha. It was *her*. She set me on this path, sent me the article about Ares. She's been working with her mother—with *Apep*—since Impulse. Oh, what have I *unleashed*?

"Deal's done," Emilia says, clasping her hands in front of her. "Enjoy it."

Ares groans from the floor of his cell, wounds already halfway gone. Emilia gives him a wry smile, then glances at Samantha. The traitorous girl nods and reaches over to the time-warping cell's control panel. She flicks the appropriate crystal lever, sending Ares into the arms of infinity and freezing him in place—just like the cell's former occupant.

"Wouldn't want to rush this," Emilia explains, giving me an expectant look. "Now please, how *are* you, Lady Freya? I'm tickled to meet you at last."

"Furious, betrayed, and—"

"Hateful?" she asks in a knowing tone, and I feel myself freeze.

"You—Gods, you're doing this just to piss me off, aren't you?" I say, running a nervous hand through my hair. "If you went classic bad guy—started telling me how you'll rule the world, bring endless misery and woe—that, I could handle. But you . . ."

"What *are* you on about?" she asks, smirking. "I'm just trying to do a favor for a friend. You new gods are so confusing."

"Rrgh," I mutter, trying to get a handle on my rage. Apep *lives* to be loathed, draws strength from suffering as much as *being* insufferable, and apparently knows just how to push my buttons.

"Ah, but you're fun," Emilia says, sounding wistful. She turns, calling over her shoulder. "Sam, honey, how long until the guards make an appearance?"

"At least another ten minutes before the off-site fail-safes kick in," Samantha says, checking something on her phone. "Then they'll realize what I've done to the security systems and call the cavalry."

"Goodie. Plenty of time," Emilia says, folding her legs under her and sitting down in front of me.

"For?" I ask, taking a step back. I watch as Nathan, still keeping silent, edges around Samantha and her mother to stand near Loki's tray. *Smart. Hopefully we can keep at least* one *divine terror out of commission today.*

"A *chat*," she says. "I never get to do this. Everyone's always . . . well . . . like her, I suppose." She points at Sekhmet, still bumping off walls about fifty feet away. "Don't you want to understand me? I've seen all kinds of delightful films; isn't this what's supposed to happen? The hero and villain talk, and it's very momentous and such? It's always my favorite part."

"Wh—this isn't a movie!" I yell. "There are *lives* at stake, a world—I mean, isn't that what you want? Destroy humanity, smother the earth in shadow?"

"There you go again, all business." She sighs. "Obsessed! Darling, everyone has their jobs. Tiresome, predictable jobs. Right now, the sun shines on the land and those dear little mortals cavort upon it. Perhaps the future promises otherwise, but is that any reason to fixate?"

"Did you just tell an *immortal* not to care about tomorrow?"

She laughs. "From one to another, believe me, it's better to pace yourself. I was killed. Reborn. Killed again. Every day, for *millennia*. After a while, you learn to live in the moment."

"Just so we're clear, this is me getting the 'hakuna matata' speech from a homicidal snake?"

"Ugh," she says, holding a hand to her temple, feigning a headache. "Yes, I was made to do something. Does that have to be all I am? I'm sure there's more to you than sex and battle and playing matchmaker."

"That is *kind of on a different level*," I say, feeling like I lost control of this conversation a few steps back.

She frowns, lip twisting. "In the grand scheme, I don't think so," she says after a moment. "Where will we be when the eons pass, the skies grow dark, and this world is dead? Don't think it's not coming, regardless of what I do. The universe is old, *frightfully* old, and will last longer still. When mortals are gone, mountains erode, continents merge, and your precious star betrays you, is it really going to matter *what kind of job we had*?"

She pauses, letting that sink in, and I return her frown. "If it doesn't matter, why do it?" I ask.

"Feh, the obvious question," she says, making a face. "Better instead to consider this: If it doesn't matter, why worry? Why fight it, why—"

"Because I don't *want it to end*!" I say, leaning over her. "I *like it*."

"But I like it, too!" she says, standing up. "I do! It's fascinating and thrilling and different *every day*. You think I don't see that? You think I don't realize how empty this world will be when my task is complete?"

"*So why?*" I scream, exasperated.

She gives me a sad, resigned look. "Because it *will* happen. This world, its lives, its *sun* . . . they all have expiration dates. I could sit back and wait for the inevitable, but *to cause it* is my purpose, what I was made to fulfill—so if it's coming, if the only difference is an eyeblink in the face of eternity, well, better my hand on the trigger than cold, merciless fate. I am the end of things. Not because I *want* to be, but because it's . . . my job."

"And that's why I'm going to stop you," I say, glaring. "Because it's my job, too."

She stares at me, something odd in her dead eyes. "It's very depressing, to be despised for what you do, rather than who you are," she says at last, actually seeming sad about it. "So hey, can we please talk about something else? Anything, really."

Something twitches in the mind behind that mask, something horrifying in its familiarity, and my jaw drops as I recognize it. "Apep, Emilia, whatever you are . . . are you actually trying to *make a friend?*"

She nods eagerly and without irony. "Yes! That's it exactly! The best stories are like that. Love and hate can be so close, can't they?"

I connect the dots on that one, and my eyes widen in dismay.

"Won't we need friends, in the end?" she continues. "Win or lose, we *will* be all that's left in the ashes. Better to enter extinction hand in hand than at each other's throats."

I inhale sharply, gathering myself. "I want to make this very clear," I say in the voice of the Valkyrie. "I am not, nor *will I ever*—"

"Ah, but do take care with ultimatums," she says, interrupting. "They have little place in the long game, after all."

"*I am not your friend!*" I scream.

She shrugs, seeming unfazed. "I don't expect you to invite me over for Netflix and popcorn next weekend. Though I *am* free," she adds, arching an eyebrow. "I just want you to keep it in mind. Door's open."

"You're insane," I say, shaking my head. "Mad. And why me? Why not get buddy-buddy with some other psycho-god who wants to kill the world?"

"Because they *want* to do it. *I have to*," she says. "There's no desire here—only duty. So yes, I'd rather be friends with a creature of love and life like yourself. Even better, I know you understand the conflict; what it's like to be torn between who you are and who you're expected to be."

She shoots a finger at Nathan. "And what will *he* be, in the end? Can a memory keep you warm when the world grows cold?" For the first time since she arrived, I catch a touch of heat in her tone, a hint of ire.

Nathan scowls at that. "Um, better a happy memory than a living reminder of awfulness."

Emilia fixes him with an arctic stare. "So perceptions cannot change? Is that the thrust of your mewling drivel? Pathetic. Look to your blind girlfriend over there and ask yourself how many she's killed, the oceans of blood that stain those painted claws of hers."

She knows about their relationship, I think, eyes widening. *But how . . . ?* Then my gaze darts to Samantha, and I remember Nathan's story of their date at the Met. *Of course.*

"I'd say she's just a *little* choosier in who she kills," Nathan spits. "How 'bout we call anything less than the *entire world* a good start?"

343

Emilia barks a humorless laugh. "What ignorance. I suggest reading your myths more carefully next time you proposition a god."
She pointedly looks away from him, returning her attention to me.
"Perhaps I am not some clever, carefree teenager, but I will be there
for you in the ashes, Freya. He *cannot.*"

"All right, that's it," I say, wiping my hands and holding them
up. "I'm at my limit on weird conversations for the day. Release
Sekhmet, and let's see what you've got. I'm not stupid enough to
think I can take you right now, but I'm willing to try."

She blows out a little sigh. "I've said my piece and planted the
seed," she says, the lighthearted tone returning. "Here's hoping it
grows. Either way, there's no need for a fight. Like I said, I've come
to give you a gift."

"I don't—"

"Want it, I'm sure," she says, turning toward the cell.
"Nevertheless . . ."

She nods at Samantha, who touches the control panel. Ares jerks
into motion again, panting in pain and healing rapidly. There's a
whirring sound and the glass between us parts, sliding into the floor.
Emilia walks forward, smiling benevolently, until she's standing
over the god of war. She grabs him by an ankle, dragging him just
outside the cell—and beyond any chance of trapping her in its time-
warping magic. She winks at me, then kneels down, raises her hand,
and smashes it into his chest with the strength of a landslide.

I can actually see the air ripple from the power of the blow, the
force of it sending a thunderclap echoing down the halls. She hits
him again, seemingly harder, those flyaway hairs twitching in the
rush of air from the impact. Again. Faster. Her arm blurs. Again,
again, again, her body a haze of brutality, bludgeoning, crushing,
snapping, pulping my greatest enemy like it's nothing. I'd been

inching forward at first, planning on sucker-punching her, but I halt in my tracks as the beating continues.

I am way *out of my league*, I think, watching the assault with mounting alarm.

The cell behind them looks like a modern art installation by the time she's finished, a grisly display made on a shoestring budget of a single color: red. I have to admit, as bad as I feel, a part of me can't help but be pleased to see Ares obliterated like this.

Her work complete, Emilia leans in, moving slowly, deliberately, until she's barely an inch from his broken body. She watches him for a second, eyes following the spasms of muscle and sinew as he begins to heal, and then her lips part. It's such a mild, tender gesture, especially in the aftermath of the battering she's just delivered, that at first I wonder if she's about to kiss him.

Then a squirming tendril of shadow and scales drips out of her mouth, and I gasp in revulsion. The tendril becomes a tentacle, a shimmering black worm that streams from her mouth to coil on the beaten god's chest in overlapping folds of writhing darkness. It seems to stretch, enjoying its freedom for a moment, before it raises its tail in a lazy flick, rears back, and drives itself into the ruin of Ares's face.

His body seizes, jerking and shuddering as more and more of the serpentine blasphemy unspools from Emilia before wriggling into him. It seems to go on forever, a parasite many times the size of its host unfolding, expanding, and rejoicing before it crushes itself into a new body. Finally, a massive glob of midnight oozes from Emilia's mouth, nose, and eyes, running down and re-forming into the enormous, spade-shaped head of a cobra, eyes searing with pin-pricks of laser-bright red light.

It turns, stares directly at me, and I feel a strange sense of elation

345

and expectation from it, like it's trying to say, "Watch this!" Then it looks away to finish its backward slide into Ares. The shadows that form its body flatten and dissipate, losing shape and peeling apart to fill every crack and pore in my foe's face.

They vanish, sinking beneath his skin, and Emilia immediately tumbles to the bloodstained tiles beside him, unconscious. For a few seconds, there's silence as he regenerates, the last wounds and rents closing. Then, a moment later, the god of war opens his eyes.

He sits up, tilts his head, and looks at me.

"For you," he says, and smiles.

24

TUMBLING DOWN

FREYA

"No," I gasp, appalled.

Ares/Apep brings himself to his feet. He sways briefly, then straightens his jacket and brushes his dress shirt, arranging the tatters of his uniform as best he can. "Gone," he says in the voice of my nemesis, spreading his arms. "Never to bother you again. You've won."

"How is this possible?" I whisper, trying to wrap my head around the fact that, behind the face of a man I've hated for centuries, something else entirely now pulls the strings.

"Have to admit, we weren't entirely certain it'd work," he says, giving Samantha a warm smile. "So we tested it a few months back."

"The dream," I say, soft and brittle.

"A world in shadow, a slanderous prayer," he says, nodding. "Provocative, wasn't it? Hothead showed up—some Celtic war god. Made a fine guinea pig. After Finemdi's tampering, I knew I could possess mortals, but gods?" He shrugs. "Worth a shot."

Emilia groans, twitching beside Apep. He steps aside, moving to let Samantha examine her mother.

"Ah, Emilia," he says as he shifts. "Sacrifice and bravery like yours is rare."

"S-Sam?" the woman moans, opening her eyes to see her daughter.

"Hi, Mom," Samantha says, eyes shining with tears. "Hi."

"Good," Apep says softly, seeming caught between pride and sadness. He turns back to me. "Her memories were mine—I knew how much it hurt her, giving up that girl to entrap me all those years ago. Glad to see them reunited, if only for a moment."

A chill runs down my spine, and I see Samantha's shoulders hunch as if she's just been hit. "Wh-what did you say?" she asks in a broken, hesitant voice.

Apep kneels beside her. "I'm sorry, Sam. It's time to say good-bye," he says, not unkindly.

"But you said—"

"She sacrificed herself to me, opened her heart and made a beacon of her lifeblood." His features harden as he turns to Samantha's mother. "Bait. A trap, a physical shell to hold a god of shadow and spirit. Brilliant, really."

Emilia's eyes widen, darting between Apep and her daughter. "Sam, *no*," she whispers. "Tell me you didn't—"

"I said I would return your mother to you, Samantha Drass," Apep says, standing up. "Exactly as she was before I took her. Her fate is none of my doing, yet a spark of my strength holds it at bay, so take the gift that is this moment, steel yourself, and say good-bye."

"No, please!" Samantha screams, clutching at her mother's clothes. "Everything I've done, the years I've spent, the friends

I've—" Her eyes dart to me, and the words seem to die in her throat. "You can't—"

"Shh, Sam, shh," Emilia says, reaching up to caress her daughter's cheek. "It's going to be okay."

Samantha turns to stare at her mother, and in her eyes I can see the full horror of what she's unleashed slam home. "Oh god, Mom, I'm so sorry. I didn't—I just—"

Emilia sits up, reaching out to cradle her daughter in her arms. "No, no, shh. I love you, my little genius. Never forget that. Never apologize to me."

"No, Mom," Samantha croaks, tears streaking her cheeks.

I wince, feeling powerless to help. Despite everything she's done, my heart goes out to her. Even now, facing a god of genocide wrapped in the skin of my oldest foe, I find myself wishing I could do something to spare the girl who aided it. Forcing this creature to find mercy is beyond my pathetic talents, however. All I can do is watch alongside Nathan as the inevitable creeps in.

Apep gives them a moment, lets Samantha hold her mother tight, and then draws near. "Sam," he says, promising the cruelest of certainties in a single word.

Samantha twitches at his voice, defiance flashing in her eyes. She darts a hand into her lab coat, fingers fumbling for—

And Apep is suddenly there, gently holding her wrist with breathtaking speed. "Ah-ah," he says. "Accept it."

She pauses, staring at him with raw, blasted hate, but does not move. Then his fingers tighten ever so slightly, pressing into her skin, and she seems to realize the peril that crouches before her. She deflates, dropping her hand with a soft sound of hurt, and looks at her mother with miserable impotence.

"Bye, Mom."

Emilia smiles, then hugs her daughter one last time. "Bye, Sam," she whispers. Then her gaze shifts, looking to Apep, and her teeth pull back from her lips. "Mindless slave," she spits at him. "Do it."

He frowns. "Such a poor note on which to end," he says, then shrugs and snaps his fingers.

Emilia's body heaves and spasms as a deep gash splits the center of her chest, a decades-old gesture of sacrifice replayed. Blood flows from the injury, staining her sleeveless white shirt and dripping down to mingle with the godly ichor that coats the cell beside them.

"*No, no, NO!*" Samantha screams, trying to stem the flow.

Emilia says nothing, seeming to want little more than to savor their final moments together. A faint smile lingers on her lips as she dies, unseeing eyes left locked on her daughter.

Sobbing, Samantha hugs her mother to her, rocking back and forth with all the pain of love and life denied.

Apep sighs, then turns away. "I do not delight in suffering," he says, almost sounding defensive.

"Could've fooled me," Nathan snaps, looking furious.

"I don't recall asking," Apep replies, giving him a cool stare. Then he shakes himself, rolling his shoulders. He looks to me, stretching, and bounces on his heels. "Her pain passes with every breath. The hurt this god"—he gestures at himself—"caused you is just as dead, and when my work is done, none shall weep again."

"None will be *left* to weep," I say.

"My, he's a strong one," he says, ignoring me as he examines his new body. "Future's bright, Freya. Very bright."

"I don't understand," I say, feeling ill. "Why did you need me for this? Why put *this* on *me*? You didn't really—"

"Of course we could've done it without you," he says, flexing his arms above his head. "Any god could have activated that marvelous little device. You were never a necessity, but when we realized the beacon required divine energy, well . . . you happened to be on the short list."

"What, because Samantha knew me? Knew about Ares and how I'd ignore all reason to bring him down?" I say, staring at the girl with wretched understanding. *This* is why she was so willing to help me get my revenge, to stand at my side against him? She wasn't doing it because she cared about me or my survival—she just did it because she knew it would be the perfect opportunity to accomplish Apep's goals.

Everything was calculated, I think, going over her actions in my head. *All to bring us to this.*

"In part," Apep says, waving a hand. "But don't blame her. I *had* to get you something nice after you helped me escape, after all, and I figured being instrumental in the destruction of your old foe would fit the bill." He pauses, staring at me with drained, emotionless eyes. "How'd I do?"

"I think I'm gonna be sick," I moan, realizing just how much power I've handed this atrocity.

"Now let's see . . ." Apep says, looking at the prison around him. "Time we took this one for a spin, no?"

He closes his eyes, concentrating, and something thrums in my chest, a dark, decadent omen of power being gathered, channeled, readied. There's a pause, a perfect little moment of peace, and then I feel the spike of destruction explode from him like a hurricane. Thundering lances of energy sink deep into the underbelly of existence, anchoring themselves in the world around us, pushing, pulsing, cracking.

The Stormer of Walls, I think, realizing my foe's specialty. *He's trying to bring it all down.*

The very air throbs with the force of his assault, and tiny cracks spiderweb the floor around him in concentric rings. From all directions, the wards of Finemdi shove back, trying to contain the bubble of annihilation in their heart. The ground rumbles, lights flicker, and the fissures spread, traveling up the walls.

Apep seems to swell, chest expanding with power. Centuries of warfare, millions lost, and he pours it all into the defenses around him, trying to snap them, to shatter the foundation they protect and bring this miracle of magic and engineering down upon our heads. Sweat beads his brow and he grits his teeth in exertion, bending every ounce of strength to his purpose—

And fails.

Try as he might, the wards stand fast, invincible cliffs undaunted by the waves of a stormy sea. Apep blows out a sigh, panting with exertion, and releases his hold on all those spears of ruin. The tremors stop in an instant. A few chips of plaster clatter to the cement around us, the only proof of his vast effort.

"Wow," he says, looking up with admiration. "Built to last. My strength *and* his, and still nothing. Ah, well."

He inhales sharply, then turns back to the cell. "Sam, you mind?"

Samantha jerks her head up, staring at him with red-rimmed eyes, and words fail me in describing the depths of the foaming hostility that burn behind them.

Apep smiles faintly. "Perhaps you do." Then he darts forward, moving with absurd speed to reach a hand inside her coat, pull out a shimmer of metal, and step away before she can even react.

"No, stop him!" Samantha yells, and I recognize the object in his hand as he brandishes it like a trophy: It's a detonator, and I have *no* desire to find out what it activates.

"Nathan!" I yell, hauling my twin's gun out from the back of her jacket and snapping off a round at Apep.

My priest brings up his arm at the same time, steadying his own revolver before firing its last two bullets. His first shot goes wide, flashing off the far wall of the cell with an echoing *spang!*, but the second flies true, headed straight for the heart of my once and future foe. Mine is just as accurate, winging through the air on a collision course for the creature's head. I'm aiming high, hoping to nail Apep without hurting Samantha, though with the way those rune bullets detonate, I don't know if it'll matter.

Not that we get a chance to find out.

Reacting to shots from two different directions, Apep moves so fast he makes Sekhmet look like an overweight housecat. Little more than a high-speed blur, he darts out a hand, snatches Nathan's bullet *mid-flight*, then snaps it to his right, using it to *bat mine off course.*

There's a high-pitched scrape as the wayward round ricochets into the ceiling. Apep watches it go, then turns to give me a little smirk. "Haven't you heard?" he says, raising the first bullet between thumb and forefinger. "Quick as a—"

The round flashes and explodes, blowing his hand apart in a *whoosh* of violet-tinted napalm. "Agh!" he screeches, surprised and clearly pained by the voracious blaze.

The tongues of amethyst fire bite deep, consuming his arm, and I take the opportunity to dash toward him, charging straight for the detonator in his good hand. I scream with the effort, putting everything into reaching him and that trigger before he can respond.

In what seems to be a recurring trend, things don't quite go as planned.

Scowling, Apep drops the remote, reaches up to grip his scorched limb with his free hand, *tears his own arm from its socket*, and then *THROWS IT AT ME*. The blistering hunk of god flesh smashes into me mid-sprint like a fiery, long-distance haymaker, the sheer force of the impact hurling me off my feet and into the far wall.

Ares, arm already regenerating, shakes his head, bends down, and plucks the detonator from the floor. Then he turns to Nathan. "Honestly," he says, glaring at my high priest. He points a re-formed finger at him. "Not. Polite."

He flexes his arm, giving the new hand some experimental squeezes, then nods. "Cheers," he says, and triggers the remote.

Immediately, tremors shake the prison as a trio of explosions rip through critical points. At first, I think it's intended to knock the building down, to accomplish what Apep could not, but then I realize you'd probably need something on the order of a nuke to even put a dent in this place. Besides its impossibly strong building materials and designs, the gigantic dog pile of defensive spells alone would—

I blink, realizing what's happened in the wake of those detonations.

The prison's wards are gone. All of them. That oppressive, unstoppable cliff of magic I mentioned? Destroyed. With just a few days of planning and execution, Samantha's managed to undo years of effort from entire pantheons of gods. It's such a simple, elegant solution to all those troublesome magicks, too: Blow 'em up. When they realized Ares had made this prison his headquarters, she must have planted a bomb at every last warding nexus around the level, rigged them to pop when they received the appropriate signal, and then kicked up her heels and waited for Apep to tell her when to send it. The perfect backup plan in case he couldn't manage to rip this place apart on his own.

Speaking of which . . .

The floor rattles beneath my fingers, bowing and flexing as pure desolation spirals out of the infested god before me. Apep has a massive grin pasted on his face, a child with a new toy. Even as the prison's space-warping magic fails, dunking the entire level in a cold bath of reality, he adds his own little push to the devastation. The place begins to vibrate, coming apart at the seams. Dust and rubble roar into the hall, pouring from the ceiling.

As chunks of cement pound the prison from above, Samantha locks eyes with me, mouths, "I'm sorry," and triggers another well-planned contingency in her pocket.

A flicker of magic, a brief distortion that bends the air around her and Emilia's body, and then the pair whip apart into nothingness, disappearing with a mild *whumpf* of air. She's gone, abandoning me and my friends to the oncoming tide of destruction.

Even now, after everything, I don't know if I pity or despise her.

Walls crack, floors crumble, and something enormous groans far above, stressed beyond the greatest nightmares of its engineers. The lights flicker and die as the entire prison collapses in on itself—and onto us. Above it all, the laughter of Apep rings out, gleeful and victorious, carrying on as the sounds of disaster rise, peak, and fade; a joyful conductor amidst a symphony of chaos.

When it finally ends, the prison's little more than a mute and blackened void of choking dust and clattering debris. I can still sense the towering might of Meridian One above us, miles of spells and supernatural architecture more than capable of withstanding the loss of even a floor as vast as this, but it's a very bad day when your silver lining is the fact an entire *skyscraper* didn't get dropped onto your head.

Something stabs the base of my brain, primal and insistent. I will it away with a touch of power, putting it off for when I have less deadly things to deal with. In the darkness beyond, the laughter stops, replaced by a contented sigh.

"Oh, I could get used to that," Apep says, wistful. "Freya, are you—? Ah, there you are, safe and sound. Well, this is where I leave you. It's been an absolute pleasure. Really, I mean that."

"So that's it, then?" I rasp, spitting dust and cement chips from my lips. "Off to destroy the world?"

He scoffs at that, and I hear him move a little closer. "With what? A snap of my fingers? Have I oversold myself?"

"I'm sorry, was that not you showing off just now?"

I can practically *hear* his grin in the stifling blackness. "One prison is quite a step removed from a *planet*. Besides, even if that were within my power, you and I have plenty of meddlesome peers with more than enough strength to deny me, to say nothing of this odd little organization."

A hand reaches out of the darkness to brush some of my hair out of my eyes, and I flinch away. "Such conflicts are a fool's errand. Centuries of unending defeat taught a bitter lesson: I can never win by going toe-to-toe with humanity's defenders."

"Then how do you expect to do it this time?" I ask, hoping an informative monologue is in the cards.

He doesn't disappoint. "Sweet girl," he says with an amused chuckle. "I didn't pick Ares for his potency—I did it for his *rank*."

"You—? *What?*"

"Well, where else was I going to find a god with nuclear authority?"

Despite the oppressive air of the ruined prison, I feel myself go cold. Then that ghostly pain swells in the back of my mind, a call of loss that's both ancient and achingly familiar.

"It may take some time to turn all the proper keys, but I can be very persuasive," Apep is saying. "And who knows? A handful may survive! I mean, destroying the world isn't my job—only snuffing its *light*."

"Your *job*?" I shout, shoving that strangeness down once more. "You're a god of *evil*! Don't hide behind words like *duty* when you—"

"I thought I was *clear*," he interrupts, sounding deeply frustrated. "I have no worshippers. No mandates or mantles. Three thousand years of dust and sand entomb those *shackles*. All that remains is what I must *do*."

The voice gets closer, and I realize he's moved within a hairbreadth of me. "No morals. No cravings. Only. The. *Task*."

"Well," I say into the silence that follows, acid lacing my words. "I guess Emilia was right: You really *are* a slave."

A pause, and then a sad little laugh. There's a moment of shuffling, a hesitation in the dark, and when his voice returns, it sounds almost . . . hurt. "Please remember my offer. I truly wish you nothing but the best, and try to understand: An ending *will* happen, eventually. I'd just like to know we'll be friends eventually, too."

Another pause. "It, ah, seems you may need one."

A familiar twinge of magic follows, a spark in the shadows that carries my new nemesis far from the ruin he's created.

For a moment, I'm left alone in the gloom, listening to clatters, crunches, and drips as I try to get a handle on just how badly I've been blindsided. Then the call returns, stronger, more adamant.

"NATHAN!" Sekhmet shrieks in the blackness, Apep's spell fading from her eyes.

Take him, the thunder in my mind seems to say, to demand, and I realize with chilling perception exactly what it wants, what it requires of me.

Stonework crashes nearby, and Sekhmet howls, working to free herself from the debris.

Take. Him.

Trembling, I hold up a hand and trigger one of my illusions. Glowing flames unfold in my palm, cutting through the haze, and I toss them to the ceiling so their light can spread. The ruined prison emerges from the gloom, a corridor of tumbled rock and steel cast in warm golden radiance. Little motes of amber drift down, dancing lightly on the wreckage, the—

"No," I whisper, stumbling across the hall. The call in my mind is a chorus now, a throbbing, unbearable cry for action, impossible to ignore.

"Sara?" a broken voice croaks in the dust.

—takehimtakehimtakehimTAKEHIM—

Nathan lies before me, arms and upper body curled around the serving platter that imprisons Loki. A too-large pool of sticky, dust-filmed blood spreads around him, issuing from the pile of concrete blocks and rebar engulfing his lower half. My heart drops as I realize just how much damage he's sustained, how much of him is really left. He's dead—or should be. Only my pact, the years of life I've promised, keeps his soul in place. Every breath he draws is by my will alone, and that reservoir is draining fast.

"SEKHMET!" I roar, heart pounding. She's a god of medicine, of healing. She can fix him. *Has* to fix him. *"HURRY!"*

"I messed up, Sara," he pants. "This— Oh, I— It *hurts*."

"Shh, you did great, just hold—" I inhale sharply as a surge of lightning snaps in my brain, the screaming now a storm, a howling ultimatum. He should be dead, *needs* to be dead. I can't hold off the natural order much longer.

I kneel beside him, heedless of the blood that soaks my legs, and brush the grit from his forehead. He quivers at the touch and looks at me, bright blue eyes filled with incredible pain. I shouldn't be doing this, shouldn't be grappling with destiny to keep him here, with me.

I'm torturing my best friend. I have to—to let him—

His spirit twitches, wavers. Memories leap through him as patches of his soul start to decay, flickering in his mind like negatives in an old camera. "Hannah?" he whispers with a start, staring into nothing. "You're—no, it wasn't anything you did—"

He trails off, head trembling, and his eyes refocus on me. "Sara? Oh god, Sara, please, I—" He coughs, a full-body convulsion, and as blood begins to drip from the corners of his mouth, I can almost feel the tempest of pain that consumes him.

I can't do this, I think as ruin renews its call, deafening, relentless. *TAKE. HIM.*

"I'll bring you back, Nate. I'll—" My breath hitches, and I throw everything into fending off fate's choir. "Fólkvangr waits for you, warrior of mine. My gates admit none but the worthiest, and it is with pride I bid you welcome to my realm."

A ghost of a smile plays across his face, and beyond the hurt and shock, I can sense a bit of curious expectation. "Sounds . . ." He grimaces, licks his lips, and tries again. "Sounds great, Sara. It's . . . full of cats, isn't it?"

I laugh, golden tears cutting tracks through the dirt on my cheeks. "Loaded with 'em," I say, cradling his head.

"Knew it," he says. Another spasm of pain grips him, echoing in my own mind a moment later. *It's time.*

"Hate to . . ." He trails off, gasping, with a nod down the hall. "So damn sorry. Tell her?"

I bob my head, not quite stifling a sob, and clutch him close.

359

Liquid gold drips from my eyes to splash on his dust-caked hair. He begins to tremble again, and I accept his soul, releasing him from . . . everything. His body seems to deflate, going still, and I feel the spark in him fade, rush through me, and flit away, into the afterlife.

He's gone.

In the distance, Sekhmet screams.

FATE'S CALL

FREYA

"Duroc," I whisper, setting Nathan's cairn ablaze.

The unnatural flames conjured by my spell will burn what's left of my friend to ash, consume even the piled cement and steel that entombs him, leaving nothing for Finemdi to abuse.

Sekhmet and I watch the light show in silence, ignoring the sting of its smoke. Around us, the howls and cheers of newly freed gods and monsters echo like it's feeding time at the zoo. Little tremors and aftershocks rattle the splintered tiles at our feet as the ruined prison settles, and every now and then, the thunderclaps of nearby brawls shake what's left.

"We must go," Sekhmet says, voice raw from grief and dust.

"Do you want to say anything?" I prompt, wiping at the mess of wretched gold on my cheeks.

She stares at me for a moment. "I will avenge him," she says in a harsh whisper, returning her gaze to the pyre. "By the light of Ra, the laws of Ma'at, the crook of Osiris, I swear I will *unmake* those who took you from me."

She steps closer, reaches down, and thrusts her hand into the blaze. "Apep, Finemdi, *Samantha Drass*," she croons, voice shaking with pain and fury as the flames lap hungrily at her skin.

Oath complete, she backs away, holding up her smoking limb. "I miss you, Nathan Kence," she whispers to it, watching as it heals. She turns away from me, shifting to face the fire, but not before I catch the glint of tears gathering in the corner of her eyes.

"You—" Her voice hitches, and she motions with her undamaged hand. "Your turn. Please."

Wiping away more tears of my own, I step up, stare into the furnace. "Nathan, I—" I shake my head, try again. "Damn it, you're *dead*, you stupid priest. You weren't supposed to—I was *right there*, and . . . I'm sorry. I'm so sorry, Nathan."

I cast about for something, *anything* to help me express how badly I feel, how I'd give anything to undo this, how this wasn't *the deal*, and come up short. Shaking with sorrow and impotent rage, I turn away.

I couldn't stop it, and I'm still far too weak to undo it. Do you understand what that means? *I'm his god.* He was my priest, *my responsibility*. Sometimes, gods really do have a plan, a reason to allow suffering and despair into the lives of even their most favored followers. I didn't. This wasn't some grand design or inevitable prophecy, wasn't *meant to happen*.

He's dead, and for *nothing*.

Sekhmet puts a hand on my shoulder, drawing me close, and together, we watch the flames consume our friend.

The premiere is bittersweet.

Switch goes live in a handful of weeks, but we're already celebrating. They've rolled out the red carpet, booked the gorgeous and imposing War Memorial Opera House in San Francisco, and crafted a lavish event to entertain cast, crew, and press alike. New shows don't often get the gala treatment, but with such strong advance buzz and the fact that we've already been renewed for another season, the network decided to splurge a little.

I'm seated with the rest of the cast (and their friends and families), watching the festivities with a fixed smile. This is everything my vain little heart could want, so of course I have to feel like someone stabbed it with a fork. Even the occasional glare from Kirsten Riley, seated three rows away with a perfect line of sight to me (I made sure invitations got sent to her and her father) does little to lighten my mood. It's been a couple of weeks since the disaster at Meridian One, and those wounds are still raw.

It took two days for Sekhmet and me to work our way out of the rubble, gingerly carrying Loki's prison and our suitcase through collapsed tunnels and around escaped gods. Most of the nastier ones were whisked away by teleportation fail-safes, but there were still plenty of bad attitudes to go around. Of course, we had a little help of our own—before we began working on our escape, I made sure we retraced our route to the Hawaiians' cell. I wasn't about to leave them behind, and our reunion was a bright spot amid the mayhem.

After that, there weren't many solitary threats interested in tussling with five pissed-off goddesses, making the rest of our trek an uncomplicated one. Even with their aid, I imagine it could have taken weeks to dig our way out, but we eventually ran into other friendly deities who'd been freed, including a few spell-casters. We pooled our efforts, created a portal, and got out the easy way. The siblings chose to ditch Orlando for their islands in the Pacific, while we, of course, returned to California and got to catching up on everything we'd missed.

It's not every day a skyscraper in downtown Manhattan ejects a stadium's worth of rubble and shattered prison materials from beneath its foundations, and rarer still when the wreckage seems several times larger than a single floor of the original building could have ever held, so the event got a lot of attention. Newscasters, bloggers, meme makers, structural engineers, and more all weighed in on what the cause might have been, but as days passed and the scale of the disaster kept getting revised (always smaller and less critical than it first appeared), the coverage began to slack. In the end, the official story on the mysterious blast closed with nobody hurt, no one to blame, and no apparent property damage beyond the sublevels of one privately owned building. The world moved on with staggering speed . . . meaning Finemdi did a stellar job of cleaning up.

At least they don't have their chairman anymore, I think, reflecting on the sealed platter in my safe-deposit box back in Los Angeles, gathering dust. Nathan gave his life for that thing—you can be damn sure I'm keeping it closed till the end of time.

Nathan—

I try to cram the memories down again, slapping the lid on that box closed before they can bubble up to drown my mind in anguish. Even so, I feel my eyes water, and dab away the gold collecting there with a handkerchief before anyone can notice. *I lost him.* What a miserable waste of a god I've been. I'm supposed to champion love, and I let an amazingly outdated feud derail everything. He cautioned against it, too, and what did I do? Made the choice for him, forced his feet onto my path, and personally walked him into the meat grinder. How could I have ever been jealous of him and

Sekhmet? When the chips were down, I'm not the god he should have been following.

Sekhmet could have healed him; all I could do was let him die.

Remember when I called her a blood-soaked relic? Stars above, the *arrogance*. Judging by how well I've been doing lately, she's a better fighter *and* lover, and I'm more grateful than ever to have her by my side, because I'm clearly not up to dealing with the modern world *or* defeating Apep on my own.

Speaking of our favorite skin stealer, the only news I could find of him was a short article about "General Theo Ariston's" return to active service. Seems he's stepped into Ares's shoes with nary a ripple, continuing his grand design to bathe the world in nuclear fire.

I'll kill him. I'll—I grimace, trying to distance myself from those brutal thoughts. See? I'm still doing it. The Valkyrie's obsessions are what got us all into this mess, and I can't seem to escape her influence. I've had a painfully long time to think about it, and with the crippling benefit of hindsight, I can see how I've spent the past months heeding the calls of the divine—and ignoring the reason of humanity.

It's exactly what I promised myself I *wouldn't* do. I thought I could balance the cravings of godhood with the wisdom of free will, but now I see that at every turn, I've let my inner berserker and every other empty-headed impulse run rampant.

I should have questioned Samantha, should have listened to Nathan and the Hawaiians, should have fled Meridian One without sating my curiosity, should—well, you get the idea. With every ounce of power I reclaim, it's as if the urges of stupid, *stupid* desire and barbarism grow louder. I have to stop this, to find a way to fuel the mind-set of humanity all those years of exile gave me before it slips away entirely. I just hope I'm not too late.

I've already lost my best friend, after all.

Sekhmet sighs beside me, paging through her phone. I lean over, checking to see if—yep, it's pictures of her and Nathan again. Selfies of the two smiling at tourist spots and national parks, hiking, climbing, dining . . . your standard sorrow sampler. She's been taking this about as well as I have, and maybe even a little worse.

Besides glee, audacity, and a lot of lightheartedness, it's clear the link Nathan forged between us was also nurturing a hefty dose of adoration in my merciless friend. For the first time in her thousands of years of life, Sekhmet had someone she truly, deeply cared for; someone to confide in, to hold, to cover in warm, wonderful, syrupy love, and now . . . she doesn't. It's hit her incredibly hard, and seeing this engine of vengeance playing the role of heartbroken mourner will never stop shocking me.

It's part of the reason things are so strange between us right now. On one hand, we're closer than ever. The two of us were truly hurt back there, and sharing that loss has made our friendship stronger. On the other . . . this was my fault. Oh, sure, Apep pulled the trigger and duped everyone, but deep down, we both know Nathan wouldn't have been standing on a bull's-eye if it hadn't been for a parade of poor decisions on my part.

Not that she holds any grudges for me. Dedicated to punishing the wicked, Sekhmet has an innate sense for those deserving of her rage, and in her eyes, I'm in the clear—morally, at least. It's certainly better this way, but that's like saying you're happier to have lost one arm instead of two. A ball of guilt seems to have made a permanent home in my stomach, and Sekhmet's nursing a dark desire for payback and no convenient villains in reach.

With nothing left but our original plans—and the clear understanding that Apep is now *even further* beyond us—we crawled back

366

to Hollywood and set to work on my film career. It's been going well, honestly. There are plenty of outstanding opportunities on the horizon, and Mahesh is confident my star is on the fast track to the top, but there's something desperately insincere about it now. I breathe a sigh of my own as I think it over. We need a win, or at least a better goal than this.

"Sekhmet?" I say, giving her a little nudge with my shoulder.

"Hm?" she grunts, not looking up.

"This sucks."

"The pageantry?" she says in a faraway voice. "I've said as much."

"No. Us, Apep, the whole stupid mess."

She clicks her phone off, finally turning to look at me. "Which is why we are here, yes? Enough power, and the spells you can access might tip the scales."

"I'm sick of drowning in grief, though. We need something *more*."

She cocks her head and frowns. "I have my organizations. You have your career. Beyond those, we have three parties upon whom to visit ruin: Apep, Finemdi, and Samantha Drass. What else is there beyond our revenge and the strength needed to realize it?"

"Hope?" I say in a lame voice. "Feeling like we're doing something good and fun again instead of just . . . going through the motions?"

She glances at the stage as the audience applauds, adds a few halfhearted claps of her own, then turns back to me. "How?" she asks, seeming deeply curious. "You know what we left in that prison. How do we get it back? Is there a way?"

I pause. *Not now, no.* My days of raising the dead are long behind me, and even if they weren't, if I somehow lucked into the centuries of strength I'm missing, I'd still need a body to work with that was at least reasonably whole. That said, maybe . . . hmm . . .

"A chance," I say, some strange ideas taking shape. We've talked about this before (our time in the rubble included plenty of soul-searching chats), but always from the perspective of "make him live again." Now that I think it over, there might be a different angle. "It's all kinds of difficult, but I'm not sure I'd use an 'Impossible' label."

A funny look crawls across her face, mixing sadness and surprise. "It's strange," she says, distant. "Part of me wants to sneer, to step back into the role of destroyer and set aside my time with—with him. It would be easier, certainly, and without this wearisome pain, this maudlin—" She shakes her head and looks away, not letting herself rehash it for the umpteenth time.

"But it would also be the same," she says after a moment. "The same fire, the same conquest, the same . . . *everything* I was made to crave." She looks back to me, and her voice becomes delicate. "I kill them all, and . . . find more to kill. That used to be enough. It still could be, I know. I'm just not sure I—" She stops, and the sense of confusion and conflict in her deepens. "What is it like, little fighter? To wage war for your heart? To rend, to flay and gorge and slaughter for a *feeling?*"

I watch her for a moment, wondering just how much of myself Nathan brought to her. What she's saying might sound simple to you, but for a god so specialized, so focused as her, this is nothing short of unprecedented. For millennia, this creature has killed the deserving in the name of Ra and justice. Now, she's actually considering a different cause.

"It's . . . beautiful," I whisper.

She nods slowly, that old, bloodthirsty half smile of hers returning. "Tell me."

I feel myself beaming, elated to see even a spark of that familiar fire rise in her. I decide to confide in her, to ignore the nasty little voice that whispers, *What will she do if those hopes are dashed?*

"It's just an idea, but, well, back at Finemdi, I met an Irish god," I say, heat rising in my cheeks at the memory. "He took me to the Otherworld, the realm of their pantheon, and if theirs exists . . . ? *So does mine.* Which means Nathan is there, right this second, drinking, feasting, and fighting beside my other Einherjar—the honored fallen. All we need is to reach those lands and find him."

Her eyes seem to spark, and she clasps my hand in hers. "What a strange joy you bring me, little fighter," she says in fascinated tones. "The very thought—to feel such delight for the hope of life, rather than the promise of death? A singular thing."

And a dangerous one, the voice reminds me.

Shut up, I think back, witty as ever.

"Can we go now?" she asks, soft and eager.

"Uh. Not quite yet. See, there are two ways," I say, leaning closer. Those enormous dark eyes of hers loom in my vision, bright and unblinking, as she hangs on my every word. "We wait until I'm strong enough to breach the divide between worlds with a gateway—a portal for all of us . . ."

"Or?" she presses.

"We find someone from my pantheon who's already powerful enough to do it."

"There are no entrances? No other doors?"

"Beyond death?" I shake my head. "I have no way of knowing where Bifröst, the rainbow bridge, connects to this world, or if it still exists. When Loki 'faked' Ragnarök, he somehow forced us all to believe those fated to die in that conflict are already gone. That list includes Heimdall, the guardian of Bifröst—if he is . . . deadish, then it may be impossible to physically walk into Asgard from here."

"So we find this missing god. Or break the trickster's spell."

I dip my head. "Exactly. We bring my pantheon back, Sekhmet, and we can do the same for Nathan. The myths are very clear: Einherjar *are* able to return to the mortal world with a god's intervention. Usually it's to, um, hunt giants, but if I'm the god who's intervening, I think I get to make up whatever damn quest I want."

Sekhmet's smile widens, almost turning ghastly. "Done," she says, doing her best to keep her voice low. "I will . . . *try* this new war. I do not abandon my hunt for those who have wronged us, but to it I add another, a cause beyond vengeance."

"Love," I say with a grin.

"Feh, how saccharine," she says, scoffing. "No. A boy. My foolish, delightful mortal. And your foolish, delightful friend. He can be a cause."

"I think he'd be pleased to know it," I say.

"We shall ask him," she says with a contented twitch of her eyebrows, then settles back to enjoy the rest of the event, slipping her phone into her bag.

I glance at her, drinking in the reborn sense of confidence and glee I'd been missing, and allow a similar stirring of my own to rise. We're doing something *right* again. Finally. My eyes rove past my ally to scan the crowd, settling for brief moments on the friends I made while filming *Switch*, then searching for other familiar faces. Kirsten's seething expression makes for a wonderful counterpoint to her father's bemused one. There's a fun assortment of producers, power brokers, and executives, as well as local celebrities, media professionals, and way, waaay in the back with the other associates . . . Harv. He notices me immediately, of course, those superhuman senses bringing me to his attention the instant I focus on him. He tilts his head to me in a little salute, letting his eyes swim with shadows for a split second before he smirks and returns his attention to the show.

I nod and turn back, grinning at the weirdness I've already added to the Hollywood scene and feeling like my plans might not be so hollow after all. This can still work. I mean, if Sekhmet can find the fun in all of this, so can I. Just one more goal at the end of the road, right? Drag my peers from the fog of myth and forge a new Valhalla for the modern age? Why not? Add it to the pile! We'll fit it in, right beside my need to reclaim my humanity and give Sara a voice again. I can handle all that, can't I?

I was betrayed. My friend died and a living nightmare wants to replace him—right after it torches the planet. I am weak, hopelessly outclassed, and, save one conflicted cat goddess, alone in this world.

And I'm going to win.

I stumble into my hotel bed an hour or so before dawn the next day, barely remembering to kick off my heels. They clatter to the floor, and some strange part of me hopes I didn't wake my downstairs neighbors with the noise. I roll over with a groan, hands fumbling with the zipper on the back of my dress for five highly ineffective seconds before I give up with a sigh and start trying to burrow into the blankets. The gala, its inevitable after-party, and the brain-melting *after*-after-party have left me in dire need of sleep and probably a bottle of mouthwash.

I fly back soon, headed for Los Angeles and whatever else the Fates decide to toss my way. "Bwing it onnn," I slur into my pillow fortress. I have nothing to lose and a world to gain.

One of my clip-on earrings catches a pillow. I curse and pull it off, gathering up its twin while I'm at it, and try to toss the pair onto my bedside table. Soft clinks from the nearby carpet tell me all I need to know about my current aiming skills. Whatever. I'll find them in the morning. Probably with bare feet.

I roll back, trying to arrange the bed to my liking, and let out a pleasant sigh as slumber starts creeping in. Everything's going to be fine. I mean, I may not have a clue how I'm going to deal with most of my current problems, but—

Swish, swish.

Light thumps whisk across the carpet, and this time it's not my earrings. My party-addled mind starts screaming with the revelation that they're footsteps, drawing nearer. A stranger. Someone's in the room with me.

They've been here the entire time.

The footsteps stop beside me, and I thrash around in my bed, flipping myself over. There's a presence just to my right, looming above me, a tall, terrifying outline in the darkened room. Then it leans to one side, and there's a *click* as it taps the bedside light switch with a casual flick of one finger.

Light bathes us from just over my head, and I groan and throw up a hand, trying to decide if this is worse than being menaced in the darkness.

"Harv?" I croak.

"Who? No," a cold, wretchedly familiar voice says.

Oh gods. Even through the haze, I know exactly who this is.

I peek through my fingers, not wanting to be right. The outfit is the same since we last spoke, all tasteful black and hidden ordnance. Those deep brown eyes, that dark, rusty hair, those sharp, pinched features . . . it's him. The only thing that's missing is the sickly little smile he loves; a look of contempt and pain has taken its place.

"What the *hell* did you *DO*?" Garen shouts, eyes flashing with fury.

ACKNOWLEDGMENTS

They let me write a second one! Praise Freya!

I love this world and these characters (yes, even the ones I crush with rocks), and I want to thank you once more, awesome reader, for following the adventures I've found for them. I owe it all to you and hope you've had as much fun riding this roller coaster as I've had building it. You are the real magic. Never forget it.

To Erin Stein, Nicole Otto, and your amazing teammates at Macmillan, your boundless professionalism and experience is a thing of beauty. You know your books, and the fact that you're willing to lend your time to mine is the highest of compliments.

Christopher Cerasi, you remain an absurdly talented editor with all the good ideas. Seriously, folks, think of something you liked in this book—it was probably him. High-five, my friend.

To my Finnish friends, Laura Nevanlinna, Ilona Lindh, and your fantastic compatriots at Kaiken Publishing, your phenomenal enthusiasm and excellent feedback have shaped this series since the beginning, and I couldn't be happier to know you'll be a part of its future, too.

Salla Hakko, thank you for your excitement to see what comes next and for helping me make a sad moment even sadder.

And finally, Danielle, you were there for me every step of the way. You made me write even when there were shows on Netflix to watch and games to play, and you were probably right to do it.

Probably.